THRONE OF AIR AND DARKNESS

Secrets of the Faerie Crown, Book 2

EMBERLY ASH

Copyright 2023 Emberly Ash, Cara Maxwell Romance

All rights reserved. No part of this book may be reproduced, or stored in a retrieval system, or transmitted in any form or by any means, electronic, mechanical, photocopying, recording, or otherwise, without express written permission of the publisher.

For permissions contact: caramaxwellromance@gmail.com

This is a work of fiction. Names, characters, places, and incidents either are the product of the author's imagination or are used fictitiously. Any resemblance to actual persons, living or dead, events, or locales is entirely coincidental.

Cover Art: Selkkie Designs

Beta Analysis: Made Me Blush Books

Map Design: A. Andrews

❦ Created with Vellum

For the warrior women fighting the darkness that just won't quit.

In case no one told you, your wrath is justified.

Make them bleed.

CONTENT WARNINGS

Throne of Air and Darkness is a fantasy romance with elements of dark romance. While it is not a true dark romance, the themes are heavy and may be triggering for some readers.

Content warnings include: child abuse, rape, murder, death of a loved one, explicit sexual content, and graphic depictions of death, violence, and torture.

Annwyn

- The Spine
- Wolf Bay
- Cayltay
- Eiriam Gaul
- The Shadow Wood
- Outpost
- The Spit
- The Split Sea
- Skywatch
- The Northern Way
- Baylaur
- The Blasted Pass
- The Barren Dunes
- Tirbyas
- The Southern Way

PROLOGUE

Seven Thousand Years Ago
The Great War

They were almost out of time.

Her mate was gone—fighting, she told herself. Not lost to the darkness. Not taken by the—

No. She would not speak their name. Would not even think it. She would not take the risk.

Behind her, the sounds of battle raged. Steel on steel was the least of it. The sounds of death, the stench of it, reached her even high in the Tower of Myda. This lonely circular room, her prison and her refuge.

Her punishment.

One she deserved.

She refused to let herself listen—to the battle or the voices screaming inside her head. If she did, she'd never finish her task. She'd never do what needed to be done—what must be done, if her kingdom was to survive.

Not just her kingdom.

Every kingdom.

She reached for the book, flipping it open to a blank page. At the edges of her consciousness, the void pulled.

But she pushed it away, ignored it, willed that ember of magic inside of her to sleep. She sang it the lullaby that she'd devised, nonsensical, repeated verses that helped ease it back to rest when her mate was not near enough to tether her.

Accolon was on that battlefield.

The hollow ache in her chest roared, demanding satisfaction. But she ignored that, too. She couldn't think of her mate, not now. He was alive, of that she was certain. It was the only thing she was certain of in that moment.

As if in reminder, in protest of the thought, her stomach jolted.

Not the only thing, then.

One hand reached for the quill, while the other drifted down to the rounded bulge below her breasts. Mate, child, kingdom. Those were the things that kept her hand moving as she began to recite the words.

She'd only heard them once, but once was enough.

"Then comes a queen," she whispered, her fingers scratching out the words across the page.

Her stomach clenched, painful and sharp. A twin spear of pain down her spine.

It couldn't be. It was too soon. The child was not due for another month.

She gripped the quill tighter, forcing out the next few words.

The clash of swords. The screams of death. Void, darkness... *Come to us, Nimue,* they whispered. But she ignored that beautiful dark she'd come to love. She'd seen the very fabric of the world, felt it shift and reform around her, known a power both beautiful and dangerous, and wholly her own.

Another stab of pain in her back.

The child was coming.

Why now? Why here? This child was supposed to be the herald of peace, of a new world reborn. Peace, prosperity, safety. Without the—

"No!" she screamed, slamming her fist down on the table. They couldn't have her—not her mate, her kingdom, or her child.

She'd win this battle. Not from battlefield, but from the tower.

She dragged in a breath, trying to steady herself. She had time. Babes took hours to come. Sometimes even days.

There was still time to seal the magic.

But first, the prophecy.

The child moved within her, a constant reminder even as she managed to blot out the pain. Maybe it was the young one's way of giving her the strength to finish, to do what must be done.

"It's all for you, little one," she breathed, setting down the quill.

She'd heard the words just once, on the banks of Avalon. But they'd been seared into her memory. The priestess who'd made them would wither and die, succumbing to her human blood. But the words would live on. They must.

Even as she prepared to make her sacrifice, she knew that it would not last forever. Another queen would come. Two queens, who would stand together to defeat the darkness and death. She would not be able to help them. But she could leave them this.

Her hand fell back to her stomach, tracing the outline. The other traced the words, a fingertip sliding along the lines, checking each one. Which might be most important... she couldn't be certain. But she would make sure they were recorded faithfully.

Then comes a queen in the age of uncertainty, when shadows cast doubt upon the realm. Born under a double moon and marked by a radiant star, a faerie queen shall rise to command the depths of the voids of darkness.

Yes, that was right. It was the easier to remember, because those voids the prophecy spoke of... she knew them well.

Twice blessed, the realm of shift and mist, when comes the awaited queen who shall possess ethereal might. With a touch, she will feel the heartbeat of her subjects, and she will unlock the secrets they guard within.

Accolon had been fascinated by the second part. A realm of shift and mist—had it meant his homeland? The misty mountains of the Spine, ruled by shifters of every shape and shade of danger?

She didn't think so; it seemed too obvious. But it didn't matter what either of them thought. They'd be long dead by the time the prophecy was fulfilled.

The quill fell from her hand as another pain racked her body.

How long had it been? She ought to be tracking the time. The healers had said...

It didn't matter what the healers had advised in those months that felt like years ago. They weren't there. If any of them still lived, they waited on the fringes of the battlefield, protected by the Gremog, to heal those who escaped that soulless force of death.

"Just a few more minutes, little one," she urged, pushing away the book.

She reached inside her skirts for the scrap of paper she'd kept tucked close to her body all these months. Months of denial, of searching for another answer, of selfishness.

Every death, every scream on that battlefield was because of her. She could have stopped it months ago, if she hadn't been so damn stubborn.

If she'd only been willing to make the sacrifice.

She could only hope that when the time came, her descendants would be braver than she.

These words were imprinted on her mind as well. Even clearer than the prophecy. A dozen words that would change her fate forever. Change who she was.

And save her kingdom.

The child within her stilled, letting her see past that precious little life to the ember of magic even deeper within her. That bright center of magic that had awoken on the happiest day of her life—her Joining to the male she loved. Her mate. Her king.

Its shining silver light had opened realms to her that she could never have imagined. Places of beauty and magic so different from her own. Realms of air and breath where she hardly materialized at all, where days lasted forever and she could walk upon rainbows.

But not all realms were made of joy and love. Some held darkness and death.

A hundred years was a blessing, she reminded herself.

A hundred years was enough to destroy the world.

She pressed her eyes closed, remembering. Letting the void pull at her one last time. Soon, all she would have were memories.

The child kicked hard.

She'd have her child and her mate and her kingdom.

It was more than enough.

A tear slid down her cheek as she lifted the scrap of paper and read the words without hesitation.

She expected a flash of pain as the magic ripped from her body. But it was slower than that. It started as a tingle, and for a moment she thought it hadn't worked. Panic flooded her. It had to work. The witch had promised it would work. Excalibur had been pressed to the wicked witch's throat; she couldn't have lied—

Tingling—no, no, no. She was slipping into the void—

But the tingling didn't pull her apart.

It burned.

Up through her fingers, her limbs, right to that shining core of magic inside of her. She felt it stripping away, an unholy fire that consumed everything in its path. It was consuming her. She was burning from the inside out, the very center of her being, her glorious magic eaten alive by the witch's spell.

She cried out, screaming—but there was no one to hear her. She didn't try to hold it in. Let her screams, her pain, merge with those of her mate and her subjects below on the battlefield.

Her magic was gone. She felt it, the hollowness inside of her. The power that had saved her, again and again. Now sacrificed, to save those she loved.

It would only be a matter of time now, she told herself. Without the void, no more of them would come. No more minds shattered, bodies stolen, and turned into dark, mutilated beasts. It might take hours or days, but eventually, they would all be beaten.

Annwyn would be safe. Accolon would be safe. Her child would be safe.

The pain ebbed, blending with the demands of childbirth. It would not be days or hours for her. The child was coming in the center of that bloody battlefield. All she could do was hope—that when she rose from her childbed, her mate and kingdom would stand victorious. Free of the darkness.

As Nimue gave herself over to the primal drive to create and bring life, the final words of the prophecy echoed in her mind—

Together they must stand, to defeat what once thought dead. Together they must give, if any shall live to the end.

I
VEYKA

This must be what death feels like.

I'd always imagined it would be the absence of feeling, the darkening of the thoughts that lurked in the back of my mind. But I was wrong. Death wasn't gentle at all.

It was like being ripped from my body. I could feel the beat of my heart in my ears. Except I wasn't in my body. My blood flowed all around me.

Me, except not. What was I?

I wasn't in my body. I was everywhere. My heart, my blood, my skin... was that my soul I saw, spinning in swirls of silver and blue?

Death was painful and exquisite. Like waking in the morning and stretching until every limb tingled.

Then I slammed into the ground.

My legs crumbled beneath me, my knees landing in the dirt.

Not dirt, I realized. Sand.

My hands landed in it as I fell forward, sinking into the wet muck. I tried to push myself up but slid instead, the wet sand coating my forearms. I clenched the muscles in my abdomen, pulling myself back up without the help of my hands.

Where was I? This wasn't the goldstone palace, this wasn't even Annwyn—

Yes, it is.

Ahead of me, still and undisturbed despite my floundering, was a seemingly endless expanse of cerulean water.

The Split Sea.

This couldn't be. It was nearly two weeks' travel from Baylaur to this coastline.

Impossible.

But there was nowhere else in the world where the sea lay still, without a single wave to break its crystalline surface. Nowhere else but the cursed Split Sea.

Unless this was not Annwyn.

No, no, no. That was even more impossible.

I had to get up. Wherever I was, I couldn't remain exposed on the shore like this. I was armed only with my brother's gargantuan sword. It would slow me down, when speed was my main advantage. I couldn't wait here for some enemy to find me, alone and exposed.

I clenched my core muscles once again, dragging one leg up out of the sucking sand.

But when I planted my foot, the world spun away again.

2
ARRAN

Mate. Mate. Mate.

The word pounded in my head, in my soul. Its staccato beat was all I could hear or make sense of. Three hundred years of battlefield training melted away to nothing. Because nothing could have prepared me for the moment I would find out Veyka was my mate. The same moment that she was torn away from me.

"Where is she?"

"The Queen—"

"Your Majesty..."

Mate.

You let her go. You failed to protect her.

I'd been holding her hand, and she'd still be ripped away from me—torn from my grasp by some otherworldly magic.

Magic.

Veyka didn't possess magic.

The beast within me growled, low and deep. A warning. He would not tolerate this separation for long. He'd wanted her before, loved her before. But this...

Mate.

This was something else. More than love or even lust. This was destiny.

Just like that explosion of power, bathing Veyka in light so bright it had burned itself into my retinas. Power, from a female who supposedly had none.

Truth between us, finally.

The truth that neither of us had known.

Veyka's wasn't powerless. She was a force waiting to be awakened.

Just like the beast inside of me, the rumblings of his roar stirring in my chest.

Veyka was my mate, and she been taken. I would shred apart the world to get her back. This realm, and all the others.

The beast's growl filled the cavernous space, building into a crescendo that couldn't be contained. I hardly noticed the shift. It didn't matter now. Male and beast were one and the same.

The others shifted too, into bears and foxes and ravens. Some threw up walls of ice or summoned tearing winds. But none of it was enough to stop me.

Mate. Mate. Mate.

My mate had been taken. *I must get her back.*

There were too many bodies between me and the exits. Too many between me and her. My beast searched for her scent on the elemental winds, trying to pick up any trace of her to chase down. But there was no whiff of primrose and plum to find.

She was simply *gone*.

So instead, I tore through the flesh of those in my way.

3
VEYKA

The cold water hit my face hard. I didn't land on my feet this time. No, I was face first on my stomach, drenched in water so frigid I was completely unsurprised by the wall of snow-capped mountains I spied in the distance.

I'd never seen a body of water bigger than the courtyard pools of the goldstone palace. But it was just my fucking luck that I landed in water not once, but twice.

It wasn't the Split Sea, I realized as I clambered to my knees. The water was still, but I could see the other shore. A ring of emerald hills, peppered with rocky crags, loomed above water so still I could see the reflection of the undulating hills clearly.

It wasn't sand beneath my knees this time, either, but rocks. Some smooth pebbles, but also sharper ones. My palms were bleeding as I dragged them up, noting the scrapes. I tried to wipe them on my gown by reflex, realized that was filthy, and thought better of it.

Thinking—I was actually thinking. My body was being torn apart from my soul, hurled from place to place against my will, and I had the ability to think.

I supposed years of torture had its advantages.

Where was I?

The Split Sea had been distinctive enough to identify quickly. I ignored the frigid water lapping against my knees and looked around.

The green hills suggested the terrestrial kingdom, a supposition reinforced by the high peaks looming in the distance. The Spine. I knew such mountains existed beyond Annwyn, though details of the continents beyond my own were sketchy at best. But this *felt* like Annwyn.

More than that, it felt... familiar.

A tug in my chest pulled my eyes away from the looming mountains of the Spine, twice the height of those that surrounded Baylaur. But something compelled me to look away, in the opposite direction. To the opposite side of the lake.

I hadn't noticed it before, the gray stone blending into the rocky lake edge at this distance. But then the mists shifted and I could see it clearly. A castle floated on the glass surface of the lake.

How was that possible? Without an elemental water wielder... maybe there were some plants holding it in place, strong terrestrial magic would be required to keep it there, but why...

Yet as I stared, my mind swirling with possibilities, a new feeling coalesced in my chest. One that I hadn't felt before, or had only just begun to contemplate as a possibility.

Belonging.

It felt like coming home.

Suddenly, the need to reach the castle overwhelmed me. It suffused every pore in my skin, every thought in my head. If I got to the castle, everything would be alright. I could *feel* that assurance in my soul. I knew it to be the truth.

I reached out a hand even as I tried to drag my weary legs underneath me. I willed my body to movement.

But instead of taking a step, a different sort of movement took me.

That dark, greedy push and pull had me in its grasp.

What is this? Why, why, why?

Ancestors, it hurts.
I don't care where I go now, just make this wrenching, tearing—
Stop.
I landed flat on my back.
I could hear the drip of water in the distance, but I wasn't wet.
Drip, drip, drip.
It wasn't water.
But neither was it blood.
I recognized that stench—the same dark death I'd encountered before. First the human in the ravine, near the mountain rift. Then again, when I'd interrogated the human supplicant. The witch in the tower.

I tried to hold my breath, but that only made it worse—because then I felt the cold.

I'd been cold before. Moments before, even, when laying in that mountain lake. But this was *cold*. It was different than anything I'd ever felt. It seeped through my skin, into the body that had just coalesced into existence moments before. I could feel the shards of ice forming in my veins, being carried through my body towards the arteries and organs.

But it wasn't just physical. The cold reached inside of my soul, towards the very essence of what made me. It snaked its tendrils around the core of my magic.

No, that couldn't be.

I didn't have any magic.

But I had no other word for it, that glowing ember inside of me that was suddenly reducing, shrinking. I was shrinking. Not my physical body, but my essence. I was disappearing, being sucked away into that creeping darkness.

No.

I wouldn't let it win.

Not now. Not after everything I'd endured. Torture, loss, death... I was not dead, I'd realized by then. Nor was I going to die. I would not allow it.

I would not meet my end in this dark, cold place without a

single soul to mark my passing. I'd fought too damn hard to let it all be for nothing, to dissolve into darkness and disappear.

I had to get out.

But how had I even gotten in? How had I ended up here?

Minutes ago I'd been in Baylaur—

Minutes or hours?

I had no idea. The world had been spinning around me, ripping me apart, and fusing me back together. It could have taken seconds or centuries. I had no conception. I just knew I couldn't stay, or I would die.

Worse than die—I would be ripped apart until no shred of my self remained.

Wherever I was, it wasn't of my world. This wasn't Annwyn. This was another realm—one of the other layers the witch had spoken of.

Out. Out. Out. Ancestors, I was so cold.

It was just like in the Tower of Myda, when the cold slipped around me and pulled me down. I'd thought I was dying then, too. Except I woke up to find that Arran had carried me out, carried me to safety, sat at my bedside.

Arran.

His name reverberated through me with a force I'd never felt. That ember of light inside of me exploded, the tendrils of darkness flinching back. The ice in my veins began to warm.

Arran. Arran. Arran.

I sang his name, a chorus in my blood and in my magic.

I felt my magic wrapping around me then, its embrace warmed by the thought of him. This time when it lifted me away, I was not afraid.

4
ARRAN

The winds whipped in off of the mountains ringing the Effren Valley, slapping across my face with the force of a hand. Maybe it was the ghosts of the dead from the throne room, punishing me. No less than I deserved.

I tried my hands, was unsurprised to find them bound with vines. But in the next breath, the deep emerald tethers loosened and slid away. I expected the voice that came next.

"You were feral," Guinevere said, her voice chilly as any elemental's ice.

My chest tightened. "How many?"

"Me, Lyrena, Elora, twenty others wielding our powers in tandem to hold you long enough for Osheen's vines to restrain you so I could knock you unconscious." She cleared her throat from behind me. "It would be embarrassing if it wasn't so horrific. The Brutal Prince, felled by only twenty fae, not even a battle unit. Clearly, you were not in your right mind—"

"How many?" I was done with her prattling. She only rambled like this when she was avoiding something.

I didn't care how many it had taken to restrain my beast. I wanted the real number.

Footsteps echoed behind me, heavier than Gwen's. Osheen, retreating now that his vines were no longer needed to hold me in place. As if I couldn't have turned those vines against him and Gwen with half a thought.

The door closed softly. Osheen was gone.

"Twenty-two."

I closed my eyes, waiting for the wave of guilt. I hadn't felt it in so long, but it came as sure and familiar as it had all those centuries ago. When I'd first come into my full power, I'd killed so many. Servants in Eilean Gayl who happened to be nearby when the beast took over; courtiers who sneered at my mother when we visited Wolf Bay; anyone, anywhere, anytime, was vulnerable.

And today, I'd killed twenty-two fae courtiers in the throne room.

But that wave of guilt didn't last as long as it should have. It was blotted out by something stronger, the very thing that had driven me feral for the first time in more than two hundred years.

Veyka.

I shot to my feet, my eyes opening and tracking my surroundings with brutal, battle efficiency. They'd taken me to my apartments, the ones I'd hardly occupied in the months since my arrival in Baylaur. They probably thought if they took me to Veyka's, I'd be unhinged further.

No chance of that. The worst had already happened.

Not the worst.

But I wouldn't allow myself to even consider that. Veyka was alive. The tether in my chest, the pull I'd felt ever since arriving Baylaur, had solidified the moment our blood was joined. The mating bond between us was intact, pulling at me with more strength and intensity than any emotion I'd ever felt, even if it wasn't quite an emotion. It was *more*.

She was alive, but she was gone.

Which meant all that mattered was finding her.

But when I spun, Gwen was blocking the door.

"Where are you going?" she asked, one hand going to the sword sheathed at her waist, the goldstone at her shoulders gleaming in the dispersed candlelight.

"To find my mate."

Her eyes widened, the black pupils nearly swallowing the gold rings.

"Mate?" Even Gwen, composed and cool, choked on the word.

"Get out of my way, Gwen." This time it was me who growled, not the beast.

She didn't move. "You and Veyka are mates," she said slowly, her eyes returning to their normal size, but that calculating keenness entering them. "There hasn't been a mated pair of fae in thousands of years."

"I don't have time for a history lesson." I stepped forward, ready to shove her aside.

The lioness flashed in her eyes. Not enough to stop me, but to slow me.

"I have to find her, Gwen." It was the closest thing to an entreaty she was going to get before I forcibly removed her.

The dark skin of her brow creased. "We don't even know where she is."

"So we start searching." It was simple. "You are one of her sworn Goldstone Guards. You should be at my back, not blocking the way."

"I am also a Knight of her Round Table. Your Round Table, Your Majesty."

The words clanged through me. Your Majesty. I was Veyka's mate—and the High fucking King of Annwyn.

"You cannot run out of Baylaur without making provisions for the safety of your kingdom," Gwen said, voice even.

Of course. Gwen, of all people, would think of Annwyn first.

I would have thought of Annwyn first. I'd been putting Annwyn's wellbeing before my own for the past two hundred and some years. But not now. Everything had changed in that throne room—before that, even. When I realized my purpose in this immortal life was not to serve Annwyn, but its Queen. Even at the expense of the former.

"I will not leave Veyka unprotected."

"Veyka is more than capable of protecting herself."

"She has no magic." It felt like a betrayal saying it aloud, even though I knew that Gwen and the others who Veyka had selected for the Round Table knew that truth by now.

For the first time in my entire immortal life, I saw Gwen's eyes soften with sympathy. "We know now that is not true."

I opened my mouth to argue—as if I hadn't been there at Veyka's side, had not felt the flash of power that engulfed her in the moment before she disappeared. I couldn't explain any of it, couldn't sort through it. Wife, mate, High Queen... it was all too much, too fast. All of it eclipsed by the simple fact that she was *gone*.

But before I could shove Gwen aside, a cascade of voices pushed through the closed doors. I recognized them. From the flash in Gwen's eyes, she did as well.

She didn't spare me a look as she turned to the doors, opening them and meeting the waiting eyes and saying with cool command: "Round Table, now."

5
VEYKA

I fell into a land of mist and quiet.

It was dawn in this realm, wherever it was. I'd watched enough sunrises and sunsets over the Effren Valley, alone in the water garden compound, to recognize the subtle differences in shades that marked the two. There was a stillness to dawn, as the creatures of the night slumbered and those of day had not yet awoken. But as I turned my head to the side, slowly taking in my surroundings, I was struck by the eerie feeling that no animals lived here in this clearing.

Everything around me was a lush green. Graceful willow trees—the kind I'd seen depicted in books and paintings, but never for myself—circled the clearing. I could only imagine what Arran could do with those long, elegant tendrils draping from the trees.

Arran. It had been the thought of him that carried me safely away from that realm of darkness and death. He'd saved me again. I didn't plan on telling him about it, either. He didn't need to add to the tally. I seemed to do well enough with that on my own.

I would get back to him, I promised myself.

Wherever I was now, wherever I went next… I would get back

to him. Back to Baylaur, the city and court I'd hated, but that now held everything I cared about.

Everyone.

Ancestors, caring for others was such a painful and beautiful burn in my chest. I still was not used to it.

But I was getting alarmingly used to the way my body was being thrown against my will from realm to realm. The ember within me bobbed happily, easing now to a low, sated glow. Satisfied, as if it were a living thing.

Every time I moved, the world tearing apart and reassembling around me, the ember softened a little. From the burning explosion of power that had consumed me in the throne room, to this amenable thing resting in my chest.

But I couldn't rest. I didn't know where I was, but it certainly wasn't Baylaur or anywhere in the elemental kingdom.

The willows swayed in the breeze. I followed their direction, my gaze tracking along the edge of the clearing to a small gap in the trees.

Not just my gaze; my feet were moving too. I stared down at them in confusion. I didn't remember standing. Had I landed on my feet?

No.

I touched my backside, confirming what I already knew. The back of my gown was wet with dew. It could have been wet from any of the watery realms I'd fallen through, couldn't it? Every one of them had that thread—wetness, water...

I shook my head, dislodging the thoughts even as my feet continued moving. I didn't have time to piece this all together now. I needed to focus on getting out, getting back, at least locating myself in whatever Ancestors-damned realm I'd been dropped into.

The grass was soft beneath my feet, squishy and wet with every step. My shoes were soaked through, useless silk slippers meant for a palace feast. I shucked them off entirely, letting my toes dig into the blades of grass.

As they curled around my toes, I imagined the blades that

Arran had summoned to disable the skoupuma. I imagined that it was his touch caressing me.

It helped ground me as I pushed aside the curtain of willows and peered out to the source of that breeze.

Another lake.

But there was nothing welcoming about this one.

It was the most beautiful place I'd ever seen. The water was a clear, crystalline blue that allowed me to see the gently swaying water plants just below the surface. Steady melodious waves lapped at the shore. The shore itself was made of tiny, rocky pebbles. But they were round and unnaturally polished, and I knew without trying it out that if I stepped onto them, they would be smooth and welcoming against my feet.

But every instinct inside of me screamed a warning.

Even as my eyes were drawn upward—compelled. I couldn't control it, just like I hadn't been able to control the movement of my feet. This place had a sentience all its own, and it wanted me to look across the water.

Through the mist. A shimmering mist of rainbows that seemed like something out of a childhood fantasy. As the first rays of morning sunlight slipped over the horizon, those rainbows danced over the blue water in a mesmerizing, undulating ripple. And then those rainbows parted, the mist melting away enough to reveal an island in the center of the lake. Upon its shore, a lady.

I had no doubt this was what I'd been drawn to see. Across the clearing, to the edge of the lake, so I could see her watching me.

Unease slid down my spine. She was indeed watching. Too far for me to make out any of her features, and yet, I felt an eerie knowing. Like I was meant to be here, meant to know who she was, but yet it was all wrong. The pieces did not quite fit together. *I* did not quite fit together.

The ember inside of me sputtered.

But then I felt the pull.

Right in the center of my chest, a tug. Hard, demanding, relentless. Like a tether had been wrapped around my heart and whoever held the other end was pulling me back.

I knew who held that tether.

I closed my eyes, blotting out the lady on the other side of the lake, focusing all my attention on that pull.

I felt the threads of my being start to fray apart. That excruciating but now achingly familiar sensation scrambled the mist and the trees and the cool dawn air, pulled it all apart into nothing. Then I was in free fall.

6
ARRAN

"You each have three minutes to make your case for where we start looking first," I said. I'd used the strategy with my generals for decades. It was the fastest way to determine where everyone stood and to find out where the conflicts were. If they couldn't articulate their reasoning in three minutes, I didn't want to hear it.

Three minutes. Four Knights of the Round Table. Twelve minutes. It was more than I wanted to spare. More than it had taken me to kill twenty-two bystanders in the throne room.

They exchanged glances.

I looked at the clock in the corner of the room.

Lyrena straightened, her merry smile nowhere in evidence. "We send out parties in every direction. We prioritize winged-shifters and wind-wielders. They will be able to cover ground the fastest, and get word back here quickly if they find any sign of Veyka."

It was a sound plan.

I turned to Cyara, who sat at Lyrena's side.

The handmaiden had recovered well from her attack outside the goldstone palace, her white wings fully feathered out again. But she still glanced around, still unsure of her place here at the Round

Table. I didn't have time for her personal misgivings. I knew my direct glare told her as much.

"There have been rumblings from the Split Sea, near the estate of," she paused, the name sticking in her throat. But she muscled past it, even as her turquoise eyes sparkled with tears. "Gawayn's brothers. They could have been involved in his plans to assassinate the Queen, or at least known of them. They might still be working to those ends."

This was the thought that had crossed my mind as well.

Gwen was next. And I knew her well enough to recognize the signs. Her palms were flat on the table, still and composed. Her shoulders set in a straight line, her lips pursed—she was girding herself for battle.

"We cannot all go after her," Gwen said. "We must leave a contingent to guard Baylaur and oversee the running of the kingdom."

Rage ripped through me. The beast roared against the tethers inside of me, the ones that were barely holding him as it was. "You are her Goldstone Guard. You are sworn to protect your Queen," I ground out.

On one side of her, Cyara was frowning. On the other, Parys stared at the table, face expressionless. Gwen ignored everyone but me, fixing her eyes in a steady stare.

"My Queen did not sacrifice her own life in the Tower of Myda to ferret out the traitor in this kingdom, to ensure its safety, just for me to abandon it."

Gwen ought to know better. She ought to have realized she could not make me choose. How could she choose? What the hell was wrong with her? Where was the loyal, unflinching female I'd known for the last two hundred years?

"You have never broken a vow." The disbelief rang in my voice.

But there was no indecision in hers. "A vow to Veyka is a vow to Annwyn."

I didn't know what Veyka would say to that. A month ago, I

would have agreed with Gwen. But not now; not with my mate's life at stake.

"You would leave her to whatever fate—"

"I would defend what she fought so hard for—what you have always believed in protecting. Have you suddenly forgotten your responsibilities now that you have a mate? You are the High King of Annwyn."

Everyone in the room froze. The gentle breeze that had swirled through the chambers—either from the open balcony in the bedroom or from Parys' latent energy—died instantly.

"Mates," Lyrena breathed, awe coating the syllables.

Gwen was as cunning as Veyka, as clever as Pays. She'd dropped the word into the middle of the conversation, knowing it would blow up the debate.

I felt the prickling at the back of my neck, sensed my fingernails turning to claws. I was a hairsbreadth away from losing control, from leaping across that table and ripping out her throat—

"It's a rift."

Three sets of eyes swung around, away from me, to the curly-haired, clever courtier who was no longer staring at the table. If anyone could figure out the three words even more disorienting than the one Gwen had dropped, it was Parys.

Fucking Parys.

"What do you mean?" Cyara said, tilting her head to the side as she considered him. As if this was a real, reasonable idea and not utter nonsense.

Parys shifted in his seat, avoiding my gaze. The stare I knew had turned lethal.

"She went through a rift," he said to Cyara.

"There is no rift in the middle of the throne room," I snarled. This was a waste of my fucking time. I had was done with all of them. Done with Veyka's cursed Round Table, done with all of it. I needed to find my mate, and I needed to find her *now*.

I shoved out of my chair, ignoring the way the gold scrollwork letters of my name on the stone table seemed to burn into my palms.

Parys' eyes went wide. "No—but yes. There is. Veyka is the rift. Sort of," he said hurriedly, stumbling over the words.

If I'd been in my right mind, I would have realized that I had never heard the smooth-talking elemental garble his speech. But my entire consciousness was a churning miasma.

"He has lost his mind," I said, summoning my commander's voice and fixing my attention on Lyrena instead. "We combine your and Cyara's plans. Send parties out in all directions, but we go to the Split Sea."

"But if she commands the void..."

I froze.

The witch's words echoed in my head—in Veyka's voice, as she'd recounted to me in those all too short days of rest and closeness after the Tower of Myda.

Why was Arthur taken?

To make way for you, Veyka.

Parys met my stare with an uncharacteristic, unflinching gaze. "I thought the Void Prophecy meant rifts all along."

Veyka had laughed at that supposition. She'd dismissed prophecies altogether, even as we sat at the same damned stone table and fulfilled the one made by Merlin at Lugnasa.

Fuck. Fuck. Fuck.

I didn't have time for this nonsense. But even as I tried to tear myself away, to push off of that table, something held me fast. A tug in my chest, visceral and real—the mating bond.

The pull of it was almost unbearable. My body was screaming out for her, reaching. What was happening to me? I ground my hands into the surface of the stone table, trying to keep myself upright even as my muscles tensed hard enough to edge on pain.

"You are saying that she is the queen from the Void Prophecy?" Cyara was chewing on her bottom lip, considering. Ancestors, she thought he was onto something.

Parys swallowed, glancing between all of us. His eyes snagged on me; I shoved away the sensations roaring through me, trying to focus on his words.

"I am saying she went through a rift. We all saw that explosion of power. I don't... none of us know what it is, or was. But she was here, and then she was gone. Just like moving through a rift," he explained, every word measured. He'd been thinking about this since she disappeared.

Lyrena was shaking her head, her golden braid flashing in the candlelight. "If there was a rift in the goldstone palace, it would have been discovered by now."

"Unless Veyka created it," Cyara said, understanding lighting her turquoise eyes. Parys nodded his agreement.

I didn't understand. Not whatever they were explaining, not the torrent of feeling crashing through me. *I could feel her.*

"Veyka."

They all looked to me now, the strangled sounds of her name coming out a rasp from my throat.

"What's wrong?"

"Your Majesty?"

"Arran," Gwen said, voice cutting through the air, sword already drawn as she edged around the table.

I tried to lift a hand to wave her off. But I couldn't. I was anchored to the table, unable to move, unable to flex a single muscle other than the one beating inside of my chest.

Veyka. Veyka. Veyka.

"I..." My entire body was consumed with fire, just like it had been in the throne room when my blood joined with Veyka's and her body was consumed with that incandescent flame of power.

Then a terrible crash rent the air and all the tension tore from my body. Gwen lunged forward, catching me from collapsing. But just as quickly, I felt my muscles responding, my legs moving under me as I shoved through the doors into the bedroom.

Their gasps behind me were drowned out by the roar inside my chest as we all saw what had crashed into the room, what now lay between the bed and the balcony in a heap of matted white and silver.

Veyka's broken body on the goldstone floor.

7
VEYKA

Pain lanced through me, hot and sizzling in every limb. More pain than I'd ever felt, all at once, everywhere.

Every bone in my body ached.

But I managed to crack open my eyes. As I peered out, familiar images filled my view. Gemstones glinted in the firelight. Goldstone sparkled, glittering orange-gold as fading sunlight spilled in from archways I couldn't quite see, but knew were there nonetheless.

Then a familiar scent swept over me. Deep and heady, roses mixed with earth, spices foreign yet familiar after all these months.

Arran.

But it wasn't him standing over me. The faces were unfamiliar, set in concentration. I tried to open my eyes further, tried to part my lips and speak. But no voice came. Those unfamiliar eyes drifted over me, just for a moment. Long enough to note my labored movements.

Arran. His name formed on my lips, but no sound came out.

He was close. If I could just see him for a moment...

But my body was being taken again. This time it was warm, gentle, like being eased into a bath. Not that terrible tearing of my soul and my self.

I tried to fight it... I reached for the ember of magic I'd felt inside of me... but it was quiet. Everything was quiet...

8
ARRAN

I could hardly see her. The bevvy of healers was a solid wall between me and my mate. Even my towering height failed me. Their bodies bent forward over her, their hands in constant motion as they mended.

Every bone in her body.

Or nearly so.

Memories stirred. Those dark, predawn hours after the Tower of Myda, when healers had stood over her exactly like this, trying to coax warmth and life back into her frigid organs, had been absolute torture. But this was worse.

To have had her safe and in my arms, clinging to my hand in that throne room, to be completed in a way I'd never known I needed... only to have her ripped away.

She is back. She is safe.

I repeated the mantra again and again, trying to hold my beast in check. Every urge inside of me demanded that I shift, that I chase away the healers standing over her and encircle her in the life-giving warmth of my fur.

But I wasn't what she needed now. She needed those healers.

The bedroom pulsed with magic. A fire wielder used their delicate flame to shape wooden splints that would brace her fragile bones. A wind wielder used their masterful gift to move her body by fractions of inches, carefully coaxing the jagged edges of the bones within her body back into place.

I wanted to roar, to remind them that this was their queen. The High Queen of Annwyn. My mate.

But they didn't need me any more than she did.

So I forced myself to stand on the balcony. Close enough to smell her comforting scent of plum and primrose, even beneath the layers of medicinal tinctures and the muck she was covered in. But far enough away that all I got were flashes of her pale skin and her bedraggled moon-white hair.

Of the Knights, only Cyara remained. Gwen and Lyrena guarded the door, their role as Goldstones clarified now that their queen had returned. Parys had disappeared—probably to the library—if only to avoid the rumors and whispers that were the currency of the Elemental Court.

Cyara was a silent, steady presence on the other side of the bed. She took away soiled, bloody cloths and returned with fresh ones and steaming bowls of clean water, heated with her own flame. She held out her hands and received the shredded layers of Veyka's gown as the healers cut it off of her. Her Joining gown, that glorious iridescent silver confection of rainbows and light, now in tatters fit for nothing but being tossed into the hearth.

It wasn't a good omen.

The beast in my chest growled, low and demanding.

It was taking too long.

Even after the Tower of Myda, the healing hadn't taken this long. There'd been no blood. But now... so much of it. I reassured myself it wasn't the kind of blood loss that could mean death, even to our kind.

But I realized... our Joining was the first time I'd seen her bleed.

In all of our sparring sessions, our forays into Baylaur, even the wicked grip of the witch's talons... she'd never once shed a drop of blood. Merlin had nearly lost her composure because of it at the Offering all those months ago.

But at the Joining, the conniving priestess had dug her blade into Veyka's hand and drawn the blood that would join us together without any trouble at all. And now, all these cuts and scrapes bled freely, crusting over to a dark scarlet, then bleeding fresh when the healers reopened them to clean and mend.

What did it mean?

Did it have to do with the Void Prophecy?

Every part of me shuddered—even the beast.

If Parys was right, what would that mean for our court? Or the darkness lurking beyond in the human realm, that Veyka had been so quick to dismiss?

She had power.

I'd seen it, felt it, just like everyone else in that throne room.

But I couldn't pretend to understand it.

Did Veyka?

Had she known all along?

Had she lied?

No.

Not after the Tower of Myda. I couldn't believe... we'd agreed that there would be no lies between us. No promises, but also no lies. If she'd known, she would have told me.

I wished for the weight of certainty in my chest to match the words I whispered in my head.

None came.

One healer stepped back; the fire wielder. As they moved to the foot of the bed and began to tidy up their implements, I glimpsed Veyka's legs. Her gorgeous, muscular calves and thighs, now wrapped in a cage of thin wood strips, carefully placed to brace and hold in place.

"How long will she be like this?" I choked out. I hadn't even seen the upper half of her body.

"A day at most," the wind wielder said, turning to face me. She looked me up and down with a boldness I'd rarely seen from the elementals in my new court.

The doubt must have been showing in my eyes.

"Bones are complicated to set, but they heal quickly. The force of the impact did most of the damage, rather than..." she paused, glancing around the room, to where Veyka had crashed onto the goldstone tiles. "Wherever she came from, her bones were not broken there."

"The nature of the Queen's return does not go beyond this room." I was hardly thinking, but some latent battlefield commander's instinct drove my words. The courtiers would be speculating enough. The fewer whispers we had to contend with, the better. "She has returned and is resting. That is all that will be said."

The wind-wielder inclined her head, then cut a look to the others. Their chins bowed in unison.

I watched in silence as the last of them stepped away to fully reveal my mate.

Veyka was naked.

The healers had draped a few pieces of pale cloth over her navel and breasts. A modesty she wouldn't have cared about, though I didn't say anything or make a move to remove them. I was too transfixed by the wreckage.

Everything was aligned once more, thank the Ancestors. Her legs and arms didn't stick out at unnatural angles, the blood had been washed away to nothing but pink cuts, already rapidly healing. But her arms and legs were wrapped in splints in careful straight lines. They'd washed her face, but her hair was still a tangled mess. Even her cheeks were marred with cuts, though her neck and head were mercifully unbandaged.

"When will she wake?"

"We spelled her to sleep while we did the mending," the wind-wielder said, watching with hands on her hips as the other healers retreated. She seemed to be their leader.

I should probably know the name of the chief healer at my

court; but I couldn't summon the will to care. Everything I had was focused on the female laying prone in the bed.

"Which means?" I felt the tug in my chest, the compulsion to be nearer to her. But my emotions held me in check. I loved her—I'd loved her before I understood the meaning of that bond between us. But the force of the feelings inside of me now was enough to give me pause. At least, some parts of me.

Entirely against my will, I stumbled forward.

Fucking Ancestors.

The bond was strong.

"It means that when she will wake is impossible to predict," the healer said matter-of-factly. "It is dependent on her body's level of exhaustion, her hunger or thirst, her own desire to sleep or wake... and her personal well of power."

The healer knew.

It physically hurt to drag my eyes away from Veyka. But I did it, pinning the healer with a look that said everything—promise, threat, and more.

She inclined her head once more. "I shall come tomorrow to remove her bindings. Send for us sooner if you have need."

Then she was gone, closing the door to the bedroom softly in her wake. Cyara gave me one glance, another to Veyka, then disappeared into the connecting rooms she'd once shared with her sisters. I didn't know what was in there now, but I knew she wouldn't retreat to the suite of rooms she shared with her parents while Veyka was bound to her bed.

And then I was alone with my mate.

I took one unsteady step forward, then another. Until I reached her bedside and my knees crumpled beneath me.

9

ARRAN

I had no notion of time passing. My knees stopped aching after the first hour. I rested my head against the edge of the bed, unable to drag my eyes up to look at her but also unable to move away. I couldn't leave her. The bond wouldn't let me, neither would my beast.

I would stay at her side until her eyes opened. I couldn't lay beside her on the bed and hold her hand the way I had in those painful hours after the Tower of Myda. But I could stay right there, waiting.

The fog of my own mind was a dangerous place to be.

The Void. Prophecies. Mates. High King and Queen.

One word overlapped another, the feelings summoned by each bleeding into the others until I couldn't parse them.

Fear.

In three hundred years, I could count on one hand the number of times I had truly been afraid. Never on a battlefield. Only in those early years, when my power had spiraled out of my control—like it had in the throne room.

I waited for the lives of those I had killed to flash before my eyes, but they did not.

Which said something even worse about me.

Veyka had been taken from me. I would never let it happen again.

I repeated the vow, let it seep into my soul, fill the crevices of fear. It didn't stop the pain, but it eased it slightly. Enough.

The door cracked open, the sound followed by careful, feline footsteps that could only belong to one female.

"The healers report that she will mend soon," Gwen said from the doorway.

Wise, not to try and approach my injured mate. Always so fucking wise, was Guinevere.

I didn't say anything.

"She needs to make an appearance as soon as possible."

I felt the growl in my chest before I heard it. "She is not even awake yet."

"But she will be soon. In the meantime—"

"In the meantime, I will stay at her side," I snarled.

"You are the High King of Annwyn. Your court needs reassurance that all is well after the spectacle at the Joining," Gwen said, her voice perfectly measured.

Perhaps Gwen wasn't as wise as I thought.

"Do not presume to tell me how to rule my kingdom. You are not the queen or the heir, Guinevere. You are a guard. Get outside the door and do your Ancestors-damned job."

I felt the roiling menace of her power from across the room. A half a thought was all that separated her from shifting into that vicious dark lioness.

"I dare you," I breathed.

I would tear her limb from limb if she dared to shift in the presence of my wounded mate. No amount of friendship, no number of years spent fighting together on a battlefield, none of it would be enough to save her.

"As you command," she said, her voice a faint snarl. "Your Majesty."

I barely heard the door close through the animal roar in my head.

A soft chuckle floated through the air, penetrating my mind, my chest, my soul.

"Do I have to call you 'Your Majesty' while you fuck me?"

10
VEYKA

Having every major bone in your body mended is damn painful. I'd endured some excruciating things, but the feeling of my own bones knitting together beneath my skin was probably the worst. I would have begged for the tea to knock me out, if I thought Arran could handle it.

But one look at his drawn face, the nearly feral set of his mouth, the fire burning in his eyes that had nothing to do with lust, and I knew that seeing me unconscious again would sever the fragile tether he had to reality.

I recognized the look on his face. I'd seen it in Cyara in the moments after her sisters' deaths. Ancestors, I'd seen it in the mirror often enough in those months after Arthur's murder.

I was the one laying broken in bed, held together with cleverly crafted splints and a heavy heap of magic. But he was the one barely holding on.

I lifted one eyebrow. I couldn't lift my hand to reach for him, still kneeling on the floor. "You can sit on the bed."

His throat bobbed as he swallowed. "I don't want to jostle you while you're healing."

"That is what the splints are for." I'd surveyed the splints when

I first woke. The extent of them said enough about the damage done to my body when I literally fell through time and space and crashed back into the goldstone palace.

Mentioning the splints was a mistake. Arran's eyes dragged downward, the worry shining in his dark eyes.

"They spent hours tending to you, to get you arranged just so," he said, voice hoarse.

Ancestors, this was bad. I thought I'd seen worry after the Tower of Myda. But this...

How long had I been gone?

I ground my teeth, ignoring the headache forming at the base of my skull.

"Arran, come and sit on this bed or I swear to the Ancestors, I will get up and drag you over here myself." Not that I could. But I'd try, and ruin all the work the healers had done in the process.

He looked like he wanted to strangle me. But he did as I asked, easing himself down until his weight was balanced on the edge of the bed near my hip.

The tension in my chest eased. It had been there when I woke, that insistent urge that had pulled me free of the clearing beside the lake and landed me back in Baylaur. But only when Arran was at my side, close enough to touch, did it relax enough that I could take a full breath.

"What happened in the throne room?" I asked. Maybe I could distract him from that all-consuming worry.

Mistake.

His black eyes darkened. An impossibility that only I could see.

"You disappeared," he said, voice little more than the growl of a beast.

"I am aware of that," I said. "But what did it look like... what happened before, and after?"

"You lit up. Your entire body was glowing, bursting with..." Arran tore his eyes away from me.

"With power," I finished, the words a tremble on my lips. It was unbelievable. But when I looked inside, I could still feel it there. The ember of power, bright and strong, at the core of my being.

I tried to shake my head, but quickly thought better of it, the pounding increasing. I stilled myself, taking a deep breath. "I don't understand. I've never had power... my mother—" A feral growl from Arran, "—tried for decades to force magic to grow in me. How is it possible that it awakened at our Joining, of all moments?"

Arran's face clouded and I realized—he understood something I did not. My mind whipped through possibilities, trying to make sense of things. But nothing materialized, nothing real.

"Our blood was Joined," he said carefully.

"So? That is what the Joining is—it is symbolic of our joint commitment to Annwyn or some other Ancestors-blasted nonsense." I was babbling, I knew it. But the fear was gone from Arran's eyes, so suddenly, and that unnerved me more than anything.

"I think the mingling of our blood awoke the magic within you... as well as the bond between us," he said, his voice full of emotion.

We were talking about mingling blood, not vows of love. *What the hell is going on?*

"What bond? What are you talking about?" I asked, hating the quiver of my bottom lip.

Arran's black eyes searched mine, delving into my soul with an intensity that I hadn't felt from him since those precious, painful minutes we'd stolen together before the Tower of Myda.

"The mating bond," he said softly.

The world shifted again. But this time I remained in one place as everything around me reordered itself.

Arran's hand closed around mine. "You are my mate."

11

ARRAN

"Mate?"

She blinked rapidly, the only damned thing she could do laying prone in that bed. I could feel the emotion rippling off of her, though I couldn't identify it.

I'd been too fast. Too much, too soon.

But when she demanded that I come and sit beside her on the bed, I thought she'd felt it, too. That clawing need that could only be eased by proximity to one another.

Veyka wasn't ready to hear that I loved her. I'd known that from the moment I recognized the emotion within myself. Why would she be any readier for this—a bond that would tie us together for the rest of our immortal lives.

We are already tied together.

I shoved that thought aside. Annwyn didn't matter—not in that moment. Only Veyka.

"I can feel it," I said, lifting the hand that didn't hold hers to place on my chest. "For me, it feels like a pull—constant, demanding. A pull towards you. I knew it the moment our blood mixed."

I swallowed hard, as afraid of my next words as I had ever been of anything in my life. "Do you feel it, Veyka?"

Her pale skin had gone ashen, the blue of her eyes bright and gleaming as if she was holding back tears and losing the battle.

It was impossible. The healers had only been gone a few hours. But she slid her fingers from mine and lifted them to her chest, right between her breasts. The fabric the healers had placed there for her modesty slipped away, leaving nothing but bare skin in its wake.

For once, I didn't notice Veyka's beautiful breasts. I was transfixed by the place between them where she pressed three fingertips. Right above her heart.

"Here," she said, her voice quaking. "What... what does it mean?"

"It means that we are mates." I knew that wasn't an answer, but I didn't have much more explanation to give.

"Why?"

"I don't know."

Slowly, she lowered her hand back to the bedside. She didn't reach for mine again, and I told myself it was because the energy she'd already exerted was too much.

"Mates aren't real. They are a fairytale." Her voice was getting stronger, edging from shock to something sharper. "There hasn't been a mated pair in Annwyn since Nimue and Accolon."

She remembered her history better than me.

"I know it is..." I paused, searching for the word to describe the feral, possessive rage I'd felt when she'd been torn away from me. The same desire to maim and kill that I'd felt when Gwen stepped into the room earlier. "Primal. Deeper than our consciousness. It is seeded in our souls."

I didn't need a thorough grasp of history to know as much. I could feel it.

Veyka's eyes widened, her gaze shifting away from me, over my shoulder. But I could sense that she wasn't looking outward at all. She'd turned her gaze inside of herself, searching for the tenants of the bond within her body and soul. I knew she'd find them as surely as I could feel their presence in my own body.

"I don't want to be someone's mate."

Her words were a whisper on the evening breeze, and a knife to my heart.

"Are you rejecting the bond?" I growled, the words too harsh. But I couldn't stop them. I was on my feet, pacing away from her, then back, menace and rage and that primal beastliness flowing off of me in waves.

Veyka's eyes went wide once again.

"I am not rejecting anything. I am trying to figure out what the hell happened to me," she cried, hysteria hovering at the edge of her tone. She didn't watch me pace, she stared at the ground, at her hand, anywhere but at me.

I see all of you. And I am not afraid.

She'd said that to me once. But as she avoided my gaze, I knew it wasn't true anymore. She was absolutely terrified to be my mate.

12
VEYKA

Just like that, the fragile thing between us was broken.

As surely as I had broken my body to shards, falling through the realms and crashing into the goldstone floor in uncontrolled freefall, I'd shredded the kernel of... *us*.

Not the mating bond. Despite Arran's words, I could no more reject that bond inside of me than I could stop the beating of my own heart.

But the parts we'd each given freely of ourselves, the bits we'd shared that were motivated by trust and affection rather than animalistic destiny... I'd ruined it.

Even if all I'd done was speak the truth—exactly as we'd said we would.

I didn't want to be Arran's mate. I didn't want to be *anyone's* mate. I barely wanted to be myself, Veyka, High Queen of Annwyn. It had taken me months to claw my way out of the darkness, to a place where I could care about something and someone other than the hollowness in my chest and the sweet taste of revenge.

And just like that, my agency had been ripped away from me once again. My body thrown through realm after realm until I was a broken, bloody mess on the floor; and my soul, tethered to another when I'd only just managed to piece it back together.

Fuck all of it.

I sat up and started unlacing the splints.

It hadn't been quite the full day Cyara had told me the healers predicted I would need, but I didn't care. I wanted them off; I wanted off of that damn bed, and I wanted a blade in my hand. I needed to stab something—or someone—desperately.

"Your Majesty," Cyara rushed forward, nearly dropping the tea tray she carried in her hurry to get me down onto my back.

"Veyka," I reminded her, an unflinching command. "I am done laying here. I am *fine*."

I couldn't hide the wince as I bent my arm to rip the splints off the other, but I ignored it.

"The healers will be back this afternoon," Cyara said. She didn't try to stop me again, but she did slide a dubious glance towards the closed bedroom doors.

Arran had disappeared through those doors last night after I broke his heart.

Based on the persistent but not overwhelming pull in my chest, I guessed that he hadn't gone far.

I ignored it, as I had been all night. "Where are my knives and scabbards?"

Cyara's turquoise eyes turned downright incredulous. "You cannot—"

"I can do whatever I damn well please. I am the High Queen of Annwyn," I gritted out, swinging my feet around to the floor.

I paused to take a few breaths. Not because I was afraid to test my weight.

My handmaiden circled the bed, the tea tray still in her hands, and fixed me with a look that was positively terrifying.

I glared right back.

Instead of battling with words, she set the tea tray gently on the side table, opened the drawer, and pulled out a hand mirror. Which she then held directly in front of my face.

I flinched harder at my reflection than I had at the pain.

"This is why I made you a Knight of the Round Table. You're as irritatingly protective and fierce as any of them," I grumbled.

I was a mess.

No, that was putting it too kindly.

I was a fucking disgusting, Ancestors-damned mess.

My hair, which had been plaited and adorned with tiny rose clips for the Joining, looked like a tangled nest for some fearsome, blood-loving bird. A few of the clips remained, but detangling them from my hair... I shivered. The cuts on my face were mostly healed, but they distorted my normally pale skin with slashes of brighter pink.

It is shocking Arran wants me as his mate at all, looking like this.

The jest wasn't even funny in my mind.

Cyara put aside the mirror and folded her arms across her chest, staring down at me with eyes full of challenge, wings quivering. The strangeness of it struck me—my tiny handmaiden, looking down on me rather than up for once, with all the command of a queen in her eyes.

Yes, I'd been wise to make her a Knight. Even if I was stupid about everything else.

"I will help you bathe, change into a night gown, and then back into the bed."

"Cyara."

"Veyka."

I regretted insisting she use my name rather than my title. "I am fine."

"Good. Be fine in the bed." Her wings flared slightly over her shoulders. I knew what that meant. I'd watched that movement a thousand times as she ordered her sisters around.

Sadness hit me hard, square in the gut, more painful than bones knitting together could ever be. I remembered then, what I'd been stupid to forget in my wallowing over the last hours. There was pain so much worse than physical suffering.

I couldn't fall back into the darkness. I wouldn't let myself.

But the sadness...

No. There was no room for sadness or weakness.

I was the High Queen of Annwyn now. My kingdom needed me to be present, not spiraling in my own sorrow.

And while I might no longer be powerless, I had no control over that burning ember inside of me. No more than I did over the tug in my chest, the male I knew waited for me just beyond the bedroom doors.

"Fine," I sighed, holding out a hand to allow Cyara to help me into the bathing room. "Do you worst, Knight."

I'd let her coddle me, if it helped her feel better. And if it helped me feel better too... well, I had a sense that even though I was now High Queen, my life was no less dangerous than it had been when I'd been the powerless Princess of Peace.

13
ARRAN

I forced myself to go back in.

Veyka had ripped out my heart and stomped on it. Honestly, I shouldn't have expected anything different.

I understood how carefully a battle sequence must be executed—moves and countermoves that took place slowly, even though the heat of battle was fast and punishing. Armies moved by inches, not miles.

But the beast within me and the mating bond tethering us together wasn't something I'd ever faced before. It felt right to me, to be near her, to claim my mate. Maybe it was because my beast form was a wolf, a species that mated for life.

The *why* of it all did not really matter—only that I'd done a terrible job of managing it. And now Veyka wanted nothing to do with me.

Too bad she was my wife and queen, as well as mate.

Once the healers left for the second time, looking frazzled in a way that only Veyka was able to achieve in her attendants, I knew I could delay no longer.

And walked in to see Veyka trying to rise from the bed, hanging on to the bedpost at the foot, legs trembling.

"Have you lost your mind?" I grabbed her without thinking. The way she jerked told me enough—she'd felt that same jolt of heat between us where our bodies touched. But she didn't try to twist out of my grasp.

Maybe she just didn't have the energy.

"It is possible," Veyka said with a sigh, allowing me to ease her back down to the bed.

I took a step back. Then another.

My beast growled. I ignored it.

"Where did you think you were going?"

She crossed her arms over her chest, framing the swell of her breasts. I barely kept in the groan. She looked a hundred times better than she had the day before, and with her breasts straining against the pale lavender of her silk nightgown, my cock couldn't help but notice.

Her mouth tightened—she knew. But she didn't say anything, or lick her lips in invitation.

"I was coming to look for you," she said instead.

I raised one eyebrow and waited.

She gave me a mocking lift of hers in return. "To discuss the running of our kingdom and all that."

"How uncharacteristic."

So, she'd decided on verbal sparring. As good a way as any to avoid the tenderness that had disappeared between us.

She bit her lower lip, and I thought she might stick out her tongue at me. Instead, she reached for the bedpost again. "I suppose I need to make an appearance before the court, to reassure them I'm still alive after that spectacle in the throne room. And we have about a thousand things to discuss at the Round Table."

As she spoke, her fingers curled around the bedpost and she heaved herself up once again. I might have admired the way the muscles in her arm flexed, if I hadn't had to rush forward and grab her elbow to steady her.

"Will you stay in the damn bed?" I said, trying to ease her back down. She found the strength to resist. Of course, she did.

"There was a time I could hardly drag you out it," I growled.

"Times change." Everything had changed.

Veyka did lick her lips then, gazing up at me, her breath coming a little too fast. "I'll stay in bed if you come join me and do very unkinglike things to me."

I wanted to take her up on it. I wanted to lay her back on the bed and make love to her, ravage her body, find our completion together. My body had been begging me for it from the moment our blood mingled together. To solidify the mating bond.

But that wasn't what Veyka wanted.

And while that had been enough, once…

"I will arrange for a feast," I heard myself say. "Once the court is assuaged, we'll see to the Round Table."

I watched the bob of her throat, wanted to lick it, taste her on my tongue. But I swallowed the impulse.

"Tonight," Veyka said, her voice steady.

I wanted to argue. But I knew she was right—the sooner the court saw her whole and in control, the better.

"Rest until then," I said. And knowing my mate well enough, I swept my arms under her knees and deposited her back on the bed before she could argue.

14
VEYKA

Cyara dressed me without asking for approval. She knew what choices to make, I knew well enough to trust her instincts. I let her drape me in burgundy silk held in place by a gold filigree bustier. The translucent fabric gave the illusion of my curves while cleverly covering the newly healed over cuts that still marked my skin. On any other fae, they would have already been invisible. But my skin was so pale, the pink stood out in horrible reference to my journey through the realms.

I'd recounted it to Arran. Knew I would have to tell the Round Table as well once we convened. But aside from a frown and rubbing his chest, he didn't have any insight to offer. Neither did I.

My magic slumbered inside me. I didn't feel like I was about to be pulled apart and flung through time and space at any given moment. I'd happily let it rest there. I had no desire to relive that feeling, the total loss of control.

Finished weaving a strand of garnets into my plait and adjusting the amorite studs pinned along the shell of my ear, Cyara turned to pour the tea she'd set to steep earlier.

The rich brown liquid splashed into the teacup, echoing louder that it ought to in my ears.

My apartments were so quiet these days.

How could it be that when all I'd wanted was silence and darkness, there had always seemed to be a bevy of interlopers chattering and giving advice. Yet when I was High Queen and needed their advice, I was suddenly alone?

Dead.

So many of them were dead—Charis, Carly... Gawayn.

My chest ached. For once, not from the mating bond.

"Pour yourself some as well," I heard myself saying, scooting around on the chair to face my handmaiden. My friend. "You ought to be attending these things with me now, as a Knight of the Round Table."

Cyara huffed, her white feathered wings contracting above her head. "I would thank you for the invitation, if we didn't both know that you dread these things as much as I would."

She handed me the tea and perched on the edge of the bed, much like the bird shifter I imagined must live somewhere in her family tree.

I smiled despite the sadness wreathing me. "My courtiers could use your clever set downs."

"Your courtiers can hardly believe you've appointed a servant to your Royal Council." She pursed her lips at the teacup.

"You aren't a servant. You're my friend. And a very worthy Knight of the Round Table," I corrected her.

Another flutter of wings. Then they eased down her back. I appreciated the sight of them, delicate and beautiful. Whole. Each white feather shimmered with iridescence like the inside of a seashell.

I let myself admire them as we sipped our tea in silence. The bitter tang on my tongue was tinged with just a hint of sweetness—the cocoa flavoring Cyara magically managed to source from the terrestrial kingdom year-round. I opened my mouth to ask her about it—

"You left out the shadowvein." The delicious tea suddenly burned in my throat.

Cyara blinked at me over the rim of her teacup. "I assumed because you were Joined that you would not want it any longer."

Ancestors.

I hadn't thought about it at all.

I'd never needed to. Cyara had dutifully added it to my tea every day since I'd emerged from the water gardens.

Before then... I slammed closed the golden gates on those memories. Nightmares.

"I... I don't..." Shit. Shit. Shit. I was a stuttering idiot. Thank the Ancestors that Arran wasn't here. What would Arran think? Would he want...

It doesn't matter what he wants. It is my body.

"Veyka," Cyara said steadily. She didn't mistakenly use my title, and I knew it was because in that moment, she spoke to me female to female rather than subject to ruler. "Would you like me to continue adding the shadowvein to your daily tea?"

I stared down at the brown liquid, already going cold in my cup. My fingers gripped it hard enough that my knuckles matched the delicate porcelain. The tug in my chest, the bond that tethered me to Arran, tightened and pulled.

A reminder. While this was my decision, he deserved to at least know about it.

But talking about something as intimate as a family, children—we barely even knew how to talk to each other, given all that had happened.

My hand was shaking as I set down the teacup.

Control. I had to keep control.

I had no power over the mating bond, no power over the magic inside of me, but I could control this.

I chanted it over and over again. *Control, control, control.*

"Yes, please," I said to Cyara. She spared me the agony of having to see her expression and turned away to brew a fresh pot.

15
ARRAN

Feasts were boring.

I'd been to more of them since coming to Baylaur than the entire three hundred years of my immortal life before that.

In the terrestrial kingdom, where the weather was cold and food scarcer because of it, meals were shared by practicality. A central dining hall was easier to keep warm than individual rooms. Food went further when served communally. Brawls often broke out. Our kind was not particularly well suited to close quarters even if necessity demanded it. But fighting was entertainment in a kingdom where brute strength was the only currency that mattered.

In the elemental kingdom, they valued entertainment of a different sort.

As we watched, dozens of scantily clad males and females entered the throne room. Music floated in on a warm wind that had their clever garments lifting to reveal tantalizing glimpses of breast and thigh.

Beside me, Veyka watched the dancers silently, little more than a wraith.

When I'd come to fetch her for dinner, she'd put her hand in my arm and plastered a smile to her face that was equal parts cruelty and charm. It was a facsimile of the one I truly loved, the wicked joy when she was about to get what she wanted in or out of the sparring ring.

If she noticed me watching her, she gave no sign. She simply stared out at the whorls of pastel gossamer.

Her eyes weren't glowing as she watched them, at least.

I'd been watching for the ring of desire ever since her return. Now that she had power, would her desire show in her eyes the way it did for the rest of our kind? The way mine burned for her? The offer she'd made in her bedroom earlier in the day had been empty, an attempt to reincarnate the dark lust between us that had existed before. I wanted the real Veyka, the real desire.

But so far, nothing.

It made sense. She'd been through something traumatic, falling through rift after rift like that, crashing into the floor of her own bedroom so forcibly she'd been bedridden for two days.

But she'd wanted me before, even in the darkest pits of her despair.

I clenched my teeth and turned back to the display, refusing to acknowledge the soft growl within me. Another thing that had suddenly evaporated—her response to my beast.

I chanced a glance, to see if maybe she'd heard it, if she'd try and soothe the feral thing beneath my skin...

Her pale face was unchanged.

I shifted in my seat, staring out at the crowd. I began calculating the number of minutes we would have to stay in order to satisfy our court. Parys was already halfway through the crescent of tables, sewing gossip about the queen as surely as he was listening for new rumors. When he made it back to the dais, we'd retire.

The courtiers had seen Veyka walk, eat, and drink. Aside from a magical display, there was not much else she could do to reassure our court that she was well.

My eyes were on Parys, but I didn't miss the collective inhale of the crowd.

Instinct had me reaching for Veyka, but her hand was already gripped around the hilt of her dagger. But her eyes were fixed on the center of the room—on Merlin.

"Your Powerful and Royal Majesties." She sank so low that her dark hair, left loose so that it fell in a dark curtain, pooled on the ground.

It reminded me of that black, noxious fluid the human had spewed when Veyka and I were interrogating him.

"I hope you have enjoyed the display." She gracefully lifted her arms to indicate the dancers, all now kneeling on the hard goldstone floor even though she was again standing.

"What do you want?" Veyka said, sitting up, hand still on her weapon.

"I simply wish to please," Merlin smiled. "All of the dancers are my acolytes. I wish to present them to Your Majesties formally."

Veyka's eyes were not burning with desire, but anger was flaring there. And the priestess was either too stupid or too reckless to mind it.

"The priestesses in Wolf Bay are allowed only one acolyte." I let Merlin watch me fingering the head of my battle axe.

Veyka drew her dagger, idly testing the tip, masking her frustration with boredom as she spoke: "That is the law here as well. Who gave you leave—"

"I did, Majesties."

I shot to my feet, but I was still slower than Veyka. Even with her newly healed wounds and bones that only a day ago had been in shards, she was standing with both her daggers drawn, the silver blades sparkling with a rage mirrored in her blue eyes.

"The Dowager Queen extended my mandate prior to King Uther's death," Merlin said smoothly, a catlike smile climbing her face.

This was the sort of entertainment the elemental court enjoyed. It was just as brutal and dangerous as the physical altercations in my homeland. I'd learned that lesson the hard way—and almost lost Veyka in the process.

My beast prowled closer and closer to the surface. I stepped back from the table, ready to shift, to leap from the dais and rip out both of their throats. I couldn't stop the growl that rumbled through me, into the room. No one could hear it, but from the faces of those nearest the dais, they could feel the wave of power—

Mine.

A single word, spoken directly though the tethers of our mating bond to the beast.

In a single flash, I understood two things—the bond was why she'd been able to connect to the beast, speak with him, even before we'd discovered the mating bond for ourselves.

Second, this kill belonged to her. Had always belonged to her.

"Then I rescind it," Veyka said, pushing back her chair.

Her movements were unhurried as she circled around the table, stepping down off the dais with crimson skirts flaring behind her. It was a prescient choice of attire. I wondered if it had been Cyara or Veyka who'd anticipated bloodshed.

"The acolytes have already begun training. To unleash them now, before they have fully mastered the mystical arts, would be dangerous to them and others," Igraine said smoothly, eyes fixed on her daughter.

The Dowager didn't care about the priestess or the acolytes. She cared about needling Veyka, wanted to exert control in any way she could.

Veyka's torture in the water gardens... it had been about her powerlessness. Realization hit me, sent the beast snarling anew. She'd never explicitly told me as much, but I fully understood it then.

As a princess, Veyka had lacked even a drop of magic. But as the new High Queen of Annwyn had displayed her power for an entire throne room. Now, the Dowager was desperate to regain control of her daughter.

I mirrored Veyka's movements, circling the other side of the table. But she didn't need me, I realized as she stepped up to the first acolyte. Determination and control were etched in every line and movement of her body as she drove her dagger into the female's gut.

Then she continued down the line, until a dozen cries of pain had rent the air. By the time she stood before Merlin, her dagger was dripping blood. The priestess's eyes flared. Veyka didn't hesitate. She stabbed her blade into the flat stomach in the exact same place she'd wounded each of the conniving female's disciples.

Veyka turned back to the line of doubled over elementals. "You are no longer acolytes. If you ever attempt to practice the mystical arts again, I will remove your heads from your bodies." There was not an ounce of mercy in her eyes as she turned to her mother.

"Will you stab me now, as well?" the Dowager said softly.

I was close enough to hear it, but none of the courtiers were as Veyka crooned in response, "When you feel the burn of my blade, it will be the last thing you *ever* feel."

Then Veyka stepped around Igraine. She paused long enough to wipe her blade clean on her dress before returning it to the jeweled scabbard at her waist.

She cut me a look, holding out her arm.

I'd been wrong, it seemed.

Stabbing someone—or several someone's—was actually the perfect way to reassure our new court that the High Queen of Annwyn was back to her usual self.

But Veyka wasn't finished. Her arm firmly in mine, she turned us as one to face the court.

"You shall not seek a healer. You shall not treat your wounds yourself. You shall stand where you are until the last courtier has finished their meal, drunk their aural, and left this throne room," she said to the bleeding elementals. Then she turned to the crowd of courtiers and flashed them that brilliant, wicked smile I adored.

"Enjoy."

16

VEYKA

"Call the others, we're meeting," I said over my shoulder as Lyrena and Gwen moved to take up their customary positions in the corridor.

They hadn't brought on more Goldstones. I never saw either of them rest. I'd do the math on that later. Just then, I was sputtering with unspent frustration.

"Veyka," Arran tried to pull me around to face him, but I shook off his arm. "We're supposed to make decisions together, now."

"Because we are mates?" I spat out too quickly.

The pain flashed on his face, and I was the cause. I instantly regretted it. But I couldn't bring myself to apologize; not when the words had come straight from my soul.

Arran glared—it was his default strategy for hiding other emotions. One he'd learned at the elemental court. My court. Our court.

Ancestors. He was right.

"We have a lot to sort through. My little journey has only delayed managing things." It was an offering, eerily similar to the one we'd made in the throne room all those months ago. But this one was genuine—to put Annwyn first, to try to be the queen that Arran had seen in me when I'd barely been able to find the will to live.

The glare didn't change.

I hated that he felt the need to hide himself from me.

But hadn't I asked for as much, with my response to the mating bond?

I hated how confused I was. Hated the fact that I couldn't even make a simple decision, or look at Arran's face, without having a thousand questions storm across my mind.

"Nothing will change between tonight and tomorrow," he finally said.

And so it began.

I was no longer merely the Queen of the Elemental Fae, and he the Brutal Prince offered as the Terrestrial Heir. We were the High Queen and King of Annwyn. Here and now, we were equals.

Gwen had gifted me her father's Round Table, but Arran and I together had sat the knights at it.

"If we meet tonight, we can start putting our plans into effect tomorrow," I said. Despite my wariness of the ever-present pull in my chest, I dragged my fingers casually along my collarbone, then down the neckline of my gown.

Arran's eyes followed the path of my fingertips, just as I'd known they would.

I thought I saw a flicker of black flame in those fathomless eyes. Could have sworn I heard a faint growl on the breeze from the open window.

One black eyebrow rose. "Valiant attempt," Arran said. "But if you want me to fuck you, we don't need an audience."

I stumbled back a step.

Oh, so that's how we're going to play.

I heard the low growl clearly, as if it was coming from inside my own body. It sort of was, I realized. Through the bond.

That was why I'd been able to hear his beast all these months, why I'd been able to communicate without words. The bond between us, this animalistic, preordained connection that I'd thought had something to do with the burning desire between us... another thing that belonged to the bond, rather than to me.

My heart contracted a little. Even as my pussy began to tingle with anticipation.

Arran stepped closer, his eyes dark with the fire that burned only for me. His hand caught mine just above the neckline of my gown, lifting my fingers towards his mouth where his elongated canines gleamed—

"If you summoned us just to watch, I'm going to have to decline."

Arran's beast roared loud enough I was sure that everyone in the goldstone palace must have heard it.

But Parys stood in the doorway unbothered, flanked by my Goldstones on either side, a glass of glittering gold aural in his hand.

"You should be so lucky," I said, stepping back from Arran and sticking out my tongue at my friend.

Parys opened his mouth, and I almost heard the retort on his lips. But one look at Arran, feral and seething with barely contained desire, and he swallowed it.

Gwen stepped into the room, closing the doors behind her.

"Be careful, Parys. If the legends are true, mates are very territorial," she said, otherwise ignoring Arran and striding for the table. "Especially when the bond is new."

"She's right," Cyara said from behind us, where I assumed she'd been waiting for my return. "I asked my father about it. He has a list of texts you might want to consider," she said in Parys' direction.

He nodded his assent, taking his seat. Cyara did as well.

"Is the mating bond common knowledge, then?" I ground out. I'd known for a matter of hours. Now it seemed the entire court did as well.

A series of exchanged, silent looks.

But it was Arran who said, "Can't we have a bit of privacy—"

"You are the High Queen and King of Annwyn. Nothing in your lives is private anymore," Gwen said sharply, her hands gracefully folded over the golden scrollwork of her name engraved on the table. She was dressed in her Goldstones uniform, but the slightly feral gleam in her golden eyes made it impossible to mistake her for anything other than what she was—a powerful terrestrial shifter.

"Especially if you intend to invite people to watch." Lyrena grinned and winked roguishly.

I looked to Arran. My partner, my friend, my lover... my mate.

He was scowling again.

Great.

I threw myself down in my chair, pretending I wasn't attuned to every movement Arran made as he took his own seat beside me.

"Merlin and the Dowager wanted to make a play for power. That's sorted for now." I leaned back in the chair, crossing my arms across my chest. "What's next?"

More silently exchanged glances. This time it was Cyara who broke the tension.

She withdrew a missive from the folds of her gown—*where did she hide the pockets?*—and held it up for the group to see.

"Word arrived from Evander this afternoon," she said. Everyone at the Round Table sat up straighter, myself included. "Nothing in his letter leads us to suspect that Agravayn or the others had anything to do with Veyka's disappearance—"

"The only one who had anything to do with my disappearance was me," I cut in. They'd discussed this, I realized from the series of looks on their faces. Lyrena—anywhere but me. Gwen—staring me down and waiting expectantly for an explanation. Parys—grim but determined, set on whatever point he'd previously argued.

I didn't dare look to Arran.

"What does Evander have to say about the missing children?"

Cyara's wings fluttered, but her voice was steady. "They found a child wandering near the shore of the Split Sea, confused and cold, but otherwise unharmed. It seems the abduction was thwarted, though they are still parsing the details. It mentions that the weather is unusual for this time of year, he suspects a connection but has not deduced that either."

It was painfully little progress after more than a month.

"Does he ask for any assistance or aide?" Arran asked.

I looked his way before I could remind myself that I wasn't supposed to do that. I was trying to hold myself separate, to keep the emotional attachment I felt to him at bay until I could determine how the mating bond changed and complicated things. And I remembered why—the way he saw into me, understood me, when no one else did. The concern in his dark eyes, the way they flicked to me, knowing how the children's abductions had unhinged me months before...

I don't deserve to be his mate.

Ancestors be damned. Another fucking thought that was going to make me lose what was left of my mind.

"He does not," Cyara said.

"We'll send it anyway. One of the airborne shifters, so we don't waste any more time." The softness in Arran's face shifted to the commander's mask, calm and brutally efficient.

Thank the Ancestors.

"What's next?" I asked before the uneasy silence could descend again.

I didn't expect Lyrena to be the one to speak.

"Several of the palace guards have complained lately," she began, shoulders loose and casual. As if she was sipping a pint of ambrosia in a pub in Baylaur, rather than discussing the running of the fae realm. "About disputes and brawls between the elemental and terrestrial factions."

"Why are they bringing their concerns to you?" I tilted my head to the side.

If it had been anyone else, they would have taken offense. But Lyrena just slashed me a smile. "Because I drink with them."

Gwen rolled her eyes. "Of course, you do."

I felt Arran freeze beside me. I understood the reaction. I'd never seen Gwen do something so... well, common. She was always so damn regal and composed.

But as quickly as it came, the casualness disappeared. Her dark brows knitted together and her tan lips pouted out as seriousness stole her countenance. "You are a Knight of the Round Table. They ought to address you as such."

Lyrena's smile faltered. "You catch more faeries with honey than vinegar."

Arran ignored them both, his large palm landing on the table with enough force to call the room to order. "We need to make inroads between the groups. If a unit is fractured, it is ineffective."

"The court is not a legion on the battlefield," I pointed out.

"I'm finding them uncomfortably similar," he admitted, his eyes on me now.

All eyes on me—on us.

"What would you do if you saw this kind of fracturing in an army under your command?" I asked. He wasn't wrong, precisely. Our court was certainly as brutal and bloodthirsty as any battlefield. The admiring looks on my courtier's faces after my display with the acolytes was proof enough of that.

And Arran's instincts had been right before.

He shifted in his seat, facing me more fully. His black eyes weren't burning. Quite the opposite; they'd turned coolly calculating. I couldn't help but admire the handsome planes of his face, the determination in his strong jaw.

The Brutal Prince.

My Brutal Prince.

My king, now.

What hadn't seemed quite so terrifying in the hours before our Joining now seemed absolutely world-shattering.

My mind began to fracture into questions. I shoved them down and focused on the male before me and the plan he began to lay out.

"I would appoint someone who is trusted by both sides, who knows the customs of both factions. Let them make inroads between them. Someone who is naturally good with people, but loyal to me above all else."

Lyrena snorted. "A bit of a shortage of loyalty in these parts, lately."

It wasn't funny, even though she chuckled.

I drummed my fingers on the tabletop, tilting my head to the side and dragging my tongue over my lower lip in the way that I knew drove Arran wild.

Preparing for battle. "So, you're thinking of Parys, then?"

Across the table, Parys choked on his aural.

At least he didn't spit it all over the Round Table.

"The terrestrials do not know him," Gwen said.

"But they like him," Lyrena countered instantly. "I've seen them drinking and chatting enough times."

"Liking and trusting are not the same thing," Gwen argued.

"It is the best we can do at the moment," I slid into the fray. "You've read enough to avoid offending the terrestrials unintentionally, and you are the most Ancestors-damned chatty person I know."

"And you are loyal." Arran's dark timbre silenced all other arguments.

I flicked him a glance.

Thank you.

A rumbling growl of approval bloomed in my chest.

Perhaps ruling together wouldn't be so difficult after all.

"Parys, we officially appoint you as Liaison for the United Fae Realms of Annwyn," I said. Arran's knee nudged mine under the table.

Approval. And perhaps an invitation.

Parys cocked a brow. "Did you just make that up?"

I shrugged. "I'm High Queen. As long as he agrees," I jerked my head toward Arran, "I can do whatever I want."

I practically felt Cyara roll her eyes. Arran's leg nudged mine harder.

"What's next?" I asked again, ignoring them all.

The clock on the other side of the room was nudging toward midnight, but I was brimming with energy.

"You are," Parys said, meeting my eyes across the table. "Tell us what happened when you fell through the rifts."

17
VEYKA

I recounted my terrifying journey through the realms as succinctly as I could. None of them interrupted, which was uncharacteristic. By the end, the smile had melted away from even Lyrena's merry golden face.

I ended with the description of the feeling in my chest, Arran's name flashing again and again through my consciousness, a persistent demand that dragged me through the realms without my consent.

Arran stared at the table as I described it. Once, his hand twitched. Like it might reach up and rub that space at the center of his chest, beneath his slate gray tunic.

I felt it as well.

Just talking about it made the bond feel stronger, the compulsion more and more demanding.

I had thought he'd been bumping his knee against mine as a show of approval and support. Now, I wondered if it was a way to take the edge off of the burning need inside of him—inside of us. A little touch, to release the tension that demanded connection with his mate. My mate.

I swallowed hard, trying to push back the rising chorus of voices inside of my head.

"He pulled you back," Parys mused, drumming his fingers on the table. "I wonder if it has something to do with your mating bond…"

"What?" Arran and I said in one voice.

We both rocked back in our chairs. Both looked at each other accusingly.

Lyrena laughed. Even Gwen huffed a breathless, half-believing chuckle.

"It appears the bond is stronger than any of us realized," Gwen said quietly, hedging her amusement well.

I tore my eyes away from Arran's. "How could that be?" I demanded of Parys. "I couldn't even control what was happening. How could Arran have been the one to pull me back, when he didn't even mean to?"

Cyara interjected before Parys could answer. "From what my father described, the mating bond is deeper than thought or intention. Arran did not know what he was doing, only that he wanted his mate back. The power of that…"

"… stretched across the realms." Arran finished. His voice was hollow, even with his glower in place.

Hollow, because he thought this mating bond between us was precious and special, while I'd all but rejected it.

Ancestors above, could I do nothing right?

Revenge, relationship, ruling. Apparently, I could only manage one at a time.

"We'll have to experiment," Arran was saying. "This is a new power, to both the elementals and the terrestrials. Or maybe it is some facet of elemental power no one has delved into before, a kind of wind gift."

"I am wind-gifted. I can move small objects using my wind, but not myself. Veyka's power is not wind magic," Parys said, annoyed.

"We'll start training, and then we'll see," Arran hedged.

"I do not want to train."

They all stared at me. Silent, again.

Good, I preferred it when they let me have my way without an argument—

"Your Majesty, that is unwise."

"Power like that will explode out of you whether you train it or not—"

"Veyka..."

A low rumble filled the room, drowning out the voices. I knew the rest of them could not hear it, but they lapsed into silence again anyway. They could feel it, I was sure. I could feel the power of it—Arran's power—dark and demanding as it coursed through the room, filling the air until it was nearly suffocating.

I felt the ember of power inside of me, tucked away so safely, flare in response.

No. Absolutely not.

I brought my fist down hard on the stone table. "It is my power. It is my choice."

Gwen was the first to get up the courage to challenge me. "The sort of power you displayed at the Joining cannot be left untrained, Your Majesty. It could be dangerous. Not only to yourself, but to those around you."

"How very rational of you, Guinevere," I said with a nod. "But my apparent power of throwing myself headlong through rifts—it only applies to me. I was holding Arran's hand at the Joining, but he did not go with me. I am the only one at risk."

"You don't know that for certain," Lyrena argued. Ancestors, even Lyrena was against me. "Power is unpredictable in the beginning. Which is why training is vital. Your wind—"

"Void power," Parys yelled.

I'd never heard him yell. Not once. Even when Arthur died—cries and sobs, but not this. This was a frustrated demand.

"*The* void power. From the Void Prophecy." He stood as he spoke: "*Then comes a queen, in the age of uncertainty, when shadows cast doubt upon the realm. Born under a double moon and marked by a radiant star, a faerie queen shall rise to command the depths of the voids of darkness.*"

Everyone was staring at him. My heart was beating so hard in my chest, I was certain that if I looked down I'd see the distention.

Parys ignored everyone else, even Arran. He held my gaze, his normally soft brown eyes hard and unyielding. "You are the queen from the Void Prophecy, Veyka. You command the depths of the voids of darkness."

18

ARRAN

"No."

One simple word.

She might as well have punched him.

But Parys, the male I'd been so keen to kill when I found him lazing in her bed—who I'd imagined gutting more than once since then just to satisfy my male pride—he didn't sit back down, and he didn't drop her gaze.

"Denying it doesn't change the fact," he said, voice shaking even as the rest of him held steady.

But his opponent was Veyka—my fierce, stubborn mate. She flattened her palms on the table and pushed herself up to stand as well. She rose to her full height, her wide body commanding the room. In an instant, she was the wrathful queen I'd lusted after and then fallen in love with.

Her full lips curved into that wicked smile, and I knew. Parys was about to lose this argument, whether he realized it or not.

"An age of uncertainty, when shadows cast doubt upon the realm?"

Parys' eyebrows rose as one. "The darkness from the human realm. You've seen it twice now—in the mountains, and the human you and the King questioned."

Veyka's hand went to the hilt of her dagger, barely cooled from the blood of her victims less than an hour before.

Ancestors save us.

"Born under a double moon and marked by a radiant star."

"You and Arthur were twins born at night," Parys countered without hesitation.

Veyka's fingers twitched. "What about that radiant star?"

I felt the swirl of wind around us, circling the table, hot and angry.

Veyka laughed ruthlessly. My cock twitched.

"Rifts, the void, call it whatever you want. But the prophecy is bullshit, just like the one Merlin made about the Round Table. Everyone has something they want, even the Ancestors who wrote that prophecy down. I don't have time for their nonsense. I have a kingdom to protect."

I wanted to worship her. She was everything I'd known she could be. More—she was my mate.

Mine.

And I would not let her be ripped away from me again.

"Then you must train." I didn't mean it to sound like a command; knew on a conscious level that commanding Veyka to do anything was a mistake. She'd dig in her heels just for spite. But I couldn't help it.

The thing in my chest—maybe it was my beast, maybe it was the mating bond—it was in full control now.

"No one tells me what I *must* do."

Power swirled around the room. Mine—I couldn't feel Veyka's, though I wasn't sure what it would feel like anyway. Instinctively, I thought I'd recognize it.

But it didn't matter. The dark, rising power within me was enough to send everyone else from the antechamber to their respective posts.

Everyone but Veyka.

She stood pinned between her chair—thrown back hastily, and the stone table. But I'd done battle often enough to recognize an opponent sizing me up. I stepped up and away, toward the middle of the room.

"Just because you are my mate does not mean you get to decide for me," she seethed. She kicked the chair out of the way and stepped wide, clearing her path.

Weapons or words, I was ready for her. "I am not trying to decide for you. I am trying to convince you to see reason."

One hand went to her hip, her chin lifting in defiance. "I have my reasons."

"Then tell me what they are." We were supposed to do this together—rule. Veyka thought that the decision to train her power was just about her; I'd have to convince her to see that it affected all of us. Every soul in Annwyn.

But convincing Veyka of anything was like trying to shift the goldstone bricks that held this palace in place, built into the side of the mountain itself. Nigh on impossible.

She didn't budge. "I already told you—everyone—I am not a danger to anyone but myself."

"That is an excuse, not a reason." She was scared. I recognized the set of her shoulders, the slight wobble of her breasts as she dragged in a breath just a bit too forcefully. But I didn't ease up on her. She wouldn't thank me for it and neither would Annwyn.

"They are the same damned thing," she spat.

"Veyka, you are High Queen of Annwyn—"

"And you are the High King. We are equals, now."

Equals. But nothing about this felt equal or right or balanced. It all felt fucking wrong. Even the mating bond in my chest, the pull to her, demanding—was unsatisfied. Unsettled. We were no longer prince and queen, betrothed, enemies... now we were Joined, mates, both powerful... and yet I'd never felt more distant from her.

I couldn't let the words sound as broken as I felt, so I said them forcefully instead, like an accusation. "What were we before?"

"That doesn't matter."

Ancestors below. Her blades were still in their jeweled scabbards, but she could slice through me just the same.

"Why don't you want to train, Veyka?" I ground out. I was suddenly so fucking tired of managing for the both of us. I just wanted her to be honest—with me and with herself.

"I am powerful enough without this cursed magic. I was always powerful enough."

"Yes, you are," I said without hesitation. But from the way her throat bobbed, from an instinct borne of months spent getting to know one another, getting closer and loving her, I knew she didn't fully believe it herself.

"You are strong, and you are powerful. And every realm should be trembling at the strength of the new High Queen of Annwyn," I said, closing the space between us. I stopped just short, leaving her that space to come to me. "I know I am."

She stepped closer, her eyes widening as if she didn't quite understand how it had happened. But I did. That same compulsion existed in my chest.

Her gaze softened fractionally. Her expression shifting to something else—the desire that had couched our anger and hate from the beginning. But there wasn't hate in her eyes anymore, now—

Her eyes were glowing.

For months, I stared into her eyes and wondered why they didn't glow for me, when I knew that mine burned so damn hot for her. I'd learned the answer—her lack of power.

But Veyka had never truly been powerless and here was the proof.

Her pupils were ringed in a glowing blue that should have looked icy, but instead was hot and demanding. She looked at me and I could *feel* the possessiveness. The match to my own. The mating bond.

"Train with me, Veyka," I said, reaching down to that tether that connected us. "Push past the fear."

I knew she could see the burning black fire in my own eyes, my desire for her shoving its way to the surface. Hate and lust were close bedfellows; but I didn't hate her anymore. I loved her so much it fucking hurt. And I would do anything to protect her—

including pushing her to train a power that clearly scared the hell out of her. Including using that bond between us, that sexual connection that long predated the Joining, to convince her.

Her lower lip trembled. She caught it between her teeth, punishing it mercilessly. "I am not afraid," she said.

And I knew I'd lost.

But she reached out, trailing a hand down the center of my throat, nudging apart the tunic I wore to reveal the uppermost branches of the tree tattooed across my chest. She traced the lines of my Talisman with her fingernail, digging it in while she dragged her gaze lower and lower.

Then she lifted her fingertip to her mouth and sucked it between her lips.

"Come find me when you cannot stand it a moment more," she crooned, swaying her hips provocatively.

Ancestors damn it all, I hated to give her the last word. But if I stayed in the room a second longer, I was going to bend her over the Round Table.

19
ARRAN

I would never be warm again.

Cold, so cold.

Cold in my chest, in my soul, dousing my magic. No, sucking it away. Feeding on it. Leaving nothing but cold, cold, cold.

A scream rent the darkness. Veyka.

The tether in my chest was an explosion of pain, demanding I save her. I couldn't see her in the darkness. Just like that night in the Tower of Myda. I couldn't see her.

But I could feel her.

I followed that tether, the ache in my chest I'd felt long before our Joining.

Close—I was so close.

"Veyka!" I tried to cry out, but the words were swallowed to nothingness.

I was so close. I reached out my hand, knowing her fingertips were a hairsbreadth away—

Then she was ripped from me again. Just like in that throne room. I reached for my magic, tried to shift, to throw out vines to curl around her limbs and keep her there. But there was nothing inside of me, no magic. Only cold.

Veyka screamed louder, sharper. The sound filled my ears, torturing me, getting deeper and more guttural with every passing second. Until they weren't Veyka's screams at all, but my mother's.

My mother was screaming. I knew that scream. It had echoed in my memory for decades until I learned to block it out. I couldn't fix it then, but I could fix it now. I could get to her, save her, protect her.

I had to protect. My beast demanded it. I demanded it. I was the beast. I was power. I was the strongest fae born in thousands upon thousands of years. If only I could get to her...

But the screams got farther and farther away.

Only to be replaced by the screams in the throne room. The screams of my victims, elemental and terrestrial alike, as I tore them apart for no reason other than they happened to be in the way of my rage.

Protect.

Mate.

Fear.

That must be what the coldness was. Fear, leeching into every corner of my soul. I could not protect her—Veyka. I couldn't protect my mother. I was powerful. I was powerless. I was nothing. I was a failure.

Once the nightmares started, they visited me nightly. Unlike Veyka, I didn't try to chase them away with aural or medicinal tea. I let them come.

Because I deserved it.

20
VEYKA

Arran didn't show up to the sparring ring, leaving me to Lyrena and Gwen. I knew he was avoiding me. Fair, I supposed. All we'd ever been good at was fighting and fucking. Lately, the former had held sway. Not that I didn't want him in my bed, but...

I'd felt that growl, the beast inside of him calling out to me. I knew his eyes burned. Did mine, now that I was apparently gifted with magic?

But it felt different. Before, it had been my choice. I'd wanted him for myself.

Now, I couldn't tell if it was the mating bond or me. Maybe the mating bond *was* me. I wasn't sure if that was better or worse.

What I was sure about was that without the fucking to drive away the noise in my mind, fighting was the only thing that would. If Arran wasn't around, then I had my blades and two Goldstones to match myself against.

Elora occasionally joined us in the ring, testing her swordsmanship against my knives. She was quite skilled, which I ought to have expected given that she'd become commander of the Elemental Kingdom's armies at only fifty years old.

I was enjoying sparring with her, until Esa showed up.

"I have some concerns, Your Majesty."

I didn't even break stride as I parried Elora's blade. "Write them down and submit them for consideration to the Round Table."

"Perhaps I may present them to you directly—"

"You may not," I said simply.

Fine droplets of water bloomed in the air. Esa was all about power and control. Something like satisfaction surged through me at the fact that I'd so easily been able to irk her.

"Thank you for the cool mist," I said, swinging upward and catching Elora unaware. I saw the panic in her eyes and felt the frost from her fingertips a half-second before my blade pressed to her throat. "It feels quite nice after all of this exertion."

The water evaporated. Esa stalked away. Elora grinned.

All in all, a decent morning in the ring.

"Where are your guards?" Parys asked without looking up.

He was comfortably ensconced on the floor, his back to the wall of windows and a sea of books around him as always. And, of course, a tray full of delicious food.

"They are by the doors, pretending they aren't listening to every word we are saying." I looked around the space, seeing no chairs, and resigned myself to sitting on the floor as well. "At least it will save me recounting this conversation to them later," I said loudly over my shoulder.

Parys ignored me, pausing his reading to write something in the notebook balanced on his left knee, then picking his book up once again.

"Aren't you supposed to be getting to know the terrestrial delegation so you can make inroads between the factions in my court?" I asked as I looked over his food to decide what I wanted to eat first.

"Aren't you supposed to be training?"

"I was in the sparring ring for an hour this morning, but then Esa showed up with a list of demands, so I had to cut it short."

"That isn't the sort of training I was referring to."

I shrugged, sliding the tray of food closer. "As I've told Arran, training my magic is unnecessary," I said as I scraped soft cheese onto a slice of toasted baguette and drizzled it with honey.

"That is what you keep saying."

"I didn't have any magical powers before. That was a dangerous secret that could have destabilized Annwyn and led to my certain death. Now I do have powers and everyone in Baylaur and beyond knows it. Threat averted, Annwyn stable." I punctuated my statements by taking a hefty bite.

"Then comes a queen, in the age of uncertainty, when shadows cast doubt upon the realm. Born under a double moon and marked by a radiant star, a faerie queen shall rise to command the depths of the voids of darkness," Parys recited. *"Twice blessed, the realm of shift and mist, when comes the awaited queen who shall possess ethereal might. With a touch, she will feel the heartbeat of her subjects, and she will unlock the secrets they guard within."*

I leaned forward to look at the book in his lap. It was about weather patterns in the Spine. He'd truly memorized not only the Void Prophecy, but the Ethereal Prophecy as well, which he claimed was really just one long prophecy parsed by time. Ancestors help me.

"Have you found any proof that I am marked by a radiant star?" I challenged.

He cut me a look sharp enough to draw blood. "Not yet."

"I haven't read any minds either." I shrugged and reached for another slice of bread, planning on drenching this one with salted butter. "I don't think we need to be worried about 'the age of uncertainty' or 'shadows of doubt' just yet."

"'*Shadows cast doubt*,'" Parys corrected, looking back down at the text. Giving up on me. Rightly so.

I didn't believe in the Void Prophecy any more than I did the one made by Merlin about the Round Table. Though the words were still eerily clear in my mind.

A table of destiny. Five shall be with you at Mabon. One is not yet known, but the bravest of the five shall be his father. When he comes, you will know that the time for the grail is near. The last is the Siege Perilous. It is death to all but the one for which it is made—the best of them all—the one who shall come at the moment of direst need.

Merlin was conniving and power hungry. The witch had said it clearly enough—one of the few things that monster had been clear about. I didn't intend to give Merlin's supposed prophecies—or any others, for that matter—any power over my life.

I had precious little as it was.

"Fall through any more rifts lately?" Parys asked sarcastically.

"Nope, not a single one," I said, licking butter off my fingers. "No soul ripping from my body, no glimpses of different realms. Just plain old Veyka."

I could still feel that ember of magic inside of me, nestled safely near the mating bond. But it seemed satisfied to glow inside of me without throwing me headfirst through rifts. I wasn't inclined to do *anything* that might wake it up.

Preparing myself another bite, I scooted back so I could lean against the bookcase behind me.

Wings flashed overhead. White, shimmering, then gone. I twisted, trying to track them, to see where they disappeared over the top of the tall bookcase. But there was nothing.

I forced the food down, my heart pounding in my throat. "Did you see that?"

Parys' eyes remained fixed on the book in his lap. "See what?"

I'd seen it before, in the throne room at the Offering and… right before Arthur's murder. The memory played across my mind as clearly as if it were happening all over again.

Arthur stood at the center of the dais, making his toast to the terrestrial delegation. Over his shoulder, I'd seen a strange disturbance. A flapping of wings, I'd thought at the time. Then it was gone, darkness fell, and Arthur was dead.

How had I forgotten?

I knew the answer even as I stuffed a few grapes into my mouth, chewing methodically as Parys stared down at his book, completely unaware of my upset.

I'd been so traumatized by Arthur's death, flung so far away from everything I'd ever known, that I hadn't been able to see *anything* clearly.

Gawayn's face flashed in my mind, followed by Roksana's.

Many, many things had gotten by me in those dismal months.

But what did this mean?

The flash of wings right before Arthur's death, another at the Joining, and then here in the library while Parys and I discussed my magic and the rifts and the Ancestors-damned Void Prophecy.

Could that strange flapping of wings have been related to Arthur's death? Were the terrestrials somehow involved? Had Arran been lying to me all along? Maybe Roksana was conspiring with them—

No.

Absolutely not.

It was insane. *I* was insane—and tired, overwrought, and confused by the mating bond that even now throbbed within me, complaining that I hadn't seen Arran at all today.

I was seeing things where there was nothing. Parys spent hours in this library. If there were any mystical winged beings, he would have seen them.

I reached for the wine, not bothering to pour myself a glass and just gulping directly from the bottle.

Parys' eyes flicked up to me, his brow wrinkling. "Very queenly."

"I aim to please," I said, wiping my lips and forcing the fake bravado into my voice.

"Will you go bother someone else?" he asked with mock politeness.

"Rude."

"I am going to prove that you are the queen in the Void Prophecy."

"Even ruder." I pushed to my feet, resisting the urge to kick his little pile of books.

Not so little, because he was intent on proving his theory correct.

I pretended to stumble on my way out. And if a few books fell... well, I ignored Parys' mumbled curse.

21
VEYKA

I tried to act normal.

As normal as the newly crowned, newly mated, newly powerful High Queen of Annwyn could act. I sat beside Arran in the throne room and listened to petitioners. I sparred in the ring with Lyrena and Gwen. I met at the Round Table and discussed how we would dismantle the Shadows' human smuggling operation. Listened patiently when Arran invited Elora to report on the status of the elemental kingdom's armies.

But none of it felt normal.

None of it felt right.

I missed Arran.

And damn it all, I couldn't determine if it was because I'd come to depend upon him, to trust his counsel even when I disagreed with it, or if it was the preternatural demand of a bond that existed outside of my control.

It pissed me off.

That was to say nothing of the desire that was building inside of me.

It had only gotten worse since our argument about training. I'd tried to tease him, to use my feminine wiles and my soft body to turn him to my point of view. Only to have him storm out and leave me to finger myself alone in my bed.

As we listened to petitioners, I'd been unable to stop myself from staring at his hand where it rested on the arm of the throne. I pictured his fingers in my mouth. Around my throat. Buried in my pussy.

While Elora talked about the composition of her legions, I watched Arran's jaw working. The stubble on his chin glinted in the candlelight, and all I could think about was how that stubble felt scraping along the insides of my thighs.

By the end of her report, I was breathing so hard that Lyrena was looking at me oddly and asking if I was ill.

This was need on an entirely different plane.

Satisfying myself wasn't enough. If I didn't have Arran soon, on my own terms, I was fairly certain I would mount him right at the Round Table, in the middle of Elora or Parys' next report.

"Your Majesty, you have that look on your face again."

I dragged my hand over my face, remembered the cosmetics Cyara had applied to my eyes, decided I didn't care, and rubbed my them anyway.

I turned toward Lyrena, standing watch at the closed doors to the antechamber, and offered her a wide, fake smile. "How do I look now?"

Lyrena returned my fake smile with a broad, genuine one of her own. "Gorgeous. Like you've just been kissed until you're deliciously mussed."

"I wish," I snorted. "I thought your desires leaned the other direction."

She rewarded my sass with her joyful chuckle. "They do. But I can appreciate beauty anywhere I find it."

"Always the optimist," I said, flopping back on the chaise. The sun was about to drop over the mountains, bathing everything in long golden rays.

Cyara arrived with a dinner tray, setting it on the little table beside my chaise. The jewel-encrusted tray was piled high with food—soft flatbread and a trio of colorful dips, crisp fried fish flown in from the Southern Way, a selection of hard and soft cheeses and nuts that already had my mouth watering. I sat up instantly, digging in before Cyara had even poured the wine.

She sank down onto the chaise next to mine, finally without hesitation. She'd joined me for about a dozen meals before she gave up trying for propriety and just enjoyed the food and the company.

Now I sighted Lyrena.

"Come and eat with us," I said in my most queenly, commanding voice.

Arran was avoiding me—and I him—but I had friends now, I reminded myself. Just because neither Arran or I could stand the tension between us didn't mean that I had to eat alone.

"I am on guard," Lyrena reminded me.

But I caught the way her eyes lingered on the tray of food between me and Cyara. I felt the grin as it climbed my face. And after everything I'd survived in the last year... it felt damned good.

"Isn't Gwen on guard in the corridor?" I already knew the answer. I'd seen her on my way in. One of them was always with me, the other guarding my chambers. I wasn't certain either of the females slept.

"Yes," Lyrena's eyes slid towards the doors to the antechamber, as if she worried that Gwen would hear this conversation.

There was no captain of the Goldstone Guards anymore. Not after Gawayn. It was just Gwen and Lyrena.

"Then I command that you eat. You'll be better able to guard me if you aren't distracted by the fact that you cannot partake in this delicious feast." I scooted over on the chaise and patted the spot next to me.

One more long glance toward where Gwen lurked outside, and then Lyrena was padding over to join us.

I popped a slice of flatbread loaded with creamy dip into her hand. "I love winning."

"Gwen is going to punish me for this in the ring tomorrow,"

Lyrena said around her first mouthful—and a groan of appreciation as the food hit her tongue.

"Gwen is a grump," I said loudly in the direction of the closed doors. "I never see either of you eat. You are always lurking."

"Lurking is their job," Cyara reminded me, nibbling daintily on a bite of fish.

I ignored her and took a long drink of wine, letting it settle into me, smooth out the jagged edges. "When are you going to bring on more guards?"

Lyrena paused, flicking her eyes back toward the door.

"We're not," she finally said, staring at her food and very efficiently avoiding Cyara's and my gazes. "After what happened, it seemed better to have less guards who could be trusted, than more who could pose a threat of their own."

I handed her a glass of wine. "It's impractical to have only the two of you. When do you sleep? And shouldn't one of you be guarding Arran, as well. He's the High King."

Damn, damn, damn.

I hadn't meant to bring him up. I'd been very adroitly avoiding all thoughts of Arran Earthborn, my king and mate.

"His Majesty is the most powerful fae born in—"

"Millennia," I finished for Lyrena, popping a grape in my mouth. "More like the biggest pain in my ass—"

"If you would train your power, then perhaps you wouldn't need a guard at all."

Lyrena swallowed so hard, it was audible. The cracker I held crumbled between my fingers. And Cyara, blast her, kept nibbling on her fish as if she hadn't just thrown fuel on the flames.

I glared at her, then at Lyrena, who was very determinedly studying the bottom of her wine glass. "Do you all get together and plan these assaults on my good nature?"

Cyara's wings quivered, and she met me with her turquoise gaze only to roll it emphatically. "I'd be inclined to honor your good nature if you would only see reason."

"I thought I was enjoying a casual meal with my friends."

"Friends don't just tell you what you want to hear," Cyara said pointedly. "They tell you what you need to hear as well."

She stood up, brushing nonexistent crumbs from her white gown. "If you'd prefer I silently nod in agreement to everything you say, relieve me of my seat at the Round Table and I will gladly be nothing more than handmaiden. Your Majesty."

I resisted the urge to throw the grape in my hand at her as she floated away.

Lyrena snatched it out from between my fingers a second before my willpower ran out.

22

ARRAN

The elemental forces were in shockingly good shape, considering the anarchy in Annwyn over the last year. As I walked the winding corridors of the goldstone palace back to my apartments, I rehashed the major points of my long meeting with Elora.

She'd been appointed by Uther shortly before his death. Very young, to be appointed to command the elemental armies—barely fifty years old. I'd initially thought it a vanity appointment, given Roksana's position on the royal council.

Maybe it had been, to begin with.

But Elora had more than proved her loyalty—cutting down her own mother for the part she'd played in Arthur's death.

She had also grown the elemental armies from a few small, peace-keeping units to a standing, well-drilled fighting force in a matter of only a few years.

The question remained—why?

Arthur's order, she'd said.

But that timeline was wrong. It had only been a year and a half since Arthur was crowned.

Had he given the order while he was still only the Crown Prince?

What would have motivated him to do so—either with Uther's blessing or behind his back?

One word flashed in my mind—one name.

Veyka.

Had he done it to protect Veyka? And if so... from what?

Her powerlessness. The ripple of instability its discovery would have sent through Annwyn.

That was the easy answer.

But it felt wrong. Or at the very least—incomplete.

None of it made sense.

Instincts honed on the battlefield through death and destruction urged me to look closer.

Those same instincts stilled my footsteps before the door to my apartments had even fully closed behind me.

I wasn't alone.

My instincts screamed, sending my hand for the battle axe at my belt. The beast inside of me growled, demanding I shift.

But not because of a threat.

Because my mate was near.

Every muscle in my body went taut—my cock included.

Ancestors, I'd been hard for days now.

Ever since I saw that glowing blue ring of desire in Veyka's eyes, everything else had been a struggle.

I wanted her. My beast wanted her.

I knew only one thing would ease the ache in my chest that extended down through my gut and gripped my balls, heavy and full.

Veyka.

My mate. *Mine.*

My beast growled, demanding I shift. The temptation was almost too much. To shift, to hunt her down wherever she'd cleverly hidden herself among the twisted vines and emerald leaves that covered the walls of my apartments.

I let my power slide free, reaching into the vines nearest me. It didn't take away the primal urge to shift, to hunt. But it did ease the pressure, just enough.

Then I heard—felt—the soft chuckle through that otherworldly connection between Veyka and my beast.

A soft, sultry laugh, followed by five words.

Catch me if you can.

My control snapped.

She was a rustle in the vines, then a flash over the edge of my balcony. I made the leap in one bound. She was already slithering away. Down, down, down, on vines I'd made myself.

Her feet hit the compacted red dirt of the courtyard below. She thought she had the advantage, going straight down while I had to leap from balcony to balcony. But I'd caught her sweet scent on the wind. I wouldn't stop until I had her taste on my tongue.

I landed hard, wide paws spreading in the dirt to brace my massive body. I could feel the whispers on the wind echoing in my large, white tufted ears. But I didn't care who'd seen my descent.

I had one thought—hunt.

Through the corridors.

Palace guards jumped out of the way. They all recognized my beast by now, elementals and terrestrials alike. They all fell away, their faces lined with fear.

All except one.

I knew where she was going.

I snarled a warning as I rounded the corner a second behind the whipping tail of her white braid.

But she only responded with a low, wicked laugh that I felt in my chest, deep within my wolf's wildly beating heart.

She slipped into the secret passages.

I did more than snarl, a deep rumbling growl ripping from my chest.

I was going to seal these blasted passages. I would not let another assassin use them to get at her. I'd failed once.

Never again.

I would never fail my mate again.

She was mine to protect.

Mine to punish for this reckless flight.

Mine.

She was going to the forest. I wouldn't allow it.

I dug in, my haunches screaming as I pushed the muscles, demanding—more strength, more speed. More, more, more.

But she was so fucking fast.

She knew the passages better. Used the sharp turns and her own momentum to propel herself faster and faster. I could bound down a flight of steps in a single leap, but my size slowed me down in the tight tunnels.

My breaths were coming sharper and sharper, my lungs burning.

Not mine—hers.

She was still recovering. Damn her. She'd been hiding it well, sparring every day. She should have been able to make this run easily. Had been able to, before she broke every single bone in her body.

Enough, I snarled, knowing she'd hear me.

Maybe not the word itself, but the feeling. The demand.

But she didn't stop. And I found a new reserve of strength and power.

I blasted the wards apart with little more than thought. We'd finish this right where it had all started—in that clearing in the woods.

Then I was in the moonlight. She crashed through the brush ahead of me, finding a new depth of energy as well. Maybe she'd accessed mine.

I couldn't begin to explain the mating bond.

All I could do was obey.

Find her. Claim her. Mate.

She couldn't outrun me here beneath the open sky.

Her hair caught the moonlight, a beacon amidst the deep emerald of the palm fronds. Another flash, her pale body catching the light as well.

Shining.

For me.

I leapt—catching her hard on the back of her shoulders.

She braced for the impact. We hit the ground, rolling together, her hands clutching my front legs, nails digging into the thick white fur.

The night spun around us. Moon, stars, the thick scent of the red dirt we kicked up as we fought our way into the center of the clearing.

Predator and prey.

You are mine, I snarled, pinning her to the ground.

One powerful paw on each shoulder, her chest heaving, those magnificent breasts rising and falling with each breath. Her eyes burned bright, even in the filtered moon-and-starlight.

"I belong to no one," Veyka snarled back, gnashing her teeth and tossing her head.

Long strands of her hair, torn free from her plait during her flight, caught and tangled around my paws. And disappeared.

The exact same shade, I realized.

My power was darkness and death to all who encountered it, but my beast's fur was moon-white. Exactly the shade of Veyka's hair, unseen anywhere else in Annwyn.

A perfect match.

I snarled again. It grew to a growl that filled the clearing. Then I lifted my head and howled it to the entire world.

Her resistance was futile.

She'd never escape me.

When I dropped my gaze back down, Veyka was staring. Temporarily stunned into silence.

As soon as she caught my gaze, her blue eyes burning into my wolfish ones, she started thrashing again.

I vaguely wondered if my eyes still burned with desire when I was in my beast form. Did she wonder— if it was male or beast in control?

It didn't matter—we were one when it came to wanting Veyka.

She wasn't afraid of me.

Veyka was afraid of the bond, of her power... but not my beast.

She could thrash all she wanted. But I could smell her desire even more keenly now, in this form.

I dropped my snout to her neck. She stilled beneath me, some instinct to be wary in the face of Annwyn's ultimate predator. But she didn't try to hide her throat.

She bared it for me.

I could see her lifeforce, thumping wildly just beneath the surface of her pale skin. My beast breathed her in, burying my snout in the nape of her neck. Sweat, need—*Veyka*.

I bared my fangs, long as a child's forearm, sharper than any blade forged by man or fae. I dragged them from the tender spot below her ear along the dancing pulse in her throat.

I let one snag on her collarbone. Just enough to draw blood. Blood that I lapped up with one swift swipe of my tongue.

Veyka whimpered beneath me. The scent of her arousal filled the clearing, sweet and hot and just for me.

I ripped away her skirts with one jerk of my beastly head, and then she was bare before me.

The insides of her thighs glistened. I lapped her up, savoring the taste of her pleasure. But it wasn't enough, not for either of us.

Veyka arched beneath me, thrusting her pussy towards my questing snout. I didn't deny her—couldn't.

She cried out, shuddering violently at the touch of my cold nose to the hot folds of her pussy. But then I was nuzzling deeper, rubbing my rough nose against her clit, gorging my animal senses on her sweetness.

It wasn't enough.

I had to taste her—really taste her. Not the vestiges of pleasure on her soft, full thighs. I wanted her burning core.

I flicked my gaze up, expecting to see her head thrown back, mouth parted to give me more of those delicious moans. But I found her eyes instead.

Veyka was up on her elbows, chin lifted so she could see over the round orbs of her breasts. So she could watch my beast pleasure her.

We were more than happy to oblige.

I dragged my tongue—thrice the size of my fae form and roughly textured—from her clit all the way down to the tight, puckered hole I'd fucked at Lugnasa.

Veyka came instantly, flooding my mouth with her sweet nectar. I licked up every drop, greedy for more.

Come again for me, my beast urged with a growl, swiping that vast tongue down again and again. Until she was bucking against me. I shoved my tongue inside of her, dragging it over that rough patch of nerves inside her pussy until she gushed all over me, wetting my fur.

She cried out desperately, arching her back and unleashing a howl all her own.

Suddenly, it was not my beast's tongue buried in her pussy, but my own.

I'd shifted without even meaning to.

Veyka demanded, and I gave.

I ripped my leather trousers aside, as desperate as she to give her exactly what she wanted.

My hands landed on either side of her head as I slammed my cock into her. I had no control. Veyka had shredded it apart.

I was in my fae form, male, but my beast was still wholly in control.

Veyka met me thrust for thrust, claw for claw, screaming her pleasure to the moon like the hellcat she was.

We were animals.

Beasts of the night.

And when we came—my cock pouring my seed inside of her,

her pussy clenching me as she climaxed and milked every drop of pleasure—

We roared our pleasure to the night like the beasts we were.

23
VEYKA

My power awoke in the middle of the night.

Arran was wrapped around me, his arm holding me firmly against his chest. I tried to breathe through it, to tell myself it was nothing more than reflux from too many miniature toffee cakes at dinner.

But I knew.

With the mating bond finally quieted, satisfied by Arran and my physical exchange, I could hear and see and feel my power unencumbered.

It started with a flicker. That ember of power inside of me that had glowed so brightly when I was thrown through the rifts had been dormant for weeks. But now, the soft glow was flickering with brightness. Just for a second, then it ebbed away. A minute passed, and there it was again.

What in the Ancestors-damned hell *was* this?

Then I felt it.

In my fingers and toes, a slight tingling that was eerily familiar and filled me with dread.

My power was awake.

I rolled in Arran's arms, grabbing for his shoulders in a panic. I clung to him, even as I realized it was futile.

This isn't going to work. He was holding my hand before—

Arran's arms tightened around me, instinctively pulling me closer. Our hips were pressed together firmly now, his cock hardening at the contact. My blasted body, more than half consumed by panic, couldn't help but respond.

A little trickle of traitorous wetness.

"Arran," I whimpered, the tingling spreading across my palms. "Arran, please—"

Then his mouth was on mine, his tongue spearing into the dark depths of me. I tried to pull away. He didn't understand. I wasn't asking for this. I needed his help. I needed him to know that I wasn't going willingly.

But he was urging my hips apart, his cock sliding into the soft folds of my pussy.

And the tingling receded.

Back into my fingers.

What in the Ancestors...

I couldn't think. Panic and desperation drove me as I locked my hips around his, clinging to his shoulders. I thrust against him hard, taking control as my tongue swirled around his in time with my hips.

It was almost gone. The tingling was fading away to nothing. I was *staying*.

Arran groaned against my mouth. He was close. Ancestors, so was I.

I rode him hard, letting his cock fill me up, letting it ground me to this reality, this world.

And when we both exploded in climax, the world around me was firmly in place, and me in it, once again.

24
VEYKA

I refused to slink out of my own bed.

Kicking Arran out seemed cruel. He was sleeping hard enough that even when I slid from the sheets and sat up on the edge, my weight dimpling the mattress, he didn't stir. I couldn't blame him; we'd taken our pleasure enough times in the night it was a miracle I could stand.

I wasn't sure I could, actually.

I gripped the bedpost and hoisted myself up. There was a definite ache between my legs, but instead of griping, that blasted bond in my chest practically purred with pleasure and satisfaction.

Arran rolled onto his back and let out a very wolf-like snore.

I snorted myself, grabbing a dressing robe off of the back of a chair and wrapping it around me. It was early still, barely daybreak. There was just the slightest chill in the air—the harbinger of autumn in Baylaur. Which simply meant instead of sweltering heat, it would be vaguely comfortable. To me, accustomed to the desert heat, it felt frigid. Especially after leaving Arran's animal warmth.

I swiped a blanket off the foot of the bed—Arran had kicked it off anyway—as well as the book I'd been reading from the table beside my pillow.

Parys kept a steady supply of books coming in from the library. I wasn't sure how he managed it, but I'd finish one only to find a new selection in its place the next day. He must be in league with Cyara.

Ironic, considering how she'd barely tolerated his presence in the months after Arthur's death.

But everything was different now.

There was a huge, unfairly muscled male in my bed, for one. Truly, just glancing at his sleeping form was enough to stir my desire again. Despite—or maybe because of—the ache between my legs.

He snored again.

I rolled my eyes and slipped through the doors into the antechamber. I settled in on the chaise, wrapping the blanket around my legs, and let myself fall into the fantasy world Parys had selected for me. For the first time since waking up in my bed, broken into a thousand pieces, I exhaled.

My friends drifted in slowly.

First Cyara, with a tea tray and a long look that told me she knew precisely how I'd spent my night. Parys arrived with breakfast, as if pulled by scents of chocolate croissants and fresh berries with cream. Arran followed shortly after—some preternatural sense alerting him to the presence of another male.

He emerged from my bedroom bare chested, hair rumpled from where I'd dragged my hands through it again and again in the night, and a glower that would have sent any other male in the kingdom running. A walking proclamation. He might as well have pissed on me to mark his territory.

Parys ignored him, drinking his morning wine and reading from the stack of books he'd brought with them. They were historical texts, not petite novels like the one in my hand. I didn't ask about them.

Gwen and Lyrena came last, taking turns eating—because the moment they picked up a biscuit, someone was sure to try to slit my throat—before turning to sparring right there in the open space of the antechamber.

Perhaps I ought to be out among my court. The Ancestors knew there were things we needed to discuss. But I clung to that moment of normalcy. There had been so few of these days in my life. None, really. Those stolen days with Arran after the Tower of Myda were the closest. Maybe the laughing walks Arthur and I had taken through the goldstone palace in the months after his coronation.

But this was different. It was special. I wanted to etch it into my memory forever.

It was all very peaceful and idyllic.

Until Parys decided to be an ass.

"I think I've found the original source of the Void Prophecy."

I thought I was hallucinating. Or that I'd been transported—against my will—to another realm by the glowing ember of my power.

Could alternate realms exist... not just different physical places, but alternate versions of this reality?

I snapped my book shut, unwilling to even consider it. I was sleep deprived already. Now Parys was going to give me a headache.

No one responded to him—probably out of self-preservation. Which only emboldened him further.

"They're human," Parys said. A little louder this time.

My teeth snagged on the inside of my cheek, ripping shreds of soft flesh away and filling my mouth with the tang of my own blood.

"There are so many things wrong with that statement," I said, pressing my index fingers to my temples.

"The prophecy was made over seven thousand years ago," Cyara pointed out astutely.

"Which means if it was made by a human, they are long dead," I finished for her. "Setting aside the ridiculousness of a human priestess."

Lyrena chuckled, barely breaking stride as she twirled to avoid Gwen's swinging blade.

But Parys' brows knit together, missing all their usual amusement. "Half human, half fae."

I rolled my eyes toward Arran, expecting to see exasperation to match my own.

Instead, he was frowning at Parys. "It happens."

Lyrena froze. Gwen didn't; pushing her advantage, she had Lyrena up against the wall in a second. I was only vaguely aware of their sparring, knowing that both females would fight till blood was drawn.

Many underestimated Lyrena, with her beautiful golden visage and whip-quick smile. I recognized that swagger was another weapon; sometimes, it felt like looking in a strange golden mirror.

"In the more isolated parts of the Spine and the Shadow Wood," Arran was saying. "Where there is little contact with the rest of the kingdom... sometimes it happens."

"Rape happens," I said sharply, understanding instantly.

Arran met my gaze, steady and sure. He would not lie to spare my feelings, even about this. I felt him through the bond. Not a tangible word or phrase, but the offering of comfort—and retribution.

But I didn't want the others to see it. They might guess, but that was different than having stark confirmation.

I cleared my throat and tossed Arran a wicked, seductive grin. Let them think that this moment was about some unknown entendre passing between us, rather than the scars that lurked just beneath my skin.

Arran responded immediately, the growl of his beast rolling through me, unleashing a dark wave of power through the room. Enough that Lyrena and Gwen turned away, back to their sparring.

Just like that, my pussy clenched, a rush of wet desire flooding through me. Ancestors... just playing with this male, just pretending, was dangerous. I ought to have known better.

I forced myself to drag my eyes back to Parys. I didn't have to fake the effort. My body was singing for Arran already.

Unlike Cyara, who was now pointedly looking the other direction, Parys met my eyes with annoyance brimming in his own.

I cracked my knuckles and reached for a cookie from the tea tray. "Even if this half-human, half-fae priestess existed, she would be long dead by now."

"Not in Avalon. No one can die in Avalon."

This time, the clatter of blades only faltered for a second. But it was enough for me to know every single pointed ear in the room was intently focused on this conversation.

"Avalon is not a real place."

"And the Void and Ethereal Prophecies are not real, either?"

"Exactly."

Parys shoved to his feet, the book that had been splayed in his lap hitting the goldstone floor with an emphatic *thwak*. "Fuck that."

Arran's snarl filled the room—not just my head, this time.

"Parys," Cyara warned, the rustle of her wings punctuating her soft but authoritative voice.

He ignored her, squaring up against me. "You are the Queen from the Void Prophecy. If I must go to Avalon and find the priestess myself in order to prove it to you, then so be it."

I could feel Arran about to shift. *Stand down*, I screamed through the bond, to the beast, to whatever form of Arran was listening.

"You are a Knight of the Round Table. You will go where you are commanded," I snarled.

But Parys was undeterred. "So much for us each having a voice, without fear of repercussion."

Some small part of me cried a warning—I'd never seen him like this. Before Arthur's death, he'd been jovial and sly, happy to do whatever his king had asked. After, we'd grieved together. And when I emerged from that darkness, he'd been there as well, giving aid without question, risking his life in the Tower of Myda. Nearly dying for me and my kingdom. He'd been my friend through it all.

But it hurt too much.

Princess of Peace, Queen of Annwyn.

Powerless, now powerful.

Betrothed to a male I hated, now mated to a male I couldn't let myself—

Everything in my life was beyond my control.

The world, the prophecies, the priestesses—they couldn't have me. I wouldn't allow it.

Parys stalked closer, his warm wind swirling around us. He was losing control as well. "Veyka, you have to see what is right before your eyes."

I reached for my dagger without realizing it, the need to arm myself against the pain springing from somewhere visceral and primal within me. But a hand stilled the motion. Not Arran's hard, calloused palm. Smaller, but warm and strong. Cyara.

"Veyka," she said softly, with such gentleness it threatened to splinter my soul.

Then it did.

I splintered apart. It wasn't Parys' wind swirling around me; it was a rift. The void. Every inch of me ripped apart and reformed. Darkness punctuated with gleaming particles of being danced around me—maybe my own, maybe the very fabric of the world ripped to shreds.

Except this time, I wasn't alone. Cyara's hand was still on my arm.

Her screams filled my ears, my consciousness, my soul.

It was all wrong. It wasn't possible. Arran had been holding my hand the first time, and still he'd remained behind. He was my mate, the connection between us unshakeable, unbreakable. If I couldn't bring him, I couldn't bring anyone--

"Veyka!" Arran's roar filled the room, the demand unmistakable. This time, I felt the tether between us clearly. It was like a rope, so physical and real I could almost wrap my hands around it.

One second, I was in pieces, fragments of soul and being spinning through darkness. Then the next, I was reassembled, my feet firmly on the goldstone floor once more.

Except that Cyara truly was in fragments.

I stood on the other side of the room, the massive Round Table separating me from my friends. Cyara was at my side, her hand on my arm. It was all right, she was all right.

But her scream—I reached for her—*oh Ancestors. No, no, no.*

Her hand was on my arm, her fingers curled around me, but the rest of her wasn't there. It was still on the other side of the room, where I'd stood only seconds before.

Before my power had overwhelmed me, before I'd given myself over to the void, plunging headfirst into my power with no thought to those around me.

Because it only affected me. I'd promised myself again and again, been thankful so many times that at least this uncontrollable power couldn't harm those I cared about.

But I was so wrong. As I clasped Cyara's hand in place so that it wouldn't fall to the floor, as blood spurted from the end of her arm across the room, as Parys sprinted for a healer... as my friend's screams of anguish filled my ears... I knew.

It was all my fault.

25
ARRAN

I followed the pull of the bond, the string that seemed to be wrapped around my heart and led to one place—Veyka.

But instead of down and out, I was pulled higher. Staircase after staircase, past the oldest parts of the goldstone palace where we'd once dined with Roksana and Elora. I'd seen the spires from the outside, knew that some of the airborne terrestrials now at court preferred the rooms up there even if they were much smaller than the luxurious apartments in the main body of the palace.

The desert wind was brutal. Now that it was autumn, the nights were turning cold. But when I found her, perched on the edge of a balcony, legs dangling over the edge as if the drop weren't thousands and thousands of feet, she wore nothing but a wispy nightgown.

On any other night, I would have hardened at the sight. The moonlight silhouetted her body, outlining her glorious curves. The roundness of her hips, the soft flesh just above them that pillowed outward as she slouched... I wanted to melt myself into the softness of her.

But tonight, I would stand firm. Because that was what she needed.

"I expected to find you beyond the palace walls."

"I don't know how to untangle the wards," she said.

Before, when she'd been powerless, they hadn't recognized her. What would happen now, with this unseen, unheard of power pumping through her veins?

Except it wasn't unheard of, though it had been unseen for the last seven thousand years. It was time we stopped pretending that Parys was stretching, that his talk of the Void Prophecy was nonsense. After what had happened to Cyara... it was anything but.

"I can teach you," I said, stepping closer.

I wanted to grab her off the edge. I could feel the torment, the pain inside of her. Another side effect of the bond. What I'd only guessed at in the months before our Joining... now it was real for me, as well. I couldn't feel her emotions, exactly. But there was a sense of her through the bond—always. When I slept, ate, sparred, even when I shifted. I could feel Veyka's presence, sense her well-being and her nearness.

The bond had demanded I find her tonight. She was too far away, the ache in my chest becoming almost painful. But that wasn't the only reason. I would have found her anywhere. I always would.

I laid a hand on her shoulder, ready for her to jerk away. Ready to catch her if she lost her balance on the ledge.

But to my surprise, she tipped her head to the side and pressed her cheek to the back of my hand instead.

It took every bit of restraint to hold myself back.

To treasure that little bit she gave me and know not to ask for more.

Once, months ago, I would have taken and worried about the consequences later.

But now... every touch between us felt important. A reminder of the bond, a way to satisfy it.

The way she'd recoiled when she found out about the mating bond... it hurt more than any wound I'd ever sustained on the battlefield.

So, I let my hand stay there on her shoulder, warming her cold skin with my rough hand. She wasn't a small female, but still my palm swallowed her shoulder.

"You're freezing," I said, realizing just how cold her skin was.

Veyka didn't move. "I needed to get out. This was the best I could do."

She needed to be free. When the darkest moments came, she needed to be free of the walls of the goldstone palace. Except now she couldn't; now, she was trapped once again.

Trapped by a power none of us understood.

Just like she'd spent twenty years of her life trapped because of her lack of power.

I didn't know what to do, how to comfort her. If I took her in my arms, we'd likely be overtaken by desire, the bond responding to our closeness. From what Cyara had told me outside of Veyka's earshot, her father had read that overwhelming lust was common in newly mated pairs.

I wanted Veyka with every breath, every beat of my heart. But that wasn't what she needed now.

Words... I'd never been good with those. I was a male of action. I was good at issuing orders and having them obeyed. Not untangling a lifetime's worth of trauma.

But I could share a bit of mine. Like I'd done in the water gardens.

"When you disappeared, I lost control."

Veyka's shoulder blades slid closer together, but she didn't speak.

"I knew the instant your blood entered my veins... what we were. My beast knew it too. Then you were gone." I had to stop, the words choking the air from my throat.

But Veyka turned her head. Just a few inches to the side, so I could see her profile in the moonlight. Her hair fell down off her shoulders, over her back, loose. Whether it had come undone during her flight up to the tower, or if she'd yanked it free of the plait that Cyara had intricately braided during the day...

I let myself step closer and inhale her scent. I needed it, to get the rest of the words out.

Plum and primrose. Perfection.

"You disappeared, and I lost control. I couldn't think. All I could do was feel—rage, fear. I shifted. And then I ripped the heads off of every courtier who stood within twenty feet of me. Elemental and terrestrial alike."

Veyka's eyes snapped to mine. She moved so fast, I reached for her without thinking, to brace her from falling off the edge. But she was graceful. Always so fucking graceful and quick.

I knew what I'd see in her eyes. The scorn, the pity.

I'd lost control so many times in those early decades.

Killed and maimed so many innocents.

But I wasn't a young male. I was the most powerful fae in millennia, and I had a power I ought to know how to control after three hundred years.

I'd failed to protect my mate, who'd been ripped away from me. But I'd also failed to protect my kingdom, killing my subjects just because they had the ill-luck to be standing too nearby.

I knew the shame was shining in my eyes.

But it wasn't in Veyka's.

The blue was shifting as a storm cloud, a window into the swirling emotions inside of her. But there was no pity or scorn.

There was knowing.

Her fingers closed around mine, burrowing beneath my hand where it lay on her shoulder until our fingers were tangled together. She pulled me closer, until our faces were inches apart.

Veyka pressed her forehead against mine.

We stayed there, balanced on a knife's edge, without speaking. A minute, an hour, an entire night may have passed around us as we shared breath, holding on tightly to each other.

Finally, she spoke.

"It is time to go," she breathed.

"Good, you're freezing," I returned, though neither of us moved.

Her other hand skated over my arm, warmth radiating from beneath my tunic even as the cold winds whipped around us. "It's time to leave Annwyn."

I started to ease back so I could look at her face. "Veyka, you can't run now..."

But her hand circled my neck, pulling me back down. "Not forever," she said softly. "But the legends say that Avalon lies in the human realm."

We were too close for me to read her expression, but my eyes snapped fully open. "Avalon?"

"Yes. If the priestess who made this blasted prophecy is there, then I will find her. And I will demand answers."

26
VEYKA

It took too long.

I was a danger to everyone around me, and yet they moved through the goldstone palace as if everything was normal—as if I couldn't rip them limb from limb with my new, uncontrollable power.

Even if Cyara had healed, had insisted again and again that she was *fine*.

I hadn't felt that burning ember flaring, nor that telltale tingling in my extremities.

I didn't let myself get angry.

I tried to summon the emptiness that had been my constant companion in the months after Arthur's death. But even that was a challenge. I'd been content to dwell in my own darkness because I didn't have friends; because I wouldn't allow myself to care.

Now, I had an entire Round Table of Knights.

An entire kingdom of subjects who depended on me.

Ancestors-damned fucking hell, I cared.

It hurt to care. It hurt so much.

The worry ate at me.

I tried to fill the ache with food—delicious pastries, creamy pasta, wine. No luck.

As for my other usual standby for dulling my emotions... Arran had been busy with arrangements for our departure. As had I. If that kept him from my bed, even as the aching need of the bond in our chests grew steadily more demanding... at least I didn't have to examine *those* emotions as well.

Arran didn't argue when we discussed who would come with us to the human realm and who would stay behind in Baylaur. Our entire Round Table was uncharacteristically quiet.

Afraid of me.

I was afraid of myself.

Gwen and Parys would remain in Baylaur. Between her menace and wisdom, his smooth talking and slyness, I knew they'd manage. I had to trust that they would.

As Esa had so presciently pointed out months ago, when Arran and I listened to her treachery from the balcony trying to find the traitors in our midst—kingdoms had long been left in the care of the royal council while their monarchs led the charge on the battlefield.

The royal council was either dead or deposed.

Good riddance.

With Elora in command of the elemental armies—Arran was confident in her skill—it would be enough. It had to be enough.

Whatever threats might emerge against Annwyn in my absence... none were as great as the one I posed, simply walking through the corridors of the goldstone palace.

If Arran and everyone else were right, and I must train this power, I would do it in the human realm. Far away from my subjects.

They'd seen my explosion of power in the throne room. They'd seen me return—mostly unharmed.

It would have to be enough.

Please let it be enough.

Because if Parys was right, and I was the queen from the Void Prophecy... then the rest of the prophecy must be true as well. *When shadows cast doubt upon the realm.*

Those shadows were coming for Annwyn, and I must be ready.

27
ARRAN

In the end, we left without ceremony.

Everyone knew the High King and Queen were leaving Baylaur. But they did not know where. They did not know why.

A visit to the terrestrial kingdom—that was what Parys whispered to the courtiers as he sipped from the aural fountain. To the Split Sea, others supposed—to address the disappearances that had first been brought before us by Gawayn's brothers. I had to believe that Gwen and Parys would manage things in our absence.

There was no way that I would let Veyka go alone.

Baylaur could crumble to dust before I would let my mate walk into danger without me by her side.

Lyrena still wore her Goldstones uniform, having added the straps of her traveling packs right over the top. Osheen looked much the same as he had during the journey to Baylaur months ago. I assumed I did as well. The same bedroll, the same traveling pack, the same leather vest and trousers. The only difference was the linen tunic beneath, the style I'd taken to wearing in the heat of Baylaur. My wool layers were tucked into my pack.

Would the seasons in the human realm mirror ours? The humans had never mattered enough for me to find out.

Parys had handed me an entire written report—because I still struggled to listen to the male speak for a prolonged period of time without wanting to relieve him of his favorite parts.

That was fine; I'd read them in camp tonight. I'd read enough reports in my lifetime as a battle commander to fill that entire blasted library built into the side of the mountain.

We waited just outside the massive doors of the goldstone palace, the same ones I'd entered through with my delegation—before cutting off Evander's arm. No more news had come from the Split Sea; Parys and Gwen would have to deal with that as well.

A movement flickered in the corner of my vision as I adjusted the weapons at my waist. "Don't go down there."

Maisri caught herself on the middle stair. "I want to see if the Gremog will respond to a flower," she said.

Ancestors save me.

Osheen had insisted on bringing her along—the orphaned daisy fae was his distant cousin of some degree.

She'd originally come with our delegation from Wolf Bay to help with cooking and laundry. A relatively safe journey. But into the human realm... none of us knew what awaited. Still, she was Osheen's ward. He'd insisted that she went where he went, and I wanted his powerful magic in our traveling party. So the child came as well.

I cast a long look at the desert around us. Not a single plant to be seen. "There are no flowers here."

The child grinned, her dark curls bobbing as she reached into her pocket and opened her small fist to reveal an even smaller flower petal. Not even a full petal. A torn scrap of one.

"The Gremog will eat a wee thing like you for its breakfast in one gulp," I advised. I hadn't seen the storied monster, but I had seen the reverence the elementals showed the thing. That was enough to convince me to stay well away.

But Maisri was undeterred. As we watched, she wrinkled her brows, eyes narrowing. The tiny flower petal in her palm erupted in a burst of color. Bright pink striped with even brighter red, folds and layers of petals expanding and curling until the bloom took up her entire hand. A rose.

I cocked an eyebrow at Osheen, but he was grinning now as well.

I understood why he did not want to leave her, at least in part. She was more powerful that I'd realized, and still only a child. Osheen was right to keep her close. Without parents to protect her, less powerful fae would try to take advantage.

Even with parents, such terrible things could happen. I was walking proof.

"Well done," Lyrena laughed, voice glowing with admiration. "That ought to be big enough," she said, nodding. "Give it a toss."

Maisri paused only long enough to glance my way. Waiting for my approval, I realized. I straightened my already upright posture. Whether she looked to me as the Brutal Prince, respected by all terrestrials, the High King of Annwyn, or merely the oldest and meanest among the group... I jerked my chin in a nod.

She turned to face the strip of sand, remaining on the safety of the goldstone stairs, and tossed the bloom as far as she could into the middle of the sandy expanse.

For a moment, nothing happened. Her shoulders dipped with disappointment.

I used it for what it was—information. The bloom, oversized as it was, was too small to entice the Gremog. It could be useful to know, if it ever came to defending Baylaur from an invading force.

A second later that nugget of information had to be completely discarded.

The Gremog surged out of the sand, high enough into the sky to blot out the early morning sun. Maisri stumbled backward, up the stairs, Osheen already there to drag her upward.

But the huge monster veered to the side, staying within its strip of sand.

Its body was similar to the snakes that slithered through the Shadow Wood, scaled and strong, muscles rippling. But instead of a snout and fangs, its mouth was a gaping hole. If it had eyes or nostrils, I couldn't make them out. There weren't even teeth.

The inside of its mouth was lined with hundreds—maybe thousands—of circular suckers that undulated in constant motion. I caught a glimpse of the rose bloom, caught against one, its delicate petals dissolving against the sucking pressure.

But it wasn't those suckers, which promised to hold its victim tight while it sucked the life from them, that were the most eerie. It was the silence.

The only sound was the swish of sand.

The Gremog was a silent death.

But the second the monster surged back into the sand, disappearing as suddenly as it had appeared, the others erupted. Maisri jumped up and down, whooping in victory from beside Osheen, who'd only released her once the Gremog had burrowed back into the sand. Lyrena's boisterous laughter filled the air, bouncing off the goldstone palace—

"I'm glad to see I haven't left you waiting," Veyka said, her voice slicing through the mix of awed laughter and cries of surprise. "If you wanted to play with a monster, you needn't have waited outside. I promised Arran he could come along."

I got one eyeful of her, and my monster—my beast—growled in appreciation.

Cyara followed a few steps behind, her usual delicate white gown traded for a long, flowing dove gray tunic that reached midthigh and a pair of matching leggings beneath. She'd belted it at her waist, and even had a knife tucked into the belt.

I'd never seen the handmaiden do more than use her fire to light the hearth. I knew she'd battled Gawayn along with her sisters. But still, the weapon at her waist felt ominous.

Veyka, naturally, wore so many weapons a weaker female would have struggled to move. But my mate walked down the stairs to meet us with her confident, steady grace.

She'd traded her long, flowing gowns that wrapped around her body like a decadent confection for clothing suited for traveling. But still, it was unlike anything I'd ever seen before.

The leather leggings were cropped at mid-thigh, cutting upward toward her hips and revealing the expanses of her powerful legs before they disappeared into the tightly laced boots that ended just below her knees. I knew if she turned around, the tight leather would highlight the wide curve of her ass. My cock hardened at the mere thought.

She wore a simple leather belt, rather than the jeweled or metal ones she favored. Her daggers in their jeweled scabbards rested on each hip. Above them, a considerable expanse of her midsection showed, the soft curve of her stomach and the indent of her belly button begging to be licked.

Her tunic was black. Made of a stiffer fabric with careful folds and pleats, it curved around her breasts and hugged the tops of her arms. It was held in place by one of the golden brassieres she brandished in the throne room. Of course, it was. Because even setting out for the human realm, Veyka couldn't help but show off that glorious body.

The body that she used to lure people into thinking less, so she could then viciously cut them down to size.

Topping it off like the cherry atop one of her favorite desserts, she wore leather armor at her shoulders, hips, and forearms. I recognized the style immediately—just like mine. She must have had them custom made. She could have demanded they be handed over by one of the other terrestrials, but they never would have fit her like this. Like they'd been crafted solely for my torture.

But it was her hair that had everyone gawking.

The waist-length braid was gone.

I'd seen it unbound before, had curled it around my wrists as I feasted on her throat and breasts. But then it had reached past her hips, swirling near the tops of her thighs.

Now the ends barely grazed her shoulders.

"Don't worry," she slashed a smile. It was the first genuine one I'd seen from her in days—since the incident with Cyara. And I felt certain it was because she was torturing me. "I packed some full leggings and long sleeves as well."

She adjusted the pack over her shoulder, the one I hadn't even noticed she was wearing. The shifting drew my eyes to the hilt peeking up over her shoulder. Not the curved blades she fought with, but a single, massive gold hilt.

Excalibur.

When she returned from the void, it had been hanging at her waist. I'd set it in a chair in the corner of her bedroom and promptly forgotten about it.

But the High Queen of Annwyn hadn't.

It was her birthright.

One she'd finally accepted—if begrudgingly.

Now, I was the one who was selfish. Who didn't care about Annwyn—only the female before me.

The female who reached me, grabbed a loose strand of dark hair that had fallen free of the knot at the back of my head, and yanked.

"You're gawking, Brutal Prince," she purred.

"King," I reminded her.

She bit hard on her lower lip, letting me scent the blood she drew. Watching with that wicked grin as my eyes darkened. "Shall I call you that the next time you come to my bed?"

"We won't be sleeping in beds anytime soon," Lyrena cut in. "Better get used to what you can accomplish on bedrolls in tiny tents."

The moment was broken, Veyka reeling back and laughing.

It was a ruse. She didn't want the rest of them to see just how worried she was. She didn't want them to think she was falling back into the cavern of the listless darkness where she'd stalled for so many months after Arthur's death.

Veyka didn't look back at me as she joined the rest of them, leading the way around the Gremog's territory of death and into the mountains, to the rift waiting beyond in the ravine.

But I knew. And I would be there when she couldn't hold the façade together anymore.

28
VEYKA

"Where is it, exactly?" Lyrena put one hand on each hip and stared across the river as if, just by commanding, the rift might appear to her.

I kept the cringe off of my face. "I am not sure."

Lyrena burst out laughing. Osheen sighed. Cyara remained silent and watchful, as always. And Maisri splashed into the water happily, entirely unbothered.

Osheen yanked her back, sighing again. Even heavier this time. I wasn't sure why we'd brought a child along. Arran had mentioned something about a daisy fae—whatever that was—and bringing someone to help with the cooking and cleaning. But the twelve-year-old seemed like more of a liability than a convenience. Though her slightly unhinged joy at teasing the Gremog had been impressive.

"It was dark, and we were more worried about making sure the man didn't kill us than figuring out where he'd come from," Arran said. Everyone went silent—as they tended to when he spoke.

He may be the High King of Annwyn, but he'd always be the Brutal Prince first.

"So..." Lyrena dipped her toe in the water and avoided Arran's eyes.

"Parys said to look for a shimmer. A visual disturbance of some kind. We might not be able to see it from all angles," Cyara said.

I shot her a look. "You and Parys seem to have been chatting a lot lately, considering how you felt about him when he—" I bit back the last few words.

Too late. Arran's beast was growling.

Calm down. The only one who gets to fuck me now is you.

The growl turned into something lower—a promise that had me squeezing my thighs together before anyone else in our group scented me.

"Parys and I both realized that while some battles are won with swords and axes, many more are won with knowledge," Cyara said.

"Spoken like a librarian's daughter." Lyrena shoved her shoulder playfully.

Cyara rolled her eyes.

"Let's spread out, then," Arran ordered, taking the first steps across the river. "The human pitched his tent there on the opposite side of the bank. So the rift must be nearby. Maisri—"

"I've got her," Osheen grumbled, the child's hand already tightly in his.

It was odd, to see Arran looking after someone. Even a child. He surrounded himself with competent beings, capable of taking care of themselves without being managed too closely.

Well, except for me.

As soon as I was across the river, he was at my side. Despite having told everyone else to spread out. And instead of looking around, scouting for the rift, he was sliding me sidelong glances that, unfortunately, were not sexual in nature.

"I am fine," I muttered, scouting along the edge of the river, scanning methodically from left to right for any strange 'shimmer.'

"I didn't say otherwise." His footsteps crunched through the gravel of the riverbed in time with my own.

Too busy scanning, so I had to eviscerate him with words instead of scathing glances. "You are hovering like a skoupuma female guarding her kitten."

He paused. "Tell me you've never gotten close enough to a skoupuma den to see a kitten."

For a moment, I thought about torturing him. "Fine, I haven't. But I read about it in one of the books Parys gave me."

Silence.

A thought materialized, even though the rift did not. "Have *you* seen a skoupuma den?"

Arran answered without hesitation. "Yes. I hunted down the entire colony after that night in the woods when it attacked you."

"Attacked *us*," I reminded him.

"They are dead, either way."

I swallowed, saw Arran's gaze trace the bob of my throat. "Even the kittens?"

"Ancestors, Veyka. You stabbed a dozen acolytes for an evening of entertainment, but you cringe at disposing of venomous beasts?"

I shot him a withering glance. "I know one beast I will gladly dispose of if he doesn't learn to give me some space."

Arran bared his teeth, the long canines flashing. "Try not to do anything stupid."

"I am sure you'll only be a few feet away when I do," I said sweetly, not even looking his direction as he stomped away.

He granted me a whole two yards. Better than nothing, I supposed.

I knew it cost him. It cost me—the bond in my chest yawning in complaint at his departure.

I almost called him back, even after ordering him away. His presence at my side... it eased something within me. Maybe it was the bond. Which should have put me off. I didn't want the bond to be making my decisions for me. I wanted some Ancestors-damned control over my own life.

Arran had been a protective pain in my ass before the mating bond. Now, it was a miracle he hadn't chained me to his side.

Maybe I should have mercy on him. And if it eased the burden within me just a little, I'd choose not to interrogate the meaning of that just now—

I felt it before I saw it.

It was like coming home but also fraying apart. Familiar, but uneasy.

The swirling darkness called to me, even as I physically recoiled, almost losing my footing in the gravel riverbed.

"There," I gasped out.

Arran was at my side in an instant.

The others came slower, skirting around behind me, scanning to see what had ground me to such a sudden stop.

Ten yards ahead, where the water tapered off into nothing more than a stream before coalescing into a pool, the fabric of the world rippled.

"A shimmer," Lyrena said in open-mouthed awe from my right.

Cyara hummed a tone that said 'I told you so' just as effectively as the words.

"We just walk through it?" Osheen said from behind, hand still tight around his ward.

"And then we'll be in the human realm." Cyara confirmed.

Just to the human realm. Passing through a rift was not the same as falling through the void. I would come out on the other side, like hundreds of others had done over thousands of years. I would not be thrown into some unknown realm. I would not go to that misty shore where my thoughts turned topsy-turvy. I would not be swallowed by cold death and darkness.

Anyone could pass through a rift. I could do it. I would be fine.

Arran's hand closed around mine.

The surge of warmth gave me the strength. I stepped forward, knowing I should go first.

But before I could, Arran released my hand and broke into a run.

One second, he was there. Then he was gone.

29
ARRAN

It was fucking horrible.

In those few terrible seconds, I realized why Veyka had been so opposed to training her power. It felt like I was being ripped apart, limb by limb.

No, it was worse than that. Limb by limb would have been a respite. This was organ by organ, fiber by fiber of my being frayed apart and reassembled, completely outside of my control.

But it was over in a matter of seconds.

Veyka had felt it again and again. She'd fallen through realm after realm, with no power to stop it. Without knowing if it would ever end.

Yet when my mate stepped through the rift behind me, her face was set. No emotion showed. If anything, the lines of her beautiful face were set into grim acceptance. While the rest of us choked and sputtered, faces ashen, she stood there stoic and strong.

Ancestors. I'd underestimated her. Again.

For maybe the hundredth time.

It ended now.

I would never underestimate her again.

Osheen came through last, a half second after Maisri. I

wondered briefly if they'd tried to step through together, but were torn apart. I would ask him about it later, add it to the growing list of facts and suppositions about the rifts, the void, and Veyka's power over them both.

Everyone was gulping down air, shaking off the unearthly feeling of being disassembled and then put back together again against their will. But we were all standing, all fine enough.

Which was a damn good thing, because less than a minute later we were surrounded.

30
VEYKA

We stood in the center of a clearing. Surrounded not by trees, but huge monoliths that towered over even Arran's head.

Another glance around, and it was easy to see where they'd come from. Unlike the red mountains that ringed the Effren Valley, the peaks circling us were all gray crags and patchy snow. But how they'd gotten here... fae, I realized as the markings came into focus.

They were carved in gray stone rather than red, but the engravings were eerily similar to the ones that marked the hidden wall behind the waterfall in the water gardens.

The mystery of when they'd been made—and why—would have to wait.

First, we had to deal with the two dozen humans peering at us from behind the stones.

Lyrena and Arran stepped forward in unison. Never mind that Arran was the High King now, that Lyrena should have been protecting him the same as me. I pushed between them. I didn't need protection, and it was best the humans realized it.

"We mean you no harm," I said loudly, tracing the faces of each human. Men, women, teenagers. A few children lurked further back, their faces barely peeking around the standing stones. Their clothing had more in common with the pieces the terrestrials wore than my elemental courtiers. Close cut trousers, tunics, thick leather leggings. It made sense, I supposed. The sun shone overhead, but the autumn air around us was distinctly colder than the one we'd left behind in the elemental kingdom.

I watched as my words washed over them as they released a collective breath. They held no weapons, which should have been my first indication that the interaction was not going to go as I expected. But I was completely unprepared for two dozen humans to rush forward without a hint of fear.

"Thank the gods—"

"Heavens above, you've finally come!"

"Please, tell us you received the messenger!"

I tried to grab for my weapons, but there were so many hands. They stroked over my skin, over the jewels of my scabbards, murmuring reverent prayers to whatever gods they worshipped. "I —stop touching me—"

Beside me, Lyrena was similarly beset. Someone reached out a tentative hand to stroke Cyara's wings, sending her jumping to the side, her back pressed against mine. Another lifted Maisri's dark curls to admire them closer.

"What the—Ancestors, yes, yes, hold for just a moment." Lyrena shoved away a questing hand.

Only Arran was spared—his battle axe and glower doing equal work to dissuade any such attempts. I shot him one look, and I knew what would come next.

"Step back or die."

They fell back as quickly as they'd come. It was then that I got a good look at their eyes. The desperation in their faces... they looked up at us like we were gods.

I hated them. Humans had killed my brother. Perhaps humans from this very village. I knew now that Roksana's forces had come through the mountain rift, the same one we'd just passed through. Whether they knew it or not, these humans had given my brother's murderers succor. They'd served them ale and bread, provided warm beds for them to sleep in.

But when I looked at those strange, desperate faces... it wasn't hatred that crept into my veins. At least, not only hatred. There was also pity.

But if they tried to touch me again, I'd stab first and pity later.

"Do as he says," a disembodied voice said, cutting through the crowd of humans.

They fell away instantly, stepping farther back into the protective shadow of the ring of stones. All except for one—a tiny woman, hair nearly as white as mine. She hardly looked real.

Deep wrinkles lined her eyes and mouth. Her whole face seemed to be made up of them. I thought at first she was hunched over, but as she stepped between the others and broached the gap of space between us, her footfalls were steady and strong. She actually *was* that tiny. Smaller than Cyara. Shorter even than Maisri, a child of twelve.

I was gawking. It was rude. Very unqueenly, I could almost hear Arran admonishing.

But I'd never seen someone who looked... old.

Arran, as usual and despite the fact that he was a battle commander and not a politician, handled things better than I did.

"Who are you?" he said, lowering his axe to his waist. A gesture of peace. Though I knew he could kill just as effectively no matter where he held his weapon.

The crone's eyes marked each member of our party, landing on Arran. I didn't need to wonder why she singled him out. He was terrifying to fae. To humans... I was surprised they hadn't all voided their bowels at the sight of him.

"I am called Sylva," she said, dipping her head in a brief bow. "I sit on the Council of Elders for the town of Eldermist. We welcome you to our realm..." A long look at the humans huddling together, watching our interaction. "Perhaps too emphatically."

"We did not expect such an emphatic welcome," Arran said. He was still scowling, his face belying his diplomatic words.

"We did not expect a welcome at all," I said sharply. *Didn't want one.* I bit back the words.

If Arran could manage to leash his beast, so could I.

The crone called Sylva shifted her gaze from Arran back to me. Her eyes flashed—recognition. I'd lived in the elemental court long enough to read expressions, especially those that were not well guarded. While she did better than the rest of the humans around her, she had nothing on the elemental courtiers I'd been surrounded with for my entire life.

"That is reasonable," she said. "Our races have lived separately for thousands of years."

"And with good reason." Diplomacy be damned.

But she didn't take the bait. Instead, she looked to the other humans. "Go, back about your business. I will see about our guests."

I didn't wait for their retreat. "We are not staying."

I wanted them all to know it. I wanted them to be afraid.

But Sylva merely shrugged. "I shouldn't think so. I doubt our little town means much to you at all, Your Majesty. But you are here—and we have things to discuss which would be better said indoors."

Arran took up a position at my side, Lyrena at my flank. Osheen brought up the rear with Cyara and Maisri in tow. They must have discussed it.

More likely, Arran ordered it.

An explosion of power in the throne room and he was still determined to protect me.

Because of that explosion of power.

I'd seen that glint of worry in his eyes. He ought to know better by now. I was more than capable of protecting myself.

Whispers followed us as we walked through the town. It took

every bit of my concentration to drown them out. I didn't want to hear what the humans thought of me, of us.

But I couldn't miss Arran's voice—low enough so the woman leading us could not hear.

"Do you trust her?"

"I don't trust humans."

"If they wanted to harm us, they certainly had the chance."

"As if you could not have killed them all," I said louder than necessary. I waited for the fear. You could always feel it, especially in a crowd. But while the humans we wary of Arran... they weren't afraid. *That* worried me. "We linger long enough to find out what they know of Avalon, and then we are on our way. The less we have to do with the humans, the better."

A soft, warm pressure against my hand.

"They looked scared to me," Maisri said, slipping her hand into mine.

My fingers closed around them instantly, without thought.

I... I'd never held a child's hand.

How strange was that?

"Of course they were scared. Have you seen Veyka when she's in a temper?" Lyrena said, laughter edging her voice.

"Lyrena—" I rolled my eyes backward.

But my eyes snagged on Maisri, shaking her head emphatically. Holding tight to my hand.

"Not scared of us. Scared... here, and here." She touched her chest, then her eyes.

I could feel the weight of Arran's gaze.

She was right. They weren't scared of us—not even Arran. And the only plausible reason was that they were scared of something worse.

I saw the tick in Arran's jaw, beneath the scruff of stubble. He understood.

But he offered nothing as we arrived at the elder's home.

The house was simple but immaculate. A single story, but from the window several feet above the door I guessed there was a loft of some kind. The stone walls were washed white with paint, glass windows and a well-fitting wooden door carved with an intricate design.

Nicer than I'd expected.

I'd imagined the humans living in little more than huts. They had no wind magic to help lift heavy timber, nor water gifts to ease the carrying of materials along the river. They lacked the strength of the fae. I knew that I could have lifted Sylva easily with one hand. But apparently what they lacked in magic and power they made up for with numbers and tenacity.

The inside of the house was as lovely as the outside. Stone walls, but lined with tapestries to keep out the cold. Comfortable furniture, if less jeweled and gilded than that in the goldstone palace. It was all... startlingly normal. Similar. Too similar.

Humans were different—less. We all knew it.

Even this sly crone.

But she was seemingly unbothered. She opened the door to welcome us in, leading us through an entryway into a cozy sitting room. The windows were closed against the cold—it was already much colder in the human realm than in Baylaur—but the curtains were thrown back to let in the streaming sunlight.

Sylva didn't even wait for us to sit before bustling over to the corner and busying herself with a delicate porcelain tea service.

"You drink tea in Annwyn, I believe."

Statement, not question.

"You seem to know more about us than we do about you." A fact that unnerved me.

She set the tea to steep, pulling water from a kettle that had been heating on the hearth. When she turned back to face our group, her eyes went right to me. "The giant takes no notice of the ant he squishes underfoot. But the ant is well aware of the giant's movements."

A rush of pain within me.

I managed to keep my voice even—barely.

"Humans murdered my brother. You are lucky I do not squish every single one of you under my boot as recompense."

Her brow knitted together, the gray-white hairs interspersed with a few darker ones that hinted at the color her hair must have been decades before.

I recognized the expression on her face.

Pity.

And I hated it.

But if she saw the hate shining in my eyes, it didn't cause to her break my gaze. "We heard of the death of the golden king, even here. I am sorry for your loss, Queen Veyka."

What she did see...

"You know who we are. Do you know why we are here?" Arran said from the doorway. He hadn't deigned to sit. Too busy monitoring for threats.

Sylva shifted her eyes in his direction. "A messenger was sent through the rift several months ago. I would assume that you have come to investigate the news he brought—the plea for help."

Silence.

The human messenger.

He'd come from Eldermist.

The human messenger I'd tortured—brutally. I waited for regret, but it didn't come. Even if this woman had known him—of course, she had, she was a town elder—he'd come to Annwyn without invitation. In violation of the treaty between our realms. Only fae were allowed to cross between, not the other way around.

I didn't question the fairness of it. I didn't care. It was a law made for the human's safety. When they came to Annwyn, they were little more than prey. Most of our kind considered them equivalent to animals. The smuggling rings—another reason for the law. So that our own kind could be punished if they brought humans into Annwyn.

But none of that mattered.

The man was dead.

And none of it had anything to do with why we were in the human realm.

We offered no response. Sylva poured the tea.

"I see I am mistaken." Her fingers touched mine as she passed me the first steaming cup.

I ignored the way they lingered in silent question.

A pull in my chest—a rumble. Then Arran's voice.

"Your messenger was received at the goldstone palace. However, he took ill. He did not survive."

"I see." Even as she tilted her head, processing Arran's words, the woman's eyes remained on me. "What do you mean by ill?"

A leading question.

We were going to be thrown out of the town without a single shred of information. It

was unfortunate, but we'd manage. Quite honestly, it was better than enduring the old woman's insufferable questioning.

My eyes swept over the room quickly, taking stock. Osheen stood beside the sofa where Cyara perched, Maisri on her knees eating a scone off the tea tray, totally unbothered. He'd see to them. Lyrena sat between me and the old woman, her fingers drumming on her knee. A half thought, and they'd be wreathed in flames.

We were in no danger, even if the woman decided that she did mean us ill.

But there was no malice in her voice as she spoke—only quiet resignation. "Did you kill him?"

She expected it. The ant knew what the giant did—it killed and maimed. I killed and maimed. I enjoyed it. And I'd never felt a single shred of guilt until that moment.

"No," Arran said forcefully.

It was true—if only technically.

Sylva sank back into the chair directly opposite of me. For the first time since we'd

arrived, I saw fear rim her eyes. The same fear that had Maisri had seen in the other townspeople. "Then it was the darkness that took him."

Cold slid down my spine. "What do you know of the darkness?"

Her eyes were empty now, distant. Thinking. Remembering. "You saw the others—that kind of desperation takes time and torture. Months and months of watching our men go mad, one by one."

Lyrena was leaning forward now. "What do you mean—"

"Maisri, go wait outside," I said sharply.

Her eyes popped up to me, crumbs littering her little lips. "But—"

I remembered the easy, trusting weight of her warm hand in mine. "Your Queen commands it."

She looked mutinous. But she tossed her dark curls over her head and went to the door, passing Osheen. He and Arran traded places, a subtle, silent communication passing between them.

Arran's eyes went to mine. I expected that cold, hard black gaze he always wore when dealing with matters of ruling. But his eyes were soft—and they were on me.

I'd had my innocence stolen.

I couldn't shield Maisri from the realities of our world. But I could make sure she didn't listen to this conversation.

I knew Arran marked the bob of my throat and the tightening of my knuckles. But when I blinked, his hard, resolute mask was back in place. It gave me the strength to turn back to Sylva.

"Your men go mad—only your men?" I asked.

She shifted in her seat. The time it had taken me to banish Maisri was all she'd needed to collect herself. "Yes. One night they go to sleep, and when they rouse... they are mad."

"What do you mean by madness?" Cyara asked, shifting on the edge of the sofa where she was perched. She hadn't touched her tea. Watching and listening, as always.

Sylva regarded her through squinted eyes. "You haven't seen it."

A low growl slid through me.

Not my own—and not for anyone else's ears.

I scooted closer without meaning too, bringing myself to the edge of the sofa. Within easy reach. Arran didn't hesitate. He reached out and laid a hand on my shoulder—the one that wasn't resting on the head of his axe.

Just like that, the roiling in my stomach eased. I could feel his tension easing too.

Through the bond.

It wasn't a tangible thing, no specific sensation I could name. But I simply *knew*.

When I looked up, Sylva was watching us closely.

"Not all of you, at least," she amended.

She shifted again, taking a sip of her tea before addressing her answer to Cyara. "Their eyes become nothing but empty holes, their mouths no more than a gaping maw for tearing and ripping flesh. They will kill anyone they encounter—enemy, friend, wife... child. They cannot be felled by our blades. Even fire is often not enough. The only true way is to behead them, like—"

"Like a fae," Cyara finished for her.

The darkness that had taken the human messenger, the monster in the ravine... they may be mad and difficult to kill, but they were not fae. They were human.

And beheading was not the only way to kill them.

But I had no reason for why my blades worked on the deranged man-monsters, and why Arran's did not. For all either of us knew, it was a fluke of luck.

I did know one thing for certain.

"This curse is not coming from Annwyn. That is what your messenger thought—he came to beg for us to stop the darkness, to pull it back. To stop punishing you all. But this did not come from us, and it is not why we are here."

The elder didn't flinch. "Then why are you here?"

"We seek a priestess," Arran cut in. An obvious attempt to diffuse the brewing argument.

Sylva laughed harshly. "The priestesses have long deserted Eldermist."

Arran squeezed my shoulder. Parys had told us as much, from the little he was able to find about Avalon and its disciples. "The priestess we seek dwells in Avalon."

If the name meant anything to her, the old woman didn't show it. She merely sighed. "So, our town is but a stop upon your journey."

"As I said, we are not staying." I stood up, unable to bear the sitting and waiting anymore. There was nothing for us in Eldermist.

Sylva waited until I was at the door. "Let us help you."

I paused. Mostly out of curiosity.

"Before you ask what help a lowly human could offer, listen, Majesty. You will find the human lands do not have great cities like Baylaur. Our communities are small, self-governed by necessity. But Eldermist is one of the oldest, our archives ancient. You may find information to help you on your journey."

I weighed her words, knowing they came at a price. One I likely wouldn't want to pay. "What do you ask in return?"

She set aside the teacup, drawing herself up to her full height—truly nothing more than an ant among the giant fae warriors in the room. Yet she still held her share of the air. "The Council of Elders meets in an hour. Come. Listen. That is all I ask."

"She thinks we will bend. That if we hear their plight, we will feel compelled to offer help," Arran said, arms crossed as he surveyed what we could see of the town.

We'd remained on the edges, while Osheen and Cyara went in to buy fresh provisions. The gold and gemstones we had brought from Annwyn were distributed amongst all the members of our traveling party, so no matter where we went or what currency we used, we'd have something to use as payment. We had more than enough traveling rations packed, but we might as well use fresh while they were available.

I let myself lean into Arran's warmth, already disliking the cold of the human world. "She's a clever old thing."

Arran didn't react. But I heard the grumble of approval from his beast as I nestled into his side. "The meeting is in an hour. In two, we'll be in the archives. By this evening, I want us far from here."

"Why?" I had my own reasons; I wanted to know his.

"We are being watched."

31
ARRAN

My beast knew.

Even with dozens of human eyes upon us, tracking our every move through the village, my beast could feel the difference. Veyka had shaken it off. I wasn't inclined to press it and give her something more to worry about.

I certainly wasn't going to say anything that drove her out of my arms. Not when she'd come there willingly.

Not for sex, but comfort.

Ancestors, it felt good to hold her.

I was becoming quite good at ignoring the ache in my chest, using it as another way of protecting Veyka. When she was too far away, the feeling of emptiness intensified. When she was pressed against me, like she had been on the edge of the town...

I didn't have the words.

Only the feeling—one I wanted again as soon as the others returned and she slipped from my arms.

We waited until the last moment to leave for the guild hall where the Council of Elders would meet, hoping to slip in the back and avoid notice. Fulfill the bargain we'd made, and be gone. I didn't want to linger here—under prying eyes—any longer than necessary.

But even though we arrived with only a minute to spare, the raised dais at the other end of the hall was empty and the humans were still milling around.

The building was twice the size of Sylva's home, but unlike her small, comfortable rooms, this was a huge empty hall. Empty of furniture. Full of humans.

A row of tall trees stood along the back; some sort of park or garden. Maybe a cemetery.

"Stay with the Queen," I said to Lyrena out. She didn't need reminding. She was nearly as fixed to Veyka's side as I was.

But it quieted the howl of displeasure in my chest.

"I can protect myself." Veyka pulled a dagger from her belt, testing the point.

The humans nearest us took several steps back.

I rolled my eyes—at them, at her, at all of it. "Good. Then protect Lyrena. I'm checking the other exits."

Veyka hissed. A human stumbled over themselves.

I worked my way through the crowded room. Everyone was already staring. So much for going unnoticed.

I towered a full foot above the tallest person in the room. It had been a futile hope.

"She's going to do something drastic if you don't give her some space," Osheen said to my back.

My logical side realized he was offering friendly advice. My beast didn't give a fuck. He turned rabid—I wrested control back.

Shifting—a fit of jealousy—and all of these humans would be dead before the meeting even began.

"I didn't realize you and the Queen were so well acquainted," I growled.

Osheen pushed open the door at the rear, poked his head outside, closed it again. Unbothered by the beast. He expected me to have control over it. A mistake. When it came to Veyka, I had none.

"She's not a soldier to be ordered around."

I clenched my jaw. "She reminds me daily."

"I've had soldiers like her under my command." Osheen worked his way to the other side of the hall. Another door—this one to a small meeting chamber. A group of humans stared at us—the elders, I could only assume. I closed the door.

"Willful and obstinate?" I bit out, sweeping my gaze over the heads of the humans to locate her in the back corner, two yards from the nearest door. Not ideal.

"Wickedly smart with something to prove.

He might be right. But I didn't like it. "What would you advise?"

The crowd parted for us, nearly jumping out of our way. But Osheen's steps were slow. Giving us time to speak. "Give her the chance to test herself. Truly."

I could feel the tick in my jaw. "At the risk of her life."

"It is *her* life."

I wanted to tear out his throat. To knock him to the floor and tell him he knew *nothing* of the mating bond. The pressure of it, the compulsion to keep her safe... Ancestors, I was so close to losing control. Again.

Three hundred years, I'd served Annwyn. I'd led the terrestrial forces in battle after battle, beating back any threat that came to our shores. Even a few preemptive strikes across the ocean. I'd always done my duty. It was how I'd learned to keep control—by knowing that I was working for something bigger than myself.

Then Veyka came along.

Even before we were joined and I realized what she truly was... even then, I'd been willing to let Annwyn burn to the ground for her.

These humans and their problems? They were nothing to me. Not when I'd seen Veyka's breath catch in her throat, the worry and fear in her eyes when she'd sighted the rift.

I would give anything—do anything—to take away her fear.

But protecting her wouldn't do it.

Because that was about *my* fear.

And that came from a different place altogether.

The only thing that would help Veyka was getting to Avalon and getting answers about the Void Prophecy—whatever she needed to help her control her power, so we could go back to Annwyn.

I'd endure this meeting and the human nonsense to get access to the Eldermist archives. That was it.

As usual, however, my mate was already complicating things.

She'd managed to clear out her entire quarter of the guild hall. Not a single human was within spitting distance. Which meant they were all pressed even more tightly into the remaining three quarters.

I lifted one eyebrow. *Not* in amusement. "Are you causing trouble?"

"If they don't stop staring at me like that, I might start." She flipped her dagger casually in her hand. I knew that she would catch it by the hilt, no harm done. The humans were not so sure. Understandably.

"You are the High Queen of Annwyn—"

"Why don't you say it a little louder, so that everyone will realize and then we can have another scene like earlier today?" Veyka hissed. She caught her dagger, slid it into the scabbard at her waist, and fixed me with a burning stare.

"Try not to kill anyone before the meeting is over."

Her eyes started to glow. "You want to punish me for my sass, do you?"

I'd made a mistake.

Veyka wasn't going to kill one of the humans. She was going to kill *me*.

Whether she was trying to distract herself or responding to the burn in our chests from the days spent preparing for the journey rather than giving in to the bond... she was looking at me with desire in her eyes. And I was a second away from losing control.

In the distance—on the other side of the hall, the town, or in another realm entirely—someone blew a horn. Veyka's grin turned absolutely wicked.

I bared my teeth, letting my canines show. "I want to listen to this meeting and get the hell out of Eldermist."

Veyka's blue eyes flared brighter in return. "By all means, Brutal Prince."

The Council of Elders was exactly what it sounded like—five humans, all in varying stages of gray with sour looks on their faces. All except for Sylva, whose expression was neutral.

They walked to the dais, standing in a line. Everyone was standing, I realized. Not a single chair to be seen in the guild hall.

I waited for the official declaration, the pomp and ceremony that I'd witnessed from Veyka's royal council before they'd been either killed or disbanded.

But no pronouncement came.

One moment there was silence.

The next, the entire hall erupted in yells.

The elders, the townspeople, everyone was yelling. There was no coherency to it at all. A sour faced elder with a long gray braid stomped his foot repeatedly, punctuating words I couldn't make out. Beside him, the youngest of the elders, a man with hair that was still mostly brown, was hunched over in a heated exchanged with another man standing at the foot of the dais. It was utter chaos.

I glanced to Veyka, expecting to see her open-mouthed amazement. Lyrena's laugh was audible through the din, disbelief mixed with the delight of pure entertainment.

But Veyka wasn't even watching the spectacle.

Her eyes were on two children, sitting on the floor a few yards away.

One could only assume their parents were among the rabble.

But the two children—a girl and a boy, perhaps aged five—sat knee to knee, engaged in a game of clapping hands in a practiced pattern.

They gave no sign they even heard the din around them. Which told me plenty—this was not unusual.

But eventually, one voice did rise above the rest.

"King Arthur promised us—"

Veyka's head snapped up. I grabbed her shoulder. It all happened in a blink.

"What did he say?" Her words were so soft, I didn't know if she'd spoken aloud or I'd heard it through the bond.

Another voice—louder. Others falling away to listen.

"King Arthur promised us succor. The guards he sent were taken by the darkness the same as our own men. They killed even more of our kin in their madness before they were brought down."

A bubbling chorus, another yell.

"We cannot trust another fae King with our wellbeing."

The humans that had met us at the standing stones were not representative. Not wholly. There were humans here who hated us, who still feared us.

"What other option do we have? The fae are the only ones powerful enough to help."

"We sent a messenger. He hasn't returned. Sending anyone else is just another lamb to the slaughter—"

The next voice I recognized.

"He was taken by the darkness. He made it to Baylaur, but it followed him even there." Sylva paused only long enough to take a quick breath. Smart enough not to squander the attention she'd gained. "The High King and Queen of Annwyn are amenable to hearing our pleas. We cannot waste the opportunity. Their alliance may prove invaluable."

Not precisely the truth.

But eyes were sliding to us.

Some of the townspeople realized who we were. If we were lucky, the word wouldn't spread until after we were gone.

I doubted our chances.

But they weren't my concern. Veyka's eyes had glazed over, her body stiff.

Arthur had known about the darkness, the madness, had been involved with the humans. Perhaps the very same humans who had conspired with Roksana to plot his death.

I knew my mate. I knew she was a second away from drawing her blades and slaughtering everyone in that hall.

The voices were closer now, the yelling.

Those nearer to us were voicing their opinions, the arguing shifting away from the dais down to the crowd.

A large man—large by human standards, at least—climbed up on a crate so he could talk over the others' heads. "Our hunting parties have stopped coming back, or are too afraid to go out at all. If one man is lost to the madness, the whole party is doomed. We cannot survive on vegetables indefinitely. We need meat."

Murmurs. Then a derisive scoff—the man turned and looked right at Veyka. "It does not seem to be a problem in the fae realm."

My body moved faster than my thoughts.

Axe in hand, weight thrown forward.

The human pressed hard against the wall, blade against his throat. "Say another word, and you die."

A hand on my shoulder. Soft but strong.

The brush of lips against my throat. "This is not the first time that someone has taken offense at my body. It will not be the last."

Maybe it was a sign of weakness, that I bowed so easily to her will. Maybe the humans would see it and think I was chained to her, subordinate, that the High King of Annwyn was ruled by his queen.

I didn't care. So long as she was *mine*.

I dropped the man forcibly to the floor and then turned my back on him. Let the rest of the humans see that even the largest among them was nothing.

Every set of eyes, limpid human eyes, was fixed on Veyka. And me at her side, by default.

Her eyes had cleared, shifted from glassy to cold and hard. But the tension still held her body in its grip. I saw her then as the humans must—taller than the men, wider, muscles strong and visibly on display. As were her weapons. A warrior queen, who might exact vengeance at any second.

One hand on each hip, framing the daggers in their glinting, jeweled scabbards, she addressed them.

And not a single human dared to yell out or compete for the crowd's attention.

"I do not care about you. I do not care about any of you, who pretend to be better than the rest of us. You are just as bloodthirsty as you charge the fae to be." She jerked her head to the children, wide eyed on the floor. "I do this for them."

"Go to Baylaur—send an entire delegation, if you like. Women only. I will write a letter of introduction myself. Annwyn will provide succor, as my brother promised."

Silence.

Even the children had stopped their game.

Veyka rolled her eyes.

She reached up her arm, pulling loose the golden arm band around her bicep. She slid it down, giving it one irreverent twirl around her finger. A glance to the man on the floor, the one I'd put there, then up to the elders on the dais. She stepped forward and dropped the trinket into the laps of the two children.

"Take this as proof. They will know the message comes from me."

I was enraged and proud and hard. My beautiful, brilliant mate. How had I ever thought her selfish?

Because she had been—she'd been different. She'd been scared and grieving and broken. Now... we were slowing healing. Knitting back together, both of us. Even if the world around us seemed determined to go to shit.

Which it did, two seconds later.

When the walls exploded and the roof caved in.

32
VEYKA

I dove for the children.

The rest of the humans could rot in the rubble.

I knew the others would protect Maisri, protect themselves. But who would protect the human children? Not the feeble, angry crowd. They were screaming, thrashing, trying to get themselves out.

Their soft, tiny bodies pressed to the ground beneath me, their tears wetting my skin. But I didn't move. I waited for it to be over. An explosion—that's what it had been. Several of them, all in rapid succession.

Chunks of roof fell all at once, hitting my back. I waited for the tangy scent of my own blood, but it didn't come. Bruises, then. The leather armor I'd had fashioned after Arran's was doing its job.

But I couldn't stay here forever. The children beneath me we quivering. I could smell urine—one of them had wet themselves.

And that roof was coming down.

One glance up—it was half gone already. Huge chunks of stone from the arches, wood as well. I could see the sunlight and flashes of blue sky. Ancestors—this wasn't a mistake. Someone had done this. Waited until the guild hall was full and then...

I couldn't think about it.

I gathered my strength, bracing my legs beneath me and scooping up the children, one in each arm. My muscles screamed as I pushed up to stand, bruised and battered from the falling rubble.

"Veyka!"

Arran.

I expected to see the beast—but my mate stood in his fae form instead. He and Osheen both, tall and straight.

Another glance and I realized why the roof was still standing—at least in part.

Massive branches snaked in from the rear of the building, where it abutted the line of trees. They formed a wide net, holding the remnants of the roof in place. People were rising, realizing that they were still alive. For now.

One look at the two fae males, the massive stone structure they held in place—this wouldn't last. Couldn't. They were powerful, especially Arran. But the damage from those explosions...the roof was coming down.

"Get out!" I screamed.

I didn't wait to see who heeded my order. Human bodies moved in my periphery. Some didn't—the dead who could not escape. I focused on the twin weights in my arms.

There was no doorway. What had been was blocked.

I turned quickly, assessing.

A half-crumbled wall. I didn't think about the consequences—the weight that Arran and Osheen would have to bear. I had to get the children out. I kicked the bricks with all my strength, the half-destroyed wall giving way to create an opening. Just as the ceiling above it yawned. A flash of wood. Another branch.

Out. I pushed my way out. Past the stream of bloody humans, into the street.

"Veyka," Lyrena exclaimed, already taking the weight of one child, then the other. I turned back to the guild hall.

My heart stopped, the bond in my chest screamed. The building was crumbling.

I surged forward, only to be yanked back. I recognized the snapping golden braid as arms closed around me.

"Let me go—"

The building exploded again.

Outward this time.

Arran's beast burst from the rubble, Osheen running in his wake. They flew over the debris of stone and wood and bodies as if they had wings.

The wolf hit me hard, knocking me to the ground.

It was horrible.

My chest ached. Pain, fear, need—oh Ancestors, it was excruciating.

I buried my face in his fur, hating the tears and still being powerless to stop them.

I'd almost lost him.

When that building collapsed, it didn't matter how I felt about the mating bond or about Annwyn or my stupid fucking void power. None of it mattered without Arran.

I heaved another sob. I hadn't cried like this, not ever. I couldn't remember this pain, wholly new. My chest ached. My heart ached.

The beast stood over me, protecting me, shielding me from view as I heaved and sobbed. I felt the nudge at my ear, then my chin. Urging me to stand again. Letting me drape my arm over his huge haunches, as tall as my shoulder. I dug my hand hard into the thick white fur.

He was vibrating, a low growl that grew by the moment.

I turned, seeking the threat.

Sylva was covered in dust, cradling her arm carefully against her body. But she walked on her own two feet. And she was alone.

"The entrance to the archives was through the guild hall. It will take us weeks to clear the entrance."

Lyrena stepped up to my side. "We can clear it in hours."

Sylva's eyes slid to me, to the beast at my side. "It is best you do not linger."

Arran rolled his head, baring his teeth. I understood them both.

The guild hall was destroyed while we were in it. It was either the precursor to something worse or a coincidence the angrier townspeople could easily blame us for.

It was reason enough to get moving.

The street around us was in disarray. If we left now, few would notice. We would be well outside of Eldermist by nightfall.

I jerked my head in confirmation. It was all I could manage

Thankfully, that was all it took for the others to step into motion, already moving down an alleyway behind us. But before I could follow, Sylva caught my gaze.

"Avalon lies beyond the Crossing. The Spit, I believe you call it in Annwyn."

I dipped my head, my fingers digging deeper into the beast's fur to steady myself as I tried to tame the tremble. "Thank you."

Sylva bowed her head. "Thank you for bringing me news of my husband."

33
VEYKA

Through the night we travelled. Long enough, fast enough, that by the time the sun set the next day we were in the foothills of the massive mountains. Arran and Osheen led the way.

Arran remained as his beast.

No one commented.

I took solace in seeing his powerful body loping along, his long fangs gleaming in the sunlight.

I hadn't been that close to losing him, I realized. Even if he'd been trapped temporarily under the rubble, he could have healed.

But the fear I'd felt... it had completely paralyzed me.

I wasn't stupid enough to think myself indifferent to Arran. The feelings I had for him... they were complicated.

An understatement.

They were a nest of tangles and trauma that a thousand years might not be enough to untangle. Atop all of that lay the mating bond.

Too much for my fragile mind. Too much for my heart, which had only just been pieced back together, the cracks still all too real.

The physical need between us was easy. Overwhelming. Impossible not to give into.

But everything else...

Soon, I was too tired to even think about it.

We finally made camp in the shadow of the great gray, craggy mountains. Arran and Osheen selected a defensible spot. None of the rest of us were inclined to argue. By the time a fire was burning—lit with a quick flick of Lyrena's fingers—we were done in.

Except Maisri, who still seemed to think this was all some grand adventure. It might also have been that she'd spent half of the journey atop Osheen's shoulders.

She roasted up the two hares that Arran had caught while scouting ahead in his beast form and we all ate silently. Gratefully.

But we were far enough that we would be able rest without fear—at least, fear of the humans from Eldermist. We'd gone too far, too fast, for them to have followed. They'd need another day at least to catch up with us, their mortal bodies unable to cover the mountainous terrain without rest.

Lyrena rallied her magic and was making little animals out of flames, sending them dancing around the perimeter of the campfire—to Maisri's endless delight. Her bright laughter was a balm to my soul after the days of endless travel and the brutal company of my own thoughts.

I was watching the fire creatures—now a skoupuma with a kitten trailing behind—when Osheen spoke below Maisri's giggles.

"What help will Parys and Gwen send to the humans?"

Arran was back in his fae form, standing behind me. I'd felt his subtle shift. "Gwen will be inclined to kill them on sight."

Cyara's eyes flicked from the flames to the child on the other side of the campfire.

She kept her voice low. "Parys will be more judicious. He has been trying to find any mention of the darkness in the library. But when we'd left—"

"I told him to leave it alone." Explicitly. Repeatedly. At meetings of the Round Table. Over flaky pastries. I'd told him that the human realm was not our concern.

Cyara shrugged, wings flicking out then back in a subtle movement. "He has never been a particularly good listener."

"Ancestors. What is the point of being High Queen if no one listens to you?"

No answers. Not a single response.

Even Maisri and Lyrena looked up from their playing.

I shoved myself to my feet. "I am going to bed."

No one answered that, either. So, I stomped off to the tents and figured my over-protective, disobedient flock of nanny goats would worry about setting a watch and cleaning up and all the other things they deemed I was unfit for.

When Arran came to the tent an hour later, I was still awake.

There'd been no question of separate sleeping arrangements. More tents meant more to carry. Everyone was sharing.

It had vaguely occurred to me after I'd gone to bed that I wasn't sure who was going to join me for the night... my handmaiden or my mate.

But I recognized the heavy footfalls, even as I drifted in and out of consciousness.

Not to mention the pull of the bond in my chest, the way it instantly eased when Arran slipped through the tent flaps.

I pressed my eyes closed, even though I knew there was a precisely zero chance he would believe I was actually asleep. Arran was far too attuned to my body.

Which meant when he shrugged off his leather vest and tunic, his broad, bare chest outlined by the light thrown from the campfire several yards away, I knew he scented the trickle of wetness between my legs.

Bastard.

But he didn't comment. Shockingly, he didn't growl either.

He slid into the furs behind me, hooking a leg around mine and sliding his arm to my torso until I was pressed against him. My eyes were closed, but even in the dark, I knew if I'd opened them he'd see the glowing blue ring. But if I didn't acknowledge it, maybe...

His hand, however, was not content to hover at my waist.

"What are you doing?" I hissed, swatting away his hand.

The growl that slipped through him was feral—and entirely male. "What do you think I'm doing?"

"We... we can't!" I cry-whispered, trying to push his hand away again. But he was pushing aside my soft linen tunic, finding no barrier beneath.

Ancestors, I should have worn my leggings to bed. It was certainly cold enough. But I'd anticipated Arran's stifling body heat, and I still wasn't used to wearing such close-fitting garments all the time. My skin was desperate to breathe.

Hot, calloused fingertips dragged over my stomach, sending a shiver down my spine that had nothing to do with the cold night air.

"We can't," I said again, my voice turning into little more than a petulant whine.

Arran's fingers skimmed lower, pausing to draw a circle around my belly button. "Why not?"

Ancestors below. He was teasing me. Unforgivable, terrible male, making me feel like this when we couldn't do a damn thing about it.

I was supposed to be angry. I *was* angry.

He hadn't reacted at all to Cyara's comments about Parys researching the darkness that plagued the human lands. Which meant he'd probably known all along. This was not how we were meant to rule. It was supposed to be a partnership between elemental and terrestrial...

Ancestors, that feels good.

He was running his fingernail along the soft fold of skin just below the curve of my belly, caressing the seam right above the tangle of curls. A half inch lower, and he'd slide his fingers into those curls, dip lower until he found my clit...

I arched out of his arms, rolling onto my back.

I *felt* the growl of displeasure in my bones.
Insatiable beast.

An answering growl—*Come and let me satiate you.*

Arran reached for me again, not bothering to toy with my stomach. His fingers went straight to my pussy, parting me so that cool air rushed in from where I'd rolled out from under the furs.

"They'll hear," I groaned, as quietly as I could. I knew it still wasn't quiet enough.

His fingers paused. "I fucked you against a column in the middle of the festival at Lugnasa and you enjoyed every damn second. You did not care who was watching."

"That is because *no one* was watching," I hissed. I had to grind my teeth to keep my traitorous hips from arching into his fingers, demanding they continue their exploration. "They were all too busy with their own exploits."

I waited for him to argue. To growl something about how he didn't care if everyone in the mountains, all the way back to Eldermist could hear us. It would have pushed me over the edge. I would have given in. I knew it. Arran knew it.

I was powerless in the face of my desire for him.

But instead, he shifted his weight, coming up on one knee so his body was half covering mine, shielding me from the cold.

"Veyka," he breathed into the pointed shell of my ear. "You need this."

A second later— "We need this."

He was right—I knew it. The ache in my chest had been building steadily for days, demanding release. I recognized it now, knew it was the mating bond demanding satisfaction.

Maybe it wasn't just the mating bond.

Maybe when he said *we*, he didn't mean the primal thing in our chests. Maybe he just meant *us*—the male and female who'd forged a trust amid a court of lies and deceit.

I needed this... because I needed him. And the only way I could admit it was with my body. The words were too painful, the emotions too raw. I'd promised myself that after Arthur, after the pain of his loss... I would never open myself up to that kind of pain again.

I'd let in my friends, my Knights of the Round Table. But though they were my friends, the part of me that Arran threatened was entirely different.

It was a place entirely untouched, even by my beloved brother.

The love of a male who was my equal, my partner.

My everything.

Today, in those terrible moments when I'd thought him dead... I'd known what he felt when I disappeared into the void. I understood how easy it would have been to kill everyone in sight, just to try and quell the roar inside.

I could almost see the word forming, feel it in my chest...

But I refused. Even now, even as I pressed up into him and let his fingers work their magic, my climax already so close, my soul reaching for his... I couldn't do it.

Couldn't think it.

Couldn't say it.

The wall I'd erected around my carefully healed heart had to remain intact. Otherwise, I was too vulnerable. I would not be in control. I would not be able to protect myself or Annwyn.

I pressed my eyes shut again.

I filtered out the sounds of the crackling fire and the murmurs from nearby tents.

I needed this escape.

I needed Arran.

Admitting that was enough.

He slid a finger inside of me and I forgot about everyone else. But Arran covered my mouth with his, devouring my moans, the ones that were for him alone.

"Hush," he breathed against my lips. "Or everyone will hear just how wicked you are."

I bit down hard on my lip. "Just like that," he said, dragging his canines over my chin. "Keep quiet while I worship you."

A challenge. A distraction.

A male who might know me and what I needed better than I knew myself.

His teeth caught on the top of my tunic.

"Don't rip it," I hissed. "We don't have a palace full of seamstresses."

I felt the soft rumble of his beast, but he obeyed, tugging the tunic up instead so he could feast upon my breasts.

We were both exhausted. It ought to have been quick.

But maybe because of that, there was no frenzy. Our movements were slow because this was the last muster of our energy and we were giving it to each other.

I dragged my fingernails down his back, tracing the rippling muscles as he shifted lower, teasing one nipple into his mouth. He pricked it with his canine, and I gasped loud enough, Arran shoved his hand up, covering my mouth roughly. Holding me down.

Another spurt of wetness.

An appreciative growl.

Oh, Ancestors, oh, yes.

I moaned against his mouth, whimpered as he sucked and nibbled on my nipple, while his other hand slid downwards. I waited for his touch, my pussy dripping with need. But instead, I felt him take himself in his hand. A rough stroke down, up, and then the head of his cock nudged at my entrance.

Just a nudge, and he pulled back.

I tried to scream my outrage, by Arran's hand clamped down harder on my mouth, pressing my head back into the ground.

"I told you to be quiet." His voice was the most erotic mixture of battle commander and wolfish lover, and I was so hot for it, I knew that no matter what sounds I made, the scent of my arousal would be floating through the camp.

Ancestors below, the thought just made me wetter.

I arched against him, desperate for his cock to be inside of me. I wriggled my hips, trying to force him inside. He punished me with a sharp bite on my other nipple. I bit his hand.

We were all teeth and need.

I was driving him as crazy as he was me. I knew it when I felt the head of his cock pressing against my pussy lips again. He was trying to restrain himself, to hold back.

Fuck that.

I pressed my hips up, locked my legs around his waist, and pulled him inside of me in one brutal, delicious thrust.

Watching the roar that should have poured out of him, instead confined to the sharp planes of his ruggedly handsome face, may have been the most erotic thing I'd seen in my entire life.

I came around his cock in an instant, the slickness urging him faster.

Arran's hand was still over my mouth. I started licking his palm in time with our thrusts. I couldn't see much in the dark, but I could feel the burn of his eyes on me. I nibbled, and he let me suck his finger into my mouth. Then another, until my mouth was as full as my cunt. Until I was fucking him with both, my cervix and the back of my throat flexing and tingling in time with one another.

Until Arran completely lost control and roared. I felt the hot waves of his come as it filled me, as he fucked me in long, slow strokes that milked every bit of his seed until he'd given me every last drop of himself.

He pulled his fingers from my mouth. I caught the last one by its tip between my teeth, one last sharp suck.

Then he collapsed down into the furs, pulling me tightly against him, wrapping his arms and legs and mouth around me until we were nothing but a tangle of limbs and satisfaction.

I let his breathing even out, his cock already half-hard against my ass again, before I spoke. "And you told *me* to be quiet."

My only answer was the rumbling growl of his beast in my chest.

34
PARYS

He hated being in charge.

Hated it.

The library was the only place left in the entire goldstone palace where he could hide from the duties of running an Ancestors-damned kingdom.

And apparently, even that wasn't sacred anymore.

"What are you doing?"

Parys jolted backward, nearly toppling the precarious stack of books at his side. He threw out a gust of wind, just managing to keep the stack—and the glass of wine atop it—from tumbling.

He wasn't scared of Guinevere.

But he most certainly was scared of the cantankerous librarians.

"I am reading." He snapped the book in his lap closed. "Obviously."

Guinevere took up most of the wide aisle, even in her fae form. It would have been laughable—and fucking terrifying—if she'd tried to fit through the narrow stacks as the dark lioness.

She didn't plant her hands on her hips the way that Veyka did, to make herself even larger. No, Guinevere didn't try to curry a particular image. She appeared exactly as she was.

And what she was—*lethal*.

Her nose twitched. Feline, even in her fae form. "We were supposed to meet ten minutes ago."

Parys eyes the plate of fruit sitting to his right and wished it was cake instead. Which made him miss Veyka. For more reasons than one. He reached for a plum.

"Then I am only five minutes late." He took a bite.

Gwen's golden eyes sparkled—not with the ring of glowing desire that marked the passionate nature of the fae race. With frustration. Anger. Whatever.

"What is the point of setting a time if you already plan on being five minutes late?" she growled.

Parys shrugged—partly because he knew his nonchalance drove her mad. "It is called a grace period. Weren't you called Guinevere the Graceful back in your home territory?"

She tensed. She didn't like that—didn't like that he'd known it.

He knew plenty about her. It hadn't been that difficult once he'd gotten a couple of goblets of aural into the terrestrials who still remained at court.

The only daughter of one of the most powerful noble families in the terrestrial kingdom, she'd prepared her entire life to be the terrestrial heir. When the time had come to fight for the title, she'd cut down every female in her path. Including her own cousin.

"That title was in reference to my battle prowess." One hand drifted down to the sword sheathed at her side. She still wore her goldstones uniform, even with Veyka gone.

Parys suspected she'd ask to be buried in the damn thing.

He took another bite of plum. "How graceful can lobbing off heads be?"

Guinevere's grip on the sword tightened. "Would you like me to show you?"

Parys wasn't afraid of her. Guinevere needed him to help rein in the elementals. Besides, she'd made a promise to Veyka and Arran. And if Parys had learned one thing about her in the intervening months since the terrestrial delegation's arrival, it was that to Guinevere, a promise was written in blood.

So, he'd live. Even if she did stab him from frustration.

"At this point, I'd be grateful. I never would have agreed to sit at the Round Table if I thought it would lead to this much work." A half-truth. Parys had known this sort of role was inevitable. He'd just assumed he would be serving Arthur, rather than his twin sister.

Unlike Guinevere, he had not trained his entire life for a place on the royal council. His mother had died bringing him into the world, her fae healing not even enough to save her. His father had been more interested in court politics than raising as on. So, Parys had made himself part of those court politics. His father still did not pay him attention. After Arthur's death, he'd left the elemental court altogether.

Guinevere rolled her shoulders, forcing herself to relax her stance. "So that is your answer. Hide in the library. Drink and eat yourself to oblivion."

"The food is good. You should try eating sometimes," Parys said, tossing his hand in the direction of the tray.

Her lips curled upward in a sneer that revealed her canines. The mark of the terrestrial fae, elongated, one step out of the forest. "I eat."

"I've never seen it." And he wasn't sure he wanted to.

"And you see everything?"

"I see enough."

"Just because you make a spectacle of yourself eating and drinking at every feast does not mean the rest of us feel the need," she didn't snap. But her composure was being tested, Parys could tell.

She was good at hiding her feelings, but he was an elemental. He'd been taught to dissemble himself and read others since birth.

"The rest of us? It's just you and me now, Guinevere," he said.

"It might as well just be me."

"And a lot of good you're doing, glowering at the elementals,"

Parys pressed. How much would it take, to get that composure to snap? Could he do it? Did he dare?

"I am giving them space. Respect. Elementals value social standing over everything, and I am not the Terrestrial Heir any longer." She straightened her shoulders—useless, since they were already perfectly straight. "I am a Goldstone Guard."

Parys rolled his eyes empathically. "You know so much about the elementals."

Her gold eyes flashed. "I spent my entire life training to become their queen."

"Not everything can be taught."

"Says the male surrounded by books."

Parys grinned. "You'd be surprised what a few drinks can do for an elemental. Terrestrials, too. While you've been glowering, I've been drinking. And talking."

Talking—and more. Guinevere's nostrils flared slightly. He could tell she was torn between wanting to know and wanting to bash his head in.

"And?" It pained her to have to ask. Parys did her the courtesy of not showing just how much he savored it.

"The elementals and terrestrials barely know each other's names. They sit at separate dining tables, drink in different taverns in Baylaur, live in separate wings of the goldstone palace." He knew none of this was new information to Guinevere. But he enjoyed drawing it out. It always got the best reaction.

He took a sip of his wine, before continuing. "They have no *reason* to know each other."

She crossed her arms over her chest and leveled him with a look so withering, it was almost physical. "You have something in mind."

"I think we need to give them a reason," Parys said, smiling. He leaned over and rifled through the stack of papers behind the stack of books. Maybe he had too many stacks.

He found what he was looking for before Guinevere started growling again.

"I've been working on something. I still have a few particulars to work out—don't need anyone dying unnecessarily."

She took the paper, eyes darting back and forth across the page. Parys watched her carefully, trying to judge her reaction. Her eyes were unreadable. But the tension around her mouth eased, slightly.

She handed the paper back to him without preamble. "A few deaths would make it even more interesting."

"Now you're starting to think like an elemental," he winked.

"In that, at least, our two races are the same." She sighed. It was so slight it could have been mistaken for a deep breath. But Parys caught it—and felt damn proud of himself for it, too.

He rewarded himself with another drink of wine.

When he looked up, the aisle was empty.

No farewell. Not even a nod of her head.

Parys rolled his eyes, even though there was no one to see. He'd find a new hiding place in the library tomorrow. There was a staircase along the northern edge that led to private reading rooms. She'd find him eventually, but it might buy him an extra few minutes.

He drained the remnants of the wine glass as he flipped open the book he'd been reading before. It took a few minutes of turning, but he found the page where he'd left off...

The sacred trinity disappeared from Avalon long ago. Legends abound regarding the provenance of the ancient items, said to imbue their master with unmatched magical power. However, many believe that each item bears individual magic in its own right...

35
VEYKA

I was woefully unprepared for the human realm.

If my companions were as well, they at least faked it better.

First of all, I hated sleeping on the ground. The lack of bathtubs? Excruciating.

At least we traveled with two fire wielders who were kind enough to heat the small bucket of water that we used for bathing. Otherwise, I might have foregone it altogether.

The human realm was just *cold*.

It was autumn, the same as in Annwyn. But whereas Baylaur would stay relatively warm all year, the nights turning brisk, the chill had already descended here. I changed my cutoff leggings for the full-length ones and dug my cape out of the bottom of my pack. The others adjusted their own clothing as well, but I never caught any of them shivering the way I did.

Before the first week was out, Osheen had crafted me a special wooden cup with a clever sliding lid using his flora-magic, which Cyara refilled with hot tea every time we stopped. I sipped on it all day, letting the heat sink into my bones. I had to stop and pee more often, but I'd pay that price willingly.

At night, at least, I was never cold.

Not with Arran wrapped around me in the furs.

The tall mountains gave way to foothills and then wide, rolling golden plains. We were headed for the Spit—the Crossing, the human equivalent was called. Arran and Osheen knew the way, at least. The geography of the human world mirrored the fae realm, but that was where the similarities ended.

Instead of the Barren Dunes of the elemental kingdom, where nothing lived in a sea of rolling red-orange sand, the human realm's golden plains played host to a whole myriad of wildlife. Even in the autumn, it was buzzing with life. Huge horned beasts with thick hides who moved in massive herds; tiny cat-like creatures that popped their heads out of the dirt just long enough to spot us and hide.

But game meant humans who wanted to hunt it.

We skirted the villages as much as we could. Arran scouted ahead in his beast form. If any humans saw him... it was as good as announcing our presence. I was certain there was nothing like him in the human realm.

But our choices were limited.

And eventually, we needed to go into a village for supplies.

"Maisri will go into the village. No one will pay a little girl any attention. I'll monitor from the outskirts," Osheen said over breakfast. We'd been compiling a list of things we required, Maisri dutifully listening while Cyara combed out her hair.

I was doing dishes. Another thing I hated about the human realm.

"What is that?"

My head snapped up. Lyrena's voice was pained—

Osheen's, however, was sour as a lemon. "A hat."

That was being generous. It was a dark blue monstrosity that bulged strangely on one side and very much looked like he'd made it himself. I bit down on my lip, forcing my eyes back to the suds.

My Goldstone felt no such compunction.

Lyrena burst out laughing. Pained from trying to hold in her mirth—not actual discomfort. "What, precisely—"

"It covers my ears."

Lyrena choked, pounding on her own chest. "What about Maisri?"

"If she can manage not to sprout any daisies underfoot, she should be able to pass for a human." Cyara tapped the little girl's shoulders. I glanced up to see that she'd fashioned her dark curls into two plaits, one hanging on either side of her head. Conveniently covering her pointed ears.

I rinsed the last cup, set it all out to dry in the feeble morning sun, and tried to rally motivation for the next chore. Camping was all about chores.

Osheen caught Maisri by the hand and started off, which meant my momentary reprieve was over. "I will start packing up the tents."

"Lyrena and Cyara can manage."

I'd been aware of my mate's approach. He'd been terrible at sneaking up on me before the mating bond. Now, my chest practically purred with satisfaction when he was near.

"If there are more dishes, you can do them yourself."

That earned me a twitch of his mouth. "We are going to train."

I'd have rather done dishes.

※

"We aren't far enough away."

"Yes, we are. No one can hear us, see us, or smell us up here."

We were, actually, very far away. We'd hiked for an entire hour to reach this spot, Arran leading the way. He must have found it while tromping around in his beast form.

It was isolated, along a ridge that overlooked the plains below. In the distance, I could see a herd of the thick-hided beasts, as well as the village where Osheen and Maisri were shopping.

Sparse shrubby trees lined one side of the ridge, shielding us from sight.

It was as good a spot as any. But I was sweaty from the climb, while simultaneously cold from the wind, and while I knew I needed to train, I didn't want to.

I edged closer to the ridge, peering down. The drop was far enough to be deadly for a human, dangerous for a fae.

"What if I disappear over the edge?"

"Then I will be annoyed that I have to climb down and retrieve you."

I tried to swallow down the lump in my throat, wishing Arran's sarcasm had any effect at all. Only because it was just the two of us, and we were far enough away that no one could see or hear or smell, did I whisper, "What if I disappear entirely?"

Arran's eyes cut to me. He'd been surveying the terrain, that brilliant strategic mind of his turning over whatever plan he'd concocted for me today.

But it all fell away.

His gaze narrowed in, focused on me with such ferocity, as if I was the only thing that mattered.

"I will find you, Veyka." He caught a strand of white hair, loose over my shoulders, tucking it back behind my ear. "I will tear apart this world, realm after realm, until I find you. I will follow the bond, dig my own heart out of my chest to find that golden thread that connects us, and then I will use it to find you. I will never let you go. Not now, not in a thousand years. I am the greatest power Annwyn has ever seen. No one and nothing can keep you from me. Not even the void."

My heart stopped beating.

Words and feelings rose in my throat, threatening to choke me. None of them were good enough. None of them could match the vow he'd made, the promise he didn't flinch from, even when we'd said that none were required between us.

I drew in a shaking breath. "Well, then. I suppose that settles it."

How could I not even try, after a statement like that?

Arran stepped back.

Did he know that I could hardly breathe with him so close? Did he feel the same?

I measured the distance with my eyes, comparing it to the feeling in my chest, that center where the mating bond lived. Maybe if I did it enough, I'd be able to place him at any given moment.

But it was a distraction, and Arran saw right through it.

"Focus," he said, quiet but firm. A command. "Close your eyes and think about your power. Imagine it inside of you, flowing through you."

I did as he said, letting my eyes float closed and trying to focus on the ember inside of me. I ground my heel into the grass. "It... that is not how it works."

"Then tell me how it works."

But he'd never dealt with anyone like me. I ground my teeth in time with my heel. "I don't know. If I knew that—"

"How does it feel?" No mocking laugh in his voice, no reprimand for my sass. Just invitation. He'd trained many warriors, I realized. And this was how—not with fear or his powerful magic. With dedication.

He was going to be a magnificent High King. Already was, though we'd hardly had time to rule before departing on this mad quest.

I knew he'd earned the title Brutal Prince honestly. I'd seen him fight, had fought at his side. I knew he was capable of death and destruction. But this... gentleness. This steady affirmation. This was new.

I couldn't help but answer him.

"It starts as a tingling. Like when you step too close to a fire without realizing it. The way it feels in the seconds before you realize you've been burnt. A tingling of awareness."

"Keep going," he urged.

"It builds, spreads. The thing inside of me... it feels like a flame, but different. Brighter, more powerful. It is always there, but sometimes it is different..."

"Sometimes it slumbers, and other times it roars to life," Arran finished.

My eyes snapped open. "Yes."

Arran hadn't moved. He still stood a few yards away, his weapons holstered, arms crossed over his chest.

I dug my other heel into the ground. "How…"

His face was firm, the lines set to hide any emotion. His voice was just as even. "The first time my beast awakened within me, I killed dozens in a matter of minutes."

I nodded, remembering. The water gardens, after I'd told him about—

No. No room for that here.

Arran spared me, distracting me with his words. Had he seen the flash of memory on my face? Or had he sensed it through the bond?

"For years, every time that my beast awoke, I lost control. Eventually I could wrest it back, but only after that initial shift, that first burst of power. Perhaps that is part of your problem."

I lifted an eyebrow.

"I had to learn to never fully release the beast. I could let him doze, let the power within me quiet, but I couldn't release my hold on it completely. Otherwise, when it woke again I had to wrestle control back."

Now both of my eyebrows rose to my hairline. "I am not a shifter."

Arran rolled his eyes emphatically. "Thank the Ancestors. I don't want to imagine the type of beast you'd turn into."

The kind that could tangle with you.

A growl of appreciation—a blaze of black eyes. I was certain mine glowed in answer.

But Arran leashed the beast within, forcing us back to the moment at hand.

"You are powerful, Veyka. Falling through rifts, commanding the void… it isn't a small thing."

I could feel the blood rushing through my veins. The gurgle of my stomach. My entire body, wanting to rebel against that knowledge. The understanding. I'd worked so hard to train, to hone my skills with weapons so I wouldn't be powerless. Now, I was a whole other kind of powerful.

"I know."

I traced the tick in Arran's jaw with my eyes. It was less visible now beneath a week's worth of stubble.

I watched his lips form the words. "Can you feel that core of power inside of you now?"

Yes.

Always.

But I didn't want to wake it. I didn't want to lose control, like Arran had implied I might.

But Arran knew my answer without me speaking it.

"Try to ease it awake."

I could feel the ember inside of me, the glow soft and steady like moonlight. I told myself to reach for it. I told myself to make it flash, like it did when the power was waking. But every time I tried, something visceral held me back. I recoiled from that core, from myself. I couldn't wake it.

I couldn't—or wouldn't.

I stayed stubbornly on that patch of grass, the ledge looming to my right, and nothing happened. For over an hour.

Arran didn't offer words of encouragement. But neither did he reprimand. He simply stood there—steadfast.

Finally, I threw up my hands, landed them on my waist, and glared. Straight at Arran. As if any of this was his fault.

He took one step closer. His eyes were... wary.

I didn't like that at all.

"Let me... I want to try something." He spoke like he would to a spooked animal that he was afraid of bolting. I wished the comparison didn't feel so appropriate.

"What?" I bit out.

I waited for Arran to take the bait. To respond to my sass. But he'd shifted into some different mode, a sort of calm that I'd seen when he commanded others, but never me. I didn't particularly care for it.

I didn't want to be another soldier he trained. I wanted... *oh fucking Ancestors. I don't know what I want.*

Arran just stepped closer. "When the assassin attacked, in your bedroom... I was able to touch him, to feel whether he was an elemental or terrestrial, to get a sense of his magic."

I remembered everything about that night. "Can't anyone do that?"

Another step. "Not exactly. I can recognize another terrestrial and determine whether they are flora or fauna gifted. I would know an elemental because they are not terrestrial, their magic wouldn't speak to mine. But I wouldn't be able to discern anything more."

He was near enough to touch me, but he didn't. A chill swept down my spine.

"So what do you want to do?"

"I want to see if I can recognize yours."

His hands were at his sides now, fingers flexing. Waiting for an invitation. For permission.

"You touch me constantly."

That earned me a baleful look. "This is different. You have to *let* me see your magic, feel it."

I remembered the body of the assassin, clothed in black, prone on the floor. From one of my knives. "The assassin wasn't exactly consenting."

"They were dead. Not much they could do to protect themselves."

The wind was picking up. I shivered again, pulling my cloak tighter around me. Because of the cold, I told myself. "We already know I'm an elemental."

"But commanding the void is not an elemental power."

The space between us had never felt heavier. Even in those months where we hated each other—hated each other, and wanted each other desperately—the space between us had always felt like an invitation.

If only an invitation to darkness.

But this... I was afraid. For the first time, I didn't want Arran to touch me. It felt wrong. I felt wrong. Everything was wrong.

"Then I will just feel... other." I forced out the excuse.

Arran hadn't moved. Not a twitch of his arm or hand. Totally still, now. Waiting for me. "Maybe. But you are also my mate. It has been seven thousand years since there was a mated pair in Annwyn, Parys said. We don't know what we will be able to feel. Our souls are connected, Veyka. It could mean we feel everything."

I flinched back. Out of my circle of tamped down grass. Away from Arran.

He didn't try to stop me. He didn't come after me. He waited until I was several paces away, clutching my cloak around me, before he spoke.

"You don't trust me."

My composure crumbled. I pressed my palms hard against my eyelids, digging my fingers into the roots of my hair. "Of course I trust you..." It was true. That wasn't the reason I wanted him far away from my magic. "Even if I don't trust myself."

I spun away.

Looked at the scrubby forest. Then turned to the ledge, considered throwing myself over just to escape this conversation and the discomfort in my chest. But when I turned back, Arran was still there.

He was still there.

And it all spilled out of me. The worry and fear and the words.

"I've barely begun to figure out who I am, *what* I am..." I gestured wildly, trying and failing to capture the enormity of it. But my eyes pulled back to Arran. Always back to Arran. I beat at my chest, at the bond that lived there now, whether I wanted it or not. "I don't even know who I am, and then suddenly I'm someone's mate. Your mate. I belong to you."

I bit hard on my lip to keep from crying. My eyes were full of tears—tears of grief that I hadn't let myself cry, because they were for me and it seemed ridiculous.

But I knew I was not the only one who was hurting.

The agony in Arran's eyes, in his heart... I could feel it.

It was there in the set of his eyes, the way the fire that burned—that black ring of fire, desire, always burning for me, even in the most fraught moments—now it was nothing more than a ring of black sparkles, just a tiny sliver around his irises. It was beautiful. And haunted. Hurt, by the way I'd flinched, the words I'd said.

I regretted them, even though they were true.

But it wasn't just what I saw in his eyes, or the slight hunch of his shoulders. His heart was twisting, dealing with the blow I'd dealt, contorting to find some sort of comfortable position within his chest and failing.

And I could *feel* it.

Like it was my own heart. Maybe it was.

I felt something else, too.

It nearly knocked me over, right off that cliff.

Love.

Not my own—Arran's.

Arran loved me.

He hadn't said it. Not those three words.

But it was right there in his heart, the heart that I felt beating and twisting. The heart that was a part of me now, because of the mating bond.

Not just because of the mating bond.

Because he loved me.

Oh, Ancestors. Why... fuck, but it hurt.

This was too much.

The power within me flared, unbidden. A panic, a response, a wild thing.

But Arran caught my chin with one hand. The other landed on my waist, pulling me tight against him. Somehow, over the roaring in my ears, I was able to make out his words—

"We belong to each other."

I felt them, the words he said and the ones he didn't. They washed over me, filled me, comforted me even as they scared the hell out of me.

Arran didn't run.

He wasn't afraid, I realized.

He knew what was in his own heart. He knew I couldn't bear to hear it. But he wasn't afraid of it. He wasn't afraid of me.

He lowered his lips to mine, brushing our mouths together in a touch so light, it might have been a summer breeze gone amiss. So soft, so tender. A gentle declaration that was deeper than words.

His tongue caressed my bottom lip, then my top. His mouth molded to mine, easing my lips apart not for a deep kiss but for a warm and soft one. Unlike any we'd ever shared. A kiss of comfort, a kiss of promise. Two souls, connected by this tentative bridge.

His hands didn't quest, didn't try to claim my body. He simply held me on that windswept cliff edge, making love to my mouth in a way that the Brutal Prince shouldn't have been capable of.

Each beat of my heart was a phrase. Repeated again and again. As if my soul was accustoming itself. Until I was wrapping myself in the knowledge and letting it soothe me, even at the same time as it scared me.

Arran loves me. Arran loves me. Arran loves me.

My mate loves me.

36
ARRAN

We were being followed.

In Eldermist, I'd been able to dismiss the feeling. There were hundreds of humans in the town, all openly gawking at us.

But this was different.

It was careful and heavy. Purposeful.

Whoever—or whatever—was watching us, it kept its distance. It stayed downwind. It was very careful not to get caught.

But I could sense it when we sat around the campfire, the back of my neck prickling.

A few times, my beast tried to chase it down. But I'd lose the scent. That was only possible through magic. A wind-wielder, maybe.

I didn't tell Veyka.

Maybe that was a mistake.

She said she trusted me. I had to believe it.

We'd promised each other truth. Was it lying, to keep this from her?

Maybe.

I'd mentioned it when we were in Eldermist. Her senses were as keen as mine, though honed by a different sort of danger. I had to trust her—trust that if danger came for her, she'd be able to fight it.

She'd called me a skoupuma mother. She wasn't entirely wrong.

But Osheen's warnings rang in my ears as well. A warning—if I held her too tightly, tried to leash her, she'd rip herself free and probably hurt herself in the process.

We'd worked back to a new sort of closeness, but it was as fragile as ever. I had to protect it... even if that meant not protecting her. Not from everything.

Maybe I'd let Veyka be the one to catch the interloper.

I'd enjoy watching her eviscerate them.

37
VEYKA

We needed a map.

We were wasting time, having to constantly try and check our direction, sending Arran off to scout and waiting for him to return or continuing to travel and hoping we were going in the right direction.

Arran didn't want to go into any villages. He wanted to keep our presence in the human realm as quiet as possible. Fae didn't come here.

The High King and Queen? Who knew what sort of human insanity that would provoke.

Not to mention the darkness that afflicted the humans.

The farther we stayed from them, the less likely we were to encounter it.

But every day we were away from Annwyn was a risk. Every day was another chance for mutiny back in Baylaur. We needed to get to Avalon, get answers, and get the hell back to our own realm.

I made these arguments nightly.

But I suspected it was the promise of a real bedroom, with real furniture and a proper bed—in which he could fuck me properly—that convinced Arran to stop at the next village.

"I would trade my sword for a real bed," Lyrena groaned, rolling her neck.

"Not much of a soldier, are you?" Osheen shot back, grinning.

Lyrena wasn't the only one looking forward to actual accommodations. The kind that you didn't have to assemble and disassemble yourself.

I was *not* made for camping.

Soft curves I had in abundance, but they did not make sleeping on the ground any more comfortable.

"Terrestrials seem to enjoy sleeping on the cold, hard dirt," I snarked, sliding my gaze to Arran. "Something in their beastly nature, I expect."

Lyrena hooted gleefully.

The soft rumble of Arran's beast filled my mind. "I shall show you my beastly nature, Princess."

"Why do you call her princess? Isn't she the queen now?"

Arran choked. Lyrena's laugh turned absolutely maniacal. I turned back to wink at Maisri, skipping along just behind me. Always skipping, always joyful.

Exactly as a child should be.

My heart skittered and skipped a beat inside my chest.

"He's old," Osheen said, sending a row of daisies up directly in Maisri's path. "It makes him forgetful."

Maisri plucked a stem without breaking step.

"I won't forget this," Arran muttered.

"He enjoys needling me," I said to Maisri, watching in admiration as she crafted the single bloom into a delicately beautiful daisy crown.

A flick of her finger, and the stem grew and twisted. A half smile, and a dozen more tiny daisies sprouted to complement the larger one.

Such beautiful magic—so different from my own.

So pure.

She held out the crown, a perfect circlet of green and white. "For you."

I tripped on a root and nearly fell on my face.

"Very queenly," Arran observed, even as he caught my arm and dragged me upright.

Maisri smiled up at me, completely unfazed, the flower crown still waiting in her palm. Arran squeezed my arm, then his hand fell away.

I swallowed past the lump in my throat. "Thank you."

I turned it over and over in my hands, admiring the delicate, sweet magic. Magic had meant so many things to me in my short life. But never this... simple beauty, solely for its own sake.

"But what is the cost?" I murmured, mostly to myself.

All magic had a cost.

Maisri grinned, and then suddenly sneezed. Again and again. I counted seven. But when she finally straightened, her smile was unbroken.

"I am allergic to daisies," she said brightly. Then she turned around and skipped back to find Cyara.

A flora gifted fae, so adept with flowers... only to be allergic to them.

I could have laughed—or cried.

Arran's hands were on mine before I could do either. He gently eased the daisy crown from my fingers. Before I could resist, he placed it on my head.

My breath caught again, but Arran's hand was under my chin, lifting my face to his.

"It suits you," he said, the slightest of smiles lifting the corner of his mouth—before it turned wolfish. "My Queen."

Two words, and he set me aflame.

Suddenly, the promise of a bed didn't matter. I'd let him take me right here on the forest floor, with the village within shouting distance.

Lyrena did shout.

At some point, she'd passed us.

But it wasn't a wallop of joy.

Arran and I turned in unison, his flora power pulling back

branches to clear the way so we could see straight through to where Lyrena stood at the edge of the forest. But it was the scent that hit me first.

    Smoke.

    And death.

38
ARRAN

I knew that smell.

If I lived for a thousand more and never saw another battle, I would still smell that scent in my nightmares.

Our blood might set us apart. Our ears and abilities and essences were fundamentally different.

And yet, the smell of burning human bodies smelled the same as fae.

I reached for Veyka, but she was already running. Straight into the burning fire, of course.

"Spread out. Find the nearest water source." I turned to Maisri. "Get up a tree and stay there until one of us comes for you."

The daisy fae looked like she wanted to argue, but I had to trust the command in my voice to motivate her. She might be the youngest terrestrial I'd ever commanded, but she wasn't the most difficult.

I stayed just long enough to watch her start shimmying up a nearby tree. The tree line was far enough from the burning town, she would be safe. Or safer.

Lyrena and Osheen were already sprinting in opposite directions around the perimeter of the village. Cyara had taken to the air, her delicate but powerful wings carrying her slight body on the wind overhead.

But my eyes were for Veyka.

I shifted, using my beast's speed to catch up with her.

Then I was on two feet again, at her side as she reached the first building—nothing more than a wall of flame. I grabbed her arm just in time to keep her from lurching forward.

"There are people in there," she said, her voice scalding as she wrenched her arm free.

I did not point out that they were humans—that she hated humans. For all that she protested, that burning heart inside of her was very much alive. Even when she wished otherwise.

"Veyka, listen." I reached for her again, but she dodged.

"I don't have time to argue with you! People are dying!" She shucked her cape, a liability among the swirling flames.

I reached for her again. She was fast, but I was faster. She drew her dagger in a flash, bringing it down on my arm with a vicious swipe.

Blood spurted from the gaping gash in my wool tunic, but I didn't release her. I dragged her closer, knocking the knife from her hand with a brutally placed fist.

"Listen, Veyka," I demanded again.

Her eyes were wild. If she could think for a moment, she would have realized. I would never have held her back from a battle.

But this battle was already over.

I knew the moment Veyka realized.

Her body went slack in my arms.

"There are no screams," she breathed, her words a horrible, tortured echo on the wind.

No screams.

No cries for help.

Because even as the flames consumed the village, everyone inside of it was already dead.

The others confirmed what I knew by instinct. No one remained alive in the village.

Our keen fae ears could hear past the crackling flame for cries and whimpers, but there were none.

It took more than an hour to get the flames out. Osheen and I channeled our considerable powers to grow thick leaves and vines that could carry water from the nearby river like miniature canals. Maisri crafted oversized, bucket-shaped flower blooms for ferrying water by hand. Cyara dumped them from overhead while Veyka wore a path in the grass between the village and river.

But Lyrena bore the real burden. Not only could she summon fire to her fingertips, she could shape and wield the flames that were consuming the village.

I paused in my own efforts more than once, in awe of the deft way she manipulated her fire gifts.

For all the months I'd spent in the elemental court, I'd never seen one of the elementals wield their magic on this scale.

Sweat slid down her temples, turning the hair at the nape of her neck dark brown rather than her usual bright gold. Watching her, I knew—we all knew—the cost of this magic would be steep.

I shot Osheen a look—all that was needed to tell him I'd return shortly. A hundred years fighting together had its advantages.

Lyrena's effort was admirable. We couldn't just let the fire burn. If it spread to the forest, it could destroy a dozen villages and even more homesteads. I didn't particularly care about the fate of the humans. But we might need their help, had needed it once already. The least we could do was rally our magic to ensure that their homes survived another day.

But Lyrena's expenditure of magic was futile. There was no one to save, no survivors who might thank us for preserving the remaining structures. Then I saw her.

Not Lyrena.

Veyka.

One glimpse of her pale face and I knew nothing would convince Lyrena to stop. No matter the cost.

Veyka's entire body was shaking.

I knew her well enough, was intimately familiar enough with her body, to know it wasn't from exertion.

I also knew better than to offer her empty words or tell her to rest. I'd just earn myself another knife wound.

She did not stop until the last flame winked out.

Lyrena was still standing, though I wasn't quite sure how. Most fae would have been comatose after an expenditure of power like that. However, she managed to throw up a hand to stop Maisri, who tried to follow Veyka as she started toward the center of the village.

"You will help me make camp." She caught the girl's shoulder, turning her firmly away from the charred wreckage.

Even Maisri didn't argue, though her eyes flashed, her head turning as she followed Veyka with her eyes. Even if she could not do so with her body.

Lyrena propelled her forward, eyes fixed on the edge of the forest over my shoulder.

I let them pass, my entire focus on the center of the village.

The stone fountain was scorched, darkened by soot and ash, but largely undamaged. Veyka stopped at its edge, staring down into the reservoir.

Long enough, I almost caught her up.

But just when I thought I'd reach her, she spun on her heel and strode in the opposite direction.

I wanted to rush after her.

But my feet stopped beside the fountain.

What had transfixed her?

The water—what remained of it—was a black sludge. Dark, swirling.

I didn't understand.

It was stupid to try.

I'd seen plenty of warriors reeling, desperately trying to cope in the wake of a bloody battle. They'd fixate on a sound or an image, seemingly random. Only important in their twisted perception.

Minds dark and damaged.

None more so than my mate.

But I wanted all the parts of her. I craved her. Even the dark and damaged parts, even amidst all this death.

I didn't need her scent on the wind to know where she'd gone.

Not to the tavern where we might have rested the night, or the guild hall where any rescue effort would have been organized.

Veyka went to the houses.

The small dwellings, no more than huts, as squat as the one she'd spent most of her life in, closeted away in the water gardens.

They were nothing more than ashen heaps. The families that had once dwelled within...

"We shouldn't have lingered over breakfast."

I ignored the yawning need in my chest to reach for her. "We had no way of knowing."

"We were fucking in the woods while families were burning alive."

We *had* fucked in the woods—slipped away while the others broke camp because we couldn't keep our hands off of each other for another second. But that had nothing to do with what had happened here.

It took all three hundred years' worth of restraint I possessed not to grab her and force her to see reason. "This isn't your fault, Veyka."

"We could have stopped this."

"You do not know that. You aren't the queen of the human realm. This isn't your responsibility."

She rounded on me, her hair flying behind her. She was caked in ash, her pale skin covered in a sickly patina of gray.

How close had she gotten while dumping those flower buckets of water?

How had I failed to notice?

Failed to protect.

Failed my mate. Again.

"This could be happening in Annwyn! And I am not there! Neither of us are!" Her chin trembled with fear or rage or sadness. "We wouldn't even know!"

"We had to come, to find Avalon—"

"We wouldn't have to if I could master my Ancestors-damned power!"

She shoved past me, away from the row of houses toward the outskirts of the village.

I wanted to tell her that it took most fae decades to master their powers. But she was the High Queen of Annwyn. She didn't have decades, not if the shadows of doubt from the prophecy were real.

My beast growled within my chest, tugging at the bond, demanding I go after her. But the male tried to reason—give her space to sort it out. Don't smother her, don't push too hard, or I might lose her again.

Footsteps.

Wings.

"The fire is out. Lyrena is sleeping. I told Maisri we'd eat a cold supper." Osheen's voice was steady. Always the diligent soldier.

I didn't answer—waiting for Cyara. She listened before speaking. But if Veyka was involved, she had an opinion.

Her steps were near silent as she came to stand beside me, eyes fixed on Veyka's retreating back.

"She blames herself," Cyara said, so softly I knew the words were for me alone.

I flicked a glance over my shoulder.

Osheen was picking through the rubble of what might have been a stable.

"It is not her fault." None of it—the wild, intractable magic she'd been gifted with, the destruction here, whatever might be happening back in Baylaur.

Once, I'd called her selfish. A waste of the crown atop her head.

As she walked, the last shreds of the daisy crown she'd worn fell away to the ashy ground.

"No," Cyara agreed. "But Igraine did her work well."

My gaze snapped to the handmaiden, ready to demand what she meant by that.

But Veyka's scream stole all thoughts from my head.

39
PARYS

It was a little pitiful to still be taking his meals in Veyka's antechamber. But he'd never spent much time in his own room, even before Arthur's death. And after…

Being alone was hard, even with the wine and aural and sleeping teas.

It had gotten easier in the last few months.

But with Veyka and the rest of the Round Table gone… sometimes he ate in the throne room, with the other courtiers. Sometimes the idea of sitting through another meal with those insipid vipers threatened to boil his brain.

So, mostly he ate alone in the library or in Veyka's antechamber. Except today, the antechamber wasn't empty.

"What is this?"

Guinevere stared at him from one of the arm chairs. There was a new table—higher than the one that had been there before—positioned between her seat and its matching, high-backed twin. High enough to make eating easy. No plates on laps. A civilized meal.

"There is one thing you are never late for," she nodded at the empty seat. "A meal."

He understood her intent instantly.

"So you intend to ruin my meals with politics?"

"If that is what it takes to get you to do the job that the High King and Queen have set for us, then yes." Guinevere didn't wait for him to sit to start pouring the wine.

Good wine. Parys could tell instantly from the rich burgundy color and the way it filled his nostrils. Full-bodied, fruit-forward, hints of cocoa that he could already anticipate lingering on his tongue. She was more observant than he'd given her credit for.

As he stared her down, the doors behind him opened. Servants bore in trays of food, the scent thick and warm, wafting into his senses. Making his stomach growl.

"This isn't fair," Parys said, even as he dropped into the chair and grabbed his wine unceremoniously.

Guinevere's composure didn't crack. She did take a sip from her own glass.

"Battles can be fought in many ways," she said. "And won."

Parys dismissed the servants with a 'thank you' and started serving himself. He'd never even seen her eat, and he certainly wasn't going to let the food get cold while waiting for that to change. "We are supposed to be working together. Not battling one another."

She watched him fill his plate and take several bites before reaching for her own. But she didn't take a bite. She left her fork untouched as she pulled out a thick stack of envelopes.

Parys pushed past the slight nausea at the sight. Smashed potatoes with cream and thick onion gravy helped with that.

"We will go through correspondence first," Guinevere decreed, slicing the first missive open with her dinner knife.

"More wine."

Parys reached across the table. The wine bottle tumbled sideways. Guinevere caught it deftly, not a single precious drop hitting the table.

She glared—so she was willing to show something other than strict composure. "You are insufferable."

He nudged her fingers away from the bottle, unfazed by her scowl. "Have you read any of those letters yet?"

"No."

He refilled her glass as well as his own.

Guinevere didn't stab him with the dinner knife. He supposed that was a positive sign, all things considered. Nor did she seem in immediate danger of shifting into her lioness form—though her amber-colored eyes were always slightly feline.

She flipped open the first letter. "It is from Agravayn."

The dancing wind that always swirled around him died.

Parys watched her eyes dart across the page, making no pretense of eating.

"There hasn't been a disappearance in over a month," she continued. Her mouth fell open—just for a second. Then she snapped it closed, just as quickly, leveling him a look. *This can't be good...* "But Evander is gone."

Parys snorted and shoved another bite into his mouth. "Good riddance."

Her jaw did drop open. Parys couldn't help but feel a bit of pride at the accomplishment. Even Veyka had struggled to break through Guinevere's cool composure.

She seemed to realize—and shove back down her reaction. Her voice was even again as she spoke: "You aren't the least bit concerned that one of Their Majesties' Goldstones has disappeared? That there could be something nefarious at play—perhaps even involving Gawayn's brothers?"

"Evander is an ass. A self-righteous, self-important, unqualified ass. The most likely scenario is he offended the wrong elemental and got himself killed." And if he came back to Baylaur, he would only cause them headaches. It was a boon... which maybe made Parys a bit more bloodthirsty than he'd realized. He forced another nonchalant shrug. "You should be grateful he didn't bolt back here as soon as the disappearances were resolved and try to oust you from the Goldstones' ranks."

Guinevere slowly set aside the letter. Reluctant, but willing to take his advice. That was something. Maybe these dinners would not be as torturous as he imagined.

"How are your plans coming?"

Parys shrugged. "Both the elementals and the terrestrials have agreed. So, well enough," he said around a thick slice of buttered bread.

He didn't plan on telling her how much drinking had been involved in getting that outcome. Or the terrestrial female whose bedchamber he'd visited, in the high upper towers of the goldstone palace. His methods were his own and they were effective. That was all that mattered.

Guinevere waited for him to say more. When he didn't she took a bite. Then a few more. She didn't speak again until she'd finished the food on her plate.

Parys racked his brain. He didn't think the silent while eating thing was a terrestrial custom. But their kingdom was large—larger than the elemental kingdom. Regional variances were to be expected.

Just as suddenly as she'd begun eating, Guinevere laid down her fork and lifted her eyes to Parys. "I am going to dismantle The Shadows."

He choked on his wine—little scarlet droplets spraying the front of his off-white tunic.

Dragging a hand across his mouth, he cleared his throat. Failed —the words still coming out gravelly. "I thought you hated humans. Letting them be smuggled into Annwyn and tortured seems like your dream."

No reaction that time. At least, not a visible one. Guinevere merely inclined her head slightly, her eyes drifting past him. Beyond. To where the Round Table sat, occupying the entire other half of the room.

"My dream was to become Queen," she said quietly.

She stared at the Round Table.

Parys was pretty sure she didn't even see him anymore, lost in her thoughts... or memories. She'd been the one to gift the table to

Veyka—an heirloom of her house intended for Arthur as a joining present.

Parys had dug up a few texts that mentioned the Round Table, in the weeks immediately after its arrival and Merlin's prophecy. Carved from a single block of stone taken from the Spine, the table was a behemoth. And said to possess mysterious powers. A magical object that behaved differently depending on who sat at it. Like the golden names now emblazoned upon it—a direct result of Veyka decreeing them all the Knights of the Round Table.

Guinevere clearly had feelings about that table... and about the lack of a crown upon her head. Parys looked at her closer over the rim of his wineglass. She'd traded the traditional terrestrial attire of woolen knits in various shades of green and brown for a Goldstones uniform. The version she wore covered more of her body than Lyrena's. She'd opted for tighter fitting leather trousers rather than the flowing pantaloons.

If she'd been born an elemental, her power would have been wind or fire. Those golden eyes were the only hint of the fiery soul that simmered beneath, but Parys knew it was there. Knew that if she had wind, it would not be the merry and joyous sort he had. It would be harsh and brutal. Deadly.

But just then, her eyes revealed nothing. Other than their lingering on the table, which said plenty on its own.

Parys cleared his throat again. "We could eat there. Veyka isn't here to chastise us."

Guinevere didn't laugh. Parys wasn't even certain she could laugh. He'd definitely never witnessed such a thing.

"That table has haunted me for a hundred years. It sat in my father's great hall for more than a thousand before that," she said.

"Must have been terrible to try and decorate around."

The barest hint of a smile. "It was, that."

She took one more drink of her wine glass, then set it aside with crisp finality. "I will never be High Queen of Annwyn. But I've vowed to enforce its laws. My feelings about the humans are irrelevant. I will dismantle The Shadows because they undermine the security of Baylaur and the High King and Queen's thrones."

She stood up sharply. Apparently, she was done eating.

Parys couldn't resist the chance to needle her one more time. Maybe he'd get another smile out of her.

He tipped back in his chair until he was balancing precariously on the back two legs. But his wind power kept him balanced easily. He gave her his best roguish grin. "Dessert?"

She rolled her tawny eyes and disappeared through the doors before the front two feet of his chair hit the goldstone floor.

40
VEYKA

My fault.

If I could have commanded the void, I could have been there in seconds, rather than hours.

My fault.

I could be back in Baylaur, warning them. Telling them everything we'd learned in the human realm. I could already be in Avalon.

My fault.

If I could do any of those things, this journey to Avalon would be unnecessary.

But reason had no place in my mind.

Guilt. Shame.

Those I deserved.

All those months spent on my own revenge, at the cost of all else. At the cost of my kingdom.

A looming darkness.

The darkness the humans feared could come to Annwyn. Already had in isolation. But if it spread...

I had to get to Avalon—find Avalon.

Demand answers.

And get back to Baylaur as quickly as possible.

Arran ought to understand more than anyone. He'd told me again and again to do my duty to Annwyn. To be the queen I was meant to be.

Was this the best I could do?

Ineffectual? Absent?

I swiped a dagger from my belt. I needed to stab something—someone. I needed to grind down the sharp edges within me before they sliced me to bits from the inside out—

The dagger fell from my hand, my entire arm seizing in pain.

I could hardly see the attacker pressing me down to the ground, wrenching my arm backward. I forced my eyes open, forced myself to see—

All the air left my body.

I couldn't breathe. I couldn't fight.

It had me.

The gaping black hole that should have been a mouth, the soulless eyes...

I was so cold. It had my arm. Then my shoulder. Forcing my head back.

Cold like I'd never felt before. Reaching inside of me, reaching for my magic.

No, that wasn't right.

I had felt this before. In that realm of cold, dark death.

I tried to throw my weight backward. It wasn't large. I outweighed it easily. If I could get it off balance, I could roll away.

But it was strong. So much stronger than me.

Stronger than it should have been.

I couldn't get away. The reality dawned on me suddenly.

I wouldn't win a physical fight.

Inside me, my magic flared to life.

No, no. Don't take me away.

But that ember of power didn't care about my feelings. All that mattered was survival. Getting away from this horrible, undead thing, even if it meant going into the void, to the Ancestors only knew where.

The monster gnashed its jaws, lunging for my throat.

The tingling began in my fingers, the void calling to me. Part of my being, deep inside, yawned awake—excited. Desperate to see that swirling darkness again, to become a part of it.

Just like that fountain, swirling with ash, I felt myself start to become the threads of the universe.

Unspool. Break apart.

Make anew.

But a tether snapped me back.

A painful, sharp pain in the center of my chest—like I was being cleaved in two.

The monster had killed me. It was ripping me apart.

But then I was flooded with warmth.

Warmth I knew. Strong, familiar, steady.

Arran.

He'd pulled me back from the void. He'd saved me.

But when I opened my eyes—*when had I closed them?*—the male who stood over me was not Arran.

"Who the hell are you?"

41

ARRAN

He may have saved my mate, but that wouldn't stop me from killing him.

From the moment he'd laid hands on her, I'd been imagining slicing his throat. That was all it took to kill a feeble human.

But the strategist, the battle commander, demanded reason.

Even while my beast roared within me.

So, I settled for a hard kick straight to his ribs. "Who are you?"

The man's face contorted with pain. I watched his legs fidget, his chin tremble, all the telltale signs of human weakness.

His response was a strangled grunt, a breathless exclamation through the pain that still racked him from my blow. "Percival St. Pierre."

Osheen had bound him to a tree—little effort, fae against human. Lyrena was still asleep, Maisri standing over her, within shouting distance if she needed us.

All of which allowed me to narrow my focus on the man—on extracting the information I needed so I could kill him and have done with at least one threat.

My booted foot caught his, pressing it backwards into the dirt until he moaned with pain. I savored it before asking my next question. "Why have you been following us?"

"He's been following us?"

Fuck.

I hadn't heard her approach.

She was so fucking quiet when she wanted to be.

I gritted my teeth, keeping my back to her. "I told you back in Eldermist that we were being watched."

Veyka stopped just short. Waiting, to see if I'd turn around and speak to her. Stubborn wench. I dug my heel in harder, until the man was whimpering.

She didn't tell me to stop. The look she tossed the human as she came to stand beside me was vaguely bored. But when she turned those searing blue eyes on me, they were filled with fury.

"Watched and followed are not the same thing."

I lowered my voice, low enough the human would not be able to hear. "You have enough to contend with."

"I see." There was no understanding in her voice—only the promise of murder, death, torture. Things my mate reveled in. "This is another way of protecting me."

She was going to make me pay, I could already feel it. Grovel, apologize, all of it. I'd be lucky if she allowed me into the tent that night. "Veyka—"

My breath caught on the last syllable as her dagger pressed to my throat.

"I told you that one day, you would meet your end at the tip of my blades."

I lifted my chin, meeting her icy blue eyes. "I told you that if you mean to kill someone, do it."

"I can protect myself." She dug the blade in harder for emphasis, until I could feel my skin splitting, scent the droplet of my own blood that decorated the tip of her dagger.

"My beast compels me to protect my mate." I knew she'd hate it. But it was also the truth.

"I can deal with your beast just fine," she purred, her voice turning guttural. "But the male? The terrestrial? You had better control yourself, and stop trying to control me. Or I will kill them both and be done with it."

I almost believed she'd do it. The gleam in her eyes... I hadn't seen that unhinged sparkle since before the Tower of Myda. When she spoke of avenging Arthur.

But I'd caught the word, the one she'd said twice—control.

That was what this was really about.

And she was right. I could protect her without making her decisions for her. I had to—or I would lose her. And quite possibly a limb—or worse.

Beneath my foot, the human writhed off the ground, arching in pain. "I want your help."

Both our gazes snapped back.

For a moment, we were both silent, trying to remember what I'd even asked.

Veyka recovered first, nudged my foot off of him, pouting out as she considered the man. "With what?"

His face clouded with pain, even with my foot gone, but only for a moment.

"My sister has been taken by a powerful fae lord who resides here in the human realm. I want your help to get her back," he said, breathless but calm.

Veyka rolled her eyes, saying exactly what I was thinking. "We don't have time for fae lords and human problems. I have my own kingdom to worry about." She cut her gaze to me. "How can we ensure he doesn't follow us?"

"Kill him."

One side of her mouth lifted in a milder version of her usual wicked smile. But just as I thought she was about to open her mouth and tell me to do it, her expression shifted. Her eyes drifted back to the ruined village.

Where she'd run headfirst, desperate to save the villagers.

Where she'd been attacked by one of those mad humans taken by the darkness.

I watched as something else took over her eyes—they shifted, setting in determination. She turned back to our captive.

"Percival St. Pierre," she said, turning the name over in her mouth. "You knew how to kill the... human taken by darkness."

This time, there was no pain in his expression as he spoke. "In my homeland, we call them nightwalkers."

A thousand questions swam in my mind. But Veyka held the young man's gaze, so I let her speak.

"You are familiar with this darkness?" she asked.

Percival inclined his head, shaggy black hair falling forward over his brow. "All humans are familiar with it. It used to be rare. But in the last few years... the last few months..." He nodded over Veyka's shoulder. "Things like this happen."

I watched her stiffen. She tried to still the tensing of her muscles, to stop the prisoner from realizing, but she failed. I saw the tick in his cheek. This human was clever. He had to be, if he'd managed to follow us for weeks and avoid even my beast. But cleverness without loyalty was dangerous.

"This..." She didn't have to turn to the village or raise her hand for all of us to know what she meant. "This was caused by the nightwalkers?"

Percival inclined his head.

Osheen's gravelly voice cut in. He was standing halfway between the tree line and the village, but his fae hearing was more than ample to follow the conversation. "How is that even possible? Humans don't have magic. Even if they did, the nightwalkers we've heard of are mad. They are devourers, not arsonists."

"It wouldn't take much," Cyara said. Quietly enough, I noted that the human had to strain to hear, cocking his head to where she stood beside Osheen. "If they attack at night, there would be plenty of lanterns and candles. It would be all too easy for them to be knocked over while the other humans fought."

The other humans. The women and children. Because the night walkers were only men.

The understanding dawned on us. The image of what had

happened here... nightwalkers awakening. Feeding on their wives, their loved ones, while they screamed and fought... upending tables, beds... destroying homes. Families.

Veyka stared at the village.

The shadows of doubt.

The Void Prophecy.

Through the bond, the tie between us that at times felt so real I could almost have looked down and seen it reaching from my chest to hers... I felt her pain. Her sorrow.

If she as the Queen meant to fulfill the Void Prophecy, if it was all true, then so were the other parts. The shadows of doubt would come to Annwyn. The nightwalkers.

She'd known. Or at least, suspected.

But the sorrow and pain of realization were hitting her now, hitting her hard enough that I could feel the tremors through the mating bond.

She insisted this was a human problem. But she'd run to their aid.

Another thought tugged at my mind... *Twice blessed, the realm of shift and mist, when comes the awaited queen who shall possess ethereal might. With a touch, she will feel the heartbeat of her subjects, and she will unlock the secrets they guard within.*

The Ethereal Prophecy. I'd been taught they were separate, but Parys insisted the two prophecies were one. What did that mean for Veyka? Did she possess ethereal might, the ability to read the minds of those around her? Would that power be unlocked somehow, the way our mating had allowed her to access the void power within her? Or did that part of the prophecy refer to another queen altogether?

If these thoughts swirled in my mind, I knew they must already haunt Veyka's.

My heart ached for her, grasping the extent of her inner turmoil. A private torture I could not stop. Not until we reached Avalon and found answers.

The smart thing to do was to kill Percival St. Pierre where he sat. He'd outlived his usefulness. His only remaining potential was to provide complications. Anywhere else, any other time, I wouldn't have hesitated.

But the pain beating in my heart, straight from my mate, stayed my hand.

I couldn't keep her from walking into danger. I certainly couldn't lie to her again. But I could protect her here, now, from the guilt that would haunt her later. I could lessen it, if only a fraction.

I jerked my chin to Osheen. "Check his bindings again and set a watch to make sure he doesn't wriggle his way out tonight. We'll leave him here when we depart tomorrow. If he's as clever as he thinks, he'll worm his way free before he starves."

Done.

I shifted the entirely of my focus to Veyka.

Bath, food, fuck.

Get her mind off of it, distract her. Until she was ready to speak.

I had no doubt our companions were making their own connections, coming to their own understanding of the stakes. Let them work it out.

I caught Veyka on the shoulder, her skin cold through her shirt without the cloak. A twinge of response, a flicker of something through the bond other than pain and sadness. But her face was still devoid of feeling as she turned her feet away from the village, toward the camp back in the forest.

"I can take you to Avalon."

Veyka froze.

Ancestors. I should have slit his throat and been done with it.

But she turned back to him before I could.

She drew her daggers swiftly, spinning them in her hands so fast they were no more than a blur. I felt—rather than saw—them as they whipped past. Too fast for Percival to move. Moving was useless, anyway.

One knife lodged in the tree with a loud *thunk*—pinning the fabric of his shirt just above his shoulder. The other landed silently in the dirt, directly between his legs. An inch higher, and she'd have made him a eunuch.

Veyka stalked toward him, her eyes as sharp and dangerous as her blades. "We have no reason to trust you."

Percival flinched, glancing down at the knife between his legs. He twitched, but didn't try to dislodge it. He dragged in a breath, managed to meet her gaze. "But you don't know where you are going. That much is apparent from your path. Less than expeditious."

Scared, but clever.

"And you know where Avalon is?"

He swallowed, the mahogany skin of his delicate, vulnerable human throat bobbing. "My homeland is near the sacred isle."

"Humans are liars. Traitorous filth, who will kill a fae as soon as they have the power." She spat on the ground.

"Yet you ran to the village. You tried to save them."

Clever or stupid.

"I have my reasons," Veyka said, schooling her face to placid evenness. Devoid of emotion. Every inch the elemental queen she wasn't born to be, but had become nonetheless. "And they are none of your concern. Your only concern, Percival, will be doing exactly as we tell you. One step out of line, and I will kill you. Not him," she jerked her chin in my direction. "Me. I have had a lifetime to picture how I will torture those who betrayed me. I will enjoy practicing on you."

His hands were shaking, but he nodded.

Ancestors help us.

As quickly as she'd turned to address the human, she left, tossing orders over her shoulder to Osheen. "Leave him tied, set a guard. He's human. I won't be murdered in my sleep by him, nightwalker or otherwise."

42

VEYKA

I would have to kill him anyway.

I knew Arran had hesitated on my behalf. He hadn't earned the name Brutal Prince by showing mercy to his enemies.

And I was certain that was exactly what Percival St. Pierre was. In addition to being human, which meant he was untrustworthy by default. He'd been following us for weeks, outsmarting even Arran's beast. No one that clever would tell us the whole truth. Which meant he wanted something from us—more than what he'd said about his sister and some fantastical fae lord.

But if he knew where Avalon was, his lies didn't matter.

We'd fight our way out of any situation.

I'd kill him before it came to that.

Since he was going to die anyway, I spared us the trouble of trudging back and forth from his tree to our camp and had him moved—to a more convenient tree. If we lulled him into thinking we trusted him, let him hear our conversations, catalog our casual references, then maybe he'd give us some useful information in exchange.

He'd be dead before he could make use of anything he learned.

No one could bring themselves to light a fire, so we ate cold provisions under the moonlight. I was so tired. Every bone in my body, tired and aching. But for once, the bedroll didn't call to me. Not even the promise of Arran's warm body awaited, knowing he'd be standing guard half the night.

I shivered on the grass, cross-legged, watching the trees swaying against the moon in the distance.

Besides, the longer I stayed awake, the more likely Cyara was to finally say whatever was on her mind.

She was as skilled at concealing her emotions as any elemental courtier. But those wings gave her away. Perhaps I spent too much time staring at them—checking them for any signs of pain or weakness. Any after effect of what had happened to her in Baylaur.

Even Maisri was quiet, content to sit and hum softly as she brushed Lyrena's long golden hair.

My golden knight had awoken just after sundown, her eyes still lined with exhaustion but at least conscious.

I felt Arran's approach. He'd been scouting the surrounding forest, searching for any signs of humans or errant fae lords. For an hour, I'd felt him slowly moving farther away, the pressure of the bond increasing. Then he'd begun circling back, the feeling easing until I heard the rustle of leaves, his shift, and the male walked into the clearing.

He walked straight to me, dropping down beside me, pulling me tight against him. As if he too had been tracking that ache in his chest all these minutes. As if touching me was the only thing that could ease it.

He was right.

Exhaustion washed over me then.

I'd been waiting for him.

Some part of me had held the sleepiness at bay until my mate was near once more. Now, with him touching me and satisfaction filling my chest, the creeping tired was taking over.

Of course, that was also when Cyara decided to break her silence.

As if she, too, had been waiting for Arran.

She sat up straight, folding her hands carefully in her lap and addressing us with an even, steady voice. "It has been seven thousand years since the Void Prophecy was made."

She had been waiting. Not for Arran—for the High King. For the High King and Queen of Annwyn to be there before her.

I rolled my eyes and leaned harder into Arran's warmth. "Parys would be very proud that you remember all the things he rambles on about."

As usual, my handmaiden ignored my antics and continued her dignified discourse. "It has also been seven thousand years since the last mated pair in Annwyn."

Maisri stopped humming.

"You think there is a connection." I felt the vibration of Arran's chest against my back as he spoke. It sent a shiver down my spine.

It was that. Not his words.

"A coincidence," I said, catching his hand and weaving his fingers between mine. Affecting ease. But my mind was in motion, flicking through what she'd said. Two simple sentences that could change everything.

Cyara's turquoise eyes, turned deep sea green by the moonlight, impaled me with their annoyance. "I think that most coincidences are explainable, but to do so makes us uncomfortable. So we write them off. I think there is an explanation here for why these two things disappeared from Annwyn at the same time."

It did make me uncomfortable.

I didn't like discussing the prophecy. It was all supposition until we found Avalon. Everything between now and then was a guess.

Guesses meant uncertainty.

Uncertainty meant surprises.

Surprises could hurt me. Worse, they could hurt my kingdom and those I cared for.

"Accolon and Nimue were the last known mated pair in Annwyn," Cyara said. Parys had mentioned my ancestors before, too.

Not just my ancestors, but *the* Ancestors. Accolon and Nimue were among the revered fae who had set the terms of the treaty that ended the Great War between the elemental and terrestrial fae. They'd stripped the priestesses of their power, killed the witches, and set into motion the generations of Offering and Joining that had led right down to Arran and I.

"We all know basic history." I shifted my gaze to my fingernails.

"But what if there is more to the history? The void power disappeared at the same time as the last mated pair... what if one of them had the void power? What if the void power disappeared because there were no mated pairs after them?"

Arran's arms tightened around me. I pressed my eyes closed.

Even if it was true, it didn't change anything in the present. Not the actions we would take—searching for Avalon. Our minds, maybe. Maybe I ought to feel grateful that I wasn't a complete aberration; that something about this void power was actually passed down to me by an ancient ancestor.

But I just felt... twisted up. Confused. Out of control—like everything in my life was a puzzle I couldn't fit together.

Arran's arms were circled around me. Cyara's eyes expectant. Even Lyrena and Osheen watching. They were waiting for me—the wielder of the void—to confirm or deny. To offer some insight.

I wished I had nothing to give them.

But unfortunately, I did.

I buried my hands inside Arran's palms, letting his larger hands entirely encircle mine before I spoke.

"When the nightwalker attacked me in the village, I felt the void. I knew I couldn't defeat the nightwalker with my own two hands... and I think my power realized it." I swallowed hard, shivering as I remembered it tearing at me, pulling my body apart. "I was going to go, whether I willed it or not. Just like at the joining."

Those arms tightened even more. Until it almost hurt.

"Why didn't you?" I heard the echo of his vow in his words—to always find me, no matter where I went. Or was taken.

I worked one of my hands free, reaching up to touch the flat stretch of skin between my breasts. "I felt you. Like a tether, pulling at the center of my chest."

"The mating bond," Cyara said, sucking in a breath. "Maybe that is part of it."

The others stared at her. I stared at her.

I couldn't say the words.

"Maybe your power only awakened at the Joining, because that is when the mating bond was solidified." She was leaning forward now, speaking in earnest. Her confidence building. "You said you felt lost, out of control. Then Arran pulled you back. Tethered you to your realm, your world. Your power is tied to the bond."

Everything in me was tied to the bond, I almost said.

Every breath I took. Every beat of my heart.

The male who held me knew it, had accepted it, loved me for and through it.

But I could hardly breathe.

I jerked out of his arms, straightening, ignoring the near-physical pain of the cold air rushing in between our bodies.

"So if Arthur had never died, Arran never would have come to Baylaur, I never would have fulfilled the Void Prophecy, and the nightwalkers would never have made it to Annwyn," I said flippantly, rolling my shoulders and my eyes in unison.

"Unless Arthur was meant to die."

Her voice was gravelly. It was the first time she'd spoken since waking.

The cost—the pain in her throat. Her hand floated up to stroke it, without realizing.

How long it would linger... if there were other costs to her huge expenditure of magic...

All of those questions paled in comparison to the words Lyrena had spoken.

I shoved to my feet.

"You have all lost your minds. We need to sleep."

I had to get away, before I started screaming. Once I started, I might never be able to stop.

43
PARYS

It was late enough that even the librarians had given up waiting for him leave.

In the small reading room tucked off the staircase built right into the goldstone wall, it was easy to lose track of time. At least when he was out among the stacks, there was the several-stories-high wall of glass looking out on the Effren Valley to help mark the day's progress. Tucked into that windowless room, though —nothing.

Nothing.

That was an apt description.

He'd spent days in this library. Weeks. Months and years, if he added up all the time before Veyka and Arran had left. And it had all lead nowhere.

Whoever had stolen the texts about the rifts decades ago had been thorough. Every book that referenced them explicitly, whether it be in title, chapter heading, or index, was gone.

But it was a big library.

There had to be things they'd missed.

He'd found some of them early on—the text of the Void and Ethereal Prophecies, the locations of the less well-known rifts.

But he'd been stalled there for weeks.

They didn't have weeks.

Yes, you do.

There was no telling how long it would take Veyka and her companions to find Avalon, get the information they needed, and get back to Baylaur.

Weeks at the very least. Likely months. Maybe as long as a year.

Avalon didn't appear on any maps that Parys had been able to find. As if those too had been purged. By the same elemental who'd removed the information about the rifts?

He'd made a list of terms to search for—things that could tangentially reference the rifts or the void or the prophecy. Prophecies. For if the Void Prophecy was true, then surely the Ethereal one was as well even though Veyka hadn't shown any aptitude for reading minds.

Portal. Nexus. Veil. Destiny. Echo. Fate. Chasm. Mirage. On and on and on.

Parys massaged his temples.

His wine bottle was empty. Probably why he had a headache.

He'd eschewed the table and chairs and sat right down on the floor in the center of the room. He thought better with books all around him. And he had... a lot. Well over a hundred, stacked to various heights.

He'd made it through perhaps a quarter of them. Every single one so far had been useless.

The list was useless.

No wine left—but some water still in the jug.

He sighed loudly—no one left in the library to disturb.

He chugged what was left of the water, then slumped.

Back, back, back. Until he was lying flat on his back, staring up at the ceiling.

He ought to go to bed. Or go find Guinevere and pick a fight. That might cheer him up. Somehow, he guessed that she was awake. It wasn't quite the same as Veyka—with her, he'd practically had an extra sense. He'd be drawn to her rooms, they'd fuck and eat, and take the edge off the pain. Like his misery had been drawn to hers.

With Guinevere, it wasn't misery that had him sitting up and deciding he'd go find her—he didn't even know where her quarters were. Maybe down near the ones the Brutal Prince had been given on his arrival.

The librarians would have a fit in the morning when they found this room, but he'd deal with that. The older one had a soft spot for cake.

A swipe of his hand, and his warm wind closed the door softly behind him.

Cake.

Maybe he'd stop by the kitchens for a slice before he went in search of Guinevere...

He grabbed the goldstone wall to catch himself, to keep from pitching forward down the steep stairs. His warm wind hadn't just closed the door. It had picked up a voice, carried it to him without meaning to.

A female voice.

No one was supposed to be in the library once the librarians left. There were rumors that the two monolithic statues that guarded the massive doors were enchanted, and would decapitate any intruders. Parys himself always scuttled quickly through those doors, using his wind to close them behind him—even though he had special permission to come and go from the library as he pleased.

But the voice wasn't coming from down below in the stacks, where the doors waited, silent and massive sentinels. They were coming from above; the top of the staircase.

Parys sent a silent, sun-kissed wind along the stairway. Up past each of the private reading rooms, then back down to whisper in his ear.

Not one voice, but two. Another female—and this one, he recognized.

The Dowager.

The door was so cleverly disguised, Parys almost missed it as he crept up the staircase. Every few steps, he sent out that silent breeze to see what it would carry back. The voices were getting clearer, though he was still only catching words and phrases.

The Dowager—*crystal... witch...*

Merlin—*getting closer... put away...*

Nonsensical, for now. Until he could get closer.

Past the reading rooms, to the very top of the staircase. Where he'd thought it just... ended. He'd never bothered to go to the top. There weren't any books up here.

But there was a door—carefully carved to resemble the goldstone, coated with a paint so accurate that it must have actual flakes of goldstone mixed into it. But it was wood, and Parys' wind was able to slip between the cracks that were invisible to the eye. The tiny gap above the floor. The seams where the wooden planks had once been perfectly fused, but had shifted over time.

His wind carried their whispers back to him. They were indeed whispering.

A covert conversation in a hidden room.

Between two dangerous females.

More words floated to him—*over the crossing... sister... chalice...*

They were getting farther away.

How could that be possible? The reading rooms were compact. Unless...

The door didn't lead to a room at all, but opened into the secret network of passageways reserved for the royal family. The same ones Roksana had used to sneak in the humans who killed Arthur, and the forces that attacked the goldstone palace.

The Dowager was not allowed access—not anymore. Not since Arthur had sealed her in her wing with fire.

Parys didn't know the exact details of what had gone on in the water gardens, but he remembered the haunted look in Arthur's eyes. His best friend. And then Veyka, his... best friend.

He scrubbed a hand over his face.

He needed to make friends with someone without the surname Pendragon.

Without Veyka or Arran to enforce the rule, however... Guinevere. He needed to find her. Tell her what he'd heard....

Which was *nothing*.

A few words whispered in secret. If they needed to meet at night in a secret passageway, that said enough about their intentions. Merlin had recovered from the stab wound Veyka had dealt her. To his knowledge, the priestess had dismissed her acolytes as ordered. But he would need to check on that. He would need Guinevere to enforce it.

He could hold his own, his wind magic strong enough to protect himself, generally. But Parys wasn't stupid enough to think his skills any match for the sort of destruction that Guinevere the Graceful could wreak.

His wind ebbed away to nothing. They'd gone too far away, or stopped talking entirely. He couldn't even hear footsteps.

As he retreated down the staircase back toward the reading room, the words flashed through his mind. *Crystal. Witch. Sister. Chalice.* He had more words to add to his list.

He wouldn't be leaving the library tonight.

44

VEYKA

I didn't miss the elemental court. Not even close—but I did miss the pastries and my ever-replenishing stack of books.

Maisri was an accomplished cook for her age—any age, really. Thankfully.

I could make tea. That was the extent of my culinary acumen. I *was* good at knocking birds from the air with a throw of my dagger.

We ate well. But not even Maisri could craft a delicate, flaky pastry over a campfire—even a magically controlled one.

The monotony of travel might have been peaceful, had it not been for one thing.

One person.

Percival St. Pierre.

He talked as much as Parys and had all the charm of one of my old royal councilors. I very much looked forward to disposing of him the same way I'd done most of them.

While all the humans we'd encountered so far had been pale skinned, Percival had deep reddish-brown skin—darker than Arran's bronze, not as deep as Gwen's brown complexion. His hair was more similar to Arran's, thick with a bit of a curl. He kept it loose around his shoulders or tied haphazardly down his back.

Not a warrior, then.

Though nothing about him indicated as much anyway. He'd carried a bow, but we hadn't given him a chance to use it. He was lean, appeared strong enough, kept pace with us. Complained about it, but kept pace.

Percival complained about everything.

The weather, the food, the rope around his hands... he may be from the human realm, but he didn't seem to like this part of it very much.

The one thing he didn't talk about was his sister.

Other than that initial promise he'd extracted from us—that we would help retrieve his sister from the supposed fae lord in return for his guidance to Avalon—he hadn't mentioned it at all. Either he didn't actually care, or he cared a lot and was keeping something from us. Waiting to spring the other half of his trap.

We'd find out after we reached Avalon.

In the meantime, I was desperate to shut him up before Arran or I lost our tempers and stabbed him. I caught Lyrena's arm when we went to relieve ourselves after a brief stop for afternoon tea.

The look on my face must have spoken loudly enough.

Within an hour, she'd devised the game.

Though I was loath to give Lyrena all of the credit. I suspected it was a tamer version of a drinking game she'd played with the palace guards back in Baylaur.

"Who do I tell my answers to?" Osheen asked, rubbing his brow. Lyrena made him do that with startling frequency.

Lyrena rolled her eyes, tossing her gold cape over her shoulder. "I ask the question. Arran says the answers he thinks you will give. Then you tell us if he was correct."

Maisri shook Lyrena's arm excitedly. "How do we win?"

Osheen's second sigh of exasperation was louder than the first. "Does someone really need to win?"

"Yes!" Lyrena, Maisri, and I cried in unison.

"The winner doesn't have to do dishes for a week," I decreed.

I was going to win.

I *hated* dishes.

The others mumbled agreement. But no one volunteered to be Lyrena's first victim.

Of course, my Goldstone already had a target in mind. "Cyara—you answer about Veyka."

"Too easy, she's her handmaiden!" Osheen protested—too loudly for a male who'd contested whether we should even keep score.

"I will make it challenging," Lyrena promised, mischievous grin already plastered across her face.

Cyara's wings contracted slightly, though her turquoise eyes remained impassive.

"What is Veyka's favorite color?"

"You said it would be challenging! One look at her and you know it is bl—"

"Dusky purple," Cyara said smoothly. Her eyes didn't so much as flicker in my direction. "Next?"

"Who is the only one of her Goldstones to ever best her in the sparring ring?"

"Guinevere."

"What creature is she most afraid of?"

Cyara at least had the decency to send an apologetic look my way. "Mice."

"Mice?" The group chorused.

"They are filthy and sneaky and too small to hit with a knife!" I shivered, remembering the time I'd tried—and taken out a chunk of the wall in my bedroom instead.

Maisri clapped in delight. "Let me guess Osheen's answers next!"

We played several rounds, with several delightfully embarrassing revelations.

Osheen's shaving routine? Twelve steps—Maisri recited each of them.

Lyrena's childhood fear? The sound of someone taking a bite of an apple—no one had a chance of guessing that.

"Lyrena," I paused, cocking my head to the side. "What is your surname?" All these random questions made me realize—I'd never heard it.

She effected a mock bow, golden hair glinting. "Lyrena Lancelot," she grinned.

When she straightened, she turned her eyes to Osheen not a second, but a third time.

"Do Arran!" Osheen bellowed.

I pulled a knife from the scabbard, jogging ahead. There was a rise with long grasses—the perfect place to rustle up a fat bird for dinner.

Lyrena's voice floated up the hill after me. "You and Veyka are the only ones with a chance..."

"Don't I get to play?"

They all went silent. I jerked to a stop, turning back to see Percival's smirking face.

He had no weapons. The knife and bow he'd carried were now distributed between Osheen and Arran. His hands were bound, even as we walked. There was no illusion that any of us trusted him. Or even liked him.

Let alone wanted to play a game.

But Arran's eyes had gone fully black—the promise of death and brutality that fae and human alike across the realms had learned to fear. "Try me."

Osheen and Lyrena exchanged a glance. Cyara was more discreet, but I saw her carefully appraising Percival. She'd been the one to brush and plait his long, dark hair for him that morning. Not a kindness, I knew, but a way to get him to ease his guard.

He was one of those types who spoke a lot, but said nothing.

But I thought I saw pity in her eyes before she refocused them on the path ahead. She was right to pity him. Especially when Arran's eyes turned dark and calculating.

Lyrena's smile faltered, but she managed to pin it back in place despite the tension. "How does the King prefer his meat cooked?"

We all noted her choice of words—the king. A well-placed reminder. The rest of us might refer to him as Arran, but Percival ought to know exactly who he dealt with. The High King of Annwyn. The Brutal Prince. The bringer of death.

Percival's smirk didn't waver. "Practically bleeding. Must have something to do with that wolf form."

That was right. Uneasiness began to form in the pit of my stomach.

Lyrena's bright smile was a match for Percival's. He didn't know her well enough to recognize the slight shift. But she'd been my guard since before Arthur's death. I knew the way her eyes wrinkled at the corners when she steadied herself for a battle.

"Which is his dominant hand?" Lyrena said.

"Trick question. He wields the axe with his right, but he's lethal with both."

"What item does he prize above all others?"

Percival's eyes slid to me. Creeping distaste infiltrated my veins. "The Queen."

All eyes slid to Arran. All except mine.

I understood a threat when I heard one.

So did Arran.

I felt the growl—but Percival clearly did not. He rolled his eyes and his matching smirk to Arran. "Care to turn the tables?"

Mistake.

The beast inside of my mate roared. Not for me, not for lust. With barely contained rage. I understood what Arran meant, about always having the beast on a leash inside of him. I knew that if he hadn't, he would have shifted and ripped Percival's throat out.

The only reason he hadn't was me.

I saw it in the brief flash of his black eyes in my direction before they landed back on Percival.

It wasn't duty to Annwyn that stilled his darkest impulses. It was his love for me.

Percival was our best, fastest way of reaching Avalon. Avalon was my salvation.

For me, Arran would leash the beast.

I also knew that if I so much as thought it, he'd rip that restraint free and worry about the ramifications later.

Arran's attention was now fully on Percival. He didn't reach for his battle axe. He didn't shift. He merely crossed his arms over his impossibly broad chest and smiled. No—not smiled. It was much too menacing for that. His canines were on visible display. A reminder that he was a terrestrial. A beast. Wild. And he didn't need his beast form to rip out Percival's throat.

"I've met clever males before," Arran said. Quiet. Deathly quiet. "Their blood all tastes the same."

***

For all that Maisri was a wonderful cook and wielded beautiful magic as if it was nothing... she was still a twelve-year-old child. And she couldn't let things go.

"I did Osheen, Cyara, and Lyrena..." She ticked them off on her fingers as she went. "That only leaves Arran and Veyka!" she cried as she collected the last bowl from dinner.

She swung her exuberant, appealing eyes straight to me. A month we'd been on this journey, and she knew exactly where my soft spots were.

Basically, anything having to do with her.

"It is time for bed," Cyara said—too sharply. She was on her feet in a second, brushing dust from her soft gray trousers and reaching for Maisri.

The child was technically Osheen's ward, but she was willful enough to take an entire group of adults to mind her.

Maisri's eyes darted to Osheen.

He was already shaking his head. "Agreed. It has been a long day—"

"Every day is a long day!" She slid adroitly from Cyara's grasp, dodged around Osheen, and curled her hand into mine. Ancestors, I was such a fool for the girl. "Veyka, let me guess for you."

I sighed. "Just a quick—"

"Ooooh no, I want you to guess for Arran!" she squealed in delight at her own idea.

My stomach tightened.

I'd been avoiding this pairing all day. I knew Arran... how could I not? His soul was quite literally entwined with my own. Which was precisely why I did not want to play this game with him. To know someone on that level... it was too vulnerable. I would be too exposed. Before all of my friends.

I bit down hard on my lower lip, trying to summon some response. It was so much harder with Maisri. I couldn't just spit a sassy retort or pull my dagger to get what I wanted. She was a *child*. And she trusted me.

"Let me start."

Arran sat across the campfire. Usually he sat right beside me, crowding into my space, silencing the demand of the mating bond in our chests through constant physical contact. But tonight he'd made a different, very pointed choice—scaring the shit out of Percival.

The clever imp was trying not to show it, but I'd caught the flash of fear in his eyes when he looked in Arran's direction.

But Arran wasn't paying the least bit of attention to our captive-prisoner-guide. His dark eyes were on me.

Was that the reflection of the campfire or a glimmer of desire?

Lyrena took a swallow from her canteen, allowing a wobbly smile to rise. She started with an easy one. "What is Veyka's favorite food?"

Arran answered immediately. "Chocolate croissants."

The tension eased slightly. Maybe this wasn't so bad. Lyrena hadn't been asking about everyone's hopes, dreams, and deepest fears. Surely, I could manage this.

"What side of the bed does she sleep on?"

His stoic glare faltered, just slightly. A subtle tick beneath the stubble. "The left."

I bit down even harder on my tortured lower lip.

Lyrena tipped her head to the side as she considered her next question. "Would she prefer an evening of sneaking out of the goldstone palace and running with your beast through the mountains or eating a meal of all her favorite foods while watching you snarl at Parys?"

That was a good question.

Lyrena knew I loved freedom. When had she realized about the sneaking out, I wondered. When didn't really matter. She'd realized, and hadn't stopped me. Even pledged as my Goldstone Guard. She would have had to keep it a secret from Gawayn.

A newfound warmth for my friend kindled in my chest.

Arran didn't take time to consider. His answer was already on the tip of his tongue, a slight smile lifting the corner of his mouth. Ancestors, his mouth. The stubble on his chin and cheeks was longer than ever—soon it would actually qualify as a beard. *What would Arran's beard feel like between my...*

"She hates running and she loves it when I'm possessive of her."

Ancestors below.

He was so fucking right.

Osheen coughed into his hand, Cyara rolled her eyes so emphatically I practically heard it, and Maisri made a very high-pitched sound that was half laughter, half squeal.

Lyrena swung her eyes to me. "How did he do?"

I realized my teeth had released their hold on my lower lip. "Close. I prefer to sleep on the right side of the bed."

More giggles and coughing and eye rolling.

Arran held my gaze over the fire. There was definitely a burning glow in his eyes that had nothing to do with the firelight. "Is that so?"

I actually prefer to fall asleep with you inside me.

His beast's rumbling growl was all the promise I needed of what the rest of my night would hold.

For the group, I answered, "Closer to the balcony, where there's more open air. He is hot as a furnace when he sleeps."

"He missed one!" Maisri finally managed to get out coherent words.

Arran rubbed his hand over this chin. "We've only been mated for a month."

For the first time, the word didn't cause a hitch in my throat. Joined—we'd only been joined for a month. But the other was true as well. And I didn't recoil from it. That was... something.

"Veyka's turn!" Maisri demanded, jumping up and down.

The rest of us exchanged glances—realizing that this would not end until we'd exhausted every possible combination of pairs within our group. Excluding Percival, of course. He was too busy listening —to whatever purpose.

Cyara and Osheen had given up trying to get Maisri to bed. She was now nestled between them for warmth as the night took over fully. Lyrena's fingers danced with firelight...warming herself against the chill, I guessed. I took a sip of my hot tea in the special cup Osheen had made me and girded myself for my turn.

"Let's have it," I sighed.

Lyrena tapped her chin a few times before deciding on her first question. "Which side does Arran use to feint?"

That one I knew instinctively. "The left."

I'd sparred with him enough times, I could see the actions rolling through my mind second by second. But I didn't need to sort through my memories for confirmation; I knew from fighting at his side. I knew his style like I knew my own.

Across the fire, Arran's face was impassive. Not quite a glower, but not friendly.

I was much too used to his glares to be intimidated by them—or anything even fractionally softer.

Lyrena's eyes darted between us. Probably trying to deduce whether I'd gotten the answer right. But Arran was revealing nothing—at least, not to her.

"Does Arran prefer his flora or fauna gifts?"

What shall I tell them? That your beast prefers me, so you prefer him?

A soft rumble in my chest, my stomach, lower. *Next time we're alone, I'll show you what my vines can do.*

I quivered.

I fucking quivered.

This male could reduce me to a puddle with a single sentence. Not even a sentence. A thought. A thought through the mating bond, a beastly growl.

"His beast," I said sharply, before I completely lost control and dragged him into our tent. Or maybe the scrubby forest around us. "He likes the taste of blood."

He wasn't guarding his expression now. Across the fire, he stared at me with raw, unslaked desire. In the periphery of my vision, I saw the others turning away from the force of it.

Through the fog of lust, I heard Lyrena's final question.

"What is Arran's mother's name?"

My stomach dropped. Like I'd been dropped into cold water. Cold like that lake north of the Spine. Uneasy, like I'd been every time I thought it might be our turn for this game. This stupid, stupid game.

It wasn't the game. It wasn't Lyrena.

It was me.

The words physically hurt as they scraped out of my throat. "I... I don't know."

Silence.

I stared at my mate. His eyes still glowed, but the expression on his face had changed, become impassive. Inside my chest, I felt a sharp pain. I couldn't tell if it was my heart or his.

A soft chuckle filled the campsite. Percival.

Quick as it started, a vine wrapped around his mouth and gagged him. *Osheen.*

If there were more vines or branches tightening around him as punishment, I didn't see them. I couldn't see anything past the burning sting in my eyes.

45
ARRAN

She stood just outside the ring of tents, staring into the darkness. Osheen was on watch, but had moved away, far enough to give us the illusion of privacy. Even though we all knew that he could hear every word if he desired.

But Osheen and I had been stationed together at many war camps over the centuries. There were many sounds—the crackling fire, the sizzle of food being prepared, groans of pain and pleasure. A good sentry knew how to filter out the unwanted noises and focus on what stood out—the unusual and the dangerous.

There was no room in my thoughts for Osheen or any of the others, anyway. All of me was for Veyka, standing there on the edge of the camp, her body tense and rigid.

"I don't even know your mother's name," she breathed, tracing the pad of her thumb along the outside of the ring.

My mother's ring.

Without even realizing, Veyka was drawn to it.

I'd thought I loved her before. But every moment, every day… there was a new facet to fall in love with.

Or to drive me to insanity.

But I'd be lying to myself if I said I didn't love that as well.

When I glanced up again, her blue eyes were fixed on me expectantly.

"Elayne," I said. "You weren't paying very close attention at the Offering."

Her lips curved into a shadow of her wicked smile. "I was far too busy imagining all of the ways I would punish you for deceiving me in the wood."

I couldn't resist her lips when she smiled like that. I leaned down, catching her lower lip between my teeth and nipping it with my canines before drawing back a fraction of an inch to respond.

"Ironic, for someone dubbed the Queen of Secrets."

She flinched in my arms, but I didn't let her pull away.

"Ask me anything," I said.

That got her to hold still.

"No promises, just truth," I reminded her. "Ask me any question, and I will give you the truth."

It was a risk. Veyka had the power to reach into my soul, my heart, and crush it. But if it could melt that ice in her eyes, the confusion and uncertainty she was trying so hard to hide… I'd take the risk.

She eyed me skeptically, one pale brow rising. "What is the catch?"

"Don't you trust anyone?"

"Are you asking *me* a question, or am I asking you?"

I wanted to spank her, kiss her, fuck her, and tell her I loved her.

Instead, I said, "A question for a question. So that maybe the next time Lyrena gets us to play her stupid game, we don't embarrass ourselves."

Veyka tortured her bottom lip, but she did finally nod.

"Then ask away, Princess."

"Queen," she hissed.

"My queen."

She shivered at the invitation and promise in my voice. I wondered what she'd do when I murmured it while my mouth was between her legs.

My gaze made it from her lips back to her eyes—only to find the pupils ringed in glowing blue. I knew mine burned in answer.

"Ask your question before I take your mouth."

Veyka dragged her tongue over her bottom lip.

I pulled her in closer, letting her feel my cock, already rigid for her. "You're almost out of time," I warned.

A breathless chuckle tumbled out of her, half desire, half nerves. I didn't have time to question how I knew.

"Why don't you talk about your family?"

Trust Veyka to cut right to the heart of things. I bit back the sarcastic retort—*Why don't you talk about yours?*—because I already knew the answer. The most important ones, at least.

And while I'd shared about my power awakening, about my capture and the attempts on my life... it wasn't the whole story. We both knew it.

My hand wandered up her shoulder, toying with the ends of her shorter hair. I wanted to feint, but even if Veyka had made no promises to me, I'd made them to her. They were real and binding, even if they only lived within my own mind.

"My mother was exiled from Wolf Bay before I was born. My father followed her to Eilean Gayl. I do not speak of her out of habit. I've seen enough terrestrials sneer at the mention of her name—and slaughtered enough of them for it." I jerked in a last shred of air. "My brother is long dead."

I could see the questions in Veyka's eyes. Either she wanted to spare me the pain of answering, or she was afraid I'd demand an equal number of answers of my own in recompense. She trailed her fingertips over my cheekbone, down around the stubble of my chin.

Her brows rose in silent invitation.

"Why does it bother you so much to be called the Queen of Secrets?"

I felt her flinch again, but not in my arms. Through the mating bond. She tugged away, the vulnerability inside of her trying to escape. Even as I watched her open her mouth and speak.

I was in total awe of her—her strength, her courage. Every facet of my beautifully flawed and yet terribly perfect mate.

"For twenty years, my secret was what defined me. My mother punished me for it. My brother tried to protect me because of it. Even you," her voice caught, her chin trembling terribly. But I knew if I stopped her, even to try and offer comfort, she may never be able to start again.

"Even you hated me because of it. Some part of me... I just wanted someone to see *me*."

The ache in that last word...

I wanted to go to my knees before her, to vow my love—my love for *Veyka*, the female, not the Queen of Secrets or anything else they tried to make her.

But I knew it was too much. I knew it would push her to the edge, the same way finding out about our mating bond had. I'd only just managed to draw her back from that.

So I offered her comfort in the only way I knew how—with my body.

"I can't be quiet," she said, thrusting hard against me. My knee rose up to give her that friction she craved, the rough inseam of her tight leather trousers against my leg leaving her gasping.

I tangled my fingers in her hair—shorter now, but still long enough to knot my fingers in—and yanked her head back so her throat was exposed to me.

"Good," I growled before lowering my mouth to the delicate column of her throat.

"Ancestors," Veyka whimpered as I scraped the sharpened points of my canines down that vulnerable expanse of skin.

Half a thought and I could have ripped out her throat. But she offered herself to me like it was nothing—she always had. Perhaps her body had known, even when her mind could not, that we were meant for each other.

"How do you want me to fuck you, Veyka?" I asked none-too-softly, tonguing the amorite studs that decorated the shell of her ear.

She choked on her breath as I thrust my knee against her pussy, again and again, determined to make her come without removing a shred of clothing. I knew how brightly she burned, how badly she needed this release. I'd give it to her, and then I'd give her everything else.

"Tell me, my love." This time it was a demand, punctuated by the bite of her earlobe between my teeth. "Tell me all the things you want me to do to you."

"Hard," she bit out, grabbing onto my shoulder so she could control the grind of her pussy against my knee. "Fuck me hard. Until I cannot breathe, until that cock of yours is so deep inside of me it feels like you are going to rip me apart."

I wasn't able to help myself. I reached down, unlacing my trousers and pulling myself free. Veyka's eyes were immediately on me, her scorching gaze on my rigid length as I pumped myself.

She licked her lips, her mouth falling open unconsciously, and it was almost enough to make me spill myself all over her.

"You like this cock, do you?" I groaned, squeezing the tip hard and then slowly fisting my way back down.

Veyka's eyes were glowing bright even in the low light, even as they glazed over with lust. She was getting close, I could tell by the increased speed as she ground herself against my leg. The pressure was building inside of her—inside of me as well. Watching her like this, taking her pleasure, hearing those filthy words on her beautiful lips—

"Ancestors," I groaned, my other hand tightening on her hip to hold both of us in place. "You're going to fucking kill me."

"Fuck yourself, Arran," she demanded, her eyes flicking between the cock in my hand and the intensity I knew was playing across my face. "Think of me. Feel how drenched my pussy is. These pants are ruined, your pants are ruined, I'm everywhere and it's because of you. Because I want that cock inside of me, because just the sight of it makes me so hot I think I'll explode."

I couldn't resist her, and she knew it.

That was what she needed in that moment of uncertainty—some scrap of control. I'd give it to her.

"I'm going to come for you," I growled softly, catching her gaze and holding it with just the force of my will. "I'm going to come all over you, and then I'm going to drag you into that tent and torture you until dawn, when I will flip you over and fuck you as hard as you command."

I didn't have much longer. My cock was so hard, I could feel my climax rising within me. It would take everything I had to hold back the roar building in my chest.

"Fuck me hard enough I cannot even remember my own name," she whimpered, her eyes flitting closed.

"As long as you remember mine," I bit back.

Her eyes snapped open. "Arran."

My name on her tongue rocked through me, speaking to beast and male alike. Nothing could have stopped me then. Not when that primal thing inside of me awoke, the tug between us demanding completion, the connection in our chests burning and glowing with ecstasy.

I came everywhere, my seed spilling from my cock, coating my hand, Veyka's stomach, the juncture between us where Veyka was riding my knee. But she didn't pause. Her wide blue eyes flared even brighter with desire, and her entire body trembled with such force, I was grabbing onto her even with my soaking hands.

She came hard, throwing her head back and screaming her climax to the wind. There were no wind-wielders among us to carry away the sound, so it reverberated between the tents, filling the ears of every being around us—fae and human and whatever lurked outside the perimeter of our camp.

I did not care. Let them hear my beautiful, wanton mate. Let them feel the power that I could feel rolling off of her, so different from my heavy darkness. I'd built a wall of trees around us, knotted together with vines so thick that nothing was getting through. Let them try. Let them lurk at that perimeter and listen as I worshiped this female.

My female. My Queen.

46

ARRAN

It began as a trickle.
Drip. Drip. Drip.
Water falling on stone.
Then it shifted. Enough water had fallen. Water falling on water. A puddle. A pool.
No longer a drip.
A steady stream. A scream.
A scream I'd recognize anywhere. Veyka.
My eyes opened. Why hadn't they been open? Was I sleeping? How could I sleep when my mate was in danger?
The scream ebbed way to nothing. Or it was obscured by the water. crashing water now—so loud it swallowed up all other sounds.
I could see everything clearly now.
I was in the water gardens. Back in the goldstone palace.
But I stood in the corner, the massive waterfall roaring over my shoulder. A place I'd never stood. Yet every inch of the water gardens was etched in painfully perfect detail.
Pain. It lined every stone, every emerald plant and crimson flower fed by those poisoned waters.
Not a dream—but a memory.

Veyka's memory.

She cried out again.

But it wasn't the Veyka I knew. The scream belonged to a child. My mate, but not. Not yet.

Yet as she screamed, the pain radiated in my chest, precisely where the mating bond lay.

Screams to whimpers.

Whimpers that should have been drowned out by the crashing water falls. But that I felt in my soul. I had to save her.

But I couldn't move.

I couldn't even lift my arm, reach for my axe—look down to see if I even had a body.

But I fought.

If I had a body, I'd wrench it free of these invisible bonds. I reached for my magic—none of the plants moved, no vines coming to do my bidding.

My beast.

Screams again—such wretched screams. What were they doing to her? I knew.

My beast surged. Wild, rabid. But I couldn't shift.

I couldn't reach her. Couldn't save her.

I couldn't make it stop.

<hr />

I arched up, my muscles tensing, breaking against the invisible bonds of memory.

Except I wasn't bound any longer. I felt my hands moving, clenched so tight I'd drawn blood from my own palms.

I waited for Veyka's screams. Was met instead by the even inhale and exhale of her sleeping beside me.

I'd lost count of the number of nights I'd woken like this since our joining. The dreams were different. Varying shades of torture, but always the same two subjects.

Veyka. My mother.

I was always helpless.

Tell her.

Wake her, let her soothe us, my beast growled.

Veyka shifted, rolling to her side.

Had she sensed my beast, even in slumber?

Take her. Let her soft body wrap around us.

That I could do. I could hold her, bury myself inside of her.

But I could not burden her with my terrors. She had enough of her own.

I could protect her from this—from the darkest parts of me. Even if I couldn't protect her from everything else.

47
PARYS

It was a simple concept. Three rounds. The first rounds were sorted between elementals and terrestrials. Elemental versus elemental, terrestrial versus terrestrial. Then the winners of those matches were paired up—with a fae from the opposing faction. Those pairs then battled another pair until there were only two sets left. The final pairs would face off against each other to be declared winners.

No matter how the competition unfolded, there would be one elemental and one terrestrial in the winning pair. They would be forced to work together—to learn about one another's magic, to respect it.

It was brilliant.

He hadn't even needed to come up with a prize. The fae were competitive enough that they'd agreed to the competition with only a bit of persuading. If they hadn't realized that they'd be fighting with a member of the rival faction rather than against them... well, he couldn't be faulted. He'd never explicitly promised anything.

If a few died before the night was over? That would only add to the entertainment and be one less ego for him to soothe later.

Parys was more than a little pleased with himself as he sipped his first—and only—goblet of aural. Leading an entire unified fae kingdom meant he couldn't overindulge. At least, not publicly. And not without the female at his side trying to cut his balls off.

They were seated on the dais, but below the thrones.

The symbolism was important—sitting on the same level as all the other courtiers would have implied he and Guinevere were the same as them, mere members of the court. The elementals would seize upon that small show of weakness in a second.

But Parys would never put his ass on either of those thrones. Not even on a dare. Not even on a promise of a month of solitude in the library.

If Guinevere had wanted to try one out, the throne that should have been hers... she didn't say. She didn't even look at them.

She was much too busy watching the first match-up. Two terrestrials, one flora and the other fauna gifted.

The fox, with its sharp teeth and quick tail, adeptly dodged the vines that shot after it. But the shifter didn't realize that his flora-gifted opponent was herding him—back and back and back towards an innocuous looking flower.

Too late. The pink bloom grew—quickly. So quickly, the shifter didn't realize what was happening. By the time the fox tried to dart away, a terrible barbed tongue had shot from the center of the flower and wrapped around its thick tail.

The fox arched, trying to snap its small but powerful jaws around the tongue. But the barbs stuck in his mouth, until the canine was yelping and whimpering.

Parys wrinkled his nose, ready to snap his eyes shut if the flower petals made one move to close. He did not intend to watch that repulsive flower devour the fox whole.

At the last second, the flower recoiled with a sharp jerk. The flora-gifted female across the room smiled widely, rolling her shoulders and affecting a mock bow to the cheering coterie of terrestrials watching from the sidelines. The fox limped off, clearing the makeshift sparing ring the center of the throne room before shifting back into his fae form.

Guinevere's eyes followed the shifter through the crowd until he disappeared from the throne room, a healer at his side.

"Did you pair flora versus fauna for all of the terrestrial matches?" she asked.

Parys frowned. "No. There's one more like this one. Then two shifters against each other and two flora-gifted for the final match." His eyes slid to Guinevere. "Why?"

She didn't shrug or look his way, eyes now back on the center of the ring where an elemental water-wielder prepared to face against her own sibling—who possessed ice magic.

"Is there rivalry, within the terrestrials?" The thought had occurred to Parys, of course. But it wasn't mentioned anywhere in the texts, and nothing had come up in all his drinking with the terrestrials. Not even a drunken barb.

"An unspoken one," Guinevere said.

They'd dined earlier, since the tables had to be moved away to make room for the competition ring. But she held a glass of wine. She'd refused aural. He had briefly wondered if it was too strong for her. Which would be the most poetic irony.

Parys lifted an eyebrow. "Let me guess... shifters think they are better than everyone else?"

Her golden eyes flashed. "There are certainly some who think so. But the most dangerous among us are not the shifters. Nor the flora-gifted who command vines. It's the ones who control animals, or who coax poison from the plants at their disposal."

Parys' skin began to crawl with prickling unease.

"Not much use in this particular competition," he choked out.

"No," Guinevere agreed. "But very effective when it matters most."

She was going to say more. Parys could practically feel the words scrambling to get out of her. But he never got a chance to hear what other horrors the terrestrials could wreak, because Elora appeared at Guinevere's shoulder.

Parys had wondered why Veyka hadn't invited the young but capable ice-wielder to join the Round Table. She'd more than demonstrated her loyalty, executing her own mother for her treason against Annwyn. But perhaps it was too fresh—Gawayn and Roksana's betrayals, the deaths of Arthur, Charis, and Carly.

Maybe Veyka did secretly believe in the prophecy Merlin had made.

A table of destiny. Five shall be with you at Mabon. One is not yet known, but the bravest of the five shall be his father. When he comes, you will know that the time for the Grail is near. The last is the Siege Perilous. It is death to all but the one for which it is made—the best of them all—the one who shall come at the moment of direst need.

Elora didn't quite seem to fit in. But then, Veyka had damned Merlin and all her nonsense to hell.

Merlin. Even as Elora whispered in Guinevere's ear, Parys' eyes tracked through the room to find the priestess. Not in the crowds of spectators, not near the aural fountain... watching from one of the arches. Her features were cast in light, the night-dark sky behind her nothing more than yawning blackness. She was smiling as she watched the bloodshed.

An elemental, through and through. A disloyal one—but as bloodthirsty as the rest.

Maybe more.

He'd brought up his concerns about Merlin and Igraine at one of his shared dinners with Guinevere. But lacking concrete details, she'd shrugged and said her focus was on the Shadows as the more immediate danger.

That would not stop him from investigating.

"Humans?"

Parys' attention snapped back to the two women. They might have been sisters—dark brown skin, black hair arranged in tight braids—but it was the cool, warrior's calculation on their faces that made them truly look alike.

Guinevere adjusted herself in her seat, making a pretense of reaching for the bottle of wine in front of Parys even though her glass was still full.

"A human delegation has arrived at the goldstone palace. They say they are from Eldermist, that they've come through the rift. At the Queen's invitation."

Parys' hand tightened around his goblet of aural. But he forced his mouth to spread into a wide, roguish grin. As if Elora and Guinevere had just made him an indecent proposal, rather than dropped another political headache into his lap.

"Can we have them quietly accommodated somewhere until we're ready to deal with them?" Even as he said it, he knew it was a bad idea.

The elementals and terrestrials alike would be roiling by the time the competition was over. Many of them would kill a human on sight and ask questions later. The worse ones would let the humans live... for a while.

The crowd was murmuring in the background—the next match had started. Parys didn't even glance down. He was smiling, holding his wine glass, and staring into nothingness as his mind worked through the possible calculations.

"Take them down to the servants' quarters under palace guard. I can break off the competition after this round and say it is to build anticipation." The murmuring was getting louder. Yells interspersed the conversation.

Then hisses. Parys' wind swirled around him, bringing one fateful word—*humans*.

"Too late," Elora said in time with his thoughts.

The attention of the spectators was no longer on the fighting ring. It had turned to the entrance of the throne room, where angry elementals were dragging in humans by their necks.

Humans were too easy to scent. And so many of them...

Parys noted three things about the human delegation instantly. They were prepared for this encounter; as prepared as humans could be against fae. Heavily armed, every single one of them. Their leader was obvious—she was old, tiny, and held a bright gold bangle in her outstretched hand above her head like it was a torch. Lastly, every single one of the dozen or so humans, of varying ages, complexions and sizes, was female.

Guinevere took care of the rest.

She crossed the throne room faster than should have been possible on two legs. Planted her feet slightly wider than hip distance, and lifted her dark eyebrows in silent command. She didn't even twitch in the direction of the sword sheathed at her waist.

"Step away."

Parys recognized the elemental courtiers holding the humans—four males, all less than a hundred years old, from noble families. Males that were bristling for a fight, who hadn't been selected for the spectacle of competition.

A mistake—Parys hadn't calculated for their disappointment.

And he certainly hadn't anticipated a group of humans.

The elemental at the front, holding the elderly human female by the upper arm, sneered at Guinevere with open contempt. *Brennar* —the name came to Parys in a flash.

"This is not how we welcome guests," Guinevere said. Her voice was deceptively even.

But Brennar was too foolish to notice. The woman he held flinched, a small sheen of ice coating her arm.

Brennar was able to control his magic. Any elemental who made it to the age of fifty ought to have a grasp on their magic and their temper. Which meant he was choosing to hurt the human.

His companions weren't much better, their holds brutal enough that the humans gritted their teeth. But at least none of them were leaving freeze burns on their victims' skin.

"They are humans," Brennar said, shrugging his shoulders.

The woman in his grip was not so easily dismissed. She tried to wrench her arm away, failed, and speared him with a glare. She might even be older than him, by the look of her thin skin and wispy gray braid.

He didn't release her. She didn't bother to address him.

She turned to Guinevere, though Parys saw her eyes dart to Elora as well. Clever, battle-ready Elora, who was slowly and carefully positioning herself to dispatch the other elementals Brennar had brought with him.

"We come at the invitation of Veyka Pendragon," the human said sharply. Her voice didn't quiver, and neither did her arm—the free one, which she stretched overhead.

The gold bangle she held—Veyka's. He'd spent enough time lounging around in her bedroom to recognize it.

Parys glanced to Guinevere, found her eyes waiting for confirmation. He nodded.

"You shall refer to her as Her Majesty, the High Queen of Annwyn," Guinevere said, taking another step forward. A couple of yards separated them. Scant—nothing, really.

The competition had halted, Parys noted. All eyes were on them—elemental, terrestrial, and human.

His gaze darted to the archway where Merlin had stood... *gone*.

A quick scan of the crowd... no sign of the Dowager either.

Fuck.

But he was trapped in the throne room. He couldn't even send his wind out to try to see if they were in some secluded alcove whispering again. There were too many other voices and conversations. Though they were quickly dimming, as all eyes shifted to the human spectacle.

Guinevere jerked her head to the side, her gold eyes staring directly into Brennar's. She'd judged that if he gave in, the other elemental cronies holding the rest of the humans would follow. A sound assessment.

But even though she'd prepared her entire life to rule over this court, the rotten bits hadn't been part of her training. If Arthur had been king long enough, he would have cut out all the pits of discontent until everyone bent to his will.

Veyka hadn't had the time before her own disaster descended.

Which left Parys to smooth things over.

But Brennar opened his stupid mouth again. "You hold no higher regard for the human filth than we do."

Guinevere's chin lifted an inch. "My thoughts on the matter are not relevant—only the orders of the High Queen and King."

Brennar rolled his eyes, the scoff scratching across his throat loud enough for the entire throne room to hear. "They aren't here—"

She shifted, her terrible and beautiful dark lioness bounding across the distance and ripping his head from his body.

None of the humans fainted—though it looked like a very near thing. The other elementals who'd held them dropped arms and necks, staring in horror at the pile of blood and gore where their friend had stood moments before.

In a second, Guinevere stood in her fae form again. She took a moment to wipe the blood from her mouth on her sleeve. "And now he isn't here, either."

She turned to the crowd. "Anyone else?"

Hundreds of heads turned away immediately, back to the fighting ring.

Parys raked a hand through his hair. The death didn't disturb him—not after all he'd seen. This was the elemental court. Death was entertainment.

At least the humans were all still standing.

He offered them a welcoming grin. "Welcome to Annwyn."

48
VEYKA

Something was wrong with Arran.

If the constant twinge in my chest wasn't enough to alert me, the hollows beneath his eyes certainly were.

He wasn't sleeping.

While I wanted to take all the credit—there was hardly a night we didn't find each other in the furs of our bedroll, crashing together with insatiable need—I slept relatively well. Multiple orgasms tended to have that effect.

But Arran was getting crankier by the day.

I was fairly certain that Percival was one ill-placed comment from having his head separated from his body—no matter how useful he claimed to be.

Even Maisri couldn't draw a smile.

Though Ancestors be damned, she was dedicated to the task.

Her most recent attempt involved creating balls of long grass and lobbing them at Percival's head, when they would promptly explode in a riot of tiny daisies.

Lyrena and I thought it was hilarious. Arran's face was set in granite.

I held my hand out to Maisri, lifting a brow in expectation.

The clever daisy fae understood immediately. Thirty seconds later, a daisy ball landed in my hand.

I tested its weight, letting the others move ahead of me.

And when Arran was separate from the rest, hanging back with me unconsciously, I threw it at his head.

He shifted.

Fuck.

I knew better than to run, so I pulled my knives instead. As if they would make the slightest difference.

The great white wolf leapt through the air.

I had half a second to reconsider the wisdom of my actions before two massive paws landed on my biceps, the force knocking my knives from my grasp and all the air from my lungs as my back hit the ground.

The beast snarled, his canines dangerously close to my face.

Ancestors.

I'd underestimated just how wound up he was.

The others were running back, weapons drawn. What would they do? Try to harm their king? Arran Earthborn? I used the fraction of an inch I had to jerk my chin to the side.

"Stay back," I ordered.

The beast's powerful tail swiped across my shins, thick and punishing. I jerked my arms hard, getting my hands up to curl around his forelegs.

I was under no illusions who would win if I tried to test my strength against the wild white wolf. But I had other ways to bend him to my will.

That's right. I gnashed my teeth. *Take it all out on me.*

The deep growl hit me hard in the chest, where the mating bond lay. *Don't tempt me.*

I licked my lips, watching the huge, wolfish black eyes glaze over. *Does my beast have a thorn in his paw?*

That vicious snout, ripper of so many throats, dipped to my neck and huffed into my ear—*Only one.*

I sank my teeth into my lower lip.

"You're scaring the others," I said aloud.

He growled louder.

The others—lingering at a distance—retreated another few steps.

I rolled my eyes. "Be nice."

A breath, and it was the Brutal Prince pinning me to the ground. "I am not known for being nice."

I tugged on a loose lock of dark hair that had fallen out of the club at the back of his neck.

"Neither are you," he growled.

"If watching Maisri hit Percival with daisy bombs cannot lift your dark mood, I know I ought to be concerned."

Arran's face clouded. I tried to read the swirl of emotions before he locked them up behind his menacing glare.

Worry, a touch of sadness... and fear.

What was Arran Earthborn, the most powerful fae in millennia and High King of Annwyn, afraid of?

I had a few sinking suspicions in the pit of my stomach. And they all centered on one thing—me.

I shoved down the guilt that rose like bile in my throat and forced one of the wicked smiles he adored so much to my face.

Arran groaned. "Whatever nonsense you are contemplating, I promise I will punish you for it." He thrust his hips against me. "Thoroughly."

My smile widened for real. "Promise?"

"There it is!"

Arran snarled again. I hoped the beast inside of him was proud. It was utterly terrifying... and more than a little arousing.

But Maisri wasn't afraid. She'd escaped Osheen's clutches and was barreling straight for us. I nudged Arran aside just in time to stop the collision.

"There is *what*?" I asked, brushing the dirt—courtesy of my beastly mate—from my clothing.

"The Crossing."

Ancestors above, Percival couldn't keep his mouth shut for five minutes.

I grabbed Arran's hand, ignoring his glare, and held him firmly in place at my side.

Heel, beast.

A low growl caressed my consciousness as we joined the others—through the trees, onto a craggy drop off.

We all sucked in a collective breath at what lay below.

"We call it the Spit," I said, though I'd never seen it myself.

"Why? Do fae stand in the middle and see who can spit the farthest?" Percival laughed at his own joke.

Luckily for him, he was so amused by himself that he didn't bother checking for anyone else's mirth.

There was none.

Not even Lyrena laughed.

What waited for us wasn't humorous at all.

The entire strip of land, a few miles long, stretching across a rippling blue sea, was moving.

Humans.

49
ARRAN

"You are going to scare everyone off. We are supposed to be blending in with the humans," Veyka hissed as we waited in line.

We'd split into pairs to make ourselves less conspicuous. Cyara and Osheen linked their arms and let Maisri skip in front of them. With Osheen's dark hair and Cyara's carefully practiced elemental smile, they passed for a happy little family. There was nothing that could be done to disguise Cyara's wings—rare even among the fae. But hopefully the veneer of a sweet little family would diffuse any overt attention.

Lyrena looked strange, with all the markings of her Goldstone rank tucked away in her knapsack. No less lovely or golden, but less threatening. Until I saw the look she leveled at Percival—her companion for the night.

Surrounded by humans, our weapons hidden from view, without backup.

This was going to go wrong.

"I am a foot taller than the tallest man. *You* are taller than the tallest man. We are never going to *blend in*."

She poked me in the side—hard.

I didn't let myself respond. Cyara had helped her pin the hood of her cloak in place over her hair, which her handmaiden had braided along the crown of her head and then knotted at the nape of her neck, the most they could manage with her shorn locks. Not as ornate as her long plait in Baylaur, but much easier to conceal.

The humans would know that we were fae. But if they realized which fae we were, we'd be mobbed. Or attacked.

I didn't care to find out which.

"But everyone is here to have fun. The least you can do is smile."

I shot her a baleful look that told her everything I needed to about that proposition.

Veyka rolled her eyes. "I'd settle for anything other than glower."

I gnashed my teeth, long canines showing.

"Ancestors help me." She looped her arm through mine and dragged me forward, to where the strangest looking human I'd ever seen stood beneath a floral archway that reached well above even my head.

The woman was completely naked.

She'd pasted exactly three leaves to her body. Large leaves, and she was a small woman, but the effect was still ridiculous. The parts of her body that weren't covered by leaves were painted bright green.

And she had the audacity to look straight up at me and smile.

"Come to pass the night away, make a wish and you may stay," she sang in a painfully high-pitched voice.

I felt Veyka twitch against me.

"We wish to enter the festival," I said. I heard the roughness of my own voice. I could try to tamp it down—but there had to be other men dragged here by their wives against their will. That was an experience universal to human and fae.

"Come to pass the night away, make a wish and you may stay." This time, the notes were a little more strained.

She swayed on her feet.

Ah—she was inebriated.

That, at least, made a bit more sense.

"Enough of this," I grumbled, steering Veyka around the woman.

She threw out an arm. Not Veyka—the human. The tiny, ridiculous woman painted bright green, whose head barely reached Veyka's shoulder, put out her arm to stop us from entering.

Veyka twitched again. I cut my eyes to her, searching for—

She was laughing. My Ancestors-damned mate was laughing at me.

"You have to make a wish," she said between gasping for breath.

The woman perked up. "Come to pass the night away, make a wish and you may stay."

"I wish for this to stop," I bit out.

The woman frowned. Was she actually going to say something other than her ridiculous little rhyme?

A purely elemental smile slid across Veyka's face. "I wish that someday, I will be able to go an entire day doing nothing but sleep, fuck, and eat pastries."

The green woman percolated with glee and waved Veyka forward.

But instead, my mate turned to me.

The humans in line behind us were starting to grumble. It was well past dusk now, the darkness of night steadily falling, faster with every passing minute. They wanted to be inside the festival, not standing in line to make their ridiculous wishes and be admitted.

Blend in. Get from one side of the Crossing to the other. Get to Avalon, for Veyka's sake.

For Veyka's sake, I could make a stupid wish.

But my mind went blank. Because of course it did.

The words coming out of my mouth were not a coherent thought at all. "I wish that you could see Eilean Gayl."

The woman frowned. So did my mate.

But then the green would-be nymph was swaying to the side, eyes intent on the group behind us. Veyka and I stepped out of the way, into the festival.

I was spared having to explain by the spectacle before us.

A nightly festival instead of sleep, to pass the darkness in revelry rather than fear of the nightwalkers coming to steal their minds. Foolish. Impractical. Irritatingly *human*.

The nightwalkers would still come for them. They had to sleep eventually.

Everyone was in varying stages of undress, I realized. Very little clothing to be had. It was slightly warmer here in the southern part of the human realm, but not warm enough to be shirking all that clothing, especially at night.

Most of the men wore little more than loincloths. Many women wore the same, their breasts proudly on display. But even so, their skin was hardly visible.

Their bodies were painted.

Every color of the rainbow and every hue in between.

Some had actually painted swirls of rainbow across their bodies. Geometric designs, faces painted to look like animals... it was wild. There were, of course, some who hadn't painted themselves. More modestly dressed, young children whose faces were painted and the rest of them clothed. We weren't the only ones with unadorned skin. But we were certainly in the minority.

Veyka's grip on my arm tightened. "We'd better find ourselves some paint," she said.

I was ready to protest that. Until I realized I didn't need to.

Either side of the Crossing was lined with booths—and a significant number of those booths were selling food. Utter longing was tracking across my mate's face. "First, food."

Watching Veyka eat made me hard.

She made the exact same face when she bit into something decadent as she did when I slid my fingers inside of her. The little huffed exhale of pleasure after she'd smelled something delicious—

the same sound she'd made when she saw my cock for the first time.

Fuck. I was hard.

It shouldn't have been a surprise, the painted, nearly naked humans around us were as unencumbered as the fae. I watched Veyka's eyes track a couple that walked by us... a woman with her legs wrapped around her partner's waist as he carried her away, face buried in her neck.

Her blue eyes went a bit hazy.

"If that is what we need to do to go unnoticed, I am more than happy to oblige." My voice was a soft growl. Maybe it was my beast growling.

Veyka's eyes flicked to me. Her tongue emerged from her mouth, dragging along her lower lip, licking away the crumbs of the hand pie she'd eaten. "I think we need some paint first."

She was incorrigible, but I couldn't bring myself to refuse her. She purchased three small pots of paint, but didn't open them immediately. We walked up the wide strip of land, teeming with humans.

The Crossing—and the Spit, by extension, was essentially a land bridge. A long, narrow strip of land that connected the two larger parts of the continent. In Annwyn, it was an abandoned, desolate stretch of land. On the elemental side, soldiers from Baylaur manned Skywatch. Across the Spit, at Outpost, terrestrials sent from Wolf Bay glared back. The Spit was the only truly neutral spot in all of Annwyn.

But in the human realm, it had been transformed into something else entirely. I couldn't see the water on either side in the dark, but occasionally I heard the splash of waves. The festival booths lined either side of the Crossing, offering everything from food to games and what appeared to be magical items stolen from Annwyn.

Humans were mad for fae-made treasures.

Like those human's in the Shadow Wood, the ones Guinevere had wanted to torture. The one's I'd beheaded and felt not a drop of guilt for. I still felt none. But I did wonder… would they have ended up here, mourning in the moonlight with the rest of humankind?

Veyka wove between the humans casually, like she was meant to be there. I kept one hand on her hip at all times. I wasn't letting her drift away from me, not even a single human was allowed to come between us. It would be far too easy for someone to slip a knife between her ribs as it was.

"You're glowering again," Veyka said over her shoulder.

"Just because the humans are drenched in paint does not make them any less dangerous."

I *felt* her roll her eyes.

She looked so damn perfect, her eyes still ringed with glowing bright blue lust, her lips bowed into a smile, her curves peeking through the cloak. Knowing I was the only one who truly knew the extent of those curves, that I could slip my hands beneath that thick fabric and touch them…

Fuck it.

I leaned down and took her mouth. Veyka's lips parted in surprise, and I was able to capture the lower one between my teeth, sucking it into my mouth. Then I sucked on her tongue, until she was as deep inside me as she could get. She whimpered—not from pain. I knew all her sounds. I knew if I slid my hand between her legs, I'd find her pussy already dripping for me.

Someone jostled into us—a man. Drunk, laughing. Not laughing when he saw who—or what—he'd bumped into.

I didn't say a word. I let a smile climb my face—the one I'd given so many opponents right before I spilled their lifeblood across the ground.

Veyka erupted in laughter, dragging me past him and further into the throng of humans. "Now you're getting the feel for it. Let's *enjoy* ourselves."

50
ARRAN

I *did* enjoy myself.

Despite the constant threat of the humans realizing who walked among them, I enjoyed the festival. The food was delicious. The music was... tolerable. And my mate was shining.

Even with her bright, beautiful hair covered in a thick cloak, her body hidden by the same, her face shone with delight. As the hours passed, she lit from the inside. Like a star had awoken inside of her and was working its way out. I wondered if anyone else could see it. But none of the humans paid us any attention.

At least, no more attention than the other fae.

I'd counted a dozen in total. Two males early on, a group of young elemental females who looked like sisters and clearly had snuck into the human realm without their parents' permission, a few individuals. A family with a child. That was good—it meant that Osheen, Cyara, and Maisri were likely moving unhindered through the crowd.

We hadn't seen any of our companions. We had no choice but to believe that all was well—we were not supposed to reassemble until we left the festival on the other side of the Crossing.

But the main reason no one noticed us was because their attention was distracted by everything else happening. Humans with musical instruments of every shape and size played—some individuals, some in groups, all with cases open collecting bits of gold and other novelties as payment.

The humans painted each other, painted themselves, had even taken to painting the lampposts. I wondered briefly if they'd been erected specifically for the festival... if they'd remain long after this nonsense ended.

When would this nonsense end? How?

When the nightwalkers finally overwhelmed them?

No one here was sleeping; for another night, the humans on the Crossing were safe.

I watched Veyka, who watched a performance on a raised stage that stood in the place that three booths would have occupied.

Maybe it was my imagination. Maybe it was just my love for her that lit her like this.

I tightened my hand on her hip, holding her a little closer. She leaned into me. My chest constricted painfully, even as the mating bond hummed in satisfaction.

Emotion—that was emotion choking me.

Seeing Veyka like this, smiling and laughing and without any of the trappings of responsibility... I understood why she seemed to be lit by an internal flame.

She was free.

Not in the same way that she was when she escaped the goldstone palace and snuck through the mountains like a leaf on the wind. Nor was it like the freedom and power I saw coursing through her when she had a weapon in her hand and that wicked grin on her face.

Here in the midst of the festival, in a land far from her own, without a preening, traitorous court, she was free from the bindings of her position. She was free to be Veyka.

I loved that she cared so deeply for her friends. I loved her clever mind and the way she turned the cunning elemental court on its head. I loved sparring with her. But more than anything, I loved the female pressed into my side, completing me.

A tremor vibrated through me, a soft growl of satisfaction from my beast.

Veyka felt it, lifted her head from my shoulder and gazed up into my eyes.

She didn't say anything. She didn't need to just then—everything was in that bright, glowing blue gaze.

She slid her hand into mine, and then we were slipping through the crowd.

I let her lead me through the crowd, between a few tents. No humans appeared to bar our way. We walked closer to the edge until we could hear the waves lapping against the sand.

Veyka paused, reaching inside her cloak—and withdrew her three little pots of paint.

"Don't you dare," I growled.

She rewarded my snarl with a gloriously wicked smile that had my balls contracting tight with need.

Carefully balancing the pots in one hand, she used the other to reach forward and unbutton me. First, the thick leather tunic buttoned at an angle from the top of my shoulder down across my chest. Then the knit wool tunic beneath. She nudged them apart until my chest was visible, as well as the Talisman inked on it.

"Veyka," I warned.

What was I warning her about? I wasn't certain. But I was sure that if she dipped her fingers into that paint and touched my burning skin with her cool fingers, I was going to die from wanting her.

Of course, she did just that.

Veyka dragged her fingers over my talisman, covering the trunk of the tree in thick white paint. The color of her hair, even though I couldn't see it beneath her hood. She dipped her thumb into a different pot—this one black. In the center of my chest, right above where my heart rested, she blended the two colors together. Mixing us together.

With the gray she'd made, she painted the branches of the tattoo that reached across my chest, up over my collarbones. Then back down, lower... lower...

I caught her wrist. "My turn."

She threw her cloak back over her shoulders, revealing the swells of her breasts and the swath of her soft stomach. "Do your worst, Brutal Prince."

I considered the three colors in her palm. Black, white, and blood red.

It was a ridiculous thing, painting each other like this. This sort of frivolity... I'd always lived on the edges of it. Plenty to be had at the elemental court. The terrestrials like to revel as well, though it had a different flavor.

But enjoyment just for its own sake—never.

Duty to Annwyn.

Duty to my family.

Duty to my mate.

Yet I knew exactly what I wanted to paint. I dipped my fingertips in the red, then the black, not caring about mixing the colors. I spread it across Veyka's chest, the thick paint providing no resistance as my fingertips caressed her skin, pebbling beneath my touch.

"You wanted me to touch you," I reminded her as I dipped my fingers between her breasts.

I covered every inch of her chest that was visible. Until her glorious breasts were the deep scarlet of the sky just before dawn. Most thought it was black. But before the first rays of sun appeared above the horizon, before the golds and pinks and oranges took over, there was that faint glow of blood. The blood of death, the blood of life. An ending, a beginning.

I leaned down and blew softly over the wet paint to dry it. Veyka shivered.

A path of warm air that felt cool against the wet paint. Over the curve of each of her breasts. Along the lines of her collarbones, just visible beneath her skin. Into the sensitive channel of her throat and neck.

Her eyes were hazy with need when I met them again.

She opened her mouth, ready for my kiss. Begging for it.

But I dipped a bare finger into the white paint instead.

I drew a star right in the center of her chest. The colors blurred slightly, the scarlet not quite dry even with my attentions. But the contrast was clear enough. Bright white and glowing against the darkness, just like Veyka.

"You are insufferable," she breathed, her voice shaking with need.

"What do you want, Veyka?"

Her eyes didn't stop glowing. No, we were both too far gone for that. We both knew how this encounter was going to end.

But she blinked and they shifted, just slightly.

"I want to stay here with you like this, forever."

My heart began to pound in my chest. An insistent demand.

"Forever is a long time." My voice was hoarse with emotions that even a few months ago, I would have been horrified to feel. But I couldn't stop them any more than I could stop the minutes from passing.

She dragged her teeth over her lower lip—not invitation, but trepidation. "We might have a thousand years, but still not a single one of them would feel like this."

I traced the star with my fingertip, my eyes never leaving hers. Somehow, I knew precisely where every line was without a single glance.

She caught my other hand, lifting it to her shoulder, and leaned her cheek against it.

Such a small gesture.

But I felt it everywhere.

I was a male made for death. I killed. I razed cities. I commanded legions of vicious beasts. I *was* a vicious beast. But with Veyka, I became something different, something more.

I would stand there and let her hold my hand hostage for the rest of the night if that was what she needed.

Veyka was special. She was more open than me, though she didn't realize it. She opened her heart easier, even if she hadn't given me the words I longed for.

Her voice was so soft, it might have been lost to the rumble of the humans reveling on the other side of the booths. I wasn't even sure I heard it with my ears. She might have spoken directly through the mating bond and into my soul.

"I never had a chance to be anything other than what they made me. The Princess of Peace. The Queen of Secrets. The Elemental Heir. The Queen of the Elemental Fae. High Queen of Annwyn."

My mate, I finished for her in my mind.

I waited before speaking, but she was waiting for me. "I had three hundred years."

The corner of her mouth lifted. "Is that so, Brutal Prince?"

"I chose that name."

Now the other side. "How vain of you."

I almost rolled my eyes—but that would have torn my gaze away from hers. Impossible. "I chose that life. I was never going to be the terrestrial heir. I could have stayed closer to Eilean Gayl. But I wanted to use my powers to defend my kingdom. I chose to do the things that earned me that name. For three hundred years, I chose." I cupped her face with my other hand, not caring about the paint. "But you never got to."

Her eyes glistened with unshed tears, magnifying the blue wring of desire that never seemed to fade.

"Whoever I am," Veyka breathed, her lips a trembling invitation, "I choose you."

It wasn't a full declaration of love. But it was damned close.

I crushed her against me, not caring about the paint. Let it mix and blend, like we were blending together. Every day, every little bit she gave freely... we were becoming one.

Her mouth was warm and soft, but her tongue made insistent demands. Curving around mine, burrowing into my mouth and claiming me for her own. I belonged to her every bit as much as she belonged to me. I didn't know where I ended and she began—didn't need to.

Her hands slid up over my shoulders, pushing away the clothing she'd already half removed. She arched against me, her body desperately seeking connection. Damn those tight leather leggings she wore—they were so much harder to push aside than the flowing garments she'd worn at the elemental court.

I needed to be with her in every way. Her mouth ravaging mine, my cock buried inside of her. My mate—I needed my mate desperately

One frenzied hand dropped from my chest, between us—she was ripping away at the ties of her leggings. But before she could get them done, an explosion rocked the world around us.

The world went horizontal. I shoved Veyka to the ground, covering her with my body, ready to die to protect her. Always.

She was shaking beneath me. Ancestors, even here we weren't safe. Fear and—

She was laughing.

Veyka was laughing, her entire body convulsing with the force of it. Rubbing her legs against me, her breasts, her pussy. I was confused and hard and an inch from death.

She grabbed my hair, tugging me down closer so our lips nearly touched.

"Fireworks," she chuckled.

Fireworks. Explosions of color in the midnight sky. It must be midnight.

I shook my head, trying to clear the protective instincts. Veyka was way ahead of me. She fisted one hand in my hair, the other digging into the muscles of my shoulder, dragging me down to meet her mouth.

I kissed her hard, let my body sink down into her.

We were by no means alone—any of the humans could have happened upon us. It did not matter. All that did was the sanctity of the moment.

But it was not a human who interrupted us.

It was Lyrena—huffing, out of breath, her hood thrown back and bright eyes wild. She appeared from between the booths, weapons already in hand.

"I'm sorry to break up... whatever this is. Or was going to be. But Percival is about to get himself killed."

51
VEYKA

If we managed to extricate him, I'd kill Percival myself.

Lyrena led us through the tangle of booths and humans, her steps quick but not hurried. We couldn't draw undue attention to ourselves or we'd have a whole other problem to deal with.

After five minutes, she swore under her breath and ducked between a row of booths. We had to climb over the detritus the humans left behind in setting up their stalls, but at least we weren't face to face with the hordes.

Arran lengthened his stride to catch up with Lyrena.

"Details." A commander's order.

The diligent lieutenant gave her report. "He's been trying to slip away all night. I recognized it immediately. Trying to ply me with wine, getting me to play the games at the booths, introducing me to humans. He knows a lot of people here. A lot. Dozens. I kept him close. But the bastard got the better of me," Lyrena scowled.

I nearly fell over. It was the crate of human shit that caught me up, of course. Not my surprise.

I'd never seen such an expression on her face. Battle ready, yes. Unqualified anger? I didn't know she had it in her.

"He lured me into this stupid House of Enchanted Nightmares.

It was dark, even to my eyes. There is some sort of magic at play in there. Something stolen from Annwyn. He slipped away. By the time I found him again, he was being dragged away by two humans, squawking about his innocence."

"Did he know the humans who took him?"

Lyrena sighed heavily. "I'd wager good aural he did."

I couldn't keep my mouth shut. "Which he conveniently did not mention before leading us into the festival."

"We knew it was a possibility." Arran's voice was even. No time wasted perseverating on Percival's motivations. That was a discussion for later. After we'd gotten him, and ourselves by extension, out of this mess.

I was still getting used to it, the battle commander. He'd gotten better at hiding his emotions, mainly his anger and frustration, since his arrival in Baylaur all those months ago.

I was coming to understand why he'd conquered what most elementals needed a lifetime to master—he already had it. The cool, calculating place he descended into when he was assessing the field, the opponents, forming his plan... it was much the same.

Lyrena darted between two booths, leading us back into the throng.

It was less dense with humans here. The Crossing naturally widened a bit, creating a wider avenue with a bulging, rounded edge on one side.

The humans had set up a larger structure there. What appeared to be several booths stitched together haphazardly.

But the image on the front was intact.

Fae.

But not like any fae I'd ever seen before. This was... grotesque. The long, graceful lines of my kind were elongated, out of proportion. Fangs like those Arran and Osheen sported, but longer, deadlier. As if the painter had transposed the jaws of the skoupuma on a fae face. There were two of them, a male and female. They were fucking... sort of. It almost looked like the male was strangling the female.

But not the erotic sort of strangling I could imagine, with Arran's hand around my throat as I gasped for breath and climax in unison. This was meant to be brutal.

This was how the humans truly saw us.

"He's in there," Lyrena said unnecessarily.

"Then I suppose he's on his own." I tore my eyes away from the tableau, a dagger already in hand. I'd stab the next human I saw just to ease the burning edge of my temper.

"We need him to find Avalon," Arran said, drawing his battle axe.

I glared at it. "We can find Avalon on our own. We have a general direction."

"The closer we get, the less helpful a general direction is. Veyka, we need him."

Rage. Rage for Arthur, for me, for the fact that I was even in this cursed human realm. "I thought I'd be the one keeping you from killing—"

Lyrena stepped forcibly between us. She didn't dare shove us apart, though her hands lifted on either side. She'd almost made a mistake.

She forced a smile to her face. It was painful to watch.

"We don't have time for your pseudo-erotic sparring," she said. "He could already be dead."

Arran and I glared at each other for the space of several seconds. Not quite hate and loathing... the anger was deeper than that once you'd seen the softest parts of each other.

"Fuck this."

I couldn't kill Percival. But I could kill every single human who stood between me and him.

I pushed past both of them, drawing my other dagger. I slashed through the tent flaps, disfiguring the painting.

Slash. Slash. Slash. Let them try to stitch that back together. If any of them were still alive.

"What is the meaning of this!" a man bellowed from inside. I didn't pause.

He was laughably easy to kill.

I was laughing.

Blood spurted. Human blood. So viscous and thin. It coated my blades, my wrists. But the effect was so satisfying. He dropped in a lump to the floor. Dead.

He was a ticket-taker of some kind. This room was lit. I pushed through the next set of tent flaps into a darkened interior.

I saw what Lyrena meant. Even with my sharp fae vision, I couldn't pick out the shapes moving around me. And they certainly were. Humans, dressed in dark clothing so they blended in. Meant to be disorienting, to confuse the person who entered.

One of them made the mistake of touching my shoulder.

Dead.

A few more died before the others realized what was going on— before the screaming started. I didn't even need to behead them. One well-placed slash to the gut and their innards spilled out. Not that I could see them.

But I didn't need to see to kill and maim. Those instincts were carved into my soul.

The next room was a kaleidoscope of light. Mirrors in every direction, reflecting and refracting the oil lamps and candles. So much light. They were enchanted mirrors, I realized vaguely. More artifacts obtained from Annwyn. These humans had broken the treaty between our realms.

They would die.

But the figure that emerged wasn't human. Not anymore. It stumbled forward with a determined but irregular gait. Black bile poured from its mouth.

A nightwalker.

How could that be?

The whole point of this Ancestors-damned festival was to escape the nightwalkers.

The movements are wrong.

I drew in a deep breath. There was no scent of death, no cloying cold.

Fucking Ancestors—only a human would be stupid enough to dress as a nightwalker.

The mirrors and bright light were meant to disorient. The pretend nightwalker could have been coming from any direction. Meant to terrify the humans stupid enough to pay good gold to enter this house of nightmares.

But I didn't need to see to fight. So I closed my eyes.

The justification was easy, not that my conscience needed one. These humans stood between me and Percival. Percival was my only way to Avalon. Avalon was the key to understanding my power, its connection to the Void and Ethereal Prophecies and the nightwalkers, and saving Annwyn. The human realm would benefit by extension.

These deaths were nothing.

A song on my blade—a hum. So easy, they barely even made a melody.

Arran was somewhere behind me. Watching my back, finishing off my leavings.

When there was no more movement around me, I opened my eyes. This was where the house of nightmares ended. The climax where humans would be pissing themselves.

But I didn't make for the exit, hanging open and easy to find if one could manage their fear.

I went for the flap that was tied up.

I slashed it open in one easy swipe, the blood on my blades spraying across the dirty ground. A few bright droplets landed on Percival, tied to the rear tent post. Not that I could have pointed out which ones were from my blade. The man was covered with blood and bruises. He'd been beaten.

Good. He deserved no less.

His eyes went wide. He tried to scramble back, away from me. "What—fucking hell! Did you kill—"

"You do not get to complain." I slashed again. He thought I was going for his throat. I freed his bindings, only to wrap them back around him just as quickly and drag him forward in the dirt on his knees.

Arran and Lyrena burst into the small storage room a half second before I leveled a kick to Percival's gut. I didn't stop myself.

He doubled over in pain. I waited for satisfaction.

None came—disappointing.

I handed Lyrena his tether. "What's the fastest way out?"

"Ancestors below—" She cursed, eyes raking over the state of him. I tracked the emotions across her face. Concern, then relief. Good, her assessment was the same as mine. He'd been beaten, but he'd live.

Arran was the who answered me.

Or rather, he ignored me and turned to Lyrena and took Percival's leash.

"Find the others. Who knows what information this traitor spouted while they were beating him. We have to get out of the festival and well away," he ordered. "Veyka, with me."

"Obviously."

He snarled. I snarled right back. Percival quivered in fear on the ground.

There was the wave of satisfaction I'd been looking for.

52
VEYKA

Arran threw him down hard enough to break bones. I wasn't inclined to care.

I was breathless, sweating, adrenaline coursing through my veins, the thin human blood still dripping from my knives.

I watched as thousands of blades of grass rose from the ground to wrap around him, holding him flat on the ground. They encircled his arms, his legs, his throat. Arran could snap his neck in an instant.

Maisri gasped behind me. Cyara and Osheen dragged her further away.

Not too far.

We had to stay close together.

We were a few miles away from the festival. That gave us some time, but not much. The humans would be able to reach us eventually if they were motivated enough. Though based on the shrillness of their screams, I doubted we'd have any pursuers.

I waited until those blades of grass were tight enough that Percival's brown skin turned lighter, a crisscross of pale brown lines underneath the earthy green grass. I stood right over him, letting the tip of my knife hang down so the blood dripped.

Down. Down. Down.

Drip by drip.

He was at our mercy once again.

His eyes flared. He was afraid of me—of us. He'd finally seen us for what we truly were.

Good.

"What was so important that you risked not only your own worthless life, but exposing us as well? We cannot very well help you rescue your sister if we are enmeshed in human nonsense."

His face contorted with pain. He'd looked like that before—when we'd caught him after the burning village. I knew humans were weak, but Percival seemed to have no tolerance for pain at all.

Tiny tears formed at the corners of his eyes but still his mouth didn't open.

"Tighter," I demanded. Arran was at my shoulder, breathing heavily, his beast's growl coming in waves through the air even in his fae form.

I savored the way that Percival clenched his hands tight, his knuckles bulging—

He was holding something. It peeked out of his fisted hand, no more than a flash of pale light. I slammed my heel down on his wrist, his howl of pain lost to the pounding in my own head as the object he'd held fell loose on the grass, rolling out of his grasp.

An opaque white crystal the length of my palm.

Before I could ask again, Percival whimpered. "It is a communication crystal. They only make them on Avalon. Just like your blades."

I was shaking my head.

Or was Percival the one shaking?

That couldn't be. He was held tight by Arran's vines.

My mind was swirling. My head was shaking. Percival *was* shaking—just his hands. Just his hands where they were visible, below his tightly bound wrists.

"My blades?" I heard myself ask distantly.

Percival's eyes turned wild. *What*—

Arran was behind me. Towering over my shoulder. One look at him and I knew where that fear in Percival's eyes came from. Percival understood it too. He would talk now, or he would die.

"They were forged in Avalon," he said, his voice trembling in time with his hands. All the bravado gone. "You did not know... I didn't realize..."

"How would I know that?" I said sharply, gripping the hilts tighter. The curved blades in my pack, which I'd replaced with Excalibur. The daggers at my waist. "That is why the metal is swirled. They aren't fae made after all."

"There are fae in Avalon," Percival said.

I flinched, Arran growled, Percival looked like he was about to piss himself.

"They were a gift from Arthur." I wasn't sure who I was talking to—no one, everyone, myself. I'd once prided myself on my ability to think clearly in dire situations. But this was different. This wasn't maintaining a logical mind under torture. This felt like my chest cleaving in two... like the way I understood the world was shifting. Up was down, aural was water, and my brother...

"Were the scabbards as well?"

Percival. Percival had asked that question.

I was afraid to answer. Afraid of what it might mean. But the word fell from my lips just the same. "Yes."

"They are special also," Arran added for me, raking his eyes over me in wonder. Over my blades. The scabbards.

"I assumed you knew. You have two of them—the scabbards, the sword." Percival was babbling. His eyes were round, the cleverness gone. I wasn't sure I could believe the words coming out of his mouth.

But apparently I couldn't believe the ones Arthur had told me, either.

I turned away. I was going to run. I was going to run far and fast, and away.

Arran's arm caught me. I *let* him catch me. I let the waves of confusion inside of me break against my mate's steady wall.

My chest was caving in. I was going to die. For once, I didn't feel the void calling to me through my panic. I almost craved it—that dark nothingness. If everything I knew was a lie, what did it matter if my soul was shredded into pieces?

"Two of what?"

Cyara's voice was soft. She held Maisri's hand a few yards away. Mostly hidden in shadow. But she'd been listening—always listening. And she'd heard what I couldn't through the fog of betrayal.

"The sacred trinity." The way the words fell from Percival's mouth... the uncharacteristic reverence... I shuddered.

I couldn't look at him. My eyes were pressed closed. I was pretty sure the only reason I was still standing was the steady grip of Arran's arm around my waist.

But someone urged Percival to continue.

"The sword, the scabbards, and the chalice... all made in Avalon tens of thousands of years ago. They have unique magical properties, each of them. It is said when they are united, the bearer will be..." he paused, his voice catching. "The bearer will be master of death."

Cyara again—"How do you know all of this?"

"I told you, my homelands are near to Avalon."

"How near?"

A grunt. Pain. Percival. Then words. "I was raised on the Sacred Isle."

I opened my eyes. I took in the hazy sunlight of dawn, the damp chill coating my skin. I heard the chirping of some small animal, or maybe dozens or hundreds of small animals. A chorus.

The others were still talking, questioning.

Percival's voice was melodic. How had I never noticed that? "My sister wears a crystal around her neck. All the acolytes do. Smaller, only good for communicating very short distances. But I thought that if I had the larger one... maybe I would be able to contact her."

"Your sister is an acolyte to the priestesses on Avalon." Arran. Rough, like scratched leather.

"She was—until she was taken."

"You could have asked us to retrieve the crystal," Lyrena said, her voice devoid of all humor. I hated to hear it that way.

"You hate me."

"You hate us," Arran growled back.

"It doesn't even matter," Percival said, his tone shifting. "I tried to call her before they caught me. It didn't work."

Cyara's heavy sigh wrapped around us. The same one she'd used to moderate her sisters—now dead. Like Arthur was dead.

Did Carly and Charis haunt my friend from the grave, like my brother did me?

"Perhaps we should try for less hate and more understanding," Cyara said.

She was a good Knight of the Round Table. The best of us, really. Perhaps because she'd never had to wield that little knife in her belt. She could still see the light, even after the loss she'd suffered.

All I let myself see was my immediate surroundings. We were at the edge of a forest. A true forest—not like the ones we'd seen in the human realm so far with their scrubby trees and barren understory. This was a tangle of branches, bushes, and leaves. A jungle, really. There were no jungles in Annwyn, but I'd read about them in one of Parys' books. Except that jungles were meant to be warm, and I was still shivering.

Shivering as a persistent word tapped against my consciousness. Against my mind.

I do not know if it was the sister, the Queen, or the female who held sway; but I knew that tapping would not stop until I said the word aloud.

"Magic." My throat hurt.

They all fell silent.

"You said each of the objects has a unique magical property." It was a lot of words, but I managed. I had to know the answer.

"The sword will only present itself to the worthy wielder. No other will be able to pull it from the stone."

Arran's grip on me tightened to the point of pain. I relished it, let it ground me. I knew he was remembering what I'd recounted, the vision now rolling through my mind as if it had happened yesterday. Killing the witch. Pulling the sword from the stone in the Tower of Myda.

"The bearer of the scabbards shall be protected from injury. Not a drop of their blood may be spilled while they wear them."

If Arran hadn't been holding me up, I would have fallen over.

Like a heavy mechanism, understanding shifted into place.

Not just for me.

Arran's breath shook out of him, skittering along my neck and shoulder as he drew me back so he could look at me. Stare at me as if seeing me for the first time. "All the times you should have bled... at the Offering, when the witch attacked you in the Tower of Myda. You were wearing the scabbards.

I swallowed hard. "But I wasn't at the Joining. I wore Excalibur instead."

My heart was in my throat, pounding wildly, as I spoke. "Arthur gave me the scabbards. They were a gift—so I would be able to protect myself wherever I went, he said. I thought... I thought he meant the daggers. But he didn't... he meant the scabbards."

Arran was staring down the space between us, staring at the jewels on my scabbards, glinting at my waist. I wore them all the time. I always felt safer with their weight at my waist. Now I knew why.

But Cyara didn't have to ask the last question. I was keeping track in my head. "What about the chalice?"

"The chalice gives life. Drink from it once, and you are healed of any ailment. Sip from it forever, and you shall never die."

I knew it was Percival's voice, but it had become something else. Disembodied, to my ears at least. Like I was hearing him through a wall, or while underwater. It wasn't a human speaking to me... it was destiny. And it was fucking terrifying.

"We don't have the chalice," Arran said.

"But Parys and Gwen might," Cyara said softly. "There is only one chalice of any note in Baylaur."

"The one used in the Offering and the Joining," I finished her thought. "The same one that has been used since Nimue and Accolon."

Arran's brow tightened, his eyes lifting back to mine. He eased his arm slightly; testing to see if I would fall over. I stayed standing. He rubbed a hand over his brow, through his hair, over his chin. Percival was still wrapped tightly. But Arran was too deep in thought to notice. His battle commander's mind was at work, his eyes tracing from the sword strapped to my back, to the scabbards on my belt, then back again.

"What is the value of any of this? We are fae. We can heal from nearly any wound, live thousands of years. This sacred trinity is useful, but it would hardly make us so much more powerful that it is worth making such a fuss about."

I wanted to agree with him.

But there were too many coincidences. Too many careful pieces being moved around the battlefield. I hated the feeling that it was all happening *to* us. To me. While we scrambled to piece things together.

"Arthur knew," I said.

This was so much worse than being pulled apart by the void. This was being pulled apart by the one person I'd trust above all others—my brother. My twin. My other half.

But I still said the words. "Arthur knew about all of it. And he lied."

53
VEYKA

I stalked into the forest. The others could deal with Percival. Punish him, kill him, set him free. I didn't care.

Arthur lied.

Arthur lied.

Arthur lied.

The words were a painful throb in my chest, my head, my heart—that echoed with each step I took.

Mine weren't the only steps.

"I have a magical sword and I cannot bleed. I think I can take an Ancestors-damned walk by myself—"

Cyara and Lyrena blinked at me. The latter's eyes were wide as saucers. The former... well, she was quite used to my fits of temper.

But neither of them was Arran—the one I'd expected to follow me. And the fact that I hadn't realized, hadn't recognized two soft sets of footsteps rather than my mate's heavy tread... it said enough about the mangled state of my mind.

Lyrena glanced to Cyara, found no help, then looked back to me. She cleared her throat. "We thought you might want to talk."

"I don't." I spun on my heel and walked away.

Of course, they followed.

The jungle was dense. I drew Excalibur from my back and started hacking away at it. I couldn't bring myself to use my brother's sword to defend myself in combat. I might as well use it for something. I slashed and slashed.

Sweat dripped down my back, my neck. I wasn't cold anymore.

I was wearing my thick leather leggings. No chafing thighs. An unforeseen benefit of the constrictive clothing. Not that I was feeling pain. At least, not the physical kind.

If I didn't have the Ancestors-damned scabbards at my waist, I'd have had dozens of small cuts on my arms from the branches and thick shrubbery. Another thing I could thank Arthur for—

"Ancestors," Cyara cursed behind me.

I swung around quickly, blade high, and took out a solid chunk of Lyrena's golden braid. I blinked. Once. Twice. Expecting her to react—to cry out. She spent a lot of time on that gorgeous hair of hers.

But her eyes focused on me—only me.

At her side, Cyara was rubbing her upper arm. A red welt peeked out from the open *V* of her tunic. One of the branches must have caught her across the chest.

"Go back to the others. I am fine." A command. They both knew me well enough to recognize it.

"The others are behind us. I believe Arran and Osheen are seeing to the flora in a less... destructive way. But they're making a path," Lyrena said.

"Great. Go back and walk with them so you do not get injured."

"We are fine where we are."

"Take Cyara back."

A sharp shake of her copper head. "No, Veyka."

"I am the High Queen—"

"You are our friend and you are in pain," Cyara said simply. Then she reached out.

She who had every reason to be afraid of me. Who I'd literally ripped into pieces when I lost my temper. She reached through the thorny shrubbery and wrapped her small hand around my forearm.

I dropped the mighty sword to the ground. "Arthur lied."

I dropped to my knees beside it. "He lied to me."

Cyara dropped right down with me.

"He communicated with the humans in Eldermist. Sent fae guards to protect them—presumably through the mountain rift. The rift that was supposed to be a secret." My head was shaking. I was shaking. Again. "The same rift that humans came through to murder him."

"I didn't know him at all. When I came out of the water gardens, it felt like I'd found my other half. The piece of me that was always missing. My twin. But everything he told me was a lie."

Cyara's hand was steady on my arm. I could only see Lyrena's goldstone-studded boots. She was still standing.

My sorrow turned to something sharper as I stared at the goldstone, catching rays of sun through the tangled trees and burning bright orange.

"You knew him. Longer than me. Better than me." I couldn't keep the bitterness out of my voice.

I expected Lyrena to drop down beside Cyara, to offer comfort. But she remained standing. Why? She was my friend, wasn't she?

I forced myself to look up. Past the blur of tears in my eyes. Maybe I would find hate there—maybe she hated me for what I'd said. Maybe she resented that Arthur had spent any time with me at all. She'd been his—

But Lyrena was smiling.

Of course she was.

Soft and gentle, and with so much caring in her eyes, I almost melted into a puddle on the ground.

She met my gaze, but didn't reach for me as she spoke. Not as soft as Cyara, but such gentleness in her voice. Such caring. I found it painful to care for my friends. A physical ache sometimes.

But it poured out of Lyrena as if it was nothing—as if she had all the love in the world to give. What must that be like? To be so completely, fundamentally *good*?

"My parents weren't courtiers, but they had power and wealth. I wasn't interested in any of it. When they brought me along on a visit to Baylaur, I saw Arthur. I didn't return home with them. I stayed, I trained, and when he became king, he selected me as one of his Goldstones."

The answers to my first question was there in her words.

"You loved him," I said quietly.

She nodded, her golden braid bobbing. What was left of it.

"Yes. I think he loved me as well. As best he could." Slowly, she lowered herself down into the mess of vines and leaves. She crouched, rather than kneeled—always a guard, always ready to spring up and protect at a moment's notice.

Still she didn't reach for me. She didn't need to, I realized. The power of her gaze was enough. I could see every emotion pulsing in her bright eyes. Gone was the elemental veneer of placidity. Here was a truly golden knight—bold, beautiful, and unabashed.

"But, Veyka, he loved you so much more. Everything..." She paused to drag in a breath. "Veyka, he was always thinking about you. Every choice was about you."

Cyara's hand on my arm tightened, almost imperceptibly. Still, I flinched.

My head was shaking again. I was starting to get a headache from the visual disturbance. "He was the King of the Elemental Fae."

Lyrena didn't waver. "He was your brother first."

"You are misremembering. Or you misheard when he told you—"

"He didn't have to tell me anything, Veyka. It was the things he did. He must have interviewed two dozen candidates before he selected your handmaidens."

A flicker of Cyara's wings—confirmation.

Lyrena wasn't done.

"The rooms and apartments surrounding yours house only the most loyal courtiers. He sealed the Dowager in her wing and banished anyone who questioned him. Powerful alliances, houses who'd been loyal to the Pendragon line for thousands of years—stripped of their titles and sent away."

But why? It was a political nightmare. Even with the Offering and the tentative peace between the elementals and the terrestrials, our kind were bloodthirsty. Arthur needed supporters within his realm. Not friends, precisely. But advisors. Allies.

Yet he'd sent them all away... because they objected to my mother's confinement?

That could only have to do with me.

Lyrena was watching me. Waiting for the gap in my thinking. I didn't bother to try and guard my thoughts as they played across my face.

She sighed, slight. Soft. "He assigned me to guard you, even though there was no precedent."

"Goldstones are for the monarch, not the spare." I'd known that, even then. But Arthur had been the King of the Elemental Fae. He could do whatever he wanted, even if it did break tradition.

But why would he?

"The ever-burning hearth," Cyara said. "He instructed us to never let it burn out, or the charm would burn out as well."

I could feel the blood rushing inside of me. Behind my eyes, the pressure was building to an intensity that had to be dangerous. I was going to explore. My head was quite literally going to explode from the influx of information.

"But why?" I managed. My voice was pitiful. A small, strangled sound. "What is so special about me? I am—I was—powerless."

"You are the queen from the Void Prophecy," Cyara said. She'd slid her hand down my arm, cupped my hands, was rubbing my ice-cold fingers between her own to warm them. "You have never been powerless."

I looked to Lyrena. "Did he know?"

Her brow furrowed. A soft shake. "I don't know. He never told me his plans."

I could hear sounds in the distance. The rest of our companions —my mate—approaching. I could feel him coming closer, the pressure in my chest I hadn't even noticed starting to ease. He couldn't stand to be parted from me any longer. He'd given me space, given me my friends. But if he didn't see me soon, with his own two eyes, his control might fray.

Ancestors, I could understand all of that from a twinge in my chest.

A tiny ray of sunlight slipped between the thick barrier of leaves overhead.

It caught on the gold—glinting brightly. Not Lyrena's braid or her goldstone—on Excalibur. The mighty, magical sword lying carelessly on the ground.

The gold of the pommel gleamed brightly. The swirls in the blade, different tones of silvery gray, seemed to shift and move in the filtered light. Ancestors, maybe they were actually moving.

It was a magical, Avalon-made blade.

I had no idea what it could actually do.

Just like I had no idea who Arthur had truly been.

There was more. I could feel the sinking inside of me, the heavy realization as I stared down at the sword that had chosen me. The same way my brother had chosen me. And I wondered aloud—

"What else didn't he tell me?"

54
PARYS

The clashing sound of metal greeted him long before he reached the dusty training ring. This was getting out of control. He was hardly sleeping. Waking hours were divided between the library, trying to unobtrusively trail Merlin or Igraine, and meetings with the human delegation. Dinners with Guinevere weren't nearly sufficient to sort through the intricacies of ruling.

Running a kingdom was so much fucking work.

Parys swiped back the curls that fell over his forehead. He'd nearly taken a pair of shears to the errant curls the night begore in a moment of weakness. But even tired Parys was too vain to cut away his thick curls.

He knew he'd find Guinevere in the sparring ring at this hour of the morning. She kept a routine—strict and predictable. He wasn't sure that it included sleep.

She worked her way through a rotation of palace guards. She even let them use their magic against her blade. To no avail.

But it wasn't one of the palace guards at the other end of her sword today—it was Elora.

And it was impressive.

Parys glanced around the training courtyard. More spectators than usual. And why not? Guinevere parried and swiped, curving her body into elegant shapes as she darted away from blasts of Elora's ice magic. Even with those constant blasts of ice, a translucent wall of ice thrown up in her path, the chill in the air—none of it slowed Guinevere down.

A scent on the wind caught his attention, though it took him a moment to locate...

The humans.

Three of them, including their leader, the elderly woman called Sylva. There were three palace guards flanking them—not to rein them in, but to protect them. Though Parys doubted the need. The court had been subdued since Guinevere had made an example of Brennar.

Parys had learned in that moment—clever maneuvering was one strategy, and an effective one... but sheer brutality and strength had its place as well.

If Sylva was here, she probably wanted to speak with Guinevere.

Too bad—Parys needed her first.

Elora shot out a blast of magic, the ice forming a spear with a wicked tip that launched straight for Guinevere. But Guinevere was already rolling, anticipating the way that Elora relied on her hands to manipulate her power and using it as a warning. She didn't roll away. She went forward, straight for Elora, and when she came up into a crouch, her sword was in her hand—the tip lodged just below Elora's breastbone.

One shove, and it would go straight through her heart. Not enough to kill her, but it would keep her down for hours, even with a healer on hand. A winning blow.

Elora took a step back, but there was an easy smile on her lips. She smiled quite often, since her mother's death. A sign she was coming into her own, or that she'd been happy to do away with her mother... Parys would have to see what he could find out about that.

Another task to add to his endless list.

And no time to be wasted.

Parys stepped into the ring. "Guinevere."

Both females cut him a look, their eyes still fierce from sparring. Guinevere straightened, sheathing her sword, but her attention was still on Elora.

"You rely too heavily on your magic. Next time, only blades," she said. Command, always such command in her voice. Even as she spoke to the commander of the elemental armies.

Elora's smile grew. "Or only magic."

Parys paused. Were Elora's eyes glowing?

It was hard to tell with the midday sunlight. But the way she angled her body, her eyes lingering on Guinevere...

But the Goldstone was no longer looking at her opponent.

Her eyes swept around the perimeter of the ring. He knew those tawny orbs were noting every face, though her expression didn't shift an inch.

The fae who'd been watching began to disperse, but the humans lingered. Definitely hoping for an audience, then.

Guinevere realized it as well, leveling Parys a look. The question was only in the slight tilt of her head. He jerked his head back down the corridor from which he'd come.

He needed to talk to her *now*.

"An hour," she said to Sylva.

Then she was striding in Parys' direction.

But Sylva didn't appear offended. She was already turning back to the other two humans with her, speaking rapidly. Parys was curious enough to send a snapping warm wind after them, but Guinevere was already at his side.

"What?" Her voice as sharp as the blade she'd sheathed only moments before.

They were alone—seemingly.

But Parys wasn't taking any chances. There were too many passageways, too many ways of listening in. He set his warm wind swirling around them as Guinevere strode briskly down the corridor, blocking off any sound from getting in and any of their words from escaping to curious ears.

"Igraine and Merlin are up to something."

"We are back to this again?" Guinevere sighed, letting her annoyance show. "Have you seen anything else?"

"No," he said through gritted teeth. "But they are smart enough to know they're being watched. To act in secret."

He'd set up tails for both of them.

There just wasn't enough *time* for him to do it himself. Not if he was going to make any headway in the library. That was pressing, though he couldn't exactly explain why. There was something he was close to figuring out... something to do with Veyka and her power. Maybe he'd already read it. He'd read thousands of pages. But it still didn't quite fit together.

Guinevere strode through the goldstone palace, her pace unchecked. After she sparred, she patrolled the corridors at random, checking that the palace guards were in place and assessing any weaknesses.

Parys had to trot to keep up with her.

"They are both vile. I do not disagree with you. And most likely have their own schemes. But the humans are the more pressing issue. The Queen sent them to us directly. Once we've settled on how we are going to provide aid, we ought to use them to get at the Shadows."

Parys blinked. "The Shadows."

"Yes."

"You are still on *that?*"

"It is—"

"It doesn't have anything to do with the stability of Annwyn!" Parys cut her off. He ignored the irritation that flared in her golden eyes. He had bigger problems. "Igraine and Merlin could be making a play for the throne. They could be—"

Guinevere didn't hold back from interrupting him, either. "*The Queen* sent the humans. That tells us enough about its importance. The Shadows' continued operation in Baylaur undermines the authority of the throne."

"Veyka and Arran don't know what is going on in Baylaur. They entrusted us with making these decisions." A headache was forming again. He always had a headache these days. When Veyka and Arran did return, he would resign from the Round Table and spend his days fucking, feasting, and—

He was slammed up against the wall with such force the air was forced from his lungs. But before he could get in a breath, Guinevere's mouth was closing over his, her tongue sliding into his mouth, her hands pinning his shoulders.

It was hard and fast and set his head spinning.

Then, as quickly as it had started, she'd ripped herself away.

She was dragging in a breath as ragged as the one he gasped for.

Guinevere's throat bobbed. "That was..."

"Awful," Parys finished.

She wiped at her lips, grimacing. "Is that what it felt like when you kissed Veyka?"

"No, she was..." he paused, trying to find the words, trying to sound clever, and failing utterly.

He sighed heavily. "It was different."

Guinevere nodded, a sharp stab of her chin in the air. She rubbed a thumb over the hilt of her sword, considering. No glowing ring of desire appeared in her golden eyes—*Thank the Ancestors*.

"I'd hoped it would diffuse the..." she waved her hand, for once struggling for words. "Whatever it is between us."

Parys managed to keep in his sputtering laugh. It didn't seem fair. Guinevere, it appeared, did have a weakness after all.

So, he merely shrugged it off. For a second, gratitude flashed in her face. Then it returned to its usual calm calculation.

"We cannot ignore any of it," Guinevere finally said.

Parys remembered to send that warm wind around them, blocking off their voices. He was still reeling from the surprise.

"Is this what you imagined ruling a kingdom would be like?" he asked, shaking his head.

Guinevere smiled—actually smiled—grimly. "It is, unfortunately. I just thought I'd have more actual authority. Trying to rule when you're not actually the king and queen... it makes things more complicated."

He couldn't refute that.

"I will focus on Merlin and Igraine. I will find out what they are up to. You deal with the humans and the Shadows," he said.

One dark eyebrow rose. "Divide and conquer?"

"More like divide and pray we don't get ourselves killed."

Another smile. Small, but there.

"I plan on being the one doing the killing," Guinevere said. "Let me know if you need help."

Parys nodded. "Same."

She adjusted her Goldstones uniform and aimed her feet away. "I will see you at dinner." Then she was gone, stepping through the invisible wall that had protected them.

Parys lingered, watching her go. For the first time since Veyka and Arran's departure, he thought he might actually be dining with a friend.

55
ARRAN

"What is this place?" Veyka said, peering around at the perimeter I'd created.

It had taken the better part of an hour, even with my significant flora gifts. But I'd managed to peel back layer after layer of the dense jungle to create a clearing approximately the size of the training courtyard back in the goldstone palace.

"I thought we'd take a different approach to training your power." I'd been thinking about it since the festival.

We'd tried again and again to summon her void power at will. To no avail. Veyka eventually got angry and either yelled at me or Percival.

I didn't mind her yelling. I did mind the fact that she was no closer to controlling her power than she had been when she'd disappeared from the throne room at the Joining.

Veyka was walking the perimeter of the circle I'd created. There was still limited sunlight, since I had only bothered to clear the four yards or so closest to the forest floor. Above our heads, the trees still laced together, blotting out most of the sun.

But I watched as my mate took a deep breath. Her chest expanded as she held in the air, savoring it. It was the closest thing to freedom she'd experienced since we left the wide-open plains on the other side of the Crossing.

She was coping with the realizations of the last few days... by not dealing with them at all. She did not want to talk about it, and I did not blame her. Aside from recounting the facts that Lyrena and Cyara had told her, she'd been quiet.

Thinking. Calculating. Her mind was always working, even in the quiet. The weight of it threatening to crush her.

Had I done that to her?

Before the Joining, she'd been focused on her revenge to the exclusion of all else—including her own safety and peace in Annwyn. I'd lectured her, I'd scorned her for her selfishness.

And now... she was the one tearing herself apart for her kingdom, while I was ready to burn it to the ground for her.

No wonder she felt trapped.

She slowly exhaled, her entire body softening with the motion.

I couldn't help watching her. I knew every curve of her body, every hollow and pucker of skin, but I still couldn't get enough. I didn't think I ever would.

"You look a little too pleased with yourself," Veyka said. She'd caught me staring.

I swallowed back my desire and threw my hands wide. "Do you like what you see?"

Veyka lifted one pale eyebrow in challenge. "Do you?"

"Always." My beast growled softly for her. "But we don't have much time. The others are expecting us back by midday."

She started tugging at the golden brassiere that held her tunic in place. "I can be quick." Her eyes gleamed wickedly.

"Use your power and I'll reward you any way you like."

Her hand stilled.

It wasn't fair—but I didn't care. She had to master her power... before it stole her away from me. For the last two months, I'd lived in fear. I still did. I couldn't protect her from her power. But I could teach her to use it.

She folded her arms under her breasts, pushing them upward. Taunting me.

I tightened the hold on my beast.

"Choose your weapon." I pulled the axe from my belt.

Veyka cocked an eyebrow, then palmed her daggers.

No surprise. I hadn't seen her wield Excalibur—ever. It remained strapped to her back, no matter what threat she faced. I knew she'd used it to fight off the witch in the Tower of Myda. But beyond that, she treated it as if it was ceremonial. Since the revelations about Arthur...

The blade might as well have been poisoned.

As soon as the daggers were in her hands, I charged.

She was ready for me. I expected her to meet me head on—she always had before. But she threw all her weight to the side, rolling into a summersault and coming to stand on the other side of the clearing.

Ancestors, she was fast. I knew it, of course. But seeing her use that magnificent body, command those muscles like it was nothing... it was fucking impressive.

She spun a knife in her hand as we circled each other. "What does sparring have to do with my magic?"

The second I opened my mouth, she ran. Launching herself at me, crouching low, going for my midsection. One knife in her hand, the other hurtling through the air. I ducked to the side, the knife singing as it whizzed past my head and embedded in a tree behind me with a *thunk*.

I didn't look to see where it had landed. I swiped a leg out, going for her knees. She dodged over me, grabbing a tree root and using it to lever herself away.

She wasn't getting away from me like that. The tree root circled her ankle, dragging her down to the ground with a crash. "You love sparring," I taunted as it pulled her closer.

Veyka still had one knife in her hand.

"I love winning." She drove it down into the root.

I flinched backward. She ripped her leg free, hitting the ground at a sprint.

But I was already there. She couldn't outrun me. Not with my blades and my powers. "You can't win against me."

"Watch me." She dodged backward, retreating.

Mistake. I'd have her in a few steps. There was nothing behind her but a wall of trees and jungle.

"You've failed to access your power in isolation. So I figured we'd put it to work." I hadn't intending to push her so hard, so fast. I wanted to draw her out, get her comfortable with the sparring.

But every contest between us was destined to become a brutal bloodbath.

"You are talking in riddles." She darted to the side, then back, then the other side. She was going to feint. "Too much time in the elemental court," she grunted. Trying to distract me by talking.

I hefted my axe. One throw. That's all it would take. I'd hit her with the handle, not the blade. Still heavy enough to knock her on her ass.

But I issued the challenge instead. "You like winning so much. Use your power to beat me."

She darted backward, circling the edge of the forest, keeping two yards between us. For anyone else, it wouldn't have been nearly enough to escape me. But Veyka was fast.

"The power doesn't work that way. I..." She huffed in a breath. She wasn't tired from the sparring. She could do that for hours. It was the crushing weight of responsibility on her chest. "It's the void... I move from one realm to another."

"Says who?" I backed her up a little more. She was running out of space, even for someone with her speed. "You are in control Veyka. It is your power. Make it do what *you* want."

Her eyes flashed.

Oh, yes, my beast growled. *Does fighting like this make you wet for me?*

I waited for her response, the seductive taunt that I knew was coming.

But Veyka knew I expected it. She used the half second to jump.

She hadn't been retreating. She'd been getting herself into position.

Her hands closed around the knife embedded in the tree. Her powerful arms flexed against the fine wool of her tunic, pulling her upward. Her booted feet sailed straight for my chest.

But I was fast too.

I caught her legs, twisting brutally. She crashed into the ground and I came down on her a second later.

"Unless you'd rather admit defeat?"

One second, she was pressed against me, caught between my arm and my body, the blade of my axe pressed to her side. No escape.

The next, she was gone.

My beast threw back his head to roar—

"I want my reward."

Two blades pressed into the back of my neck. One swift, punishing movement, and they would cross each other—and remove my head from my body.

I dropped my axe. "You did it."

The blades on my neck dropped away. I swiped up my axe, spinning as Veyka retreated a few steps.

She stared down at her hands—still clutching her knives—at her arms and then down at her own feet. As if she couldn't quite believe that her entire body was there.

"I did it." Half sigh, half sob. "I held onto the tether—to you. I went into the void, just enough, then I came back out. Here. In this realm—in this Ancestors-damned clearing." Tears were rolling down her cheeks.

My own eyes burned.

Relief. That's what this feeling was.

She would master her power. It might take another month, another year. But the void would not steal my mate from me. She was born to command it.

56
VEYKA

I was unleashed.

Maybe it was seeing the humans, their unbridled joy in the face of such danger and death. Or maybe it was Arthur—the rage I felt propelling me once again. Once it had been rage at his murder. Now it was rage at him—for all the things he hadn't told me. All the actions he'd taken for my protection without a whisper to me.

The questions he'd left behind.

Or maybe I just really wanted to wipe that smug, self-satisfied smirk off of Arran's annoyingly handsome face.

Moving between physical locations in the realm I was already in was infinitely easier. After the first few times, I hardly felt it at all. The less distance I went, the less tingling there was. But even when I disappeared from one side of the clearing to the other, I was only in the void for a moment.

I could still feel the other realms. They were hovering there on the outside of my awareness. Like layers of paper in a book. But instead of ripping a hole in the ones above or below, I moved along the same line of text.

It was easier. It was less terrifying.

And it made that ember of magic inside of me very happy. It was glowing. I was glowing. Or at least, I felt like I was.

Arran reached for me.

I summoned the void and reappeared behind him.

His beast growled. I spied a tree over his left shoulder. A blink, and I was behind it.

I couldn't hear his beast when I was in the void. But I could still feel the mating bond in my chest—the tether. I knew my mate was close, that I was hovering near him, near the realm he occupied.

Maybe that was why it was easier—because I could feel Arran there with me.

Even if I never let him get more than single finger on me.

After an hour, there was murder in his black eyes.

Today might be the day he actually turned me over his knee and spanked me.

I was wet just thinking about it.

"Enough!" Arran bellowed.

My cheeks were beginning to hurt from grinning. "You wanted me to use my power."

He stalked closer, the beast showing clearly in his eyes. "Is this the reward you wanted? To torture me without consequences? Because there *will* be consequences, Veyka."

I shivered.

Yes, please.

I felt that next rumbling growl, so deep it sent tremors through my chest, down to the soft mound of my stomach, straight to my pussy.

I dragged in a breath. I couldn't take much more. The desire in my chest was becoming a physical pain. I needed my mate. I needed him inside of me. This teasing was burning me up just as badly as it was him.

One last time, I told the dancing ember of power inside of me.

I felt the tingling in my fingertips—

Hot fingers encircled my wrist.

"Arran, no—" I screamed. Blood and gore and Cyara's pained face all flashed in my memory.

But there was no screaming. The tingling was gone.

I was flat on my back at the very edge of the clearing. Arran was over me—intact. Whole. Staring at me in shock.

"What—did you feel that?"

My heart was hammering inside my chest. "I felt you," I managed.

Arran lifted the hand that was grasped around my wrist, holding himself above me with the other. "It felt... it was like going through the rift in the ravine."

His gaze snapped back to me. "Were you... were you going to take me with you?"

I blinked. "I wasn't trying to."

"No... but you weren't trying that day with Cyara, either. But maybe you could." I recognized the expression on his face. Battle applications. He was eminently practical. He was thinking about the implications of me being able to move not must myself from one spot to another, but to bring someone with me.

I couldn't think about it. Couldn't risk it. Cyara's pain had been enough. We didn't have a healer with us. If I tried it and ripped Arran in half, there was no one to save him.

The ember in side of me sputtered and dimmed.

"We should go back. It is almost midday."

My words snapped Arran from whatever bloody scenarios he was constructing in his mind. He shifted his weight away, giving me room to stand up. I folded my legs under me, leaning forward and bracing my arm. I reached for one of the thick branches that had created a border along the perimeter of the clearing, using it to pull myself to my feet.

But my eyes snagged—through the curved branches and leafy vines.

Something I recognized.

"Arran," I breathed. Was I breathing? It felt like there was no air at all in my lungs.

"I told you I would spank—"

"Arran," I demanded harshly. "Look!"

He was glaring at me—thinking it was another joke. Another way to torture and tease. But I knew when he realized, when he saw it as well.

He sucked in a breath, sharp and quick. Followed by a growl.

The vines and leaves peeled back. The branches were a little slower, but in less than a minute the way was clear.

"It was overgrown," I breathed, laying my hand on the stone. "Creating the clearing... you must have unearthed it."

A single standing stone. A monolith.

Almost identical to the ones that marked the mountain rift in Eldermist. Except this one had different carvings.

Different than the ones in Eldermist—but not unique.

I'd seen this before. We both had.

In the water gardens.

***

"They aren't completely identical," I said, several steps back in the clearing.

A ball of fire in Lyrena's hand lit the dark niche off of the main clearing Arran had created. She held it up as Cyara and Osheen peered at the carvings.

"But the differences are almost indiscernible," Arran said at my side.

He had one eye on Percival—still tied up, useless crystal in his hands. The man was clinging to it, even though none of us had seen it do anything remotely magical.

"The content is the same, but the style is slightly different. Like a letter written by one person, and then copied by another," I said.

We'd poured over every inch of the inscriptions before fetching the others. The Great War, the humans, the fae... the repeated outlines of Annwyn hovering over one another. All of it was there, just like in the water gardens.

"Which is the original?" Cyara wondered aloud.

Osheen quirked a brow. "Does it matter?"

A slight quiver of white wings. "Maybe."

"Whoever carved that didn't think very highly of the humans." Osheen returned to the larger clearing, one eye on Maisri. She was making tea over a small fire on the other side of the circle.

We'd wasted enough of the afternoon on the monolith and its carvings. We might as well make use of the open space for our campsite. A few more days' travel, according to Percival, and we'd emerge from this jungle in the shadow of the mountains.

"I noted that the first time, in the water gardens." Arran's arms were crossed over his chest. They had been, ever since that initial inspection.

He was glaring at the standing stone. As if he might scare it into revealing its secrets to him. "But this is the human realm. Why would a human depict their own kind so viciously?"

"Because they aren't human." Percival and his fucking revelations.

This time, I had a sinking feeling I knew what was coming.

"They are nightwalkers."

Percival was the new recipient of Arran's glare. "This stone is thousands of years old."

"So are the water gardens," Cyara said, stepping back into the main clearing. "They date from the original construction of the goldstone palace, around the time of the Great War."

"The nightwalkers were in the human realm before," I said. "And in Annwyn."

Lyrena started talking quickly. Cyara's voice was steady. Percival had apparently decided his opinion was needed. Osheen made loud inquiries about tea.

Our eyes met.

The chaos was just the beginning.

The nightwalkers had come to our kingdom before. They were an old pestilence, a dangerous one if the carvings were accurate. Entire legions of them, facing off against the fae in battle.

But if they'd come before, they'd also been defeated.

If I could control my power...

If we made it to Avalon and found out what the prophecy really meant...

If we made it back to Baylaur before the darkness fell...

Maybe we would stand a chance.

With Arran at my side, I stood a chance.

57

ARRAN

I love you.

I love you.

A cruel, cunning laugh sliced through me.

"How could she ever love you? How could anyone? A male of beastliness—a male of death?"

I didn't recognize the voice, but still it felt eerily familiar. Like it had haunted my nightmares before. But this wasn't a nightmare. This was real. This was Veyka, standing at the edge of the forest, staring at me.

Walking away from me.

"Where—where are you going?" I didn't care that I was stumbling over my words. Stumbling over tree roots—roots that should have bent in my very presence.

All I cared about was getting to her. My mate.

She kept walking.

Didn't turn back, even as I called her name. Or was that the beat of my own heart?

Veyka. Veyka. Veyka.

"She never wanted you. It was the bond that held her to you all along."

So many times, the fear had flashed in my mind. In these nightmares. I loved Veyka more than life itself. More than Annwyn or my family or the terrestrial kingdom. I had loved her before the mating bond.

But she'd never said the words. Never given me any indication that she loved me as well. That she was even capable of love.

And she was walking away.

"Veyka!" I screamed—but no sound came out.

I ran faster, forced myself to get to her. I was so close.

I summoned my vines, pulling the trees out of the way, clearing a path. I'd shift into my beast. She'd always connected with the beast, even when she couldn't connect with me.

Closer. I was almost there—

Beasts surged from the trees. Terrible beasts—panthers and leopards, skoupumas, deadly carnivores that only a cursed male could dream up.

But then the beasts were gone.

Not gone—transformed. Terrestrials shifting back to their fae forms. Holding my mate down. Ripping her clothing from her.

"You can do nothing to protect her."

Vines closed around me, holding me back as they hurt her. I shifted, but even the beast was not enough.

My chest was exploding. Veyka's pain was my pain. Her soul was fracturing from the violation, mine from being unable to reach her. Everything was fraying apart at the edges. I was fraying apart. I was losing my mind.

"You cannot protect anyone. You are not worthy." The voice laughed again, dark and cruel. I'd never heard it that way. That voice had only spoken kindness and love. My mother's voice...

"Wake up! It is a nightmare!"

It wasn't. Veyka was dead—no, worse than dead. Violated. Just as she'd been raped as a child, now taken and raped again and again. Because of me.

I roared, throwing my fists outward. Throwing the heavy weight of vines off of me.

They loosened, but didn't release me. I gnashed my teeth, ready to rip them free with my fangs. I sank in deep, savoring the taste of their blood.

But vines didn't bleed.

"Arran, Arran, please. Please, listen to me."

It wasn't vines wrapped around me. It was Veyka.

Veyka.

Whole. Skin nearly as pale as her hair. Shaking.

Maybe it was me who was shaking.

The tang of blood filled the tent.

Veyka's blood.

I fell backward, scrambled away. I swallowed, wiped at my mouth, loving the taste of her even as I nearly retched at what I had done.

"No." What was wrong with me. Was I destined to hurt everyone I loved? "No. No. No."

It built and built until I was screaming it. Over and over. The rage pouring off of me.

I lunged away, seeing nothing but darkness and blood, trying to get away, to get out.

But two strong hands caught my shoulders, dragging me back. Climbing into my lap. She slid her hands down my arms, never easing the intense pressure.

She was so strong, my mate.

Not strong enough.

My head snapped up. Her fingers tightened on my wrists, eyes meeting mine. Eyes that burned—not the blue glow of desire, but something primal and even more powerful. She pressed one of my hands to her chest. The center, where her heart pounded beneath her skin. She held it there for several long beats.

I felt every one, in every tired, broken corner of my soul.

Holding my other hand tightly in her lap, she lowered her mouth to my face. But not to kiss me. Her tongue dragged across my chin, right over the stubble of several days without shaving. She covered the lower half of my face in long sweeps.

Licking away the blood.

Her blood.

It would have been erotic, if I wasn't so fucking broken.

But every touch, every rough path her tongue tracked over my skin, brought me closer back to reality.

Cyara had said that I was Veyka's tether, when she disappeared into the void.

But Veyka was my tether. She was my reason for existing.

The reason for every nightmare.

Finally, her task done, she leaned in and pressed her forehead to mine. "What is it?"

"It is nothing." A lie, even when I'd promised myself I would never lie to her again.

If the others heard me lose my mind, they must have heard Veyka as well. Wisely decided to stay away.

My hand was still pressed to her heart. I felt the long breath she dragged in, felt her mustering the strength to say, "You said we could ask one another anything."

I had said that.

I had meant it.

Ancestors.

"I started having nightmares," I said. Maybe she'd leave it at that.

But my nosy and persistent mate was having none of it. "Obviously. You've been shaking me awake with them since we came to the human realm." She paused, squeezing the hand that was still cradled between us. "Did they start before that?"

I swallowed, the small sound suddenly huge in the close space. "After our Joining."

After you disappeared.

She tilted her head in enough to press a kiss to my cheek. She didn't pull away, letting her soft cheek linger against my stubbled one. "Tell me about the nightmares."

Not a question. An order.

"I don't want to hurt you."

She leaned back, held up her arm. The wounds where I'd sunk

my teeth into her were visible, her arm still smeared with blood. But they'd scabbed over, already beginning to heal.

"I am stronger than you think."

"I know exactly how strong you are."

"Then stop trying to protect me."

I'd promised as much—to myself and to her. We'd said no promises, and yet we seemed to make them to each other with every other breath.

We were tied together. Our souls bonded.

Maybe that was why I couldn't stop the rising tide of agony in my chest as it crested, broke, and spilled out.

"I dream that you are taken from me. That you are raped. Brutally. Repeatedly. That I'm forced to watch. That there is nothing I can do to save you. Until I wish that you were dead, just to spare you the violation."

Her eyes flared wide—glistening. Fuck.

A second, and then she was blinking back the tears.

Her hands didn't flinch away from mine, her body still slotted in tightly against me. She looked me straight in the eyes as she spoke.

"If we are ever in that situation, I give you permission to kill me," she said gravely.

I shook my head. "I would never be able to."

That was the truly devastating part of the dreams—the part that tortured me the most. That I would not be able to save her.

She pressed her head down to my shoulder. "I used to dream of the water gardens," she said softly. "Of what happened to me. I'd relive it, again and again. It was only after you came... that the nightmares stopped."

Her sigh was heavy enough to rock us both.

"It seems so unfair. Why should you ease my nightmares while I make yours worse?"

I slid one hand free, wrapping it around her shoulders, plastering her tight against me. I couldn't look her in the eyes as I said the words, but if I held her tight, maybe I'd be able to get them out. "Because of my mother."

"My birth was foretold, just like yours. After my mother came of age, received her Talisman... a priestess foretold that she would bear a powerful son. The most powerful male to be born in millennia. She didn't last a week after that."

Veyka's hand lifted to my back, stroking down the bare expanse of skin repeatedly over the tight muscles. Urging me on with quiet comfort.

"She was stolen. And passed around. For years. Every terrestrial fae male wanted to be the one to sire that powerful child upon her."

I expected her to shiver or cry or buck away.

The agony and torture I described was so horribly close to her own. But Veyka was steady. She held me through it, her hand turned warm by the repetitive circles she rubbed on my back.

She gave me the strength to continue. "After my brother was born—not weak, but not remarkable—she was discarded. She returned to her ancestral home."

"Eilean Gayl?"

I nodded, my chin digging into the soft flesh of her shoulder. I could have sunk into her and stayed there forever. But I forced myself to finish the tale. "My father followed her to Eilean Gayl. It took him a hundred years, but he convinced her of his love. They were Joined. And eventually, I was born.

"She was raped. Again and again and again. Because of me."

I waited for her to realize the truth that I'd known for months now—loving me was too dangerous. I'd failed to protect her—would continue to fail. She'd never admitted that she loved me, to begin with. But there had been times when I thought I saw it flash in her eyes.

But now, I'd never hear those words from her.

I was the cause of my mother's pain. I'd been unable to protect her, shield her. Just like I had been when Veyka was ripped from my side by an ancient, unknowable power.

She rocked back in my lap, putting just enough space between us so that she could look into my eyes. It was dark in the tent, not even a sliver of moonlight through the tightly laced flap. But I could see her nonetheless—some strange, extra sense.

The mating bond.

I felt her reaching down it, reaching for me.

Embracing me—not just with her arms, but with her soul.

The very essence of Veyka wrapping around me—twining us together.

Until we were one soul in two bodies.

I felt her words, rather than heard them.

"You are no more at fault for your mother's torture than I am for mine."

I tried to recoil, to argue back. But she pressed her fingers to my mouth.

Not a shred of fear, even after I'd nearly torn her arm apart with my fangs.

How could she be so brave, when I felt like nothing more than a shaking coward?

"It has taken me... years, to say that, Arran. And some days I still do not believe it. But it is the truth, whether I believe it on any given day or not." She leaned in and pressed her lips to my forehead. "What happened to your mother is not your fault."

I pulled her tight against me, burying my mouth in her neck. I needed to be with her, in every way possible.

He throat was so soft, so smooth and tender.

So easily, I could have ripped it out. Yet she offered it to me freely, arching so I could kiss the delicate column.

I couldn't hold her tight enough, couldn't kiss her hard and fast enough. I wanted our bodies to merge in time with our souls.

"Arran," Veyka moaned. "Arran, please."

It wasn't an entreaty for more—it was a pause. I recognized the difference instantly.

I drew back, abashed.

"I hurt you."

"No!" She grabbed my shoulders, holding me fiercely. "I just... for once, we have to say the words."

The words.

The words.

My heart stopped in my chest.

"Arran, I... after Arthur died, I promised myself..." Her breath fell from her lips in quivering waves. I was too paralyzed to respond.

"It hurt so much," she said. "I thought I'd never come back. I did not want to come back. You forced me. You dragged me back to reality, to the world of the living. You made me care about something other than vengeance."

And because I was a self-sabotaging fool, I couldn't keep my mouth shut.

"Hate is only a step above vengeance. You ought to hate me now. Being with me... it could get you killed. Or worse."

The trembling stopped. Or maybe it didn't.

Maybe it was just that Veyka was shaking her head so hard it was indiscernible.

"How could I ever hate you? Or be scared of you?" She grabbed my hand and pressed it to her chest, right in the center. Where the mating bond lay. "Arran, you are a part of me now. Being scared of you would be like being scared of myself."

But I wasn't the only one whose demons had been circling since our Joining. "Isn't that what's been happening, since your power awoke?"

"Being scared of my power is not the same."

She tugged my other hand up, the one not pressed to her chest, and pressed those fingertips against her lips. "I was scared my power would take me away from you. That I would never find my way back."

There was no more space between us.

I couldn't allow there to be.

I wanted her tucked against me, at my side, for the rest of eternity.

"I will always find you," I vowed. The sweet scent of her plum soap drifted through the air as I spoke against her hair, flooding my senses. My sweet, perfect mate.

"We have to face these things together," she said softly. "If we are going to protect Annwyn from the nightwalkers... if we are going to truly be mates... we have to trust each other enough to share the things that scare us most."

She was baring her soul.

I understood the implication. We would show one another our broken, twisted souls.

In their entirety.

And we would not walk away.

It was more than I could have ever hoped for—everything I hadn't even known to hope for in my first three hundred years of life.

But I'd never been a patient male. And I couldn't resist.

"Since I answered your question, does that mean you must answer mine?"

The soft rumble of her laugh filled any rough edges left inside of me. "I suppose you've earned it."

My stomach turned over in fear—anticipation.

"Veyka, do you—"

But the words died on my lips. I didn't get to ask my mate if she loved me.

Death had found us.

58
ARRAN

We moved in tandem—fast, sure, the language of battle and blood that both of us spoke so well. The words that came easily even when no others did.

One slash and Veyka had sliced open the tent, emerging like a fearsome beast from its shell, ready to conquer and kill.

The scent hit me even before my eyes had fully adjusted to the darkness.

Nightwalkers.

That noxious smell of death that had spilled from the human in Baylaur. It had been missing in the village—cleansed by the flames? It didn't matter. They were here. And those were Lyrena's screams.

We should have been safe in the thick ring of trees. The jungle was dense—too dense for them to move with any speed. And it was thicker still around the edges of the clearing, where I'd turned the branches and vines outward.

But they came.

Unhindered by the twisted branches—they contorted their bodies sideways, legs and arms sticking out at all angles as they forced themselves through with no regard for sharp thorns or splinters.

They felt no pain.

But they knew how to hunt their prey—and we were it.

I didn't even have time to drag my mate against me, to kiss her one last time, before we met the darkness. I shifted—my beast was better for ripping off heads than any weapon. Veyka was already running to Lyrena's aide.

She could manage. I didn't let myself run after her.

All of the others were focused on a dense pack of nightwalkers on the other side of the clearing. I headed for the tree line instead.

They came and came and came.

Leap. Sink in my fangs. Kill.

There was no time to retch at the terrible taste of that black bile coating my throat.

No time—only time to kill.

Kill, kill, kill.

My mate was on the other side of the clearing. I could feel her fighting, sense the distance. Close enough that I could reach her in two bounds. Close enough, I could protect her.

Protect.

Protect my mate.

Kill.

59
VEYKA

Lyrena could barely stand. Her leg was a mangled mess I couldn't bring myself to look at. I fought with her at my back, Osheen on her other side. But even clinging to a tree, my brave golden knight fought on.

Slash, thrust, deflect.

She might not wield Excalibur, but her sword seemed pretty damn magical to me. Especially once she sent a wave of flames down the blade.

Her burning blade lit the clearing.

Worse.

So much worse than I'd realized.

The nightwalkers were *everywhere*. How had they—

I slashed with my knives. Ancestors damn it—the knives were all wrong. They let them in too close.

I narrowly dodged the gaping maw of one of the monsters. I shoved the daggers back into the scabbards, pressed my back hard into the tree behind me, and used the force to kick away the two advancing nightwalkers.

It wasn't much time.

But it was enough to draw Excalibur.

The hilt was impossibly warm in my hands.

Arthur?

I had no time to wonder—three more nightwalkers lunged for me. They couldn't make me bleed. I knew that now. But they could break bones. Worse, they could hold me down until I was useless to my friends.

Lyrena would not last long against this pack, even with her flaming sword.

One head rolled. *Two. Three.*

Counting soothed me.

Excalibur was heavy; much heavier than my daggers or my curved rapiers. But it sliced through the nightwalkers as if they were the softest custard.

Eight. Nine. Ten.

I was making quick work of them.

Where were the others? It was so dark, the trees overhead blotting out the moon and stars. The only light was from Lyrena's sword. Even my sharp fae eyes could only see the yard or two immediately around me in the cloying darkness.

Twelve. Thirteen.

The void was calling to me, the power inside of me jostled awake by the excesses of battle. But I couldn't leave Lyrena. If I could take her with me…

No. I couldn't try that and risk injuring her more.

I needed help. I couldn't keep all of these nightwalkers back on my own, even with Excalibur. Eventually, they would encircle—

"Arrgghh!" Pain ripped through me.

My arm wrenched backward, behind my back.

My eyes started to close against the agony, but I forced them to stay open. To take in and focus on the hazy images of fighting above me.

My fingertips began to tingle.

No!—I wrapped myself around the tether in my chest, the mating bond connecting me to Arran. He was near. Just a few yards away, on the other side of the clearing. I would not go. He would not let me go.

A body crashed to the ground beside me. Another, half on top of me.

I shoved away the abhorrent body on instinct. I pushed myself up on my good arm. Not my dominant fighting arm, but all that I had left.

Percival stood over me, panting.

He was covered in the black bile.

He'd saved me—again.

I blinked.

That was all the shock I could allow myself.

He offered his hand, and I took it with my remaining good hand. He hauled me up to my feet.

Nothing more than a knife, I realized. A single knife, that was all he held. And he'd faced down those two nightwalkers who'd attacked me from behind. Faced them, and downed them.

I drew one of the daggers from my waist.

"Two knives are better than one." I pressed it into his hand.

It was too dark to read his expression.

But he nodded. Then he turned and disappeared. To fight, I hoped. Rather than escape. Though I supposed it didn't matter at this point. We might not survive the night.

Another scream—then a whimper.

My heart stopped in my chest.

Maisri.

I didn't even have time to fully swing back to Lyrena. "Go!" she screamed.

Another whimper.

Close, but not close enough I could see.

Ancestors, I would have given anything to be able to sense the child the way I could Arran, in his beast form shredding apart nightwalkers on the other side of the clearing.

Up, the sound was coming from above my head. The trees.

She'd tried to scale a tree. Of course, she had. That's what Arran had told her to do when we'd first found the burning village. But she wasn't far up, not far enough to—

Her whimpers turned to sobs.

I sprinted—she was in a tree. Less than a third of the way up, just above my head. But there was a cluster of nightwalkers at the bottom. They were too uncoordinated to climb up after her, but they could leap. One of them had her by the leg, was dragging her down.

The feet between me and Maisri felt infinite. I knew I was moving fast, but I'd never felt slower.

Too slow—Cyara got there first. She was a blur of wings, flapping behind her as she half ran, half flew through the clearing. Then she flying, snatching Maisri out of the tree and going up, up, up, depositing her high above our heads where no one, nightwalker or beast, would be able to reach her.

Relief coursed through me as she soared back down in a flash of wings.

Relief that turned to horror.

It wasn't Cyara that dropped into the clearing.

It was a beast of wings and claws. Terrible and beautiful.

Talons sprouted from her fingertips, her wings turned a deep coppery brown—the same color as her hair, wild and tangled, ripping from its plait as she thrashed. There was nothing of my friend in the monster I'd only read about in fairytales.

A harpy.

I'd always supposed there was a terrestrial fae ancestor tucked away in her family tree. Not this—never this.

But Ancestors be damned, it was impressive.

And lethal.

She tore out three throats before my next breath, severing heads from bodies with a swipe of her vicious claws. A flap of her powerful wing, and then her eyes were on me. The sparkling turquoise eyes—Cyara's eyes.

But there was no recognition in them.

Ancestors, please.

I wouldn't be able to kill her. Even if she attacked me, even if my death meant Annwyn's doom.

A roar ripped from her chest—high pitched. Not a roar but a screech. She dove for the next wave of nightwalkers. Not for me.

I decided to leave her to it and focus on my own attackers.

Time ceased to matter. Only the next kill, the nightwalker in front of me.

Excalibur was still warm in my hand, even as the temperature in the clearing dropped. Colder and colder. So cold—a cold I recognized. From that realm of death I'd seen when I fell through the rifts for the first time. Understanding began to solidify, somewhere in the back of my mind. But I couldn't spare it any more attention than that—I had to keep myself alive for the next second, the next minute.

I killed another one. Black bile coated Excalibur's gleaming blade.

The swirled, Avalon made blades held true—they killed the nightwalkers when the other blades did not. Severing their heads also seemed to kill them. Lyrena's fire could beat them back, but not for long. Soon, they'd rise again, this time flaming omens of death.

I couldn't see Percival or Osheen. I hoped they were still alive.

Occasionally I heard Cyara's screech—if that harpy and Cyara truly were one, the way that Arran and his beast were.

Another nightwalker. *Twenty-four.*

Where did they come from?

The humans hadn't said anything about this—masses of them, all together, like a legion of doom.

The humans hadn't—but the carved stone now shrouded in darkness had told this story. We'd been stupid to disregard it.

From the periphery of my vision, I caught a flash of moonlight.

It should have been impossible, this deep in the jungle. Maybe I was seeing the end of my own braid. No—I didn't have a braid anymore.

I slashed again. Where my blades went, nightwalkers fell and didn't get up.

Thank the Ancestors for these blades. Thank Avalon. I'd even thank Arthur, if it meant my friends would live.

I hadn't seen Maisri in too long.

No, it was good that I hadn't seen her or heard her. It meant she was still up that tree. Safe.

Another flash—how could that be?

I kicked the nearest nightwalker hard, giving myself a half-breath of space to whip my head to the side.

It wasn't the moon—it was a person—and they were waving.

What in the Ancestors-damned hell—

"Veyka!"

Just like that, I was surrounded again. Arran's yell was swallowed by his shift, his wolf powering through the nightwalkers like they weighed nothing. They rose back up, uninjured, unable to feel pain. But he'd bought me precious seconds.

He shifted. How much energy did that take? How much magic? I'd never asked him. He never seemed to suffer any pain or exhaustion—what was his cost?

I'd think about it later. Arran fought at my side again. The pain in my chest eased.

I felt safer—for myself, and for him.

But that damned flash.

"Look to my left," I cried harshly between beheading and stabbing, trying and failing to modulate my voice. It wouldn't have mattered—nightwalkers didn't appear to think. They only wanted one thing—to kill.

Arran spun to the side, much more efficiently than I had, taking out several nightwalkers as he did. "Who—they are signaling us?"

They continued down on us. Waves and waves of them.

So many humans—all turned to nightwalkers. How had they gotten through the dense forest? It should have been impossible. We should have been safe in the clearing.

But we weren't. We were stuck without an escape.

Maybe not. "Do we go?"

An assessing glance. A battle commander, surveying the field. "There are too many of them."

If he said it, then it was true.

I trusted him completely.

"To me!" I screamed. I drew the attention of the nightwalkers, but it didn't matter. I needed my friends' attention more.

But fighting across the clearing was painfully slow. They emerged one by one—Cyara with Maisri clinging to her back. Percival, my dagger clutched in his hand.

"Go!" I motioned them all behind me. Arran guarded my back as my eyes scanned.

Where were Osheen and Lyrena?

Lyrena could barely walk. I needed to go to her.

"Veyka, no!" Arran bellowed. But I ignored him. I cut my way through the wall of nightwalkers. I trusted Arran to get the others to safety—to wherever our mysterious rescuer was taking us. But I would not leave Lyrena.

Suddenly, Osheen was there. He thundered past me. The instant his foot left the dirt, a tangle of vines and thorns sprung up from the impression left behind. Not enough to kill a nightwalker, but enough to slow them so he could retreat.

But I sprinted past him. I dodged the vicious plants. I could see the glow of Lyrena's sword through the mass of dark human bodies writhing and lunging for me.

They couldn't have me. They couldn't have my friend.

I tunneled deep into reserves of energy that I hadn't known I had—new reserves. Magical ones.

Why am I running?

I let my eyes drift closed. I summoned my ember of power. I became the void. The world spun around me.

Then I was at Lyrena's side.

"What—"

"No time," I said, slipping my arm around her waist. I didn't stop to question my instinct. If I had, I'd never have been able to do it.

Lyrena leaned into me, not a hint of fear in her face. Complete trust for her queen, her friend.

I closed my eyes and commanded the void to let us pass.

Just like that, we appeared on the other side of the clearing.

Lyrena's flaming sword had winked out, but she was close enough to me that I could see her face clearly. She looked like she was going to vomit.

There was no time for that. Arran was suddenly there, taking Lyrena's weight.

I turned to follow him, bracing my muscles for a difficult flight through the trees.

But instead, the ground fell away below me.

60

PARYS

He trusted the female he'd assigned to tail Merlin. She was a cousin, though distant, another wind-wielder—the most useful of the elemental powers for subterfuge. But she also provided an opportunity that he couldn't afford to squander.

She could alert him if Merlin returned while he was searching her sanctum.

The temple was open to anyone, elemental or terrestrial alike. But priestess's sanctum was her own—private. Locked.

Parys had anticipated as much.

He closed his eyes, sending a tiny wisp of wind into the lock. Not all wind-wielders could manage this sort of delicate work. His wind moved through the mechanisms, feeling the levers and pins, the heft of the bolt. He constructed an image in his mind. He wasn't particularly familiar with locks, but he was able to push and pull and manipulate the tiny metal mechanisms until finally the bolt slid free.

Parys paused on the threshold, waiting. A priestess wasn't quite the same as a witch, and they'd been stripped of their spell books after the Great War. But he would not discount anything when it came to Merlin. Ambition was a powerful motivator—and she'd already shown disregard for the laws of Annwyn.

But nothing in the room seemed to change as he stepped in. More importantly, nothing about *him* changed. No intense pain like the riddle room in the Tower of Myda. No illusions living in mirrors like Arran and Veyka had faced.

Just... a room.

A single room that served both as bedroom and living space. That made sense—the temple was in the older part of the goldstone palace, situated in the mountain itself. Tens of thousands of years ago, the priestesses had been known for the asceticism. A room like this would have housed half a dozen priestesses and acolytes.

Now, it was richly appointed. Not large, but plenty lavish.

Rich gossamer draperies on the bed, embroidered with intricate golden thread on the scalloped edges. A jeweled chalice sat atop the mantle, along with a ceremonial plate of pure goldstone and a large, opaque white crystal. Gilded mirrors hung on the wall. The kitchenware was all studded with gemstones.

A clear example of why the Ancestors had discharged the priestesses of their power—they imagined themselves equals to the King and Queen. A sweeping glance of the room was enough to tell Parys that Merlin was of the same school.

He went to the work table first.

He couldn't linger here; Merlin was unpredictable in her routine. The only times that were reliable were when she went to pray to the Ancestors in the temple. But the temple directly adjoined her sanctum, and Parys wasn't stupid.

He'd be gone by the time she returned for afternoon prayer.

A book of rituals with incantations... a folder of correspondence with other temples across Annwyn...

He recognized the Offering and Joining ceremony in the book. As well as the words for Lugnasa. Generally unremarkable. The letters...

Nothing untoward there either. Requests for particular texts to be exchanged, and sending acolytes...

The acolytes.

The ones Veyka had stabbed and threatened. Not dispersed back to their families, but to other temples.

Fuck.

It was enough to call Merlin to account. Directly disobeying the queen. But instead of picking up the letter that was his proof, Parys slid it back into place.

Acolytes were not the root of this. Maybe some small part of a bigger scheme. But whatever Merlin was plotting with Igraine was more dangerous.

Time. He was running out of time.

What else...what else...

Where would she hide things? These were her personal quarters, but Merlin wasn't stupid. She knew that someone could get past the lock. She was a powerful water-wielder herself. But there were too many spaces to search—a cabinet of small drawers that stood as tall as his head, the bookshelf built into the wall.

But those were workspaces, where the singular acolyte she was allowed might stumble across some evidence of treason. Where, then...

Maybe in plain sight?

Where is the most obvious place to put something when you want visitors to see it...

The mantle.

His reflection stared back at him from the gilded mirror. He ignored the slightly frantic look on his own face and examined the items on display. A golden plate larger that his face, ceremonial, surely, with inscriptions. He had to tilt his head to read—*to beseech the Ancestors for blessings and plenty...*Ostara, when the High Queen and King would take the ceremonial first bites and mark the beginning of a plentiful spring.

A small painting he hadn't noticed before. A female who looked strikingly similar to Merlin herself—porcelain skin, up-tilted black eyes, straight sheet of black hair. Her mother, probably.

He marked the other items quickly. The chalice that had caught Veyka and Arran's blood at the Offering and a crystal that appeared to have been left on the mantle casually. It wasn't arranged in any particular way, or set up to display. Just a pretty white crystal, large enough to fit in his palm. Unremarkable.

His attention went back to the portrait. There could be something behind the canvas in the frame. He eased his wind forward, letting it seep into the cracks, trying to sense if there might be layers—

Footsteps echoed through the room.

Sent on a brisk wind—Merlin was coming. His cousin had sent the breeze, amplifying the sound. For half a breath, Parys considered shoving the portrait into his pocket. But it was a personal item—Merlin would surely mark his absence.

He made for the door, pausing just long enough to sweep his eyes over the room, trying to memorize every detail so he could dissect it later. His eyes caught on the chalice, a ruby in its stem glinting in the light slipping through the open door from the temple.

Parys closed the door and hurried out into the corridor, carrying away the too-loud sounds of his own footsteps in the opposite direction.

He was running out of time.

61

VEYKA

I counted the breaths around me, even as I heaved in my own. Arran, Lyrena, Cyara, Osheen, Maisri, Percival. All safe, all accounted for.

But maybe safety was an illusion, because we weren't the only ones there in the dark cave. The only light should have come from the outlines of the narrow opening far above. But not a yard ahead of me, flames danced.

Pale, white flames I'd only seen in the middle of a candle, just around the blue center. And those white flames illuminated what had been nothing more than flash of moonlight in the darkness above.

A white face. Not pale like mine, but truly white.

White hair in a hundred tiny braids.

Glowing white eyes around a black pupil that did nothing to make them any less unnerving.

And delicately curved, perfectly pointed ears.

"You're fae." I could hardly believe it. But the pointed ears, the magical flames dancing at her fingertips...

"I am a faerie," she corrected, her syllables sharp as the sword sheathed down my back.

We were all armed—even Cyara and Maisri. But there wasn't a blade on the woman—*female?*—nor a hint of fear.

My eyes went back to the flames at her fingertips. I watched as they winked out, one by one, revealing the fingers beneath. Fingers tipped in brutally sharp claws.

"Aren't they the same thing?" I asked carefully, keeping one eye on those claws even as I examined the rest of her once again.

She returned my stare, slowly perusing my form from bottom to top. Her expression didn't change, that same challenge in her gaze as it returned to mine.

"What do you think, High Queen?"

I cut a look to Arran, but it was Lyrena who said, "She'd fit right in at the elemental court with cryptic questions like that."

I felt Arran and Lyrena shifting behind me, positioning themselves to defend and protect. They ought to know by now that I was as likely to stab them as any of these supposed faeries.

"Friend or foe?" I asked, raising my eyebrows and casually crossing my arms beneath my breasts—in easy reach of my dagger.

The female slashed a smile I almost recognized from the looking glass.

"That depends, Majesties." Her sharp eyes flicked to Arran.

He didn't miss the implication. "On?"

"If you hold the same prejudices as your precious Ancestors," she said, taking a step back into a wall of darkness.

A tunnel.

A tunnel so dark, I was immediately drawn back to that realm of cold and death…

I stepped back, knocking into Arran just behind me. His left hand—the one not wielding his axe—landed on my hip. Steady reassurance.

I was not in that realm.

I was not alone.

I could control my powers—sort of. At the very least, I had Arran—my tether back to reality. *My reality*, that was.

The white female was already several steps down the tunnel,

would have already been swallowed up entirely were it not for the pale, reflective quality of her skin and hair.

Arran's warm fingers pressed into the strip of flesh just above my leggings. I recognized the message—*my decision.*

One word from me, and we'd climb back up and face whatever terrors awaited on the surface.

I let myself savor that comforting warmth for three seconds. Any longer, and I'd show weakness. Any longer, and I might curl up in his arms and try to hide from the world.

I took one step forward.

Wherever we were going, it could not be worse than what we'd survived above.

"Where are you taking us?" Arran said from behind me, close enough that his warm breath lifted the strands of hair brushing the nape of my neck.

"To safety," the female said.

"Cryptic once again," Lyrena sniped. The scent of her blood underlaid everything. She was upright, but still bleeding. "The least you can do is tell us your name."

The female paused, pale eyes flickering right past Arran and me to place Lyrena. Her mouth curved. "Much will be revealed soon, Golden Knight. But I can do as you ask," she said, looking back at me and Arran. "I am Isolde of the White Hands."

62

ARRAN

None of it made sense.

We were deep underground. I'd fallen too quickly to keep precise track, but the force with which we'd hit the ground told me enough. And we were only going deeper.

Veyka walked directly behind the female, Isolde, the stark whiteness of their heads acting as beacons for the rest of us to follow.

Except that one was nearly twice the other's height. Isolde was tiny. Smaller even than humans. Even Maisri was taller, though it was clear she was not a child, but an adult—a faerie.

Faeries.

A memory flashed in my mind.

My mother, reading to me when I was very young. My brother was there as well. *The faeries were charged with keeping harmony in nature...*

It couldn't be.

Yet the proof was walking before me.

And the deeper Isolde led us into the tunnels, the more apparent it became.

The faeries were much more than a bedtime story.

I let the others walk ahead. Percival was still armed—*was that one of Veyka's daggers glinting in his hand?* Lyrena was hobbling. She wouldn't be much use if it came to a fight. Osheen had a tight hand on Maisri's shoulder. And Cyara...

A harpy.

Another impossibility to be unpacked later.

Veyka at the lead, me at the rear. Guarding, protecting. I had no doubt she'd draw her weapon at the first sign of danger. She didn't need me to protect her.

My beast grumbled within me.

She needed a partner. Not a protector.

I could do that. I could be worthy of her.

We'll kill anyone who lifts a—

I leashed my beast. Though it was true. She'd fight her battles—with me at her side. At her back. With her. Always.

I tightened the restraints. I didn't need beastly instincts. I needed a calm, calculating head. I needed to observe.

What sort of defenses did the faeries have? How many guards? What powers could they muster and how strong were they? Could we defend against them?

The path started to slope downward, the angle increasing sharply. Sharp enough we had to pause and climb down a ladder. It took Osheen and Veyka's careful maneuvering to help Lyrena down with her wounded leg.

Another tunnel. This one, however, was actually lit. Soft golden light glowed on the walls at intervals. Lamps.

For Isolde, they were far overhead. But for me, they were level with my chin. I peered in—

And reeled backward at the indignant squeal. It wasn't a lamp at all. It was a tiny, glowing faerie. Exactly like Isolde, from the pointed ears to the sharp clawed fingers. But small enough it could have fit in the palm. *She* could have fit it my palm.

But her entire body glowed with incandescent light. Including her wings.

A faerie.

"They bite," Isolde's high-pitched voice said from ahead.

I glanced at the other faeries lighting the way as we continued down the tunnel, glowing with their soft golden light. They too, were entirely monochromatic. All pale gold.

What other color faeries would we see before this was over?

I didn't have long to wonder.

The tunnel was widening. Thus far, it had been narrow enough to act as a natural deterrent. It would be nearly impossible to push a force of any size and power through those narrow passageways. It would take too long, and the faerie fighting force could merely wait at the end and take out those who emerged one by one.

But now the tunnel was wide enough that three of us could walk abreast—three fae, taller and wider. And the walls weren't sheared black stone.

There were alcoves.

Small openings, built for beings much smaller than me or my companions. Carved for the faeries who occupied them.

I didn't duck down to see better—it seemed like an intrusion. Because those were not warriors or guards standing in the curved entrances to the alcoves, but families. A pale pink faerie with slightly translucent skin held one tiny child on her hip, another by the hand. All with claws, all with the same all-over coloring of the others.

They watched us with varying levels of interest. Children poking out heads, males with their claw-tipped hands crossed over their chests. But it wasn't just the colors that were stunning—shades of vermillion, forest green, white like Isolde.

It was the magic.

Water dribbled from a mother's fingertips into the child's waiting mouth. Magical hands lit hearths that I only saw for a moment, at a sharp angle through the small archways that led into the alcoves.

My companions were as awestruck as I. Maisri was grinning, reaching into her pockets for mangled flower petals, growing them into blooms, and then tossing them to the faerie children. Cyara's white wings were in a constant flutter, which meant her eyes were darting around as well.

Only Percival was stoic, eyes straight forward. He'd known they existed, then.

It is an entire civilization. A peaceful one.

My gaze flew over the heads of the others, finding Veyka. Her back was still turned to me, but I'd heard her words in my mind as clearly as if she'd been standing at my side.

My beast immediately let loose a soft, purring growl. *They could have warriors tucked away.*

I watched Veyka tilt her head to the side. *They are leading us through the residences, the families. They know we are not a threat to them.*

My beast growled louder. *That doesn't make them peaceful. Just stupid.*

Veyka's shoulders rolled. She turned her head to the side again—she was speaking to Isolde. Only an elemental would be able to hold two conversations simultaneously—and one of those happening entirely in her head.

Or chest? That was where I felt the force of the mating bond that allowed the strange intermittent connection between us...

"How long have you been down here?" Veyka was asking.

They'd slowed down. Veyka and Isolde were side by side, the others just behind them. My instincts told me we were close—

To what?

"Seven thousand years," Isolde said in her high pitched, tinkling voice. "Since the Great War."

Suddenly the tunnel widened and then fell away entirely. We were in a huge atrium. Stones stacked carefully along the walls to support the height. Higher up, ornate carvings depicting landscape and forest scenes—lakes, waterfalls, rolling hills. At the apex, some sort of carefully woven cover let light shine through from above. It was hard to judge based on the little bits of light, but I thought it might be dawn in the world above our heads.

"Who is your leader?" Veyka asked, her eyes more focused on the female at her side than the grandeur overhead.

Isolde smiled, revealing long canines reminiscent of my own that glowed as brightly white as the rest of her. "You are."

63
VEYKA

"You are."

I blinked. Maybe my mind was addled. Maybe I'd been hit over the head by one of the nightwalkers and this was all a dream.

A nightmare. "That is not possible."

Isolde's smile didn't falter an inch. "I misspoke."

Oh thank the Ancestors. I was able to drag in a breath—

"The two of you," Isolde amended.

My head was shaking. It was constantly doing that lately. Like I'd lost control of the muscles in my neck.

More like my mind couldn't believe the new information and the rate at which it was coming in, so my body wasn't waiting anymore. My mind was unreliable.

The vision of wings flapping flashed across my memory.

Isolde's smile softened to something closer to a smirk. "Are you not Veyka Pendragon and Arran Earthborn, High Queen and King of Annwyn?"

Arran finally stepped up, pushing past the others and planting himself firmly at my side. "Yes. But we are not in Annwyn."

It took you long enough.

But before his beast could growl back at me, another voice sliced through the tension.

"No. You most certainly are not."

Overhead. I reeled backward, Arran's hand pressing into the base of my spine. But I found the voice quickly. The female was overhead, wings keeping her aloft. Some of them had wings. I sucked in a breath. It was extraordinary, an entire race of beings—

Then she shifted, and suddenly she flew on different wings entirely. A gull with pale white and blue on the undersides of her wings. She sailed down through the massive atrium in sweeping circles until she reached the center. She shifted again and landed on two pale blue feet.

Not just elemental powers—some of these faeries had terrestrial powers as well. Shifters who kept their wings even when in their fae form. *Faerie form? Ancestors, I don't know.*

Isolde, at least, was unimpressed. She folded her white claw-tipped hands in front of her and waited for the other faerie female to turn and face us.

She did—slowly. Surveying the room as she rotated, nodding here and there. Even a smile at some children clustered off to the side. But when she came to face us, there was no welcome in her small features.

That didn't deter Isolde. "Taliya. We have guests."

One brow arched. Her skin was pale blue, so were her eyes, hair, and clothing. It was difficult to see where her clothing ended and her skin began. They were so close in color and so finely made. The only part of her that didn't match was the little amulet that dangled from her throat. A single gem—either diamond or amorite. It was small enough I couldn't tell.

Taliya, Isolde had called her.

The true leader of these faeries.

I recognized her stance. The same one that Arran took when issuing orders for defense. The same one I used when I stood in the throne room of the goldstone palace.

She stared us down, utterly unimpressed. "I can see that. But where did they come from?"

Isolde's arms dropped. "They were beset above by the—"

"I understand," Taliya cut her off abruptly. She didn't have to wave her hand or say anything else; the dismissal was clear enough.

Isolde dropped back a step, but didn't disappear entirely.

But it was clear to me—and judging by the low growl rolling through me, to my mate—who would decide what happened to us next.

I tried to think of Arthur. Of Gwen. I tried to summon their graceful, political smiles.

"Thank you for giving us refuge." My voice sounded strangled and gravely. But at least the words were right.

A second eyebrow joined the first. "I have not agreed to give you refuge."

My patience was fraying. I resisted the urge to cross my arms, but then they went to my hips instead. Not really any more welcoming.

But then, neither were my words. "Taliya, is it? I am Veyka Pendragon."

There were faeries all around us. The large atrium appeared to be a communal space of some kind. There were children playing a game with balls and spikes, a large cooking hearth near the center, benches lining the walls.

There were no thrones, I noted.

There were eyes—so many eyes. All watching us.

Quite literally half my height, Taliya set one hand on her hip to match mine. She stared up at me from a yard away, and it should have been comical. She might weigh as much as one of my legs. But there was command in those pale blue eyes—eyes not so different in color from my own. An unnatural shiver slid down my spine.

The shadow of a smile passed over the female's face; as if she'd detected my quiver.

"I know who you are, Majesty. We all do. As Isolde said, your titles hold meaning here. At least, among some."

But not all—not her.

Taliya opened her mouth to say something more, but two children stumbled between us. One was holding a torch, tripped, dropped it to the ground. Before the flame could spread or burn, it was engulfed with ice.

Ice which had blasted straight from Taliya's fingertips.

My head was shaking again.

But it was Arran who asked, his voice gruff. Half growl, really. "How is it possible—you have both elemental and terrestrial magic."

"You thought you were the only one twice blessed, did you, High King?" Her intonation told me precisely how she felt about that title.

Arran didn't bristle. He just glared—I knew that meant there were more complex emotions at play in his mind. But the faerie female did not—and she was more than happy to glare right back at him, High King or no.

"We are the Faeries of the Fen. Our magic does not hold to the rules of your elemental and terrestrial factions. We are older. We have existed since long before your kind came to dominate Annwyn."

Why did it seem like everyone knew about us, and yet we knew nothing?

I suddenly wished I'd spent more time in the library with Parys—doing something other than eating his cake and drinking his wine.

Arran's frown deepened. Not just a glare—a frown. Something about this was bothering him. I tried to speak to his beast, but the rumbling growl reached me before I could.

A warning. He was right.

We didn't know what kind of magic these faeries had. Ethereal powers were long extinct in Annwyn... but void magic had been as well. Until it awoke within me.

We had no way of knowing that one of them wouldn't be able to tap into the bond between us.

Arran's voice was smoother when he spoke again, his scowl

firmly fixed. "We do not wish to cause you strife. We ask only for time to bandage our wounds, and then we will be gone."

Taliya laughed mirthlessly. "Is that all you will ask?" She shot a look my direction. "No, I think you will ask for much more than that. More than you have any right to."

It might come to a fight.

I hadn't seen a single weapon on any of the faeries. But they possessed magic, that much was clear. There were probably more shifters among them. I doubted any were as fearsome as Arran's beast. But I'd rather not find out.

Not with Lyrena still injured, and Cyara... *fucking Ancestors. Cyara is a harpy.*

It was a miracle my head didn't go flying right off of my shoulders.

Another growl.

Calm, it said.

I can't be fucking calm.

Another rumble in my chest. *Be a queen.*

Whatever the hell that means.

Taliya knew. "Isolde, see that our guests are given appropriate accommodations."

Good for her.

I gritted my teeth. This battle would be fought on another day. After Lyrena had healed and Arran and I could talk. "Thank you—"

"You are not free just yet, Your Majesty." A doorway opened behind her. "Come."

Arran's hand touched my waist. An unspoken signal, just like when we'd first come skidding down into the tunnels. *My decision.*

I was going to have to speak to him about this—we were supposed to rule together. I was getting damned sick of making decisions.

64
ARRAN

Veyka was all striding sass, swaying hips and hotheaded posturing as she followed the tiny blue female through the arched doorway.

I was more reticent.

A look back to my companions. Osheen would protect Maisri. Lyrena would fight through her pain. Cyara was more than capable of defending herself, apparently. Percival... I could not say what he would do. I'd encountered males like him on the battlefield—conscripted by family woes to a battle that was not their own. They could go either way—become loyal, gifted soldiers; or run at the first sign of bloodshed.

Percival, at least, had fought with us against the nightwalkers.

That was something.

More than something—I let them go with the Isolde, the tiny white faerie beaming once again. But I had somewhere else to be.

The bond in my chest was thrumming. My mate wasn't far, but I didn't know what we were walking into. She'd use sarcasm and bravado to arm herself—for now. I fingered the head of my axe.

The small room had been carved out, the arched doorway similar to the entrances to the alcoves that had lined the tunnel on the way in. This entrance was slightly taller, but I still had to crouch. Thankfully, once inside the ceiling opened up again. I briefly wondered what sort of accommodations we'd be given—whether we'd be crawling into them.

There were benches along the walls, but generally the space was sparse. Again, no throne. A hearth in one corner, topped by a rudimentary stone chimney. This was not a temporary residence. This network of tunnels and rooms had housed the Faeries of the Fen for a long time. Thousands of years, maybe.

The Faeries of the Fen.

Quite literally, figures from the pages of my childhood fairytales.

Veyka and Taliya squared off in the center of the room. The latter was hovering several feet above the ground, her iridescent wings flapping rapidly to keep her in place. To bring her face to face with Veyka.

Who looked like she'd sooner stab than talk.

Not much of a diplomat, my mate.

"We will speak later. My companion needs care." Veyka planted her hands on her hips—not even bothering to play at a conciliatory tone.

"Isolde is a healer. Your friend will be better tended in her care than anything you could hope to achieve." The bite in Taliya's words was vicious enough to draw blood.

Veyka angled her chin.

Fucking Ancestors.

"You think your magic is a match for ours." A challenge. A brilliant one—to find out just how powerful the faeries were.

"We don't pretend to be as powerful as the mighty fae of Annwyn," Taliya spat. "Our magics are small, but they are vital. How has your realm fared in our absence?"

"Annwyn has gotten on just fine for the past seven thousand years," Veyka returned.

"Has it? How are the summers in Baylaur? Or the winters in the Spine?" Taliya laughed, not an ounce of humor to be found. "Without the faeries to moderate the weather, to bring the mild rains of spring or nurture the long autumn harvest?"

"You are keepers of the land, just like the fairytales."

Both females cut their eyes to me.

Fuck. I hadn't meant to speak aloud.

I wasn't much better at diplomatic relations than my mate. Give me a battlefield any day.

"The terrestrial kingdom has not forgotten," Taliya said, her eyes softening slightly. She didn't dissemble like the elementals. She didn't follow any of the rules and customs of the fae I knew. Another indication that she'd spoken true—that she and the other faeries were not held to our conceptions of power and magic. "We are the keepers of balance and harmony. Without us, the lands become inhospitable. Extreme. But the fae can adjust to anything, it seems."

The derision in her voice might have burned if I didn't recognize it. The same sort I'd held for the elementals. Still did, generally.

Didn't I?

"Yes, yes, we are a cunning, brutal bunch," Veyka said sharply. "Why does Isolde seem to think that you answer to us?" She jerked her head in my direction.

Taliya hissed through her teeth, her wings flapping faster, carrying her higher. "We answer to no one."

Veyka looked vaguely bored. *Ancestors above.*

"Isolde doesn't seem to agree."

"Isolde is a young fool!"

"What about the other faeries?" Veyka cast her eye meaningfully back toward the arched doorway. It was the only one we'd seen fitted with a door, and that door was closed.

How keen was the faeries' hearing? They had the same pointed ears as Veyka and I.

Veyka wasn't done. She pulled her remaining dagger and tossed it up casually. Taliya twitched as if she might try to snatch it from the air. The hilt landed perfectly in Veyka's palm.

"You left Annwyn—were you forced, or did you flee? Did you

once answer to the High Queen and King? Should I go out there and see how many of them will follow me?"

Taliya snarled, a terrifying, high-pitched sound. She might be tiny, but I could see the damage she'd inflict with those long fangs and needle-sharp claws. She would try to tear apart my mate—try and fail.

Then we'd have a dead faerie leader and a whole other host of problems.

"We don't want anything from you," I said, stepping up beside Veyka.

I didn't try to take her dagger—I didn't feel like testing Isolde's healing prowess—but I did loosen my hold upon my beast. I let him growl softly, let him rub up against Veyka's consciousness through the mating bond.

Ironic, that the growl that had made so many fae warriors piss themselves with fear seemed to calm and soothe my mate.

Fitting, really.

I lifted my gaze to Taliya—not an experience I relished. "Show us a way out and we'll take it."

"Not until Lyrena is healed," Veyka said.

I didn't break Taliya's gaze, but I lifted my chin an inch.

Her pale blue eyes were similar in color to Veyka's—even to her mother, Igraine. But they felt wholly different. Maybe it was all the blue around them—skin, hair, brows, even her eyelashes were a pale milky blue.

"You'd like to rejoin your *friends* above?" Taliya hissed.

She knew.

The faerie knew what we'd escaped above ground, even though I hadn't seen anyone give her a report.

"You've encountered the nightwalkers."

"We are familiar with their kind, Majesty. For seven thousand years, the Faeries of the Fen have lived in these tunnels, growing a mighty jungle overhead to protect us. Since your precious Ancestors cast us out, along with all the others—witches, priestesses. We have been preparing for the return of the succubus."

65
VEYKA

"Seven thousand years of building our fortress, and you've led the succubus right to us. The fae bring nothing but darkness and death to the faeries," Taliya snarled.

She was a vicious little thing. I wanted to squash her beneath my boot.

But she was the leader of the faeries, despite what Isolde said. I'd seen the way the others in the atrium watched our interaction—watched her. The children who'd dropped the torch had bowed their heads in respect before running off. She was the leader of her people, even if some of them believed in an ancient allegiance.

That didn't mean I couldn't subvert her insecurities.

Or find out who, exactly, among the faeries believed that Arran and I had a claim to them.

But none of that mattered. It was all happening in the back of my mind; calculations and posturing that seemed to be part of the elemental fae blood that ran in my veins.

Only one word echoed in my consciousness—

Succubus.

"You mean the nightwalkers," I said.

A feral toss of her head. "A human name—from humans who

do not remember their own history. They are so short lived, it is no wonder. But the fae—what excuse do beings who live a thousand years have for forgetting the name of their greatest enemy?"

"There have been other threats," Arran said. He was thinking of Arthur's murder. The battles he'd led the terrestrial armies into over the centuries—disputes and conquests with far away continents.

"You fight amongst yourselves, positioning for power. That is all the elementals and terrestrials have ever cared about." Taliya's wings slowed. Was she tired already? I was certain Arran noted the change as she lowered herself to the earthen floor. Farther away this time.

Smart female.

"The real threat is the succubus." I said it aloud, and knew it was the truth.

Arthur had known it too. He'd sent aid to the humans in Eldermist. He'd put the weapons in my hands that could defeat this new darkness.

But it wasn't new. I'd seen the carvings—in the water garden and then again in the jungle. "The succubus have come before."

Taliya's face wasn't quite as angry. She looked more tired—exhausted, really.

Anger was an excellent way to get information—exhaustion worked nearly as well.

"What do you think the Great War was about?"

Understanding flooded through me. The carvings in the water gardens. The human forces had looked strangely disfigured—because they were not human at all. They were succubus.

A soft snarl flooded through. Soft, but full of menace. Death. I *felt* Arran's overwhelming urge to shift, to wrap his beast's huge body around me. To protect.

Down, beast.

The snarl turned into a growl.

A strangled, horrible sound ripped from Taliya's throat. I hadn't looked away from her, but my attention had been elsewhere. She earned it back in a second.

Her mouth hung open. "You are mates."

Somehow, she'd felt the connection between us. *How*—not the time.

"Yes," Arran growled.

Taliya shot into the air, buzzing around the room so quickly I almost lost track of her. She landed again, much closer. And though she hit the ground hard, was several feet shorter, the rage in her eyes was enough to give me pause.

She stared directly into my soul. "You. This is all your fault."

Arran shoved me aside, battle axe drawn.

I shoved him back, raising my dagger. "Explain yourself, faerie, or I will cut your wings from your body."

"You have the void power. It only appears in mated pairs—you are the reason the succubus has returned. You are the reason for the death. You! Always the fae, bringing death upon us all!"

She was insane. As she spoke, her wings started flapping again, pulling her backward. I had a million questions, but Arran was already in front of me, advancing.

Ready to make good on my threat and damn the consequences.

"Veyka has done nothing. She has no control—"

"Of course she has no control! She has summoned them! Where do you think those ghastly monsters come from—"

She shot into the air to avoid Arran.

Whether he would have actually killed her with the swipe, I didn't know.

I stepped forward.

Lifted a hand to his shoulder.

I understood.

"They come through the rifts, using the void." That realm of darkness and death. The smell was the same. The cold that reached inside and tried to steal my magic. The same. "The succubus come through the rifts to the human realm, to Annwyn. To take over or possess the humans. They use the void, and I am the one who opened it."

Arran stared at me.

The intensity in his stare, the fear... fear for me. Fear of Annwyn.

I couldn't hold it. I looked away, turned away, trying to pace.

The room was too small. I was trapped. No air, no sky above my head. I had to get out.

But I couldn't.

Duty held me in place. My kingdom.

This was no longer about posturing. This was about finding out everything Taliya knew.

"How did they get here seven thousand years ago?"

Taliya was now circling overhead. Her version of pacing, I supposed.

But she answered me. "Your ancestor possessed the same power as you."

Something wasn't quite fitting into place. Taliya looked at me with derision—more than derision. Not hate, not exactly. Blame. My fault.

My fault.

Arran and my blood had joined, my power had awoken. I'd been unable to control it, falling headfirst into the void, through the rifts. I had visited the succubus realm without even realizing it. I'd opened the way.

Except that wasn't the first time I'd seen the succubus.

"You are wrong."

Her wings flapped faster.

"We encountered a nightwalker—a succubus, before we were mated."

"Twice," Arran corrected. "The man in the ravine, and the human emissary from Eldermist."

Now Taliya's head was shaking in time with her wings. "That cannot be."

"Are you calling us liars?" I glared up at her. I wished I had

Percival's bow and arrow. I was better with my knives, but I only had one and I was loath to risk it.

"All fae—"

"You are fae! We are all fae!" I shouted.

That shut her up.

I waved my hands around like a fucking idiot, as if I could pluck her tiny, infuriating body from the air. I was close to losing my temper, losing my mind.

"They only possess humans, only when they sleep. Why?" I demanded.

"If your own kind have not fallen prey to them yet, you are lucky. Human minds are weaker, easier to steal. Even more so when they slumber. But they will come for your males just the same. Unless all of you are as well gilded with amorite."

I froze. Arran's eyes found mine. *Amorite.*

I pulled Excalibur from my back in one brutal sweep.

The swirls of metal seemed even more pronounced now that I knew what I was looking at. The blades weren't merely made in Avalon; they were forged with amorite.

"These blades can kill the... are they humans? Or are they succubus?" I flicked my eyes upward. Taliya was now hovering high up, directly above our heads.

"They are humans still, but they are slaves to the succubus. The succubus wait in their realm of death. Were trapped there until you began opening the void. They never leave it, only use the void to take over the minds of our males." She lowered herself down, close enough to see the blades. "Only the amorite is effective against them."

"And fire," Arran said.

Taliya nodded. "It is not as effective, but yes."

I met the faerie's blue eyes, suddenly mere inches from my own. "Why are you telling us all of this? You could leave us to our deaths." I paused. "Unless you want our help."

Her eyes flickered. "We do not need your help. Our males wear amorite amulets. They are protected from invasion by the succubus."

"Perfect. Amorite necklaces for everyone."

But Arran was shaking his head. "Amorite is rare. There are a few mines in the terrestrial kingdom, but not enough. Not for every fae, or every human."

He looked at me, waiting for me to say it.

Fuck the humans.

But the words didn't come. I returned Excalibur to its sheath down my spine, the knife to my scabbard.

Arran's fingertips brushed the shell of my ear. The amorite studs that reached from the soft rounded lobe up to the sharply pointed tip.

You're getting a piercing tonight.

His beast didn't even bother to growl back at me.

"We will only stay long enough for Lyrena to recover. We are bound for Avalon," I said, my eyes never leaving his.

Taliya was shuffling or flapping nearby. "We will take you back above when the threat of the succubus has passed."

Which meant we might be here forever.

But that wasn't what she meant. She thought we'd led them here, that horde that had driven us underground. Maybe we had.

Even with everything Taliya had told us, everything I'd pieced together, we still knew precious little about the succubus.

Taliya was clever, even if she was shit at managing her emotions.

When the threat of the succubus has passed.

She meant that we would leave when she allowed it.

I wasn't going to argue with her about it—not yet.

But no one would keep me from Avalon, not now. We needed answers. My kingdom needed answers.

"We'll lodge with the others," I said, finding the blue female hovering near the door we'd come through minutes or hours before.

"I am certain Isolde is waiting to speak with you." Contempt— Taliya didn't think much of the other female.

Another bit of information to dissect—*later.*

The door opened, sounds floating in from the atrium. Before I ducked through it, I looked up at Taliya one last time.

Her face was unreadable. Not because she was able to dissemble —but because there were so many conflicting emotions at play.

I felt a flash of sympathy.

"Why only males?" I asked.

A few quick flaps of her shimmering blue wings. "Because the succubus are all female."

66

ARRAN

We did have to crawl.

I didn't ask how they'd gotten Lyrena inside.

But there she was, along with all the others, sitting on benches that lined the inside of the circular chamber.

At least once we crawled through the passageway, the alcove was big enough for us to stand.

Barely.

I watched Veyka's eyes dart around the space, noting the same things I did. A circular center room that opened back onto the tunnel. Not the one Isolde had originally led us through during our descent, but another one of the spokes branching off from the central atrium.

The walls were reinforced with carefully stacked rectangular stones, fitted together carefully. The best I could see, there was no mortar holding them in place. Magic, maybe. The powers the faeries possessed… Taliya had said they didn't match the sort magic that ran in my own veins, in the veins of my companions.

But I wasn't going to trust a single, very volatile faerie's words.

Aside from the entrance back to the tunnel, there were four more openings. Presumably leading to additional rooms. None of them had doors—the only one I'd seen in the entire tunnel and cave system was the one leading to the chamber where we'd spoken alone with Taliya.

Apparently, the faeries didn't have much use for privacy.

I wished we had a wind wielder with us.

They at least could carry away the sounds, create a whipping wind around us to prevent our voices from drifting away into waiting ears.

But Parys was back in Baylaur. Gwen with him.

I hadn't thought of them much.

Hadn't thought of Baylaur, or how Annwyn at large fared.

For three hundred years, duty to Annwyn had driven my every action.

Until Veyka.

What did that make me? A battle commander—but whose motivations were tainted. I wouldn't have trusted myself on the battlefield, not with the shifting allegiance. Defending a kingdom meant letting everything else go.

Ancestors fucking hell. I don't have time for this kind of musing.

Cyara and Maisri sat opposite the door, preparing breakfast and tea.

Osheen sat just inside the opening to the tunnel, his sword across his lap. He cleaned the dark succubus bile off of it, but slowly. A show. An excuse to have his weapon out.

Percival wasn't in sight, but I knew Osheen would not have let him go far. Probably in one of the connecting rooms.

Near the hearth, and another stone chimney built into the wall, Lyrena's mangled leg was bare. Isolde was bent over a pot beside her. Veyka went right to them.

"How bad is it?"

"I am fine," Lyrena said, cracking a smile.

Veyka nudged her foot. Lyrena winced.

"Not fine." Veyka turned her eyes to Isolde. "You are a healer."

A slight smile on the white face. "Yes."

"Then why haven't you healed her yet?"

The scent of Lyrena's blood wasn't as overpowering as it had been in the first minutes after we'd slid down into the caves. It had clotted and there was a thick cloth tied around her thigh to stem the flow. Isolde had done something. But Veyka wasn't in the mood.

"You are not in battle, Majesty. We have the time to tend to her carefully."

"What do you know of battle? I do not intend to linger here."

But Isolde merely smiled at Veyka. "Has Taliya given you leave already?"

Veyka gnashed her teeth. She may lack the elongated terrestrial canines, but I had no doubt she could rip the faerie's throat out with her teeth if she wanted to.

My feral, vicious mate.

Need stirred. It had been a few days.

Ancestors, why weren't there doors on those adjoining chambers? Veyka would never let me fuck her with a thousand faeries listening in—

"Heal her." A command from a queen.

Isolde's smile grew, but she inclined her head. "Of course, Majesty."

She handed Veyka the earthenware pot she'd been holding. Veyka was fast—if she hadn't been, the contents would have sloshed all down her front.

But Isolde wasn't even looking at Veyka. All of her attention was on Lyrena. She lifted her tiny, childlike hands—except for those lethal claws—and skimmed them over Lyrena's wound.

Lyrena arched back, clearly in pain.

But just as suddenly, her body sagged. Relief washed over her face. Then her eyes widened.

A collective gasp.

Isolde wasn't manipulating wind to hold the skin in place as she stitched it, or fire to cauterize the wound. Her hands were glowing —bright white.

Isolde of the White Hands.

Not because of her white skin, but because of the glowing white magic. Healing magic.

I hadn't realized such a thing existed—it was impossible. It wasn't elemental or terrestrial magic. It wasn't even Void or Ethereal. Those were supposed to be legends, but at least we'd heard of them.

This was entirely different.

And completely in keeping with what Taliya had said.

The Faeries of the Fen may be some version of fae, like the elementals and terrestrials. But their magic was totally different—ungoverned by the laws of nature we'd simply learned to accept somewhere over the last seven thousand years.

As quickly as the glowing had come, it winked away. Isolde removed her hands, revealing an expanse of slightly pink skin. But whole, knitted together. Not even a scar.

She held her hands out to Veyka.

"Taliya is my cousin," Isolde said as white flames sprang from her fingertips, heating the little pot to boiling before I could count to ten. "Our families have... differences of opinion about loyalty."

"She called you a young fool," Veyka said.

"She is my elder by a few hundred years."

"Are you a fool?"

The faerie turned to face Veyka, tilting her head to the side. Then she looked at me, gave me the same perusal. "I hope not."

She dipped her fingers into the pot and scooped out some of the mixture, now thickened, onto Lyrena's leg. Lyrena hissed through her teeth, but didn't complain.

A good soldier. As good as Gwen, I could admit. Even though I'd questioned Veyka before.

"I will come back tomorrow to change the dressing. But you can walk and crawl and do whatever else you want." She nodded to Lyrena and the others.

She paused at the door, her eyes finding Veyka's, then mine. Then she bowed.

Deep. Respectful. A subject to her Queen and King.

Ancestors.

Instead of finding answers, we were gaining new subjects to protect.

But as soon as Isolde was gone, the others turned their eyes to us.

Veyka rolled her shoulders. *Can we escape and take a nap?*

I have a few things I'd like to do to you before we sleep.

"If you don't have anything important to tell us, then go to your room. At least we won't have to watch," Lyrena groused.

Veyka flashed me a wicked grin and settled down on the bench next to her golden knight.

I took the spot on the other side of the entrance, opposite Osheen.

My beast growled in frustration. Veyka's squirming on the bench didn't make matters much better.

Soon, I promised my beast. And myself.

And *her*.

We briefly recounted what Taliya had divulged about the nightwalkers—the succubus.

Having a name for it made it less fearsome. The things we'd learned... had the opposite effect.

Veyka may not have been the one to bring the succubus back to Annwyn and the human realm initially, but the connection was undeniable. Both creatures of the void.

The void that had taken my mate.

The void that she was just now learning to command.

Learning to love.

I'd witnessed the joy on her face as she used her power against me in sparring. I had sensed that brutal satisfaction in her when she used the void to battle the nightwalkers. She wasn't just learning to control her magic—she was coming to love it.

It was what I'd wanted. Only by embracing that power inside of her, letting it become a part of her, would she truly be able to master it. She wasn't there yet, was still teetering on the precipice.

But we'd unblocked something in that clearing. Moved past a barrier. Veyka was fast and clever and brilliant.

No matter what awaited in Avalon, her power and her control of it would only grow.

I thought that training her power was essential, the only way to keep from losing her to the void.

Now I wasn't so certain.

Now the void contained monsters.

Percival appeared from one of the connected rooms. He must have been able to hear us all along, even with his more limited human hearing, because he didn't ask any questions.

None of them did. They listened, they offered an occasional comment for confirmation. But it was all quiet.

So quiet, that when she finished speaking, Veyka looked to me.

What do I do now? Her eyes asked.

My beast had a few ideas.

"The faeries are wrong about the succubus," Cyara said abruptly.

Veyka's eyes whipped to her. "What do you mean?"

"The humans, this Taliya... they say it can only get into the minds of males. But the witch in the Tower of Myda was female."

Veyka lurched, grabbing onto the bench to hold herself steady.

I moved forward to catch her, imperceptible to everyone else. My mate shot me a warning glare.

"Everything you've described... the strange discordant movements, the blackness, the cold that seems to drain your magic, it all fits with how you described the witch," Cyara pressed on.

She was right.

My heart froze in my chest.

"And the assassin."

Veyka's eyes swung to me—they all did. But I only noticed hers.

"The assassin in your bedroom. When I touched him, to determine if he was elemental or terrestrial. My magic recoiled. The succubus must have been within him, or some vestige, after you killed him."

Veyka was shaking her head. Her hair, heavy with sweat and grime, swayed limply over her shoulders. "That cannot be. He moved with purpose. He climbed the vines to get to my balcony." Her voice faltered. "Roksana sent him."

We stared at each other, but Veyka's eyes were distant. She wasn't looking at me. She was back in Baylaur, sorting through a thousand memories.

"Maybe it was something else," Cyara said quietly. "It doesn't quite fit."

It didn't.

But it was connected.

Cyara had said it herself more than once—coincidences did not exist. They were an excuse when we were too uncomfortable to admit the truth.

We were silent then. Even Percival. Even Maisri. She passed us each a plate of food. Cyara brought tea. We ate in silence. Exhaustion began to creep over the room.

Too much fighting. Too much new information.

If we were a unit on the battlefield, I would have commanded us to the rear and brought a fresh unit forward.

But we were it. We were all that stood between Annwyn and the succubus.

And we all knew it.

The plates were cleared. The yawns became more frequent.

When Maisri actually fell over sideways from exhaustion, Cyara stood up. "To bed with you," she ordered the child, tugging her to her feet.

The daisy fae didn't argue—proof enough.

"Aren't you going tell us about your little secret, Cyara?" Lyrena said, stretching her arms high enough above her that even in her seated position, they nearly brushed the ceiling. She was definitely feeling better.

The handmaiden turned Knight of the Round Table and secret

harpy rubbed her hand over her face. It struck me—odd. Cyara was always composed. Even when her wings had been mangled, her sisters murdered... she was always graceful, even-keeled.

But now she just looked tired.

A cost of the harpy that lived beneath her skin, maybe.

"Later," I said. "We are all tired. Osheen will stand guard. The rest of us need to sleep. We are no use to one another if we cannot even keep our eyes open."

"Always the commander," Veyka said with mock sweetness.

My cock hardened in answer. *I have a few commands I'd like to give you.*

Her wicked grin was enough to make me nearly spill myself in my trousers.

67

VEYKA

Arran did not take me to bed.

Much to my chagrin, he went to check the perimeter and find out what additional sorts of defenses the faeries had against the succubus and any other threats.

Always the battle commander.

I slept hard.

No dreams came to me—no nightmares either. And I was damned grateful. My consciousness had plenty to work with, after all I'd learned in the last day or two. But exhaustion was effective, if nothing else.

When I emerged into the central chamber of our little alcove, only one person was awake.

Percival.

He watched me warily from the other side of the room, his chamber directly opposite the one that Arran and I had claimed. But he didn't retreat.

I wasn't sure whether that was an improvement in relations or not.

I rummaged around the packs that had been tossed down near the hearth. "Food?"

He nodded toward a tray with a thin cloth draped over it, near the archway to the tunnel.

"One of the faeries left it."

I lifted the cloth, examining the offering. Some sort of creamy dip with a spoon. Crumbled grains. A pot of honey. Crab apples. Good enough for me.

If it was poisoned or dosed with something... what would we do, starve?

I took an apple, heaped some of the other food onto a small dish, and retreated back to sit opposite the human.

I never would have imagined I could sit across from a human and eat a meal. Civilly.

Nothing made sense anymore.

My entire world was a jumble of lies, half-truths, revelations.

Witches, assassins, nightwalkers, faeries, humans, succubus.

Percival watched me from behind hooded eyes. He'd brushed his hair—a rare occurrence. But there were dark circles under his eyes.

He hadn't slept.

No one would have trusted him to stand guard. Osheen was probably out in the tunnel, guarding the rest of us while we rested.

But Percival still sat here. He hadn't eaten from the tray. He hadn't slept.

I finished my food. Set aside the dishes. Maybe one of the faeries had water powers and could magic them clean.

Half an eye on Percival, always.

I wasn't surprised to see him draw the dagger—and though I was fast, I didn't draw my own in response. He held the blade—offering me the hilt.

My dagger. The one I'd tossed him during the battle with the succubus.

"Here."

I stared at the blade. The hilt, shaped into a wolf with a glinting eye, seemed to stare back at me. "Keep it."

Percival's eyes widened. He shook his head, slowly at first, then more empathically—until his dark hair was spinning wildly around his shoulders. "I can't."

I lifted one brow. "You can. As a thank you for saving me from the nightwalkers, not once, but twice. You'll have a better chance of doing it a third time if you have a blade that can actually kill them."

It was a risk. He might very well stab me in the back with my own blade.

But I had the scabbards.

He backed away, though he didn't tuck the blade back into his belt. He held it firmly in his hand, but across his knee. It was then that I noticed the other hand—and what it clutched.

"Have you had any luck getting it to work?"

Percival blinked. Then he turned his hand over, uncurling his fingers to fully reveal the large white crystal waiting in his palm. He stared at it accusingly.

"No."

The vehemence said more than the word.

"But you've been trying."

His chin dropped a fraction of an inch. My chest ached. Not the mating bond, for once. Which meant that wherever Arran was, he hadn't gone far. Maybe he was the one standing out in the tunnel on guard duty while Osheen and Lyrena slept.

"I lost my brother," I said.

The understatement of the millennia. Lost didn't even begin to describe how I had felt when Arthur was murdered.

As if half of me had been torn away—the better half. The king that Annwyn needed and deserved. Leaving me, the pale, disappointing, dangerous imitation, in his place. But now... now I had power. Now I was High Queen, with a strong and powerful mate at my side.

It didn't ease the pain. It didn't make it feel any more... right.

Percival was still staring at the crystal. As if he couldn't hear my words.

I recognized that too.

I knew what words he would hear.

"After Avalon, we will find your sister. I promise."

His gaze snapped up to me. His hands tightened—around the blade and the crystal. He didn't say thank you. He didn't need to, really. It was part of our bargain.

But I'd planned to kill him, rather than honor it.

I knew Arran had as well.

Who knew what plans the rest of our companions had made.

And looking into Percival's eyes... he understood exactly what had changed.

I shoved to my feet, picking up the dirty dishes I'd made. I may hate doing dishes, but I wasn't going to leave them for someone else to do.

"Sleep," I advised as I dropped to my knees to crawl out of the alcove. "At least for today, you won't have to worry about the succubus coming for you."

68
PARYS

Veyka's antechamber had become a makeshift council room. It wasn't as striking as the actual royal council chamber, but Parys didn't have any desire to go back up there. For all he knew, it was in the same state of disarray it had been after Elora struck down Roksana in the aftermath of the massacre at the goldstone palace.

He hadn't been in any condition to check after the Tower of Myda.

He was early for dinner, but he couldn't stay in the library any longer. It was unusually busy that afternoon and he didn't feel like talking.

But his luck was shit.

Because Veyka's antechamber wasn't empty either.

Gwen was in the armchair she preferred; dinner nowhere to be seen yet. She wasn't alone. Two palace guards stood inside the doors, and the elderly human named Sylva sat on the chaise, several feet separating her from the lion shifter.

Parys wondered who'd chosen their seat first.

They both started to stand as he entered but he waved them off.

"I'm not staying," he said, swiping an apple from the bowl by the door.

But he didn't go back out. Instead he strode across the room, opened the door to Veyka's bedroom, and crossed to the balcony. He threw himself down in one of the padded lounge chairs and closed his eyes, the apple already forgotten in his hand.

Maybe he could sleep. He was having a hard time at night, staying up late in the library instead. But he was so tired...

"Any guards we send are just as likely to be taken by the darkness, are they not?" Gwen said, her voice floating easily through the slight opening he'd left to the antechamber.

He didn't even need to summon a breeze.

"Yes," Sylva was saying. "That is what happened to the ones that King Arthur sent."

A beat of silence.

Not that it mattered—Gwen was nearly impossible to read even if you were standing right in front of her. That part of the elemental court she'd arrived with already mastered.

"What if we only sent females? That is why you came as an all-female delegation, is it not? So you would not risk being set upon in the night?" Gwen's words were even. Giving away nothing.

"Yes." Sylva paused. "But even if they aren't taken by the darkness, they cannot prevent it from coming either."

A slow exhale—Gwen's. She did that when she was contemplating whether to give voice to her thought.

"What about bringing the humans into Annwyn?" she said slowly.

Parys' eyes flew open.

But Sylva spoke before he could even sit up. "They would not be any safer here. My husband was taken by the darkness, even in this realm."

Shit.

"Your husband was the human messenger."

"Yes."

Parys pushed to his feet. Gwen wouldn't do anything to harm the woman... but if Sylva attacked, lunged, would the dark lioness take over?

But the conversation continued. "Were you there when the darkness took him?"

Gwen's voice was tight. She could show emotion—it must be gnawing at her. But what emotions, precisely? "No. But I was pleased to hear of it."

Silence.

Parys stopped just short of the door. Even if he was in the antechamber, he doubted he'd be fast enough to spring between them.

Shifting of cushions, nearer to the door—the chaise. Sylva.

But it was Gwen who spoke. "I would have killed him, if the Brutal Prince had not stopped me."

More silence.

Then quiet words, farther away this time.

Gwen made a soft sound, purely feline. Somewhere between a growl and a purr. As confused as her mind must be.

"May I make an offering of advice, from an old woman?" Sylva said.

Parys found himself leaning in closer to the door, trying to hear her quiet words clearly.

"I am older than you are," Gwen said. Even again—she was regaining some control.

The old woman chuckled. Actually chuckled. Ancestors, humans were resilient creatures. Parys supposed they must be; their lives were too short to spend years lingering on a hurt or grudge.

"Age is relative, is it not?" Sylva said. "I am near the end of my life, while you are in the prime of yours."

Gwen didn't argue. She didn't move at all, if Parys guessed correctly.

So, Sylva spoke again.

"Forgive yourself. Even a year is too long to bear those burdens."

Parys could hear his own heartbeat. Ancestors, he could hear Sylva and Gwen's as well. All three, thundering wildly.

As he counted them, another minute passed. Then Sylva stood, her skirts brushing over the ground noisily as she curtsied and left, the guards at the door following to escort her back to the human delegation's quarters.

Parys used the sounds to cover his retreat back to the night dark balcony, settling himself onto the lounger he'd vacated minutes before. He'd wait until the dinner trays were delivered. Give Gwen those few minutes of peace and silence, without his intrusion, to resettle herself. He'd pretend he hadn't heard her throat clench with emotion. It was the least he could do, as her friend.

But the door from the antechamber opened. Soft footsteps, then a whoosh of air as Gwen folded herself onto the chair beside him.

Parys slid his gaze her way. Stiff as a board, in a lounge chair. He supposed that made sense; he'd never seen Gwen at any kind of ease.

She stared straight ahead, though he was sure she noted his stare. He was a male of many words, but something in that moment held his tongue.

Her golden gaze did not shift, staring into the darkness of the Effren Valley beyond as she spoke softly. "Would I have made a good queen?"

Parys' throat clenched, but he forced out the words. "Better than Veyka?"

Gwen's dark braids swayed in the moonlight as she shook her head. "That is treason to even think," she said. "But that is not my question."

Again, Parys could not bring himself to speak. Listening was not his strength. Silence liked to be filled, and he was damn good at filling it. But if any of the gods the humans believed in did exist, perhaps the human delegation had brought one with them from Eldermist. For it seemed as if some greater power held his tongue silent at that moment.

"I fought my entire life to become the High Queen of Annwyn." Her hands clenched tightly around her weapons, as if she might be able to physically fight the emotions clawing their way to the surface. "I cannot stop wondering whether I would have been good at it."

Parys could not stop the hoarse, shocked chuckle. "Gwen, you are calm, composed, strategic, loyal, dedicated to Annwyn. You put aside your own feelings to do what is best. What the hell else could be required?"

She blinked. "A heart."

Gwen might struggle to show emotion, but Parys didn't. He could keep them locked down when needed, like any true elemental. But he did not try to stop himself from sitting up, from staring straight at her as he said forcefully, "You have a heart, Gwen."

Her mouth twitched. "Do you know what I felt when Arthur died?" A beat of silence. "Relief."

Parys rocked back on the lounger. Surprise, confusion, hurt... no, not hurt. He expected the hurt, waited for it, but it did not come. And what did that say about him?

"He was your friend," Gwen said, her voice coated in pain now. Pain she wasn't holding back. "How could you ever be mine, knowing I felt that way?"

Still, the hurt did not come. A low ache in his gut, the echo of a memory. The place inside of him that would always belong to Arthur. But that searing pain he expected, was waiting for? It did not come. And he knew what that meant... that he'd finally accepted it. That he had started to move on.

"How do you feel now?" Parys asked, giving his full attention and heart to the friend who sat in front of him, rather than the one who was gone.

Gwen closed her eyes tightly. "Empty," she said softly.

Even with her eyes closed, he knew she sensed his movement. But she held still, let him reach for her. Let him clasp her hand between his tightly. "You deserve friends, Gwen. No matter what you did or who you were."

A single tear rolled down her cheek.

Parys let his eyes drift closed, so that any more tears she shed might be hers alone.

A rush of warm air washed over him. He opened his eyes—to find a massive black and brown lioness sprawled at his side. The huge, menacing head rested on folded paws, golden eyes staring out at the night. Slowly, he let his hand come to rest on the thick, warm fur.

Parys reached for the forgotten apple in his lap. Somehow, he knew that Gwen would not be eating tonight.

69
VEYKA

"It is this way, I am sure of it!" Maisri cried, tugging my hand in earnest.

"You said that about the last tunnel. And the one before that."

"It isn't my fault that you stopped to talk and I got distracted—"

"*I* wasn't talking—the faeries were," I corrected. Which was mostly true. I couldn't go anywhere in the tunnel and cave city without being stopped.

Some were content to bow or whisper behind their claw-tipped hands. Others were desperate for news of Annwyn.

A home they'd left but never forgotten.

Then there were the glares. The disapproval. The hate.

I could stand that easier than the fawning. I'd spend twenty-five years at the elemental court. Even closeted in the water gardens, I'd learned how to withstand that sort of judgment and distaste.

Maybe because of the water gardens.

And I may very well spend the next hundred years of my life trapped in the maze of subterranean tunnels.

As soon as Lyrena was back to full strength, we'd leave. The wound had been deeper than I'd realized, even after Isolde came to heal it. My golden knight tried to hide her pain, but I saw the way she grimaced as she tried to crawl and navigate the compact tunnels.

We'd been there for two days. We could spare a few more.

If we emerged from this sanctuary and found the succubus waiting, at anything less than full strength, we would not live to find Avalon.

"Maisri, we aren't going to find it—"

"But it is the only one and all the other children have seen it! Please, Veyka—"

"Perhaps I may be of assistance."

The walls were talking.

Or I'd lost my mind.

At this point in my life, anything is possible.

"Here."

"Oooohh," Maisri cooed, her eyes going wide. Her hand dropped out of mine.

Not the walls or my imagination.

A faerie.

Her skin was black, but when she moved it shimmered with starlight. Starlight she very well may have never seen, trapped in this foreign refuge.

I am not responsible for the actions of my ancestors.

I felt pretty damn responsible for the half of the residents of the faerie caves who bowed whenever I walked by.

"You're beautiful," Maisri declared, completely unabashed.

A soft smile. "Thank you."

It would have been easy for anyone to miss her.

It certainly was not because I'd let down my guard in the relative safety of the faerie caves.

Ancestors below.

If Arran found out I was being so careless, he'd chain me to his side.

The bond in my chest hummed approval at that prospect.

"Where are you going?" The shimmering silver-black faerie asked.

She was tucked into a small alcove off the main tunnel. Though this wasn't really a main tunnel, was it? Maisri had led me through a dizzying number of twists and turns to arrive here.

"The crystal waterfall," Maisri said, her smile bright.

She stepped closer, into the alcove, examining the faerie without a hint of reticence. Being a child had its advantages, in any realm.

"You have taken a few wrong turns, I'm afraid," the faerie said. She inclined her head back the way we'd come.

Every movement was graceful, unhurried.

All the Faeries of the Fen were beautiful, I'd noticed. Unnaturally so. But what was natural, when it came to legendary beings?

Once I got over the surprise of seeing her—and the female herself—I was able to notice more.

She sat at an altar. Several crystals were arranged atop it—one an opaque white like Percival's communication crystal. The others were pretty, but otherwise unremarkable.

They all seemed inconsequential before the flames. Black, sparkling flames. Like the color of Arran's eyes. Like the faerie's skin. Beautiful.

Eerie.

"Who are you?" My words were garbled, scratching their way across my throat.

But I knew she understood me.

"I am someone who can help you."

Definitely eerie.

A strange prickling crept over my senses. *The void.* It was coming for me against my will—

No. This felt different. A tingling of awareness. As if every sense was amplified—all of a sudden, all at once.

"Veyka!" Maisri yelped, jumping back.

The fire.

The black flames danced over my skin. My arms, my hands. I held one up in front of me. Mesmerized. Horrified.

I opened my mouth to demand—

It stopped.

No flames. No awareness.

It might have all been in my imagination.

"Real," the faerie said calmly. "As real as the wings you see flapping on the breeze."

I grabbed Maisri's hand.

I had to get out.

"I can help you," the soft voice followed us through the tunnels.

I glanced down at my hand, expecting to see it wreathed in glittering black flame. But there was nothing.

Nothing but the sound of our retreating footsteps and the echo of my own fears.

70

VEYKA

"Maisri found cake," Arran said, pushing into the tiny chamber serving as our bedroom.

I never thought I'd miss our tent.

I peered at the small metal plate he held out. "That is not cake."

One black eyebrow rose.

"It doesn't have any frosting."

The other rose, in time with a soft rumbling growl that filled the small space, pushing in on me from all sides. "I'll frost it for your, Princess."

I reached for his shoulder, digging my fingertips hard into the wool covering his bronze skin—and shoved him backward. "That is disgusting."

He was on me in a second.

Where the 'cake' went—Ancestors, I didn't care.

"That's not what you thought last night," he growled against my mouth. "When you were begging for every drop of me."

I notched my knee between his legs.

Ancestors below, he was already so hard. Heat flooded my pussy instantly.

"Who is begging now?" I said against his mouth, rubbing my knee roughly across his length.

He snaked a hand between us—shoving my leg down, cupping me roughly through the tight leather leggings.

Ancestors, it was almost enough to make me forget—

"Forget what?"

I jerked backward, grabbing Arran's shoulders, pushing him back far enough that I could see his face.

"I didn't say that out loud."

Arran swallowed. It had been days since he'd shaved. Maybe a week. I wanted to see that ragged beard glistening with my juices —*fucking Ancestors, Veyka! Focus!*

Arran had heard my thought. Not one I'd said intentionally to his beast. He'd plucked it right from my fucking head!

Was this the Ethereal Prophecy, finally taking shape within me? *With a touch, she will feel the heartbeat of her subjects, and she will unlock the secrets they guard within.*

But I hadn't seen Arran's thoughts. He'd heard mine.

"How did you know?" I stammered.

Arran shook his head. Did I look that absurd when I shook mine?

"I just... felt it. I felt your worry. I felt you trying to forget... what? What happened?" His head wasn't shaking anymore. His eyes were intent on me, still burning black. Still wanting me—always wanting me.

But just now they summoned the memory of those eerie black flames. I half expected Arran to see the memory. But he just kept staring at me, expectant.

I grabbed the back of his head, curling my fingers around the tight club of hair, and dragged him back down. "We can talk about it later."

He stopped me with his mouth an inch from mine.

Powerful. In control. Eyes nearly feral with need.

Yet somehow, he managed to speak. "I think we need to talk about it now. It seems the mating bond agrees."

I glared up at him. "I am High Queen of Annwyn. I won't be governed by an intangible... thing in my chest."

He'd braced himself for vitriol. For my vehement rejection of the bond.

But it didn't come.

Not from my lips, nor my head. Not from my heart.

Arran leaned down, closing that inch. He caught my lower lip between his teeth, dragging it out, dragging it away, scraping his canines over the soft flesh of my mouth.

"Tell me."

Because I'd promised. I'd said we shouldn't keep secrets. That we should share our burdens.

"I see things."

I wasn't trembling. I wasn't afraid.

I wasn't.

"Things that no one else sees. Things that are not really there."

Arran said nothing.

It was painfully difficult to read his face when we were pressed this close.

"Am I mad?" I was trembling.

One hand came up. Massive, as big as my face. Broad. Strong. Yet so gentle as it swept aside the loose strands of white hair from my face.

"You're not mad, Veyka. But you should have told me sooner."

Just as he should have told me about his nightmares. Months, spent too afraid to share the parts of ourselves we thought would scare the other away. Months spent alone—not in body, but in spirit.

"Maisri and I stumbled across a strange faerie. She knew about the wings—the visions. Wings—I always see wings. I think she is a priestess of some kind. She said she could help me."

Arran's fingers paused for a moment, then resumed rhythmically stroking my face. "Help you how?"

I let my eyes drift closed. Let myself melt into his touch. It wasn't even dinner time yet, but I felt like I could sleep for days.

A familiar feeling—an escape.

"I don't know."

Arran's lips replaced his hand. A gentle but firm scrap along my jaw.

"We will figure it out. Together."

71
ARRAN

Veyka would not actually be content to go to sleep for the night without dinner. If I didn't get her food now, she'd wake me in the middle of the night. First to fuck, then to find food.

The first I'd be more than happy to oblige.

The second I'd find, begrudgingly. And only because if she didn't eat, that lovely round ass of hers would shrink and there would be less of her to worship.

I couldn't have that.

Lyrena's voice greeted me. "I thought she might hold you hostage in there all night."

"He cannot be a hostage if he is willing," Cyara said, not bothering to glance up from the tea she was grinding.

I ignored them, pulling myself up to stand, ever conscious of how close the top of my head was to the ceiling. "Where are the others?"

"Maisri was invited to dine with one of her new friends. Osheen went with her." Cyara lit the hearth with a flick of her fingers and set the tea to steep.

Lyrena glanced in the direction of Percival's connecting room.

No one had wanted to share with him. "He's closeted himself in there most of the day."

I hadn't needed to tell Lyrena to watch him. Ever since he'd gotten away from her at the festival, she'd become his shadow. A point of honor.

Even though he now had one of Veyka's daggers tucked into his belt.

"More food for us," Lyrena said, shaking off the heaviness that had perched briefly on her shoulders.

"What food?" Cyara said sharply, turning and placing her hands on her hips. For all that she was tiny, she was fearsome. I always enjoyed watching her square off against Veyka. My mate would fight with me to the death, but her handmaiden could cow her in a matter of seconds.

"I will go fetch some." I was already standing. The short walk to the main atrium, the heart of the faerie caves, would give me a chance to think. To ponder what Veyka had told me—visions of wings, mysterious faeries.

But as I grabbed the bench by the open doorway to crawl through, a bright flash of white appeared. Isolde.

"I beg your pardon, Majesty." Her white braids swung as she bowed, shrinking her already tiny stature. She didn't wait for a response—moving right past me for her target—Lyrena.

Isolde was among the faeries who acknowledged Veyka and I as their rulers, even after seven thousand years in the human realm. But it wasn't the same sort of acknowledgment I'd experienced in the goldstone palace. None of the faeries were afraid of us. Their awe wasn't of our powers, but the fact that we'd somehow appeared in their hidden home after millennia.

In Annwyn, my power was what set me apart. Here, it seemed inconsequential.

What did my power over vines and trees matter to the beings who were responsible for the season that allowed those plants to even sprout into existence?

It was unnerving.

If Isolde noticed, she was unbothered. She swung a knapsack off her back and began unpacking food onto the bench, along with a collection of herbs.

"Have you applied the ointment?" she asked Lyrena.

Lyrena snapped her fingers, letting fire dance at the tips. A distraction—for herself or the healer, I was not sure. "I have been busy."

Isolde lifted her smaller, claw-tipped hands and mimicked the motion. Made pure while flames dance in an effortless facsimile of Lyrena's magic.

Lyrena's flames winked out.

"Trousers off."

This time, Lyrena did as she was bidden. Her smile was nowhere to be seen.

Cyara began preparing the food Isolde had brought—the two of them seemed to understand one another implicitly. Maybe because they were both... other. Faerie. Harpy.

Harpy. I still couldn't quite believe it.

Veyka's quiet, observant handmaiden could transform into the harbinger of female rage and cruelty.

"It would be faster if you used your claws," Isolde observed drolly.

Cyara paused over the block of cheese she'd been cutting—with the little dagger from her belt. "I cannot summon them at will."

Isolde knew.

Had she seen in the clearing, during the battle with the nightwalkers? The succubus.

We didn't know how long she'd watched before offering aid. Maybe she'd seen everything. My stomach tightened. Maybe she'd heard my nightmare and screams in the night.

"How can you summon them at all?"

Veyka sat cross legged, framed in the small archway to our quarters. She'd managed to get herself there without anyone noticing—

or at least, anyone saying. She hadn't bothered with the intricate gold brassiere that usually held her tunic tight. Instead, it was loose around her shoulders and breasts, concealing the soft rolls of her stomach.

Not her tunic.

Mine.

Fucking Ancestors. My cock hardened instantly. Thank the Ancestors all eyes were on her.

I resisted the urge to stalk over there and drag her into my lap. I settled for the bench beside the main alcove opening. The few feet of space between us weren't enough. Not nearly. But I wanted to hear Cyara's answer.

Veyka dragged her tongue over her lower lip. Just for me.

She knew what she was doing. She always did.

But her gaze remained on her Cyara, who was still determinedly preparing the meal.

"You are an elemental fae. I have met your parents." She paused, swallowing down the pain that she wouldn't allow to show in her eyes. "Your sisters. How can you be a harpy as well?"

Cyara tossed her long copper plait over her shoulder. "Harpies are not born, they are made."

Isolde nodded over Lyrena's dressing, tightening it back down. She knew.

"Who made you?" Veyka asked. Her voice was carefully even.

"Gawayn. When he slaughtered my sisters."

"But you've always had wings," Lyrena commented, gritting her teeth and not-so-subtly shifting away from Isolde's ministrations. Golden knight, terrible patient.

"From my mother." Cyara dumped the vegetables she'd sliced into a pot on the hearth and set the tray with bread, cheese, and butter aside on the bench. "The wings come no matter what. Only in the females. It's why my mother only had daughters."

Her hands twitched. I slid my gaze to Veyka, who was tracking each of her friend's movements carefully.

"But for the harpy to emerge, one must suffer a great tragedy. A great wrong."

Like the murder of her sisters by the male who'd sworn to protect their queen.

I could sense the questions in the air. Had a thousand of my own. But Veyka didn't ask any of them. She unfolded to her feet—graceful, even with her larger size, even in these tight quarters, and went to sit beside Cyara. She took her hand, unafraid of the monster that lurked within.

So brave, my mate.

"I am sorry."

It had been for her. Carly and Charis had died for her.

Veyka would never let go of that guilt, not entirely. I'd sent enough warriors into battle to know.

Cyara didn't offer platitudes. She didn't tell Veyka it wasn't her fault. But she let her hold her hand.

"When the succubus went for Maisri, I felt the change. Like the harpy had been inside of me, waiting. I would not let another person I loved be taken from me."

Love.

We all cared for the child, but Cyara and Maisri had forged something deeper. Love.

What would happen if Osheen decided to return to the terrestrial kingdom, taking his ward with him? I'd seen no affection between the sentinel and the handmaiden, but...

Since when did I even wonder about such things?

But they were my subjects.

My friends.

Mine to protect.

Just like the female that sat at her side, clutching her friend's hand.

Such capacity to love lived inside of Veyka, if she'd only unleash it. If she'd learn to trust it—to trust herself.

Was I any better?

I loved Veyka.

And it threatened to cripple me at every turn.

I'd always felt my duty to Annwyn driving my actions.

What would happen if I truly loved it and its citizens? What would it cost me to love my kingdom?

72

ARRAN

"The last time I followed someone down through these tunnels, it didn't end well."

"I am not sure whether I should be flattered or insulted by the comparison." I didn't break step. Veyka's fingers were laced through mine, and though she spouted skepticism, her steps did not falter.

"Where are we going?"

"You will see in a few minutes."

"I don't like surprises."

"I thought you trusted me."

She stopped, her fingers tightening around mine, not letting me go. "I do."

We were alone. Far from the nexus of activity around the central atrium that buzzed with faerie life even late at night.

Osheen and I had scoured the underground city over the last few days, mapping out the exits and points of weakness. There were very few of either. The faeries had spent seven thousand years perfecting their subterranean refuge. A day or two more, and Lyrena would be at full strength. Then we would take one of those passages out, out and away before the lingering inaction ate away any more of my sanity.

None of that was my focus, not with Veyka at my side.

Not with what I had found in my explorations.

Veyka glanced over her shoulder. I didn't need to read her mind to know what she was thinking, this time. She was remembering when Maisri had dragged her down into the remote tunnels and they'd stumbled across the mysterious faerie.

I'd asked Isolde about it. She'd confirmed the faerie I described meant no harm. Still, Veyka hadn't felt inclined to take her up on her vague offer for help. I wasn't going to push her.

Not on that.

But things had been building between us.

We were so very close to the precipice. Not the edge of darkness where Veyka had lingered when I'd first met her.

No, we were on the edge of something bigger.

More.

More dangerous.

More important.

More.

I could feel the insistence in my chest. The bond—unfulfilled.

We'd been together dozens of times, but I knew that was not the fulfillment the bond was looking for. It wanted true satisfaction. Acceptance.

And none of that would be achieved tonight.

Tonight, I had only one goal for my mate—to give her a hot bath.

73
VEYKA

"Where are you taking me?" I repeated for the hundredth time. We were going up, which felt ominous. Closer to the world above, where a thousand horrors waited.

"Why do you keep asking?"

"Because I want to annoy you," I saw sweetly.

Arran cut me a glare. I smiled. He groaned. I squeezed my legs together.

Wherever we were going, I was going to throw him down and mount him. Whether there was an audience or not.

"You constantly annoy me," Arran said without looking back. He walked on, completely undeterred. Not even a glance in my direction.

That wouldn't do at all.

I stopped at the next intersection. Three paths forked out. I planted myself directly in the middle of them. I tugged my hand loose from his and planted one of each of my generous hips. Drawing attention to them. He loved my hips. He held them tight, digging his fingers into the soft flesh while he thrust inside of me. He traced the soft curves and rolls when I bent to one side or another in sleep.

The very thing that had earned me so much scorn fascinated him endlessly.

And why shouldn't it?

I was just as obsessed with every muscled line of his magnificent body. I'd never met a male who was my match—who could lift me and toss me around, who could match my strength with his own and revel in it, rather than being intimidated.

We are made for each other.

The thought darted across my mind.

I tugged it back. Let it sink in. Let it fill me up.

We are made for each other.

Our bodies had known it from that first meeting in the clearing outside the goldstone palace. The rest of us had taken longer to catch up.

I had, at least.

Arran loved me.

I'd known that for weeks. I'd felt it, I realized. The same way that he'd felt that emotion inside of me, that desire to forget so strong that it permeated right through the bond.

Every day, we were a little more intertwined. Every breath.

"I'm not going anywhere until you tell me," I said, lifting my chin.

It was a bluff. I'd follow him to the ends of the world.

But Arran didn't argue.

A low growl filled the tunnel. Filled me.

"I won't be intimidated by your beast." As I said it, wetness trickled down between my legs.

I'd left off my tight leather leggings, instead fashioning a skirt out of a gauzy fabric gifted to me by Isolde. It was white, which was unfortunate. But there were no elementals or terrestrials here to send gossiping. No Parys to charm them for rumors.

I felt a pang of sadness.

I missed my friend. His quick laugh, his wit, his taste in food. I missed his counsel, even when it drove me to distraction.

The beast's growl deepened—a snarl.

Had he read my mind again?

"Why are you being contrary?" Arran growled. He stalked closer, across the yard of space I'd created by stopping abruptly.

I let my lips part, an open invitation.

Another step.

His head tilted to the side. He inhaled deeply. He caught my scent in the air—my arousal. Slowly, he dragged those ominous dark eyes back to me. He looked... wolfish.

"I will undress you right here in this tunnel. I will lay you back on the cold, hard ground and fuck you until you're screaming loud enough for all the Faeries of the Fen to hear you." He stepped closer, covering my hands with his own. Holding my hips in place. He was in control now. I was under no illusions. "But I promise that if you follow me a bit longer, you will not regret it."

I regretted many things in my short life.

But not Arran.

I leaned into him, pressing my body against his, arching my hips slightly so they skimmed over his leather trousers. I could feel the hard length of his cock, already straining to reach me. If he could torture me, I could more than return the favor.

"Lead on, Brutal Prince."

His hands tightened over mine. I watched him struggle and savored every second of it. He wanted to throw me down and ravage my pussy as badly as I wanted him buried inside of it.

But he managed to pull himself away.

Whatever he had in mind, it better be damn good.

My knees went weak.

I had never swooned, not once in my life. Survivors didn't swoon. Neither did warriors. I couldn't allow that kind of vulnerability a place in my life, even once.

But seeing those steaming pools of water was nearly enough to make me forget a lifetime of discipline.

Arran's arm snaked around my waist, pulling me in tight against his side. Smart male.

For a few seconds, I just let myself look. Savor it.

I'd never seen something so beautiful. I doubted I would again anytime soon.

The dark stone and dirt that the faerie's city was carved from gave way to black stone with thick veins of white running through it. Obsidian. Black so dark, it swallowed all other light. But yet, there were those tendrils of glowing white, spreading across the dark surface like a spiderweb.

The black and white stone sloped down to pools of water. They dropped down, one into another, in tiers like a cake. But that wasn't mist lifting off of the surface of the water, but steam. Hot springs of some kind. Magical ones—a soft blue glow emanated from their depths. Nearly the same color as my eyes.

Mist coated the stone around us, the cave walls. Up and up and up I followed the walls until—

The sky was open above our heads. I could see the stars. I could smell... freedom.

It ought to have reminded me of the water gardens. The tiered pools of water, running down into one another in small waterfalls; the open air above our heads. But we were an entire realm away from that nightmare. And Arran was at my side.

For the space of an inhale, I worried about the succubus. But the edge above was a sheer drop. Anyone—or anything—that stumbled over it would be smashed to bits on the ground hundreds of feet below. From that height, even the steaming water in the pools would feel like granite.

Or amorite.

I reached up, bypassing Arran's silky hair and catching the soft lobe of his ear between my fingertips. I snagged my fingernail on the small amorite stud. I'd taken one from my own ear, heated a sharp sewing needle provided by Cyara, and pierced it myself.

My mate would not be taken from me.

I would not allow it.

He tilted his head to the side, letting me caress his ear, then his neck and shoulder. Until I was toying with the edge of his wool tunic.

Arran turned his face toward my hand, nipping at my palm. "I am surprised you still have your clothes on."

I let him sink his canines into the soft mound of skin at the base of my thumb. "Someone thinks a lot of himself."

"I meant the faerie pools."

Faerie pools.

Yes, that was an apt name.

I stepped backward, already hooking my fingers into my belt. But Arran caught me, dragged me back. The soft growl in his throat said what he wanted clearly enough—*mine*.

And I was.

I was his.

My body. My soul. And my heart.

"What do you want, Brutal Prince?" I said, echoing back the words he loved to say to me.

He caught me against him, burying his mouth in my neck. His words rumbled against the delicate skin of my throat. "I want to hear my name on your lips."

I tilted my head back, giving him better access.

He took it in a second. His mouth fitted over my throat as if he would tear right into the pulsing artery and drink my lifeblood. I was so lost to need, I'd probably let him. He'd tasted my blood before and been driven nearly feral for it. I wanted to see him like that again.

The scrape of his rough, unshaven beard wasn't enough. Neither were the canines he dragged over me, nor the sucking pressure of his mouth. He'd leave a mark on my pale skin, and I'd wear it proudly for all of the faeries to see.

But it wasn't enough.

"Bite me, Arran," I moaned.

His moan reverberated through the mating bond, through my body until it reached my pussy. Until my pussy was quivering in time with the tremors of need racking his body.

"Not yet." He tore his mouth away from my neck, sending terrible shivers of need and loss through him. I clung to him, afraid I'd lose control. Lose myself.

Had already lost myself to him.

Arran caught me, let me press against him for the space of one long breath. Then he was pushing me away. It was the most interminable loss.

But his hands were on me.

His huge hands, hot hands. Seven feet of hard steel, that's what my mate was. And his hands were a perfect extension of him. Palms as large as my face, fingers as thick as any other male's cock. All other males were nothing before him. Those powerful fingers skated across my tunic, and all I could think about was burying them inside of me. Riding them.

"Arran," I moaned again. He'd wanted his name from my mouth. He'd have it, a thousand times, if only he would—

"Greedy thing tonight, aren't you?"

I was grinding myself against his leg. I hadn't even realized. My thin skirt did nothing to disguise my wetness. My arousal was already dripping down my thighs, wetting the top of Arran's thigh.

"I can't wait." Urgent demand. I wrenched the fabric closure of his leather vest, hearing the buttons pop and fall. I'd sew them back on myself. I needed his skin. His chest. His cock.

Arran caught my hands in a steel vice. "Yes, you can."

I snarled in his face. If there was a secret beast inside of me hiding alongside my ember of void power, if I had some remnant of harpy blood, it would have exploded out of me right then.

But nothing.

Not nothing.

I disappeared.

As easy as thinking, I was out of his grip and on the other side of the cave. Right on the edge of a pool. Standing in a puddle.

Not the best use of my magic. But I was where I'd intended to go.

"Running away, now?"

Arran didn't move. He didn't chase me. Bastard.

But my skin was burning even in the cool air. I needed release. I needed it desperately.

I reached up and unfastened the golden brassiere that held my tunic in place. It looked complicated, but it was just two fasteners on either side of my ribcage. I dropped the metal on the stone with a *clink*. A sharp tug, and the tunic it had held in place was gone as well.

My skin pebbled with gooseflesh, but I didn't allow myself to shiver.

I forced my mate to stare at me, just out of reach.

My breasts hung heavy and full. I swayed my hips slightly to the side, knowing it would make my breasts sway as well. My rosy brown nipples peaked against the cold, standing out sharp, ready for his attention.

I watched as his eyes turned to glowing black embers.

But I wasn't content with that. I wanted to torture him like he'd intended to torture me.

I skimmed my fingertips down between my breasts, careful not to touch them. I lingered over my belly, circling the soft flesh around my belly button a few times. Then I traced the outlines of my hips, up to my waist, and back to my breasts. Up to my mouth. I sucked two fingers between my lips, staring straight down at him.

Arran's hands were fists, his stance tight. Every corded muscle tensed. "Take off your shirt."

"You are not the one giving orders," he snarled.

I rubbed my wet fingertips over my lips until they were glistening. "If you say so."

I dropped my hands to my breasts, toying with the nipples. I pinched them hard enough to draw a little whimper from my throat. Arran tossed his head—an unconscious mimicry of his beast.

"Enjoying yourself?" he said. But the words were hoarse. He was struggling.

Good.

"Very much," I groaned, drawing out the syllables. From beneath half-closed eyes, I watched his nostrils flare. He could scent my arousal. One of his fists loosened. Drifted downward. Toward his cock.

Mine.

The ferocity of the thought startled me, making me drop my hands from my breasts. Had it come from Arran?

No. That thought—that possessiveness—was all me. All mine. Just like Arran was mine.

I inhaled and stepped back through the void.

I wasn't interested in playing games anymore.

Whether Arran sensed it through the mating bond or read it in my eyes, I didn't really care. He stepped closer to me, reached for me, took my hips with his hands. That was all that mattered.

His fingers dug into my waist, through the soft layer of skin to the thick muscle beneath. The other unfastened my belt.

The gauzy skirt fell away. It might very well dissolve on the wet ground. But I didn't care. My legs were bare to him now; so was my pussy. Both were trembling with need. I knew if I looked down, I'd see the glistening of my own wetness.

But I caught the belt before he could shuck it away. My fingers closed around the two familiar appendages. Encrusted with jewels, intricate and beautiful. The scabbards.

How many times had I curled my hands around them, finding peace and comfort in their presence on my hips?

Before I'd even known what they truly were, I'd hated to be parted from them.

Yet I felt no hesitation at all as I twisted my hand, snapping one free of the belt.

I held it out to Arran.

He stared. Blinked. Then his eyes flooded with understanding and he shook his head sharply. "No."

"Yes." I reached for his hand, shoving the scabbard into it.

"You don't know if they will work when parted."

"I don't care," I said simply. "If you bleed, I bleed."

"I'd rather neither one of us bleeds."

"Then take the scabbard."

"Veyka."

"You don't get to choose for me," I said sharply. "You can listen, you can protect. But my choices, my life... they are mine. I choose."

His gaze shifted from the scabbard, up to me. I felt the weight of those dark, burning eyes as the traced the swell of my stomach, the curve of my breasts. Over my chin. They lingered on my lips. When he reached my eyes, there was such understanding there. Such depth. Myself, reflected. Me, truly seen.

He didn't hesitate. "I know."

"I choose you, Arran."

He didn't glare, but his face was unreadable.

I waited.

I was waiting for the words. For the first time in my life, I was ready for them.

Twenty years of torture. The pain of loving Arthur—of losing him—of finding myself. I was ready.

But instead, Arran caught my hand and stepped toward the faerie pools. "I promised you a hot bath."

My chest contracted. But I managed a smile. "Yes, you did."

74
VEYKA

I was already naked. And despite the heat of desire flooding my senses, I was cold.

Walking into the hot water of the faerie pool was almost as good as an orgasm. My entire body trembled. Arran wasn't holding on to me. I took every bit of muscle control and concentration to guide my steps carefully down the stone steps built into the wall of the pool rather than just flinging myself straight down into it.

It was exquisite.

I groaned as my feet finally found the bottom. It was deeper than I'd expected, the water coming all the way up to cover my breasts so that only the very top of my chest was exposed. The tips of my hair dipped into the pool and floated all around me. I still hadn't fully adjusted to the shorter hair.

It was convenient for traveling—I wore it loose most of the time, and Cyara and I could brush it out in a few minutes rather than spending an hour on an intricate braid. It felt lighter—it made me feel lighter. And nowhere was that more evident than in a pool of water.

But I didn't waste time looking at my own hair.

My body wasn't nearly as fascinating as Arran's.

I drifted back into the pool, savoring the heat as it permeated my limbs. My eyes found Arran, watching me from the edge of the pool. And still wearing all of his clothes.

"Unfair."

He cocked an eyebrow. "I'm enjoying myself immensely."

"You cannot even see me."

The other eyebrow rose to join the other. "Look down."

I did—and gasped. I could see every curve of my body, all the way down to where my toes touched the bottom of the pool. The glowing blue light lit my body in an iridescent glow. Every angle, every roll of soft skin, every curve—on display. And Arran stood up above me, enjoying himself immensely—as he'd said. The evidence was in his burning eyes—and the rigid outline of his cock against his leather trousers.

"Unfair," I said again. Sharper this time.

I wanted him naked and pressed against me. No more games.

"You were torturing me. Maybe I should torture you." But he tugged off the leather vest. Then the tunic. Until he was bare-chested.

I didn't get to see him like this enough. Too many stolen kisses in the darkness of our tent, quick and brutal fucking in the forest, with our clothing pushed aside. I stared up at his Talisman. I knew Gwen and Osheen must have their own markings, though I'd never seen them. I was vaguely curious. So vague, the thought barely registered.

How could I think of anything else with Arran before me, staring down at me with lust and love in his eyes?

"Get in."

The corner of his mouth twitched in a smirk.

But he didn't argue. He unfastened his trousers, kicked off his boots. My breath caught in my throat as the glorious length of his cock sprang free.

Twelve inches of perfection. So thick. I'd had his fingers inside of me, thick and rough and so skilled at manipulating my pussy until I was quivering and squirting everywhere. But nothing compared to that perfect cock. The slight curve. The heaviness of his balls pressed against me when he sheathed himself fully, deeply.

Thank the Ancestors I was in the water already. The stream of wetness flooding from my pussy was entirely out of control.

"If you do not get in the water and fuck me now, I think I will die."

Arran's rough laugh echoed off the walls, up and up and up until it mingled with the starlight. But he didn't torture me any longer. He climbed into the water on feet much steadier than mine had been. Before I could draw in another breath, he'd crushed me against his chest.

My breasts pillowed out against his hard chest, my entire body curving around his harder one. My legs went around his waist, letting him take my weight. He was so tall, he stood easily in the deep pool. I felt his legs bend beneath me, seating me in his lap as he leaned back against the edge of the pool.

"Ancestors, oh, oh, oh." His cock was rubbing up against my clit. The heat of the water, the roughness of the wiry hair around his cock, the rigid length… it was so much. Too much. Not enough.

"I told you the only name I want on your lips is mine," he growled against my mouth. He caught my tongue between his teeth and bit down hard. My mouth flooded with blood. Arran sucked it up greedily before the immortal blood in my veins healed the small wounds.

He didn't have to tell me again.

He flicked his thumb over my clit, and I tilted my head back until my entire upper body was floating in the water. And I roared.

"Arran, Arran, please," I heard myself begging. If there were any faeries nearby to hear, I didn't care. He wanted to hear me crying his name? I'd give him that.

That and more.

"Arran, I want to come. I need to come. Please, please, please." I'd never begged for anything like this in my life. But I knew in that moment, I'd always beg for him. Him, and nothing else. No one else.

"Yes, my love," he growled, increasing the pressure of his thumb as I ground myself against him. His other hand held my hip, keeping me from bucking out of his grip entirely. "You belong to me. You are *mine*."

I couldn't argue with that.

Neither could my body.

He scraped his thumb over my clit and I exploded. The force of my orgasm sent me back, floating in the water, my eyes hazy with half-sated need. The water was so warm. So deliciously hot. I could lose myself to it. Except that my pussy was still pulsing, still desperate for him.

I let my legs drift down, my toes drag across the bottom of the pool.

Arran hadn't moved. He was still resting with his back against the wall. But his breathing was ragged. As affected as me.

My feet hit the ground. Instead of stepping toward him, I stepped toward the stairs at the edge. I crooked my finger, and he came.

"What are you up to?" he murmured as I planted my hands on his chest and guided him up and back. Until his muscular ass was firmly seated on the stairs and his entire chest was above the water.

He didn't shiver, even with the stark difference in temperatures.

I wasn't sure I could feel temperature at all anymore. I just felt pleasure and need.

I slid my palm up his chest as my mouth dipped lower. The muscles of his abdomen were defined enough for me to catch my teeth on. So I did. I tasted his flesh. I longed to have the sharpened canines of the terrestrials, so I could taste his blood at the same time that I tasted the precum dripping from the end of his cock.

I traced the outline of his muscles with my tongue.

I love you.

I grazed my teeth along the slice of his hip bone that jutted out, trailing down to his magnificent cock.

I love you.

I dug my fingernail into the skin of his chest, savoring his low groan, as I left my own mark atop the talisman that spread across his chest.

I love you.

His cock was still below the hot water. Arran braced a hand on either side of the pool's edge, holding himself in place. His breathing was so heavy now, each breath he dragged in shaking his chest and making the sprawling tattoo almost seem to come to life. As if the branches were moving, controlled by his power.

Such power, inside that body.

Power that was death.

Power that should scare me.

Instead, it completed me. He completed me.

A whole different need flooded my body. The words I'd held inside of me for weeks. Maybe months. How long had my heart known what the rest of me refused to acknowledge?

Such pain. I'd lived through such pain.

I'd been raped and tortured. I'd seen my brother, the only being I'd ever loved, murdered brutally before my eyes. I'd teetered to the darkness, until my own life seemed forfeit. Worthless.

But I'd pulled myself from that darkness.

And Arran had been the one to reach out his hand.

I didn't reach for his cock or try to lose myself in him, to spare myself the moment. I set my chin on his chest, our bodies half-submerged, half exposed to the cool night air. The stars glinted overhead, giving just enough light for me to see the outlines of his handsome face.

I dragged my tongue over my lower lip. Caught it between my teeth. And finally felt my face soften as I stared up into his eyes, burning with black flame just for me. Always for me.

"I love you," I breathed.

Arran's face didn't change. No softening of his mouth or flare of black flame in his eyes. He watched me steadily, unflinchingly.

"Finally," he said, his dark timbre a low rumble I recognized on an instinctual level. Half beast, all male.

My breath caught in my throat, a strangled sound halfway between a laugh and a sob.

"Finally? After all these months... everything we've endured—"

He pressed a finger to my lips, but I could swear I felt him in the corners of my soul.

The bond.

I could feel him because of the bond. My body was the question, his was the answer.

Two halves of a set, a pairing foretold and prophesied and infinitely precious.

He pressed a finger to my lips, still staring down at me with that same expression.

I realized what that solid, unshakeable expression on his handsome face was.

It was certainty.

"I have loved you," he paused to drag in a breath, "Since I found you after the massacre of the goldstone palace. The first time I thought you might be taken from me, I knew."

Months and months. Before the Joining. Before the mating bond.

A bead of wetness formed at the corner of my eye. I couldn't even lie to myself. It wasn't mist or condensation. It was a tear.

For myself. For Arran.

"All this time," I half-sobbed.

Arran slid down into the water, bringing me with him, wrapping my legs around his waist and pressing his forehead against mine. "Always, Veyka."

I couldn't breathe. My entire chest was caving in.

Arran's smirk grew into a smile. A real smile. I leaned back so I could see it, even though that meant showing him the tears streaming down my face. True smiles, true laughter... so rare from my mate.

My mate.

I let the word sink into me.

"You are my mate," I breathed shakily.

The smile grew. "Yes."

"You are mine."

It deepened. A husky growl, almost like a purr, rumbled low in his chest. Rolled through me. "Yes."

"You waited for me."

He was tugging me closer. He must have been moving me while we spoke, slow and steady, because suddenly the head of his cock was nudging at my entrance.

"I would have waited a thousand years for you to realize what was right in front of you." One thrust of his hips, and he was inside of me.

My head went back, my mouth falling open as I savored the fullness. There was so much of him, so much of me. A perfect match.

"I am going to be terrible at this," I said through my moans.

Arran rolled his neck, then his hips. "I think you're quite good at it."

I managed to swat his shoulder. A gargantuan effort. Thinking was becoming harder by the second. Let alone controlling my limbs.

"We'll learn together," he said.

Together. How to be more than lovers, more than mates. How to love one another.

A journey we'd started that first day in the clearing. All those months ago.

Enemies. Lovers. Mates.

More.

"I love you," I said fiercely.

I gripped his shoulders, levering myself forward so that I could take him deeper. That smile on his face was gone, replaced by a look of deep concentration. He was trying hard not to spend himself quickly. He needed me as badly as I needed him.

Lucky for both of us, I was already so close.

"I love you, my fierce and headstrong mate," Arran groaned.

I tangled my fingers in his hair, shredding apart the leather thong that held it in place. "I love you more."

He set his teeth to my throat. "Why do you always have to argue?"

Then he sank them into my neck.

I came instantly, the sharp bite of his canines in my throat just above my collarbone—the heat of the water on my clit—that magnificent cock inside of me. It was too much. It was everything. I was floating. I was dead, but still breathing. I was in another realm—one of pure bliss and pleasure. Where everything else ceased to exist. Just me and Arran.

The male that I loved—the male I would love until the end of my life. Whether I be in this realm, in Annwyn, or any of the others I'd glimpsed when thrown through time and space.

Arran tried to hold on, but I couldn't have that. I wanted him there with me on our own private plane of existence.

I rocked against him, hard and fast, tugging on his hair, edging our fucking with that brutality that I knew sent fire shooting through his veins. He threw back his head and howled his pleasure to the night sky above. As he coated my pussy with rope after rope of thick burning come, I came again. My pussy quivered around his cock, pulsing in the hot water, my flood of wetness lost on the decadent heat that enveloped us from all sides.

Arran caught me around the waist, pulling me tighter against him. I didn't resist. If I could stay like this, with him buried inside of me and his words ringing in my ears for the rest of my life...but...

His mouth crashed against mine in challenge and promise. To keep me in the moment, to remind me that we were far from done with the faerie pools.

When I finally laid my head on his shoulder, my mind was blissfully blank once again.

"I love you," Arran murmured into my hair. "I would have loved you for a thousand years, even if you were never able to say it back."

"A thousand years and a thousand more," I whispered, reciting the words of our joining. But this vow wasn't for Annwyn. It was for us.

75

VEYKA

I walked around in a daze for the entirety of the next day. Arran? He was functioning just fine. Apparently because he'd had months and months to deal with the fact that he was in love with me.

But me? I saw my mate, and my legs turned to jelly. I woke up in the morning, smelled him in, and my mouth started to water in league with my pussy.

Lyrena had taken to making rude gestures every time she saw us together.

I stopped counting the number of times we'd fucked in a twenty-four-hour period when I got to five.

I was sitting alone in the central chamber of our quarters, trying to pay attention to the sensation in my chest. I was determined to quantify the ache of the mating bond. Arran had left to find Osheen, who'd been casually talking to the parents of the faerie children that Maisri had made friends with. They usually played in the main atrium. How far away was that?

The rustle of clothing.

A soft flutter of wings.

Cyara crawled through the archway from the tunnel into the alcove.

She took one look at me and rolled her eyes. "It's the mating bond."

I blinked. Was everyone able to read my mind—

"I can smell it on you—Arran. I can smell *him* on you." She said it so casually, not even pausing as she went to prepare tea.

My gaze dropped to my chest. I tried to take a covert sniff.

More eye rolling. "Not like that."

"It is your essence. It is not just you anymore." She lifted one copper brow. "You've accepted the mating bond."

"Arran and I have been mated since the Joining," I said, adjusting my seat. The seam of my leggings ran straight between my legs and was rubbing against my...

"Yes, but that is physical. Your blood mixed. This is different. Deeper," Cyara explained, flicking her wrist and lighting the hearth so she could set the tea to steep.

"How do you know so much about the bond?"

She shrugged, her wings moving with her shoulders before she seated herself on the bench near the hearth and tucked them in tighter against her body. "I asked my father before I left."

I tipped my head to the side. "I remember that."

"The rest of it is intuition and observation. It is difficult not to draw conclusions when I spend so much time in close proximity to the two of you—rutting like stags."

I cringed. "Sorry."

Cyara rested her head back against the wall, letting her eyes drift closed. "Don't be. Mates are rare and special. You deserve to be happy, Veyka."

I let those words wash over me.

We sat in silence for a few minutes while the tea steeped. When the kettle whistled, I shooed Cyara away and fetched it myself, pouring two cups.

We sipped in silence for a few more minutes. There was precious little of it in these tiny quarters. Despite all they'd done to make us comfortable, the faerie city was not built for fae. Even the more petite ones, like Cyara and Maisri.

But even still, I found myself breaking it.

"I told Arran that I love him."

Cyara's eyes popped open. A flutter of wings and wafting steam from our tea, and she was upon me. Somehow, she managed to get the hot tea out of the way while she threw her arms around my shoulders.

I blinked several times. Quickly, then more slowly. I let my arms come up from my sides and embrace my friend in return.

When she sat back, her turquoise eyes were glimmering.

"That was... more than I was expecting," I said, reaching for my tea—desperate to cover my awkwardness.

Cyara settled back on her part of the bench, taking a long sip of her own drink. Her lips curved into a smile. "Lyrena and Osheen owe me a week of dishes each."

I didn't know what surprised me more—her effusive show of affection or the fact that my quiet, observant handmaiden had wagered on me. The other two didn't shock me at all.

"I should be the one who doesn't have to do dishes," I grumbled.

Cyara chuckled soundlessly. "Does this mean we will be leaving soon?"

I frowned. "What does one have to do with the other?"

"Arran has wanted to leave since we arrived. He's only lingering here for you."

"What?" I nearly spilled my tea. Ancestors below. "Did he say that?"

"Of course, not. But he sees threats around every corner. Whereas you are relaxed here in a way any of us have rarely seen," Cyara said.

I had been relaxed. I'd felt safe here. Free of the expectations of the elemental court. Trapped by the succubus above our heads. No one pressuring me to make decisions or to rule. But there was no way of knowing what waited above ground. It was just as likely the succubus had dispersed; probably more likely than not. I ought to be pressuring Taliya for information, making Percival divulge what he knew about Avalon so we could get moving, now that Lyrena was healed.

Where was Percival? I'd barely seen him since that first day when I'd gifted him the dagger...

"What do you think we should do, Cyara?" I asked abruptly—as quickly as the thought occurred to me.

She straightened—still not used to being a Knight of the Round Table. She'd offer her opinions about my personal life without hesitation. But weighing in on the ruling of Annwyn did not come as naturally.

"We need to find out what the faeries know. Osheen has been working on the ones he's met. I've asked Isolde a few things, but she's hesitant to divulge too much. Her family is loyal to the Crown of Annwyn, but she lives here and is cognizant of not upsetting Taliya."

I laughed softly. "All of that from observations and carefully placed questions."

Cyara nodded.

"So what is our next move?"

"Taliya knows more than she is letting on. The Faeries of the Fen cannot have lived in the human realm for seven thousand years without learning the precise location of Avalon, and how to get there."

Cyara was right. Taliya knew more about the history of Annwyn and the succubus than we did. It followed that she'd know the location of Avalon as well.

"It is time to talk with Taliya again," I sighed.

Cyara nodded silently.

"There is one other thing I want to do before we leave." I shifted my weight, setting aside the tea. "Have you heard anyone speak about a priestess among the faeries?"

76

PARYS

The origin of the sacred trinity has long been lost to the annals of time. The legends and myths surround their making are as shifting as the mists of the Sacred Isle itself. Nearly as mysterious are the locations of the items themselves, each having been lost—or taken—long before the Great War...

Parys rubbed his temple with one hand while the other tipped the wick of the taper candle to relieve its nearly spent companion.

Why wasn't he a fire-wielder?

If he were, the librarians would never have left him alone in the library. No matter how highly ranked he was or what the Queen decreed.

He was about to have a bed installed in one of the private reading rooms. Spare himself the effort of even walking back to his quarters—quarters he only visited to sleep and relieve himself.

He hadn't even slept the night before. Too busy meeting with Gwen and the humans before their departure that morning.

They'd left Baylaur with less spectacle than they'd arrived, but infinitely better prospects. Ten female fae warriors, seven elemental and three terrestrials, all hand-picked by Gwen and Elora.

Female only, to guard the males of Eldermist while they slept. To assist with hunting parties. To put down any human males consumed by the darkness.

A temporary solution.

But better than the humans had dared to hope for.

Some have theorized that the sacred trinity is not of the fae or human realms at all. And that their disappearance is merely the return of the items to their proper, other-worldly home. While still other scholars believe they are fae-made, and as such have been reclaimed by the fae kingdoms of Annwyn. The only thing that scholars agree on...

His eyes were going to start bleeding. He'd sifted through dozens of texts about the sacred trinity of Avalon. If it was tied to Avalon, perhaps it was tied to Veyka's power as well.

But not a single text identified what in the Ancestors' name the three items actually *were*. Why yammer on about them for an entire chapter without actually naming them?

Did the scholars not know?

It would be so perfectly elemental—not to admit ignorance, but skirt around it in the most prosaic way possible.

He needed to find a terrestrial text that mentioned the trinity. Which meant dragging himself out of the comfort of the reading room and down to the stacks. To the embarrassingly small collection of texts that the elementals had cared enough to procure from the terrestrial kingdom.

He trudged down, down, down the staircase built into the wall.

Along one of the spoke-like aisles.

Past the massive doors—long since closed for the night by the librarians.

He squinted to read the spines illuminated by starlight rather than bring the candle too close.

Flora and the Human Realm.

That was at least in the correct realm.

The Travelers. The Once and Future King. Faerie Tales for Lost Souls.

Parys grabbed as many as he could, prioritizing anything that mentioned or alluded to the human realm. He'd come back and look through the chapter headings of all the others in the daylight.

He hefted the stack back past the doors, down the aisle, started back up the stairs.

And just—stopped.

He was so damn tired.

Maybe this was far enough.

He sank down onto the steps. Flipped open the very top book. *The Travelers.* He hadn't even meant to grab it. But his eyes began scanning the table of contents by habit.

The chapters were all titled in the same strange, concise manner as the book itself—*The Passing. The Nightwalkers. The Three.*

The Three.

Parys flipped through the book, turning pages quickly. Wax dripped off the tip of the candle, but he kept going until he found it.

Not all travelers are welcome. Some invade the body, others the mind. For this reason was the sacred trinity created. What once was one then became three. The sword. The scabbards. The chalice. Only united can they banish the darkness. Three kingdoms created them. Only when wielded as one can they serve the purpose for which they were made...

Parys snapped the book shut. He waited for a drip of blood to run down from his eyes—or maybe drool from his open mouth.

Excalibur. Veyka's scabbards. The chalice Merlin had used at the Joining.

The sacred trinity.

The sacred trinity could banish the darkness.

He had to find Gwen.

They needed to send someone after Arran and Veyka. This couldn't want for them to return. It was too urgent.

He sprang to his feet, the candle winking out.

It didn't matter.

He clenched *The Travelers* under his arm, energy replenished. Warm wind swirled around him, his magic dancing in time with his pounding heart.

And carrying back a voice.

Two voices.

Merlin and the Dowager.

The same hidden door.

The same passageway.

Voices, drifting further and further away.

Merlin possessed the chalice.

She must know something about its significance. She was too cunning—the coincidence too improbable.

And Igraine was involved.

His wind eased open the door. No lock barred his way.

A bit of luck, finally.

Parys carried away the sound of his own footsteps, walking quickly. They were far ahead of him, but he was gaining.

He focused every scrap of his power—bidding one wind to carry their words back to him while another hid his footfalls.

A bead of sweat slid down his temple.

Headache forgotten.

Book still tight under his arm.

"She is getting close…" Igraine.

Quick footsteps—descending stairs.

Then Merlin— "I already have all I need."

Could she already possess the sacred trinity?

No, that was impossible. The scabbards and the sword were with Veyka.

But who was '*she*'? Another conspirator in whatever plot they'd hatched?

Was it a bid for power... a coup? He had to warn Gwen—

They collided so hard, Parys barely managed to wrap them in a torrent of air to keep the sound from escaping. He was no good with a dagger, but his wind could steal the air from—

Gwen.

She grabbed his forearm, pulling him to his feet.

"What—" he stammered.

"The Shadows. I caught one of their runners. I am following his scent to find how he entered the goldstone palace.

Scent. Of course—her dark lioness would sense such things, even when she was in her fae form.

"Merlin and Igraine," Parys said. He tilted his head in their direction. Touched a finger to his lips.

He'd tell Gwen the rest later.

Now they had to follow—

Gwen nodded her head sharply. Parys dropped the wall of air, falling into step behind her.

Gwen didn't need wind to silence her footfalls. Each step was confirmation of who she was—what she was—at her very core.

A predator.

And tonight, she was stalking her prey.

Parys stayed behind her, letting her track them through the winding passageways, down another set of stairs.

The Shadows, Igraine, Merlin, the sacred trinity. They'd been chasing the same trail all along. All those weeks ago, the first time he'd heard Igraine and Merlin, they'd mentioned the chalice. He should have known then, should have realized when he'd searched the priestess' quarters.

The Shadows... they'd been using these tunnels as well. Too perfect to be coincidental. Igraine and Merlin wouldn't have used them unless they were sure they were safe. Unless they knew exactly who else might be in them.

What was the connection?

The passageway branched off in two directions. Gwen paused, tilting her head to one side and then the other.

Parys sent a warm wind whipping over her shoulder, searching out...

Hushed whispers. Right.

He stepped forward, intent, nodding. But Gwen didn't move. She was looking to the left, her nostrils flaring slightly. Parys didn't wait—couldn't wait. He couldn't let them get away.

His walk turned to a jog, his wind carrying away the sounds as his steps got heavier and heavier. He was going down, he was going—

He burst out of the goldstone palace, stumbling as his feet hit sand instead of compact dirt and stone.

Thoughts tumbled through his head. The wards—where were the wards? Someone had disabled them. Igraine or Merlin, surely, and it was evident why.

He tried to count the figures in the dark as he stumbled backward.

One, two, three, four... and a flash of silver. Igraine—four Shadows dressed in dark cloaks and the Dowager, now circling around him.

The warm wind dropped away to nothing.

"You always were a clever thing," the Dowager said, her voice as cool as the frigid water that she sent flowing from her fingertips, slithering across the sand in a thin stream towards his feet.

"Not clever enough," Parys choked out.

"No," Igraine smiled. "Not this time."

Even as he realized it, he refused to give up. The Shadows nearest him were moving closer, but stopped a yard or so away on either side. The other two stood talking to each other, voices low enough even his fae ears could not hear them, and apparently uninterested in his presence.

But the Dowager was interested.

Her thin lips drew up over her face in a wide, viper's smile, the moonlight glinting off of her too-white teeth, her alabaster skin.

Pale and cunning, like her daughter and yet so utterly different in every way that mattered.

"Tell me, what have you figured out, clever Parys?" Igraine asked, her water starting to pool at his feet.

He wasn't about to reveal himself to her. He was caught, but she was the one fishing for information. He could keep his knowledge from her, on the chance that he'd made some connection she hadn't yet.

The sacred trinity, items of mythical power that could be used to banish the darkness from Annwyn and the human realm. Veyka already had two of them. The chalice... he had to find a way to get the chalice from Merlin. To get a message to Veyka and Arran. He had to hold out against Igraine.

He gnashed his teeth, as he'd seen Gwen and Arran and Veyka do, looking so intimidating. "That Arthur was right to seal you into your wing." That powerful magic had died with Arthur, and only in that moment did Parys realize the true implications of its loss.

Igraine's pale blue eyes flashed—but Parys couldn't identify the emotion in the limited moonlight. No matter what it was, Parys seized upon it.

"Where is Merlin?" he demanded.

The two Shadows' heads snapped up at that—he was of interest now.

Igraine's eyes had never left him. He stood in water up to his ankles now. "She is gone."

"Where?"

A slight crinkle at the eyes. The first harbinger of aging in a nearly immortal race. "To ensure the chalice is safe."

A stream of water snaked upward, covering his face, shoving itself past his lips and into his nose. He tried to spit it out, but the force of the water was too intense. He tried to swallow, but his lungs—

A roar echoed through the mountain, shaking the very foundations of the goldstone palace where they stood.

The water was gone, the dark lioness no more than a blur overhead as it leaped over him, swiping easily at the two Shadows.

She turned to Parys, and he nearly collapsed back to the sand.

There was nothing of the friend he'd come to know in those burning amber eyes, or the jaws dripping with thick fae blood turned black by the night.

But still he managed to say, to point, "Follow Merlin. Catch Merlin."

Gwen's lioness needed no more urging. She bounded away between the trees, leaving Igraine to him.

The Shadows got to him first.

He splashed through the deep puddle the Dowager had created, spinning wind all around him. He managed to knock one of the Shadows away with the force of that wind, but the other held on tight—tighter by the second. Tight around his neck.

But if he could create wind, he could take it away as well. He ripped the air from the Shadow's windpipe and deeper, straight from his lungs, until his organs were popping and he fell unconscious to the ground.

His power was flagging. He'd used it to cover his approach in the tunnels, too much of it, not anticipating it would come to this. The other Shadow broke through his wall of wind with a spear of fire, grabbed Parys from behind.

Gwen understood—had always understood that ruling Annwyn would mean sacrifice. Parys hadn't expected this... not again... not after surviving the Tower of Myda. He'd thought that sitting on the Round Table would mean reporting rumors to Veyka and Arran, spreading the ones they wanted to the courtiers. Never this.

But he'd do it all again.

Not a single choice changed.

For his friends.

For the male he'd loved. For Arthur.

He rallied the last of his strength, his magic nearly depleted. He sent a punch of wind into the face of the Shadow holding him. The male reared back, loosening his grip just enough that Parys was able to get himself free.

Only to be hit with a wall of water.

It caught him.

That was why Igraine had created the pool of water—for this moment. So she could summon it upward with a swipe of her hand into a waterfall, but opposite. Water going up. Water flowing around his limbs and holding him in place.

Water down his throat. Into his lungs.

Air. Wind. Fill my lungs with wind. Long enough for Gwen to get back. I have to tell Gwen, so she can find Arran and Veyka, so they can banish the darkness...

Water until there was nothing left.

I need more time. To figure out the Ethereal Prophecy, to help Veyka. To save Veyka.

Through the water, he imagined he saw the blur of a dark feline body.

To save Annwyn...

Then he saw nothing at all.

77

ARRAN

I didn't like the idea at all.

The Faeries of the Fen had been nothing but good to us. Provided refuge, food, and information. But priestesses were dangerous in any race or realm.

A priestess had foretold my birth and led to my mother's rape at the hands of dozens of brutal terrestrial males.

Another had made the Void and Ethereal Prophecies, sending us on this mad flight across the human realm in search of answers.

The witch in the Tower of Myda, mind stolen by the succubus, had almost killed Veyka.

I was beginning to think we were better off not knowing what the future held—or the past.

But Veyka hadn't been able to stop thinking about the glittering faerie's offer. It had weighed on her conscience, even in the most joyous moments.

I can help you.

My mate wanted answers. The half-human priestess who'd made the Void Prophecy was in Avalon, still no more than figment of possibility on the horizon. But the faerie priestess was here, accessible. I couldn't deny Veyka the chance to quiet the possibilities that terrorized her.

"Stop growling."

I hadn't realized I was.

"My mistake, Princess. I thought you enjoyed when my beast growled for you."

Her hair whipped over her shoulder, the white gleaming almost silver in the low light of the tunnel. "He's not growling for me."

Yes, he was.

Just not for lust.

"How much farther?"

Veyka dragged a hand along the stone and dirt wall. "We are nearly there."

"If you haven't gotten us lost."

She stuck her tongue out at me and turned back around without another word. But she was right—less than a full minute passed before she stopped right in front of an alcove. I could see why it had surprised her when she and Maisri first stumbled across it. It was shallower than the other alcoves, and didn't appear to lead into a network of rooms like the others. It was just one room, a yard or so deep, and largely unadorned.

The only items within were the altar with crystals, as Veyka had described, and the low fire. It wasn't lit—not yet.

The faerie sat directly between the altar and the unlit hearth. "You have returned sooner than I expected."

"Not much of a seer, then."

If I'd have said it, Veyka would have embedded her elbow in my side. But she ignored me entirely, regarding the faerie from beneath skeptical eyebrows

The silvery-black female merely folded her hands in her lap. "I did not need the sight to know that you would come searching for me Veyka Pendragon."

Veyka's mouth tightened. "You said you could help me. I have many questions. I need answers."

"But which ones are the most important to you—the ones that will save your kingdom, or the ones that will save your soul?"

I didn't need the mating bond between us—I knew Veyka. I knew the guilt that must have roared to life in her gut at the implication. Because it was the same one I'd been living with for months now. I stepped up to her side, pressing one palm to the small of her back.

I saved her from answering. "Can you truly help, or are you going to continue speaking nonsense?"

The priestess's mouth stretched into a grin—but there was no happiness in it. Amusement, yes. At my expense. "Hello, Brutal Prince. You can take your own journey if you'd like."

Veyka was having none of it. She stepped fully into the alcove, dominating it easily with her height and width. Not to mention the gleaming weapons that were always strapped to her beautiful body.

"We are only here because Isolde vouched for you. If you truly have nothing to offer, then we will go."

She didn't even wait for a response. She grabbed my arm as she turned, giving the faerie her full back. Not even deigning her worthy of notice.

"I can help you," the silvery voice said. "Sit. I will speak as plainly as I can."

Veyka's face was trained in a carefully unmoved mask—the sort of disinterest she hadn't needed to feign when I first met her. But she sat, cross-legged on the ground on the opposite side of the hearth. I dropped down beside her, though I pressed my back to the edge of the alcove and settled my battle axe across my lap.

I wasn't leaving our backs unguarded.

"You are a priestess," Veyka said, looking carefully over the crystals then back to the unlit hearth and finally the faerie. "I have dealt with witches before."

The seer's smile flickered. "Priestesses exist in many forms, many races. There are human priestesses, fae and faerie priestesses. And of course, the witches."

"What remains of them," I said.

"Indeed."

She didn't offer an opinion about that—whether she sympathized with the other beings that had been driven from Annwyn at the same time as the Faeries of the Fen. Or whether she recognized the witches as dangerous.

What she thought didn't matter.

Helping Veyka did.

"How does your power work?" Veyka asked, eyes drifting back to the crystals.

"That would take longer to explain than you or your mate will tolerate." The faerie reached behind her, selecting a pale pink crystal veined with streaks of darker scarlet that looked eerily like blood. She held it out in one hand. In the other, she produced a small vial of liquid.

"The Faeries of the Fen are gifted with physical appearance to match their power. I am the starlight, the heavens, time itself. I can move beyond those restraints which bind you to the here and now."

Like Veyka's void power. Too similar. Unease began to unspool in my stomach.

She looked directly at Veyka. "What do you wish to see?"

My brother.

I heard Veyka's heart answer as clearly as if she'd spoken the words aloud. Maybe it wasn't the bond connecting us. Maybe it was simply that after all these months, I knew her so well, I knew what her answer would be.

For although she'd let go of revenge, she hadn't let go of Arthur. Especially not with the revelations of the past few weeks.

"What can you show me?" she hedged.

The faerie's smile did not waiver. "I am merely the conduit for your journey. What—or who—you see is entirely determined by you."

"I wish to see Avalon and what awaits us there," Veyka said.

My hand tightened around hers.

Strange—I didn't remember reaching for her.

But hardly surprising. The bond demanded constant closeness. Or perhaps I was getting better at comfort.

All that really mattered was that she didn't pull away. She let me hold her hand tightly, even as she glared at the priestess.

"Do it."

The priestess whispered a few words—words in a language I didn't understand. From the unshifting glower on Veyka's face, I guessed that she didn't either.

Then she tossed the crystal into the hearth. Instantly, it burst into flame. They flared pale pink, then deep scarlet. Then the scarlet turned darker, like old blood clotting and drying until it was black. The glittering black that Veyka had described.

When I looked back up, the seer was holding out the vial.

"One swallow," she said as she pressed it into Veyka's hand.

"Then wha—"

But Veyka had already tipped it back. She fell back instantly. The priestess caught the vial deftly, but I had to catch Veyka. She nearly toppled over, her muscles suddenly useless to hold her upright. She was gone—in a trance.

I laid her back as gently as I could, trying to arrange her body so she wouldn't wake up in pain. But the alcove was small—Veyka and I were not. I moved so her head was in my lap. But as I stroked a hand over her cheek—no reaction.

Even in sleep, Veyka turned into my touch.

This is wrong. All wrong. My mate—

She started shaking. Her entire body, shaking terribly.

"What is happening to her?" I demanded, terrified to look away for even a second, but needing to search the priestess for answers.

Her voice was steady as ever, unbothered. "She is safe. Her body is here. Only her mind travels."

I was going to slit her throat when this was over.

"Her mind is as important as her Ancestors-damned body. Make it stop!"

"I cannot. The Queen is the only one who can decide when her quest is complete."

"Like hell. I will bring her back." I reached for the half-empty vial. "Send me as well."

She tilted her head to the side—an insect considering its options before it was squished. "It will not be your journey, Brutal Prince. You will not be able to intervene."

I didn't answer her. I didn't care what the fuck she thought. I grabbed the vial from her hand, drained it, and disappeared into darkness.

78

VEYKA

I couldn't move.

The feeling was so intense, I half expected that when I looked down I would find I did not have a body at all.

But there it was. My breasts. I couldn't see past those, so I had to assume my stomach and my legs were below it. I was about the right distance from the ground to be standing. But I could not take a step forward, and I could not lift my hands to look at them.

That didn't stop me from trying.

I grunted from the exertion. If I had a body, I should damn well be able to move it.

Nothing.

My muscles relaxed suddenly, still trembling slightly from the exertion. Except they hadn't moved at all? None of it made sense.

Warmth suddenly flooded me.

Warmth—*was I cold before?*

No, I hadn't felt anything. But my muscles had relaxed and trembled. And I was now warm. My mind was spinning. At least the rest of me was standing still.

And I wasn't shivering.

I was warm.

That warmth... *I know that warmth.*

I whipped my head to the side—except that I didn't move at all but somehow could still see what was alongside of me. Not what. Who.

Arran.

He could see me, too. Was looking at me with such intensity. I watched his eyes flash through all the frustrations I had over the past few minutes—trying to move, failing, realizing he could see but not feel, all of it.

His dark eyes flickered—he was trying to use the bond to communicate with me.

I waited.

Nothing.

Panic seized in my chest.

No. No. No. No. Not the mating bond—

But there it was, in my chest, whole as ever. I was able to find it, to sense it. The golden thread that stretched from my heart to Arran's.

My mate's eyes softened as well. He'd found it, made the same conclusions. We couldn't communicate, but we were tethered together still.

Relief washed through me.

I didn't have time to consider the irony.

This... vision? Dream? Whatever it was that priestess had conjured up with her crystals and tinctures and magic, it wouldn't last forever. I'd asked to see Avalon—so this must be it.

I recognized it.

The soft green grass, the unnaturally rhythmic kiss of the waves against the crystalline sand. The willows that draped gracefully on each side of the clearing, framing the isle in the distance, just visible through the mists.

I'd seen it before.

When I fell through the rifts for the first time, torn apart and reassembled within the void... I'd come to this unknown shore. Except it wasn't entirely foreign—it was Avalon.

Of course, it was.

Some instinct had brought met here even before I understood the source of my power or its meaning. Another confirmation—if I needed one—that the Void Prophecy was true, the darkness was real, the Ethereal Prophecy must be genuine, and that the answers I sought waited in Avalon.

What else awaited us?

I lifted my eyes to the distant shore. The last time, there had been a strange compulsion acting on all of my senses. Now, I was without a body. Or at least, without a functioning one. I couldn't walk closer to the edge of the lake or lift my hand in greeting. I could choose where to look—and there was only one place that drew my eyes.

Across the water, on the edge of the island.

The same female stood.

The Lady of the Lake.

The words reverberated in my mind. How did I know that?

I looked to Arran; he stared at her as well.

She hadn't moved. Simply appeared through the wall of mist. Around her neck—a white crystal, exactly as Percival had described. A priestess on Avalon. Was she... was she the one we sought? The priestess who'd made the prophecy that had saddled me with this power—and foretold the return of the succubus?

She looked eerily familiar. Something in me shifted, some sort of recognition.

I *knew* her.

But that wasn't possible. I'd never been outside of Annwyn, outside of Baylaur, until a couple of months ago.

I opened my mouth, trying to call for her even though I knew it was useless.

She stood on the edge of the lake, unmoving. Watching us as we watched her.

I started taking in the rest of the scene. There were trees behind her, still shrouded in mist. I couldn't see anything beyond the island in the middle of the lake—not the landscape in the distance or the other shore. Everything was shrouded in mist. I only knew it was a lake by instinct.

I tried to look at what was around me. Because I was not on that island. I was not in Avalon. The priestess's vision of the future —*was it the future?*—had brought me to the shore, rather than the island itself.

The beach gave way to thick grass, wet with dew, the long drapery of willows in the periphery of my vision swinging in the breeze—

Blood. The grass at my feet wasn't green at all. It was scarlet. Soaked in blood.

Suddenly, I could lift my hands. They were covered in blood. Thick. Fae blood.

My vision flickered.

Time was up.

It was less jarring than the feeling of being pulled through the void. It felt more like waking up. Like those moments right before full consciousness, when you can sense the world around you, but you resist its pull and try to remain in dreamland.

The scenery around me flickered and blurred, until it was nothing more than mix of colors and light. I couldn't make out the female on the shore.

But the next flicker was clear—only for a moment. Emerald and gold. A smile that was as much a part of me as my own. Then it blurred away.

My eyes were open. I stared up at the dark ceiling.

I gasped for air, Arran's scent flooding my senses. I was in his lap. He was slumped against the wall of the alcove, his hands loosely around my head. He seemed to come awake at the same moment as me, stirring and trying to right himself.

His hand tightened in my hair. I touched my fingertips to his and he eased his hold. I carefully sat up, grabbing the wall and then my mate to steady me. We were tucked in tight together against one side of the alcove, farther away from the priestess and her altar and fire than we had been when I had swallowed down the vial.

But I didn't try to move away. I let every inch of my mate's warmth sink into me, let his arms close around me. He needed to hold onto me as much as I needed his strong, steady touch.

The priestess pressed cup of water into my hand. I drank, then passed it to Arran.

I was about to ask why he'd joined me, what had happened, when we heard the echo of footsteps in the tunnel.

"I apologize for interrupting."

I knew the voice even before I turned.

Isolde stood just outside the alcove, head tilted to the side as she considered us. Her normally bright smile had softened. But it was her hands that gave her away—clasped tightly in front of her. Too tightly.

"What is it?"

Her lips pressed into a straight line. "Taliya insists that she must speak to you urgently."

Arran's eyes were waiting for mine. The look we exchanged—What had happened? Had the succubus breached the underground city? Did she have news from Annwyn?

A glance at Isolde told me she had none of those answers.

I felt rather bereft of them myself—considering the vision I'd just seen.

But there was no time for more questions, not on my own behalf. Not ones that weren't directly related to saving Annwyn.

Arran was already on his feet, stooping slightly. He offered me a hand. I accepted, pulling myself to my feet. He murmured something like thanks to the priestess, but then he was in the tunnel. I lingered a moment longer.

I stared directly at the seer as I spoke, determined not to miss any facet of her reaction. "I thought I saw my brother."

Her chin dipped. "That was one of your desires."

"Is he alive?"

"You have already asked and received the answer to that question." Yes, she could see into the past and the future. She knew what I'd asked the witch in the Tower of Myda.

"Is he part of my quest?"

Sympathy sparkled in her eyes. "That is for you to decide."

An answer that was not an answer. Naturally.

"Priestesses are no better than witches," I grumbled as I climbed out behind Arran.

79

VEYKA

Same room off the main atrium. Same fluttering, sour-faced blue faerie darting around above our heads.

"Where have you been?" Taliya asked before the door had even closed fully behind us. I wondered about its existence at all.

But I wasn't about to be cowed by a snippy faerie half my size. I could quite literally have sat on her, and that would have been the end of this argument.

I planted one hand on my hip. "We are getting to know our faerie hosts."

Annoyance edged with something sharper flashed over Taliya's face. I'd been accused of having a temper, but this faerie... "You were with the priestess."

I rolled my eyes. "Why do you ask questions you already know the answer to?"

Arran was at my side, nudging me with his arm. Subtly—as he reached to resettle his own hands near his weapons. A show; we both knew he would never draw them against Taliya or the other faeries. Our subjects... sort of.

But it was his way of reminding me that I was supposed to be playing the part of the diplomatic queen. Something I was utterly terrible at.

Taliya's gaze darted between us, as if she would somehow be able to access the unspoken messages that flowed so easily from Arran to me and back again with just the brush of a hand.

She planted her own claw-tipped hands on her tiny hips as her wings slowed and she lowered herself to the ground. She waited until her feet were firmly planted to issue her edict. "It is time for you to leave."

I lifted my chin. "We are in agreement."

"We are healed and provisioned, for which we are grateful," Arran cut in. Always the more diplomatic of the two of us. Ironic as hell for someone who'd earned the title Brutal Prince. "We will leave tomorrow morning."

I ignored Arran, my eyes pinned to Taliya. "The priestess showed us Avalon."

"I see." She blinked, but other than that, did not react. I doubted she'd suddenly learned to hide her reactions. Which meant she'd expected as much.

"You knew all along where it was."

Her lips curved slightly. Little monster. "I never claimed otherwise," she said.

I was done waiting for her to judge us worthy of her help. Time to start demanding. Time to get to Avalon, before the blood from the priestess's vision started flowing.

I took a step forward, emphasizing how I towered over her when both our feet were on the ground. "We need a guide."

Taliya didn't flinch—she shook her head sharply. "I will not send faeries to their deaths."

"If I ask, they will come. Some of them, at least."

Taliya's face transformed, her long blue claws splaying wide.

A wild, feral beast. Beautiful, magical, but dangerous nonetheless.

"The Faeries of the Fen have survived for seven thousand years by avoiding risks, not seeking them out," she snarled, her wings flapping again. She lifted a few feet into the air. Without really meaning to, I guessed.

But before I could argue or order, Arran was at my side. Stepping into the space. Face to face with the faerie, even as she hovered several feet above the ground.

His voice was dark and cold—every bit the warrior of death I'd fallen in love with. "The succubus will come for you too, eventually."

Taliya jutted her sharp chin upward. "What do you know of it, Brutal Prince?"

Arran ignored her irreverence. Her blatant snub—he was the High King of Annwyn now. But titles didn't matter to him, a terrestrial. He'd earned the title she used—and when he leveled her that black glare, I was reminded of why.

"I know that I have stood on hundreds of battlefields and faced foes that would make most fae shit themselves with fear. The succubus are something different. They are a few now. If we can stop them before they take over the human realm, before they bleed into Annwyn… then perhaps the worst of the devastation can be avoided. But if we fail… eventually, the jungle you've made above your heads will not be enough."

Taliya's wings quivered, her voice a little desperate as she said, "We have the amorite."

"That will stop succubus from possessing your male's minds. It will not stop them from ripping your bodies apart limb by limb." His black eyes flicked over her shoulders, the timbre of his voice merciless. "Wing by wing."

She dropped to the ground. She looked at Arran, not me. Fine. I didn't care who she listened to, so long as she listened.

"I will not force anyone to go. But if there are volunteers, I will not stop them from guiding you to Avalon."

"Thank you." Arran inclined his head. Actually inclined his head. I nearly fell over.

He turned to leave, satisfied.

But I wasn't done.

Taliya was already flitting overhead again. I didn't try to follow her with my eyes. I just spoke loud, clear, channeling all the queenliness I didn't feel.

"Will the Faeries of the Fen answer, if Annwyn calls for aid?" I asked.

"No."

Arran exhaled. I didn't.

The flutter of Taliya's wings filled the space, but I could hear her well enough over it as she spoke. "You are not poisoned by the prejudices of your ancestors, Majesties. I have seen that well enough. It is why we have allowed you to linger here. But no. My first allegiance is the faeries."

I threw my hands up in frustration. So much fur queenliness. "We are all faeries. Fae. We are one kingdom."

She paused, landing on a small metal perch set into the stone wall. I hadn't noticed it before. She looked down on us, but for once, it didn't feel like she was actually staring us down.

Her voice was resigned. Resolute. And a bit sad. "Once, that was true. But the Faeries of the Fen will not die for the elementals and terrestrials. Not again."

I'd expected her answer. Known it.

If I walked out of that room and made an announcement in the atrium, a call to action, some of those faeries would follow me out. They saw me as their queen.

But I wasn't just responsible for those faeries. I was responsible for all of them.

Their queen, whether they wanted me or not.

I would not force them to die for us; not yet.

The day might come when we'd have to call upon the Faeries of the Fen. I could only hope that by then...

I wasn't sure what I hoped.

Part of me wanted to leave them here in their underground sanctuary forever, protected from the evils above.

But Arran was right.

If we couldn't stop the succubus now, if we didn't get the

answers we needed in Avalon... they wouldn't be safe. None of us would.

"We will leave in the morning," Arran said, opening the door.

Taliya inclined her head. She was far above us, but I thought a bit of that sadness remained in her face as she said, "Luck be with you. You shall need it."

80

ARRAN

Maisri crossed her arms, jutted out her lower lip, and glared with the ferocity that only an adolescent feeling themselves so deeply wrong could muster. "I want to go."

Osheen shrugged his shoulders, the picture of unmoved parental nonchalance. "Too bad."

The child didn't stomp her foot in the dirt, but a flower did burst out of her pocket. Followed by another. How many petals did she have in there?

"*You* are going," Maisri said accusingly.

He straightened from where he'd been bent over one of the traveling packs. "No, I am staying here with you."

That gave her pause. Calculation gleamed in her bright eyes.

The decision hadn't been hard. Bloodshed awaited us in Avalon. It was one thing to bring a child along on a journey that might include any manner of encounters. It was something else entirely to knowingly expose her to danger.

We'd asked. The priestess had shown. Now we knew... precious little. But enough to cement that Maisri would stay behind the in safety of the faerie caves. And where Maisri went, so did Osheen.

I'd miss his steady presence, the easy interactions between us as soldier and commander. But he had something—someone—to protect. I understood that.

Maisri was having a harder time.

"Veyka!" Maisri squealed, struck with brilliance. She dove for the opening to the alcove.

I threw up an arm to catch her. If she got free into the tunnels, we'd spend the next several hours tracking her down. She might miss our departure. Neither she nor Veyka would be able to stand that.

"Sorry, young one. But you stay."

She squalled in my arms with the voracity of a skoupuma. But I managed to get her down onto the bench—and block the exit with my much larger body.

"Why?"

Because we will risk our own lives, but not yours.

Because you are good and whole, and we want to keep you that way for as long as possible.

Because we don't want you to die.

Evading the truth served no one. But I could choose a softer one. "You know about what we face up there."

Maisri bit her lower lip. Then nodded. The mutiny faded slightly from her eyes.

"One day, we may need the faeries fighting at our side. When we call, we need them to answer." Veyka and I had failed to convince Taliya. Maybe Maisri would have more success.

I waited a few breaths, letting her process the implications. She was a smart child—and she'd been listening for the last two months as we wended our way across the human realm.

I took a chance. I stepped away from the doorway and sat down on the bench opposite her. "Do you understand what I am asking?"

Maisri's teeth still worried her lower lip, but she didn't make to escape.

"Yes, Your Majesty," she said quietly.

Good soldier.

But not yet.

"Arran," I corrected gently.

That earned me a small smile. "Arran," Maisri repeated.

A slight tingle began in my chest. I stood up, rubbing at the spot. "Go pack up the food. We'll be cooking for ourselves soon, but I want as many of your oat cakes in that travel pack as will fit."

Maisri's little smile turned into a fully fledged grin as she jumped into action.

I ducked out of the alcove, wanting a moment of respite and knowing I would get none—because I knew what that twinge in my chest meant.

My mate watched me from the other side of the tunnel, arms crossed under her breasts and blue eyes turned sapphire by the faerie light.

I let myself savor the sight of her.

Even relaxed against the wall, legs out in front of her and crossed casually, she took up a significant portion of the tunnel. But then, she always did.

Any room she walked into. Any tunnel or encampment under the open sky. No one could fail to notice Veyka.

A flick of her white hair over her shoulder. Her long black lashes. The impish half-smile that told everyone she was watching. That dared them to look back.

One hand casually wandered down her chest to rest at her hip, just above the scabbard and blade—twin to the one on my own hip, now. She thrust that hip out—a threat, and a promise, depending who was watching.

Her gaze caught mine, and lit a little more, the sapphire glowing with barely contained desire.

Done enjoying the view?

Never, my beast growled.

She circled one foot in the dirt, cocked her head back slightly to expose more of her throat. An invitation.

My beast propelled me forward. Licked up the column of her neck until I was sucking her ear between my teeth.

"You are shockingly good with children."

I jerked back. Her eyes were glowing fiercely. If I inhaled deeply enough, I'd be able to scent her arousal.

She was trying to diffuse the burning lust that threatened to overwhelm the tunnel. I could indulge her—for now.

I cleared my throat and shifted my weight to my back foot. Still close to her—but not close enough.

"At some point we'll be expected to have one," I said.

She cocked her head to the side. "I still take shadowvein each morning."

Rational thought deserted me. "Good."

Veyka's chin dipped sharply. "Good."

It was good.

Children were rare among the fae. Not rare in the way that they didn't exist at all—most couples had at least one child over the course of their lifetime, often two and sometimes more. But unlike humans who rarely lived to see a hundred years, who couldn't reproduce for half of that, fae could have children anywhere over the course of five hundred years or more. One child born every hundred years was considered impressively fertile.

The last thing Veyka and I needed was a child. Even if the odds were against it.

But that wasn't what had me wondering— "Why are you telling me now?"

Veyka shrugged. Casual—but not really. She'd uncrossed her legs, her hand rested on my wrist. Was she monitoring my pulse? She wasn't certain what my reaction would be. She was nervous.

"It seems like the sort of thing one should share with their mate," she said.

That's what this was about—the shift between us. The words we'd shared in the faerie pools. This was another way for my mate to tell me that she loved me.

But I couldn't resist needling her.

"Yet you haven't said anything before," I pressed.

Her eyes narrowed. "Is this going to be an argument?"

"No," I said, dragging her against me. "We have a thousand

years, Veyka. I plan on spending the first three hundred or so fucking you on every surface in the goldstone palace."

"Then we'd better get this nonsense with Avalon finished. That is a lot of surfaces to cover."

"Are they always like this?" Isolde's high-pitched voice cut in from behind me.

Isolde and Cyara stood side by side at the entrance to the tunnel. But it was Lyrena who answered, clambering out of the alcove itself.

"This is mild," she grunted.

Isolde just smiled. "I suppose I shall have to accustom myself to it, then."

Veyka's hand landed on my arm—a preemptive attempt to quiet my beast's complaints about being interrupted.

"Why is that?" she asked.

"Taliya did not tell you?" Isolde's white eyes sparkled with excitement. "I will be your guide to Avalon."

Veyka's gaze cut to me, sharp as a razor. "This should be interesting."

81

GUINEVERE

There was no need for a dungeon.

Gwen wanted the entire elemental kingdom, all of Annwyn, every realm that might exist, to hear Igraine's screams.

There was no punishment great enough for what the Dowager had done.

Murdering Arthur.

Torturing Veyka.

Killing Parys.

She'd been too late. Seconds. Seconds she'd wasted running after Merlin. Futile.

By the time she'd roared back into that clearing, he was gone. Not even the fae could heal the dead.

Let them all hear her screams. Let them be carried away on the wind, cooler now that winter was descending upon Baylaur.

If they'd been in the terrestrial kingdom, Gwen would have tied her to one of the parapets of the castle on the edge of Wolf Bay. She would have let the cold wind whip at her, flaying away her pale skin layer by layer until she was nothing but exposed muscle and blood.

But they were not in the terrestrial kingdom.

So she'd torture her here.

"What is it?" she asked for the second time, holding up the opaque white crystal.

She'd found it in a concealed pocked of Igraine's gown.

The Dowager's eyes were unshifting. Her mouth unmoving. She was bound to the chair, perched in the center of the balcony, where everyone could hear her screams.

Oh, how Gwen would savor those screams—when the time came.

For now, the Dowager held her silence.

A thrum of excitement coursed through Gwen as she reached into the leather satchel attached to her belt.

"What other secrets are you hiding?"

Gwen didn't wait for an answer. She leaned over the Dowager and slashed across her stomach. The former High Queen of Annwyn blanched, her nose wrinkling at the foul scent. Her eyes widening.

"Do you like my new tool?" Gwen purred. "The skoupuma fought valiantly, of course. A vicious creature. Strong. But she bowed to my lioness before it was over. They all do."

That was a bluff.

Merlin had gotten away. Spirited away through that mountain rift by the Shadows before Gwen's lioness could reach her.

But Igraine didn't know that. Let her believe she'd torn the priestess apart with her teeth before returning to the goldstone palace to finish her off.

Gwen held up the white crystal in her other hand. "Tell me what it is, or I'll puncture that pretty skin of yours."

The Dowager's eyes flashed. But not with fear... with calculation. "If you kill me, you won't be able to question me."

Gwen clicked her tongue, letting the feline smile climb her face. "Try me."

The Dowager stared right into Gwen's eyes and closed her mouth.

Excellent.

She stabbed the skoupuma fang into the Dowager's thin, pale arm, shoving it deeper and deeper until it hit bone. Then she dragged it down, past the indent of her elbow, until she'd flayed her open to the wrist.

"What is it?" Gwen asked again.

Igraine couldn't hold her mouth shut. She threw her head back and screamed, hollow, piercing sounds like the darkling wraiths of nightmares.

Gwen crossed her arms expectantly.

More screaming—Gwen let each trill of it fill up the aching emptiness inside of her. It was fuel, better than any food she could ever hope to eat.

The Dowager started coughing, struggling to breathe between her screams. Gwen reached for her, catching her chin in her free hand. *What is it,* she mouthed without making a sound.

"Comm..." Igraine heaved, spewing bile all over herself. Gwen got her hand away just in time. But she nudged the Dowager with her foot—reminder. "Communication... crystal."

"A communication crystal?" Gwen turned it over in her hand. She'd heard of them, though she'd never seen on herself. They were exceedingly rare, even in Annwyn.

The Dowager's head lolled to the side. Gwen sighed and motioned the healer forward. Stood by impatiently while she patched Igraine up, just enough to keep her conscious. To stall the skoupuma's poison. *For now.*

"Who are you communicating with?" Gwen asked as soon as Igraine could hold her head up again.

Her blue eyes were mutinous now. Her hands tugged uselessly at the restraints. Even if she had her water power, Gwen would shift and rip out her throat before she got a chance to use it.

For Arthur, the betrothed she'd lost.

For Parys, the unexpected friend she'd found.

He'd been carrying a book. It waited on the armchair where he'd sat during their many shared dinners. It's significance... she'd think about it later. When her composure wasn't an inch away from shattering.

The others thought her control was inexhaustible.

But she was as tired as they were.

The only difference was what fueled her.

This—the torture—it was everything she needed in that moment. For all the ones that had come before, and to give her the strength for what would come after.

Igraine hadn't answered.

Gwen raised the skoupuma fang.

The Dowager's reaction was immediate. She grimaced so violently, she almost upended the heavy chair in which she was restrained. Satisfaction richer than any sauce or wine flowed through Gwen's body.

"The human realm," Igraine choked out.

Gwen's heart skipped a beat, but her voice was even. "Veyka."

Igraine's mouth twisted into a cruel smile.

There was no confusion between them. It was not Veyka she communicated with... it was Veyka she plotted against.

"What are you planning for Veyka?"

The smile sank deeper into the Dowager's face. Gave her strength, resolve—Gwen recognized it immediately.

Knew she would not get an answer from her. Not again. Not for a while.

Gwen tilted the skoupuma fang so the noxious poison glinted, reflecting the first rays of dawn as they peeked over the mountains surrounding the Effren Valley.

The light reflected in the Dowager's eyes. The fear there was tiny now, no more than a speck. Gwen would enjoy watching it grow. Punishing her.

For Arthur. For Charis and Carly. For Veyka. For Parys.

She drove the skoupuma fang deep into the Dowager's gut.

82

ARRAN

Two days of darkness, without even the faerie lights to mark our way.

Isolde led us, white flames flickering constantly at her fingertips. In the rear, Lyrena and Cyara alternated lighting and carrying a torch. Those of us in the middle had to rely on our sharp fae eyesight to navigate over the uneven ground. These tunnels were not used by the faeries. They were an evacuation route.

Percival stumbled along just in front of me, Veyka's dagger still tucked in his belt. I'd argued for leaving him imprisoned with Osheen and the faeries. My mate had insisted we might need his help when we actually reached the sacred isle.

It would not matter, I told myself. We would not be wasting time looking for a wayward fae lord, no matter what we'd agreed to with Percival. As soon as we had answers, we must return to Annwyn. There was no telling what had happened there in the nearly two months we'd been away.

I doubted our court was behaving as civilly as the Faeries of the Fen had for the seven thousand years they'd been left unattended.

Step after step, I wondered how many thousands of years it had been since anyone had traversed the ground we walked over.

But there were no obstructions. And two days later, we emerged on the other side of the mountains. The human counterparts of the Spine were every bit as daunting. Just as barren of civilization.

If fae could hardly survive among those icy peaks, the humans had no chance.

In Annwyn, Eilean Gayl waited just beyond the Spine. But instead of craggy green hills, here the land had filled in with lakes. Lakes everywhere. If we'd been able to stand atop the mountains, the land might have looked more like a river winding between the waterways.

Where did Avalon hide, among the labyrinth of water?

Maybe the priestesses of the sacred isle had summoned these lakes, to help hide them.

But when we crested the hill that looked down over that sacred island, shrouded in mist, there was no mistaking the power that hummed from its center.

We had found Avalon.

It took a few hours to wind our way through the other lakes and waterways to the shore of the sacred isle. But then we were there—so sudden. We'd spent nearly two months—and it felt... anticlimactic.

Not that I would ever say that to Veyka, who was staring at that lake like her entire future awaited there. It very well might.

"I've been here before," she said quietly.

The others were fanning out, scouting the area for defenses or signs of magic. Even in the dull human realm, Avalon was clearly a place of magic. The ground we stood on thrummed with it.

"In the priestess's vision," I said, coming to stand beside her. I could see the gooseflesh rising on the small slashes of skin she'd left exposed. But instinct held me back from reaching for her.

"Before that," she said, her eyes fixed on the wall of mist at the center of the lake. "When I fell through the rifts, I came here. I didn't realize what it was."

Her power... the implication hit me squarely in the chest.

She'd traveled through realm after realm, but this wasn't just falling through the void. She'd moved through the void and covered a distance that had taken us nearly weeks and weeks to traverse. We'd encountered plenty of diversions, but if she could move between realms... over long distances in a matter of seconds or minutes...

She could go to Baylaur. Or Wolf Bay.

If this conflict with the succubus escalated, she could coordinate movements of armies on a massive scale—an unheard-of advantage. Not to mention, the power of moving herself—a capable warrior. And if she could bring others along with her...

But Veyka wasn't thinking about any of that. Her eyes were fixed on the mists.

"The area is clear," Lyrena reported.

"I circled wide," Cyara confirmed as she dropped to the ground, tucking her delicate white wings in behind her.

I nodded sharply—once for each of them. Isolde stood a little further back, watching the proceedings, not intervening or offering comment. I half expected her to melt into the trees and disappear back to the underground city now that she'd fulfilled her task. Still, I wasn't going to complain about having a skilled healer at our backs.

But all of that was for later. Now, there was one concern—crossing that lake and getting the answers my mate needed. That Annwyn needed. "Percival, how do we—"

"Cyara, what are you doing?" Veyka yelped, jumping backward. "Get her off of me!"

Shock held the others in place. Instinct propelled me forward.

Cyara clutched Veyka's throat, her small but strong hands digging into the flesh. Veyka didn't reach for her weapon—wouldn't. She'd die before she harmed her friend.

But it wasn't Cyara looking out of those turquoise eyes as Veyka got a hand around her arm and ripped her off before I could even intervene.

The smaller female fell backward into the grass, but her feet never touched the ground. Her wings flapped wildly and she rose into the air.

An otherworldly screech, and the harpy ripped from her flesh.

I shoved Veyka behind me. She shoved right back, Excalibur now in her hand, a dagger in the other.

"What in the Ancestors—Lyrena?"

Cyara dove for us, talons outstretched. Veyka was faster than me—in motion at the same instant as Cyara.

Not diving away from Cyara—diving *for* Lyrena.

Lyrena had dropped all her weapons. Shucked off her cloak and goldstone armor. She was down to her thin tunic and pale leather vest. Veyka shoved her out of the harpy's path, knocking her flat on the ground.

Veyka rolled, coming up in a fighting crouch.

But Lyrena didn't move. She laid flat in the grass, staring up at the sky with a distant look of wonder.

"What is happening?" I roared, covering the ground to Veyka in a few steps. Isolde stood at her back, watching Cyara circling overhead, no doubt coming around for another dive.

We had seconds.

I didn't try to shove Veyka to the side this time.

She hefted Excalibur above her head, but not in a fighting stance. She held it aloft, one hand curled around the pommel, the other around the top of the blade just below the tip. It should have sliced her hand open, but she wore the scabbard.

"Get away!" she yelled as Cyara dove.

Isolde moved fast for her size. I gave Veyka just enough space—enough that she was the target. Cyara's claws closed around the metal blade and a screech of pain ripped from her throat. But Veyka was already throwing her body to the side, using her weight and size to her advantage, the momentum enough to send Cyara crashing down into the grass.

Ten thousand blades of grass surged up from the ground, encircling the harpy's wings, then her limbs and her claws. Until she was prone in the grass, unable even to thrash.

Veyka was back on her feet in a second, Excalibur hanging from her side and murder in her eyes.

"What is happening?" she screamed—to whoever or whatever might answer.

"It's this place," Percival cried. He was near the tree line, almost obscured by the long trailing tendrils of the willow trees.

He fell to his knees, clutching his head. "You must resist it. It is enchanted, as a protection. It will drive you mad, to prevent you from getting too close to the sacred isle."

"I remember..." Veyka grabbed my arm. "When I was here before. I felt... compelled. Out of my mind. I couldn't control my movements."

My eyes darted between Cyara and Lyrena, both on the ground now—to the faeries, wide-eyed. "Then why are the rest of us unaffected?"

"The amorite," she breathed. She began ripping the studs from her ears. "You, me, Isolde—we all have on the amorite jewelry."

Lyrena didn't resist at all. Veyka ripped the gold hoop from her ear and shoved an amorite stud through. The effect was nearly instantaneous. Her eyes cleared and she shot upright. "What in the—"

"No time." I dragged her up and half-across the clearing. We'd need her help to get one into Cyara.

All three of us—Veyka sitting on her chest, pinning her down with her knees—but we managed it. I didn't release the grass binding Cyara until the last vestiges of the harpy slipped away and the fae female lay in her place once more.

Percival's ears weren't pierced, but Isolde was able to fashion a necklace.

It ended as suddenly as it had started. The only sounds punctuating the quiet clearing the heavy inhales and exhales of our breaths.

"Thank the Ancestors for your taste in jewelry," Lyrena laughed, falling back in the grass.

Veyka's mouth twitched in a half-smile, but she didn't respond.

She was sitting up in the grass, cross-legged, thinking. I could see her mind at work as her eyes tracked between our companions —affected and unaffected, the dagger in her hand, and the island still shrouded in mist.

"Percival had my dagger—it has amorite in the blade. I had Excalibur when I was here the first time... but neither protected us from the enchantment," Veyka said, turning over the blade in her lap. The swirled amorite and metal glinted.

"You must have to be wearing it to protect from the enchantment," I said. Useful information—if we ever came to Avalon again.

But Veyka was shaking her head. "Wearing the amorite protects from possession by the succubus. That cannot be a coincidence."

All eyes slid to Percival.

For once, there was no artifice or attempt at cleverness in his dark gaze. He merely shrugged. "I do not know."

Veyka pulled herself to her feet; a silent signal to the rest of our entourage. The interlude was over.

"I suppose we'll add it to the list of questions to have answered in Avalon." Veyka walked to the lake's edge. "How do we get there?"

Percival pointed past her, to a slight disturbance in the otherwise regular curve of the beach. "There is a boat beneath the water. You need to find the chain and pull it up."

He made no move.

No more delays.

Answers. That was what we needed. And we needed them now.

But my foot didn't even break the water.

I wasn't held by magic or enchantment—but my surprise.

Out of the mists, as if floating on the fog itself, a female appeared.

A female of incredible beauty. Dark brown hair interspersed with streaks of gold, falling loose around her shoulders except for two braids that fell straight down—behind her pointed fae ears. She was tall—as tall as Veyka. But where my mate was corded muscle and soft hips, this female was so thin, a strong breeze could have felled her.

No wonder she could float upon the mists.

Her pale blue robes—the same color as her eyes—hung in drapes all around her, disappearing into the mist at her feet. Feet we couldn't even see. The mist was all around her, as if it came from her.

Maybe it did.

Around her neck hung a singular white crystal, the size of her fist, glowing and beautiful—and tied simply from a piece of twine. Not an acolyte, wearing the small crystal that Percival had described.

A priestess.

A powerful one.

Who looked straight past the others—Percival, eyes wide; Lyrena, gawking openly; Cyara, wings fluttering. Past the faeries.

There was no doubt who she addressed when she spoke—"You have reached Avalon, Veyka Pendragon."

83
VEYKA

"I've seen you before." Falling through the rifts. In the priestess's vision. In my memory. There was something so familiar about her nagging at me, brushing up against my consciousness like an animal.

Just out of reach.

She opened her mouth just enough to speak, her lips barely even moving. "Yes."

"Twice."

"Yes."

I was already tired of the games. "Do you know any other words?"

"Yes."

It felt like a joke. But there was no humor in her pale blue eyes. Blue eyes that reminded me...

No. That wasn't possible.

I squared my shoulders, standing tall with Arran at my side. "We are the High Queen and King of Annwyn. We wish to visit Avalon."

She stared right back at us, unmoved.

It felt... strange. Like speaking to a painting, or one of the gods the humans worshiped. She was fae, that much was obvious. A priestess. I'd dealt with Merlin and her ilk. But she was more —*other*.

And she didn't seem to care one bit that she spoke to the rulers of the fae realm.

"That is not possible," she said simply. Her gaze flickered, just for a moment, toward the lake's edge. "A fact which Percival St. Pierre is quite aware of."

Arran's beast took over, growling loud enough for everyone to hear. "You said you were raised on Avalon."

Percival's red-ochre skin had gone pale. "I was, but—"

"Once an acolyte leaves us, there is no return. Percival made his choice," the priestess said. She didn't have to raise her voice, not a single octave. We all heard the implication—but Percival's face turned wretched.

"I did not have a choice," he said viciously.

But the priestess was undaunted. "Only acolytes may visit the sacred isle."

Arran was losing his composure. I could feel the beast beneath his skin, howling and straining at the restraints he kept upon it.

"Yet you come and go," he snarled. "What does that make you?"

I knew the answer. "The Lady of the Lake."

Not just a priestess. *The* priestess.

Our companions had fallen back. They made a semi-circle around us, without realizing it, hemming us in so that Arran and I stood at the center, the priestess a few feet across from us on the lake's edge.

For once, I was the one in control. Arran was about to leap out of his skin. I could feel it—his need to shift, to inspire fear, to get what he wanted. What he wanted—answers, for me. But the priestess was not scared of my mate.

Maybe it was a mistake. But I took a step forward.

"We need your help. We seek a priestess who is known to dwell on the sacred isle."

Her blue eyes fixed on mine. "We cannot help you. Avalon is neutral."

Arran's growl roared through me. We'd come so far. Survived so much... only to meet with disappointment. It was more than he could handle. For love of me, Arran Earthborn would rip part the world. Starting with the sacred isle and the Lady of the Lake.

I should have been as enraged as he.

But something about this place... it called to me. Focused me.

Like all the other debris was cleared away. Emotions were distant. Thoughts clearer than they'd ever been before.

The word spilled out of me, without planning or artifice.

"The succubus has returned to the human realm and to Annwyn," I said. "We must speak with the human priestess who made the Void and Ethereal Prophecies."

"Avalon is neutral," she repeated.

Arran growled in frustration. But I couldn't feel frustration.

Avalon was neutral... "Can you answer my questions?"

Something flickered in those placid blue eyes. "That depends what you ask."

Understanding lit inside of me. "We cannot go to Avalon and speak with the priestess. Can you bring her to us?"

"No."

Arran snarled. "Why not—"

I dropped back a step, enough that I could lay my hand on Arran's arm. "Avalon is neutral."

"I can hear just fine."

"She's answering my questions."

"She's evading your questions."

"Just... just let me try."

Arran's black eyes were murderous—and that dark intent seemed to be evenly distributed between the Lady of the Lake and myself. But I thought that maybe... just maybe... I knew what to do.

I turned back to face her. She watched us, but there was no indication of interest or malice or anything.

Neutral.

Arran was the rational one. He was the calm commander. But that male had deserted him—in this moment, he was not the High

King of Annwyn or the Brutal Prince. He was a male, primal, intent on one thing—protecting his mate.

I would have to be the Queen that Annwyn needed.

And I knew the next question I had to ask.

"Is the priestess alive?"

The blue eyes flashed with an emotion I recognized—approval. "No."

I felt my mate's devastation. But I couldn't let it pull me down. I could stand strong. Arran had been so strong for the both of us, for so long. I could do this for the male I loved.

"Am I the queen from the Void Prophecy?"

"Yes."

I expected my blood to turn cold—for my veins to fill with dread. But something else was lighting inside of me.

Purpose.

"And the succubus... it is the shadow?"

I knew the answer. Before she said it, her eyes changed, just slightly. In a way that I recognized—from the mirror.

"Yes," she said.

"What about the Ethereal Prophecy?"

She was already shaking her head—as I'd expected. But she surprised me, even so.

"Avalon is neutral. I can confirm what you already know, but no more."

I paused, thinking of how to rephrase the question. "The Ethereal Prophecy mentions a queen. Am I that queen as well?"

A slight tilt of her head in response. "No."

Relief slid through me—that responsibility, at least, I'd managed to avoid. But there was more to ask.

Two questions still haunted me. In sleeping, in waking, in the liminal moments between. Maybe she wouldn't be able to answer them. But I had to ask.

"Does my brother Arthur dwell in Avalon?"

Lyrena gasped behind me, the sound fraught and searing straight to my heart. But I didn't let my gaze waver.

Even as the priestess shook her head. "No."

One left. One to save my soul or to damn it.

"Is my void power the reason the succubus has returned?"

Pain spread through the center of my chest—Arran. He stood still at my side, but inside he was roaring. His beast was begging me—take back the question. Do not do this to yourself. Don't let this take what we've only just found—

But I ignored it.

It took every ounce of my will. But I'd been tortured before. I knew how to withstand the pain.

Besides, the ache in my chest was nothing compared to what came next.

Nothing to the agony as her pale, perfect lips formed the word. "Yes."

I remained standing only because Arran was holding me up.

Everything else slipped away. My fingertips began to tingle. The void wasn't coming for me. I was summoning it. Begging it to rip me into a million tiny pieces, so that I didn't have to stand the agony of being in my own body, my own mind.

Voices...

Arran was speaking. Making demands. Cyara said something. Isolde's high-pitched titter. Then the priestess, silencing them all.

"The priestess you seek is dead. She was brought to these shores at her own request, rather than live to see the return of the succubus."

Brought to this shore, outside of the protection of Avalon, to die.

"A coward," Arran spat.

The priestess didn't react visibly. Only pinned Arran with her silvery-blue gaze. "The succubus has returned. None of us here knows the true cost of the Great War. Not even me. But we shall soon see for ourselves."

She turned back to me. "I return to Avalon."

Arran had more to say, but I gripped his hand. There was nothing more she could—or would—give us.

I had one last question as she drifted back toward the mists. "What is your name?"

Her eyes met mine. Inside of me, something slid into place.

"I am called Morgyn le Fae," she said. Then her gaze lifted—over my shoulder. "Remember. Avalon is neutral."

My senses prickled in warning.

I turned just in time—just in time to shove Arran out of the way and take the arrow straight to my chest.

84
ARRAN

I couldn't feel the arrow, but I could feel her fury. It paled in comparison to my own—for her, shoving me out of the way. For the one who'd launched it.

But Veyka didn't fall.

She screamed loud enough to be heard across every realm, fae and human and every other blasted place, but she didn't fall.

She didn't bleed.

She ripped the arrow from her chest. Screamed through the pain of it—the scabbard was safety from bleeding, but not from the pain.

No blood dripped from the pointed tip as she lifted the arrow into her line of vision.

The scabbards worked, even separated.

A small mercy—infinitesimally small as they appeared from the tree line. Dozens of them. Line after neat line. Humans and fae.

And at their head, a singular male. Striding across the clearing, a bow knocked with an arrow held loosely from one arm.

Unbothered.

Fifteen, twenty, twenty-five, thirty... we were outmatched.

But Veyka wasn't looking at the lines of soldiers dressed in matching silver and sky-blue armor. Her eyes were fixed on the male at the center.

Wrong.

More wrong than an advancing force, a foe that had already fired on us.

Wrong at the core of my being. Wrong that wiped all reason and understanding from Veyka's face.

Wrong.

"This cannot be," she whispered.

She was so white. Her skin was nearly the same shade as her hair. The dark blacks and browns of her clothing were stark against her skin. The only color at all was her eyes. The bright blue was ablaze. Not with the glowing ring of blue that spoke of desire. But with wrath.

"You are dead." She stated it like a fact. Even as the fae male drew himself up tall before her, still several yards away.

His brown hair fell forward rakishly over his brow as he tilted his face toward her. "You certainly thought so."

Her face was blank, unreadable. To everyone but me. I knew Veyka like I knew myself, her soul an extension of my own. I knew what lurked behind the wall of ice she'd constructed.

She was calculating. Soon, she'd reach for her power. She didn't care that we were outmatched. A blink, and she'd be behind the male. She'd slit his throat and then sever his head from his body. Lyrena would blast him with flame. It would be done.

Once my mate finished him, I'd shift and dispose of the unit of soldiers behind him. Human or fae—I could rip them apart all the same.

I'd demand answers about who the male was, why he'd shot at us, but later. After he was dead. After the soldiers were dead. I reached for my battle axe, the need to kill thrumming in my veins.

But Veyka did not move.

This conversation... she wanted something. To stall, but why?

Unless... she really did want this information.

"I killed you." She was so still. No trembling. I could hardly feel her through the mating bond in my chest. The rage that she'd descended into was so deep, even I couldn't reach her.

"You tried." The male smiled. A vicious, sickening smile that made my stomach turn. "But no one can die in Avalon."

She didn't want to ask. I watched her mouth form the single word, the pain of it etched in every feature. "How?"

"I opened a rift."

The battle scenarios running through my mind dissolved to nothing.

The male's smile was growing. He was laughing. "Come now, Veyka. You did not think you were the only one who could access the void."

A snap of his fingers. A shimmer. And a woman suddenly appeared from nowhere.

My heart throbbed in my chest. A rift—she'd stepped through a rift.

One glance—that was all it took to realize who she was. The same mahogany skin, though hers was marred with scars. The same long, dark hair. She was softly curved, her body similar to Veyka's but shorter, less muscular.

Human.

A white crystal hung around her neck.

"Diana," Percival croaked.

The sister. The fae lord. Pieces were sliding into place. But this male was known to Veyka. Someone she thought she'd killed, but had lived. An elemental, then.

One more minute. I'd give her one more minute to make the kill, and then I'd shift.

He dragged the woman closer. Her hands were bound.

Closer—so he could rub himself against her, drag his nose through her dark hair and breathe in her scent.

Awareness began to awaken within me.

"It took practice, of course. And using the witch's considerable gifts. It is not a true void power... not like yours, Veyka. But it is enough. For now."

Witch. The young woman was not human—she was a witch. That meant Percival—

Lyrena's body hit the ground hard.

The knife Percival shoved beneath her goldstone armor, right through her back and straight into her kidney, did its work well.

Too well. Lyrena spurted blood. It was everywhere. Thick, rich fae blood. It only flowed like that for the gravest of injuries. We had to get her back to safety, somewhere Isolde could work. One look at the golden knight, and my battlefield experience told me that only the gifted healer would be able to save her.

Veyka was fast, but just this once, Percival was faster.

He darted away, toward the male, his hands upraised. Veyka's dagger still clenched in one palm—still dripping with Lyrena's blood.

"You are a witch too," Veyka hissed.

It all made sense—painful, excruciating sense.

He'd only been willing to answer our questions when we'd had him pinned down with the immediate threat of death. I couldn't remember the conversations exactly, but I'd wager Eilean Gayl that each time, he'd answered exactly three questions truthfully.

Fuck.

Veyka didn't move. Her eyes darted between Lyrena, Percival, and the male.

"Her fae blood will not save her," the male said casually. "Not here. All magic has a cost. The cost of immortality in Avalon is that here, in this clearing, no healing can happen."

He smiled again—brutal. Cunning. Worse than any expression I'd ever seen on my own face, reflected back in the mirror.

"I did as you asked, Gorlois," Percival interrupted. "I destroyed the archives in Eldermist. I earned their trust. I brought them here. Not give me my sister."

Gorlois.

I searched my mind. Gwen would have known—she knew all about the elementals. She'd trained for this. Not me—I was a poor excuse for a king. I didn't care about my kingdom. Not anymore. Not with my mate standing before me, paralyzed.

She wasn't going to attack.

She would have done it by now.

She wouldn't—or couldn't—access her power. But why not? Fear? I tried to sense it through the bond, but all that I found was burning wrath.

Gorlois rolled his eyes, shoving the young woman into Percival's waiting arms. "What does it matter, now that I have the real thing?"

The real void power.

Veyka.

No one would take my mate from me ever again.

The beast inside of me roared. Pulled against the restraints. One by one, they began to snap.

Mine.

Gorlois lifted his bow and arrow, making a show of examining it as he spoke. "I had nearly given up hope, you see. After so many years, no magic had appeared within you. Igraine and I did everything we could think of to seed magic within you. You met all the other requirements of the prophecy. Born under a double moon, marked by a radiant star."

My beast growled—not a sound inside of me. Not anymore. It filled the clearing. And that male, that sent every instinct in me roaring, finally looked to me.

"It was your mate all along, wasn't it? He was the one to awaken the power within you. I couldn't do it no matter how hard I tried."

No.

Veyka screamed the word—inside, through the mating bond. It reverberated in my chest.

No. No. Please, no.

Make it stop.

I didn't understand. *Make what stop? No to what? To me, my beast? To this male, Gorlois? What—*

"Ah, I see you haven't figured that part of the prophecy out yet.

Shall I tell you, Veyka? I was the one to mark you. I am your radiant star." He shifted. A starling.

Against the shimmering mist—a glowing, radiant star.

Veyka's knees gave out.

I understood.

It was *him*.

85
VEYKA

I was frozen.

Frozen with rage.

With fear.

Trapped, like the child inside of me.

Make it stop.

They moved around me—my mate. Ferocious, brutal mate. Arran. Oh, Arran.

I should have told you what I suspected all along. *It is me…*

Not just the queen from the Void Prophecy.

But the Queen of Darkness.

The Queen of Death.

The succubus had come because of me, because of my power. I was the cause of the darkness that would come for our kingdom, our subjects. Eventually, it would come for us.

But I loved him too much to burden him. Too much to let him realize that understanding my power wasn't the key to solving our problems. I was the cause of all our problems.

Me.

For me, he would die—and willingly.

I couldn't say it all, couldn't think it fast enough or communicate it through the bond to male or beast.

I was not afraid of Gorlois. Not anymore.

But I remembered killing him. Even as Arran dragged me to my feet, holding me tight as my legs remembered how to function, I remembered.

My father was dead. But for me, that had changed nothing. I was still a prisoner. Still held in the water gardens. That was when I'd decided to do it. To kill him, to escape, or to die trying. Never again would they hurt me, Gorlois and my mother. I laid in wait, the water-smoothed stone I'd fashioned into a dagger over months and months clenched in my hand. When he came without my mother, alone for once, I struck. I drove that dagger into his heart with the rage of twenty years of torture to strengthen my hand. That was where Arthur found me hours later. Covered in blood. Reached for me without hesitation. Led me out of the darkness.

But maybe I'd never really escaped the darkness. Maybe it had been inside of me all along.

Arran shifted. He sprang for him—the male who'd tortured and raped me. Arran Earthborn, my mate, my love, the most powerful fae born in millennia.

It should have been nothing. No contest. As easy as his beast ripping his head clean off. Like he'd done with Gawayn.

But I knew it wouldn't be like that.

Not this time.

Gorlois hadn't plotted for twenty years to go so easily. Not twenty years, I realized. Hundreds of years. He was the one who'd removed the books on rifts and the Void Prophecy from the library in Baylaur. He'd been planning and preparing... he and my mother both. There was more he wasn't telling us. More power that he was hiding. Waiting.

My mate was going to die.

The rage that had held me fixed changed. Sharpened. I didn't need the blade—I was the blade. I was death.

I reached for my magic, that burning ember inside of me. And found it waiting, ready. Hungry.

86

ARRAN

He shouldn't have been able to move that fast. The starling circled in the air, around and around, above the battle. Out of reach.

I would end it.

Veyka could have Igraine.

Gorlois belonged to me.

Beasts came. Beasts I'd seen in my nightmares. Terrestrial fae, outcast from Annwyn from one reason or another. I didn't need to recognize their faces to know their kind—unruly, vicious. Unable to be trained into an army unit. Spurned by their families. Bears and panthers, I met in that clearing. Ripping them to shreds until the grass ran with blood.

Cyara met the hawks, the birds of prey. She caught them between her claws, tore them with her beak. She was a monster, high above the ground.

The starling circled lower.

Percival was gone—his sister with him. I'd hunt them down, later. Distribute justice.

But first, this. First, death.

The soldiers knit together, shields up. Approaching me in a

solid wall. As if I couldn't leap well beyond their lines. Eat them alive from their flank.

But I never got the chance. A flash of white—Veyka.

The line fell, one by one. She cut through them from behind, just as I would have done. By the time one realized the man beside him had fallen, she was already sliding her dagger between their ribs. Humans were easy to kill, and she wasted no time. No need for beheadings here. These were simple, weak humans. They died like it, too.

The line fell. Not a single human left standing.

A second of reprieve.

Where is Lyrena? Veyka cried through our bond, even as she repositioned herself, ready for the next attack.

My beast rolled his head, throwing his snout back toward the water's edge. Isolde had dragged Lyrena off to the side. Stood over her, throwing her white flames out like spears. She was keeping them at bay, if only just.

And beyond... Morgyn le Fae.

Floating on the mist—watching it all.

Avalon is neutral.

I roared and sprang for the next fae that dared get too close.

87

VEYKA

There were too many of them, not enough of us battling. Arran's beast was fast, brutal. The humans were easy to fell. The fae were harder. Isolde could barely keep Lyrena safe. Was Lyrena even alive?

No—I cannot think like that.

If I do, I will die. We will all die.

Far above our heads, Gorlois circled.

The starling.

I'd never suspected. I'd never seen him use magic—he hadn't needed to. My mother was a perfectly capable captor all on her own. But I'd assumed he was an elemental. How could a terrestrial dwell at the elemental court for centuries without anyone suspecting?

All those years of torture, they'd been trying to get magic to take root within me. I'd thought it was because I was an embarrassment, a liability. But it was more than that... they'd wanted my power. Why? Why did they want the void? What did they need it for?

The battle was dragging on. For every fae I killed, another sprang up to fight me. It was just Arran and me on the ground, Cyara in the air. It wasn't enough.

But Gorlois didn't want me dead.

What did he want?

I had to get him down, somehow. Back into his fae form. I tried to reach for Arran, to communicate with his beast. But he was too far gone, sunk too deep into that feral part of him for me to reach.

A fire-wielder threw out a spear of flame. I stepped through the void, dragging my dagger over his neck. Another tried to shove water down my throat. But I'd already disappeared before she could try and drown me from the inside out. I sliced her hand away, then her head.

Excalibur moved with me. No longer my brother's sword that I wielded out of necessity. It sang for me—the song of death. I was Queen of the Air and Darkness; I may as well be the lady of death as well.

Arran's beast lifted his head to the sky and howled.

Gorlois—he wanted Gorlois.

Wait—I tried to tell the wolf. *We don't yet know his game.*

But Arran wasn't listening—whether he was more beast than fae, or he'd simply closed off that connection between us somehow. He started circling the clearing, running on his four massive paws, faster and faster—he leapt into the sky as the starling swooped down.

It didn't work. It didn't—

Arran shifted as he crashed down to the ground. It was a feint. The starling swooped away from the beast's jaws, careening into a wall of branches and tendrils of willows that Arran had called to battle.

The starling ripped through the vines as Arran tried to strengthen them. Gorlois shifted, snapping loose as his size doubled, tripled, more until he stood on the ground a male once more.

And he shouldn't have been able to do it, not without the witch. Not at all. How could he create rifts without the void power—

But it didn't matter how.

Because he did.

Gorlois' hands closed around Arran's head, one on either side, in perfect position. Blades came from everywhere—sentinels who'd been waiting within the forest rushing forward now. They pointed them at Arran from every angle. Every vital organ covered.

They didn't know the significance of what hung at his waist, but it didn't matter.

The scabbard would stop him from bleeding. But it wouldn't stop Gorlois from snapping his neck.

The soldiers might not know it. But Gorlois did.

"Such lovely scabbards," he said, grinning at my glance. "Where did you unearth them from, I wonder? I'd searched for so long... but it is no matter. Once you open those rifts for me, you can hand them over."

I had to buy time. I had to figure out a way to get Arran free.

"You want the sacred trinity. You want to use the rifts, my void power. But what use is it to you?" I flipped through options, each one less likely than the next.

Asking the questions was a distraction. I could live without those answers. I could not live without Arran.

Isolde was with Lyrena. Cyara had landed atop one of the willows, watching. But she was all harpy. I could count on her for outright bloodshed, but not for any sort of complex strategy maneuvers.

Gorlois toyed with Arran's long hair, knocked loose in the fight. I watched Arran flinch, and my heart clenched.

"This is about Annwyn, and taking my rightful place. Uther Pendragon came too late for his bride. Igraine was already mine."

I stilled. "I don't understand."

"I should have been the terrestrial heir. But I was born too early." Gorlois shrugged, as if we were having a casual conversation. As if my mate's life didn't hang in the balance. "But I came to Baylaur, anyway. I met Igraine, and we both knew. We were more than the agreements between the elementals and terrestrials. We were not meant to rule one realm, we were meant to rule them all. And with the void and the sacred trinity, we will. We thought it would be our child that would fulfill the Void Prophecy. I am a starling. Igraine is the descendent of Nimue, the Elemental Heir. Alas... Morgyn was a disappointment."

I blinked. That couldn't be.

Yet I knew if I slid my eyes behind me, to the edge of the water, that she still waited there. Watching only because Avalon was neutral.

My sister.

"Morgyn... Morgyn le Fae," I heard myself say.

Gorlois' oily smile slid beneath my skin, reaching into the recesses of my memory. The smile he'd given me so many times, before he took what he wanted. What my mother had given him freely. "Le Fae is the surname they give fae bastards in this realm."

"You abandoned your own daughter." The eyes I recognized—my mother's eyes. So similar to my own.

But Gorlois was already bored, dismissing the mention of his daughter as easily as he'd dismissed her existence. "Only a queen can fulfill the Void Prophecy, so Arthur had to go. All of it had to happen—you had to come into your power, break free, come to me here. In this clearing, where not even the fae magic in your blood would be enough to protect you."

I thought I'd moved past revenge.

Maybe I had—maybe this was something different. It didn't blind me. It didn't break my heart. It fueled me. More than food or drink ever had.

"You killed Arthur."

"Igraine arranged it all. A marvelous female, your mother. For years, all we've had is the communication crystals. A pale imitation of true connection, but enough to do what we needed, after Uther's death. But we will be reunited soon."

I was breaking into a million pieces—and I was going to bring the world with me. I was going to shatter it all.

"Every step in your life, Veyka, every path you've walked down has been orchestrated by me. To bring you to this moment."

The void was in me, pulling me apart. I was ready—

"Ah, ah, ah," Gorlois clucked, dragging me back.

Back to that grassy clearing. Back to reality.

A reality where he twisted Arran's head to the point that the bones began to strain. Arran tried to cover his face, to hide the pain, but he couldn't. Not from me.

"Gorlois," I choked. "Please, stop."

I had no plan.

Nothing that wouldn't end in my mate dead.

My muscles failed me. My arms fell to my side, my weapons useless. "Anything. I will give you *anything*."

Victory roared to life in Gorlois' horrible face. "Haven't you realized, Veyka? The only thing I ever wanted was you."

Bile rose in my throat.

I choked it back. I couldn't be weak or sick. Not now.

He didn't realize—without Arran, I couldn't touch my power. I couldn't command the void without Arran to tether me back. Not just as my mate—but the male I loved. Without him to come back to, I would be lost in the void forever. Falling. Aimless. Unmoored.

Gorlois wanted the void power, but he did not understand how it worked. It grew from my connection with my mate. If Arran was dead, that magical ember inside of me would die too. I knew it instinctively, without question.

I knew I shouldn't reveal anything about my power—shouldn't give an inch.

But I'd do anything to save Arran.

I opened my mouth—

Go now.

Arran spoke into my mind as clearly as if he stood beside me. We'd communicated through the bond—growls, admonishments, a few traded sentences and feelings. But this was clear.

Get to Lyrena. Take her, and go through the void, he said.

I didn't want to give us away. But I couldn't keep from looking at him. His dark eyes burned, not with lust. With something deeper —love.

I felt my heart starting to break. *I can't.*

Arran didn't shy away from my gaze. He met me, unafraid. Ready for me—as he had been from the beginning.

You did it before. You can do it now, he said.

Cyara will fly away, safe.

Isolde will retreat to the faerie caves.

I was shaking my head. Gorlois could see it, but I couldn't see him. I barely even registered his existence. The entire world, this realm and all the others, had condensed down into that singular golden thread that connected me to Arran.

Go, Veyka.

I shook my head harder. *I won't. I won't leave you. I can't.*

Yes, you can.

A soft growl rumbled through me. It caressed my consciousness, comforted my soul with its soft song. *Please. I love you, Veyka.*

I won't let him take you away from me. Not after I've found you. We are supposed to have a thousand years.

Veyka, please. Save yourself.

"No."

88

VEYKA

I am a whisper in the night.
I am in the air you breathe, all around you, no escape.
I am darkness and despair.
I am death.

I'd always been fast. As I matured and my hips widened, my breasts grew, I forced myself to get faster. I was strong, but I wouldn't always be the strongest. I could be the fastest. I didn't have magic, so I had to be able to get out of the way of water and flame and wind on the strength and speed of my own muscles and reactions.

If I was fast enough, I'd be able to save my mate.

I didn't let the void come slowly. I plunged myself into it, faster than I'd ever done before. I let the strength of Arran pull me to him —not just to his realm, but right to his body. Right behind Gorlois.

I lifted Excalibur—

Pain ripped down the side of my face. I watched—as if from another body, another place—as the entire shell of my ear fell away to the ground, sliced away by one of the guard's blades.

All the amorite in my body, gone.

But the sword had already left my hand.

And it was too late.

Too late to keep it from veering off course, wobbling sideways as my hand jerked away, as the pain and confusion consumed me.

Fight it. Percival's words echoed in my head. Fight the madness.

The soldiers were retreating. I grabbed one, dragged him down, clawed at his face. The madness was taking me, turning my already frayed mind into mush. An amulet—a sparkling amulet. I ripped it from his throat with such force, he screamed.

Screamed and disappeared.

I didn't care. I only had enough control to get the necklace over my head, to tie a sloppy knot...

Awareness flooded back into me.

I checked the amulet. The amorite sparkled, the delicate chain held. Of course, otherwise I wouldn't be able to think. It's a miracle I could over the shouts of a hasty retreat.

If the soldiers were retreating, then Gorlois must be dead. Excalibur had flown true.

I turned, ready to walk into the warmth of Arran's arms—

Two bodies were on the ground.

Gorlois did not move.

But neither did Arran.

89
VEYKA

"Veyka."

A gentle voice. A gentle demand.

"Veyka, let Isolde look at him."

Cyara. She was tugging on my shoulder.

"Don't touch him!" I screamed, shoving her away. "He is fine. He has the scabbard. He has the scabbard. He cannot bleed. I cannot bleed. We... we saw it work, when they shot the arrow at me... he cannot bleed," I sobbed.

But I was covered in blood.

Arran's blood.

Thick, scarlet, coating everything. The grass, my hands... the priestess's vision snapped into my mind. *This*. She'd seen this.

Dead—Gorlois was dead. Really dead this time.

But Arran...

A white hand covered mine. I thrashed, throwing it away. Suddenly, I was being pulled back. A set of pale hands. Cyara, dragging me away.

"No! Do not take me from my mate!" I screamed, bucking, desperate. Arran could not be dead. I could feel that golden string in my chest. I could feel him. He couldn't die. If he died, I would die. I didn't want to live—

"He is alive."

Isolde stood, hands at her side.

Everything inside of me splintered.

"But he won't be for long," she said.

No hands could have held me then. No magic. I threw them off. I crawled across the ground to Arran. His chest... Excalibur had gone straight into his chest. Straight through Gorlois, dealing a death blow there before continuing on to my mate.

My throw.

My sword.

That was why he was bleeding like this—why he was injured. The scabbard could protect him from the world—but not from himself. And that is what I was... the other half of his soul.

The bleeding was slowing. *That must be a good thing. He is going to heal. He is powerful. The most powerful fae alive. He is going to heal, despite the cursed clearing.*

The blood slowed enough, from a spurt to a steady flow. I could see each heartbeat... slower... fewer.

That golden thread between us was stretching, fraying. I threw my head back, feral as the beast within him, desperate for anything, for anyone.

And I found it.

My salvation.

The strength was all my own. Arran had none. He was unconscious in my arms, bleeding from the wound I'd given him. I loved him. More than I'd ever loved Arthur, or Annwyn, or myself.

But the strength was in me. Had always been—and Arran had helped me find it.

I carried his broken body to the edge of the lake, where Morgyn le Fae stood with the swirling mist.

My sister. I didn't need to open my mouth and ask. She knew what I wanted.

"We are neutral," Morgyn said, her blue eyes unshifting.

My eyes.

"You stood by and watched us get massacred from the safety of your little lake. The least you could do—"

Her nostrils flared at the impertinence. "We are neutral—"

"Is it neutral to stand by and do nothing as he dies? The strongest fae male in existence? My mate?"

I would beg. I would kill. I would tear down the Lady of the Lake herself if it saved Arran.

An acolyte appeared at her side—in a boat. There was the boat Percival had spoken of, and several acolytes sat in it. But only one stood, turning to Morgyn.

Even as Arran's lifeblood seeped from his body, covering my hands, wetting my leathers, they spoke as if nothing were amiss. They whispered in hushed tones that even my fae ears could not hear. As if my mate, my love, had all the time in the world.

I couldn't bear it.

"Enough!" I cried, sinking to my knees. "If he dies, what of neutrality then? There will be no defense against the succubus. I cannot use my void powers without my mate. There will be no one to lead Annwyn. Ancestors above, I am your sister! Help me!"

It would be a challenge to hold Arran close while also using Excalibur to sever my head from my body. But I'd manage it. It was no less than I deserved.

A flick of her slender hand and Morgyn dismissed the acolyte at her side. "You have assembled a Round Table of capable knights who would carry on in your stead."

Her words were shards of ice to my soul. I hung my head, the strength required to hold it up beyond me.

My fault.

All my fault.

My blade, my mistake. My fault.

"Please."

I was sobbing, my tears mingling with Arran's blood.

"He is the one that Annwyn needs. Not me. I am selfish and

temperamental. I am new to my power. He is wise, and experienced, and dedicated. He is everything. He is *my* everything."

I wouldn't need the sword. My heart was already slowing.

It was fitting, really. Our lives had been irrevocably changed with that first mingling of our blood, when our souls recognized one another as mates. Now, we would die with our blood mixed once again, this time on the blade of Excalibur.

Soft hands landed on my shoulders. My forearms. The weight of Arran's body was suddenly gone, lifted away by dozens of capable hands.

My fingers tried to close around the leather of his tunic, but it slipped away, slick with his blood. My body ached for him, even as gratitude rose in my heart.

I staggered to my feet. One shaky step, another. The acolytes carried him to the boat, lowering him gently. There was no room for me.

Fine. I'd swim behind it. I started to shuck my boots.

"No."

The finality of Morgyn's voice filled me with dread.

"Only he shall pass."

Every fiber of my being protested. "I have to be with him."

Even as I spoke, the boat slipped away from shore.

For the first time, something like emotion flitted through Morgyn's eyes.

"He shall return to you, Queen of Air and Darkness. It was foretold." Then she turned, descending to the lakeside on phantom feet. She needed no earthly vessel. She walked on the very mists themselves.

I reached out for the golden thread, now so thin and stretched it was almost impossible to find. But it was there. And it hurt—it ached in a way it never had before. I deserved it.

I love you. I knew he wouldn't hear it. But I'd say it again and again, every day, every hour, until that bond was strong again. Until I could hear him say it back.

He shall return, Morgyn had said.

I would be waiting.

For a thousand years, and a thousand more.

But just then, I was helpless to do anything but watch as my mate disappeared into the mists of Avalon.

THE END

***Court of Vines and Vipers*, Book 3 in the *Secrets of the Faerie Crown* series, is coming April 2024.**

Can't wait that long? Sign-up for my newsletter at https://1link.st/emberlyash to receive a FREE steamy bonus scene. You'll also be the first to find out all the official release details for upcoming books in the series—including exclusive excerpts, cover reveals, and more.

Not ready to leave Annwyn? I share excerpts, character bios, and giveaways on my social media accounts. Follow me on Instagram and Tiktok @emberlyashauthor

ACKNOWLEDGMENTS

Writing Veyka and Arran always feels like taking a chunk out of my soul and splattering it across the page. These two have so much of my own struggle in them. The number of messages I've gotten from readers in the short time *Crown of Earth and Sky* has been published... I cannot even begin to explain what it has meant to me. To see you all respond to the trauma, the healing, the plus size representation... it has given me the fuel to keep writing this story even on the hard days. And just like Veyka, just like so many of you out there, I have plenty of them.

Thank you to every single reader who picked up book one. Thank you to the reviewers, to those of you who have sent messages, posted on social media, harangued your friends about this series. Thank you to the readers who keep reminding me how desperately they are waiting for this book. And to my street team, the most dedicated little group that ever could! I am so thankful for you all.

Throne of Air and Darkness, even more than book one, is about love. It's about trusting another person with the ugliest, most broken parts of yourself and realizing that even though that is so fucking hard, it can be so worth it with the right person. Bryan, you've been that person for me for more than fifteen years. When I fall apart, you're always there to pick up the pieces and help me fit them back together. You make me want to fit them back together, even on the dark days.

To Fenna, Sadie, and Briar—thank you for support in all the little moments. Whether I am so frustrated I want to throw my computer against the wall, I'm celebrating a new high, or when we're laughing together about ridiculous reviews, you are always one message away. I feel so incredibly lucky to be on my author journey with you all.

Always last but never least, thank you to my girl. E—being your mom will always be my favorite, most important job. Thank you for your hugs and kisses as I chase my second most important dream.

ABOUT THE AUTHOR

Emberly Ash stole her first romance novel off her mom's bookshelf at the age of ten and never looked back. The author of 12 romance books under her first pen name, Emberly craved something darker and steamier—enter the world of fantasy romance. Her books are dark, twisty, and not for the faint of heart. In the real world, she manages a fire-breathing five-year-old and a grumpy mage of a husband. But you'll most often find her in her hot-pink writing cave, dreaming up your next book boyfriend. Spoiler alert: he's fae.

Find Emberly online at:

https://1link.st/emberlyash

https://www.amazon.com/stores/author/B0C55YXHS8

https://www.instagram.com/emberlyashauthor/

https://www.tiktok.com/@emberlyashauthor